Through The Wormhole, Literally

David Winship

ISBN: 1508718407
ISBN-13: 978-1508718406

For all who have had close encounters with me on this planet, and especially for those who managed not to snigger when I left it behind occasionally to write this book.

Contents

1

THE WORMHOLE REPORTS

The Voyager 1 space probe was launched by NASA on September 5, 1977, to study the outer solar system and, ultimately, interstellar space. It carried a gold-plated audio-visual disc in the event that it might be found by intelligent life-forms from other planetary systems.

The disc carried photos of the Earth and its life-forms, spoken greetings from people including the President of the United States, Jimmy Carter, and a medley of sounds from Earth, including whales, a baby crying, waves breaking on a shore and music, including works by Mozart and Chuck Berry's "Johnny B. Goode". It got picked up by two itinerant spacecombers from Morys Minor.

One of them, smolin9, was subsequently dispatched to Earth to assess the suitability of the planet for colonisation...

Planet Investigation

Investigator: smolin9
Target Planet: The Pale Blue Dot
Date Investigator Assigned: 12.19.18.11.6

Investigation Scope:

The investigation will focus on the suitability of the target planet for colonisation. The objective of the investigation is to determine the credibility of the referral source (Jimmy Carter, Voyager 1).

Investigator Diary 12.19.18.11.6:

How are you all doing back on Morys Minor? This is smolin9 here with my first wormhole report from the Pale Blue Dot. First of all, it's ridiculously easy to get in here. Nobody stopped me to ask for ID. I could have been a green-snouted goopmutt from Ynonmaq Decimus for all they knew. Their wormhole controls are an absolute joke. I came in under a Mark II Craterkite cloaking device. Hell, that was cheap, supplying me with equipment like that! Tell polkingbeal67 I'll have his blips for belt-nozzles when I get back. There are other illegal aliens too. I've seen a whole army of those ant-like chillok creatures from Oov. I wonder what they're up to.

Anyway, I'm here. According to my research, a lot of earthlings believe this planet was created in six days – frankly, I'm surprised it took that long. I haven't found this President Carter yet. Do you think he's human or some other life form? You never told me there were so many species on this damn planet.

I managed to get one of our foxp2 speech-conversion implants into a small furry creature with a prehensile tail that I've just identified as a mouse. He hasn't had too much to say for himself yet. Just keeps asking for chocolate and cheese. I hope I haven't wasted an implant. When I work out what chocolate and cheese are, I should be able to do a trade. More of him later, no doubt.

Chances of finding intelligent life here? Pretty remote, I'd say. There's no evidence that the life forms can even control the basic elements. I did a reccy around one of the bigger land masses earlier today. A house caught fire every 45 Blue Dot seconds. No, it wasn't the same house! Ha ha. Tell polkingbeal67 that was a joke. No don't bother, he wouldn't understand.

I'm going to follow this mouse for a while. Perhaps he'll lead me to Jimmy Carter eventually.

Okay, that's the end of this report. Keep the wormhole open.

Investigator Diary 12.19.18.11.10:

Smolin9 here again with another wormhole report from the Pale Blue Dot. I definitely wasted a foxp2 implant on that mouse. He still hasn't welcomed me to his planet and won't talk to me unless the subject is chocolate or cheese. I've tried to widen my circle and meet new Blue Dot life forms. I've deciphered some primitive datagrams on my microwocky and made 202 friends on something called Facebook. I don't know what species they are yet. I think it's a combination of humans and farm animals. Some keep poking me but others are quite friendly. I thought they'd be alarmed to encounter an alien life form from a distant galaxy, but they say they like my status. Not many mice on there. I'm not surprised.

Tell polkingbeal67 he might be right about earthling humans. What I've seen on Facebook suggests they haven't got enough neural circuits in their brains to power a standard phase one microwocky. I offered my Facebook friends the chance to share reflections on the more challenging aspects of string theory and gluon particles, but the only reply I got suggested I go and seek sexual congress with someone. I really fail to see how unleashing primitive biological urges contributes to the debate.

Anyway, this planet is a mess. Who does the planetwork here? The land masses have got forests growing all over them. Yuk! There's snow all over the mountains and nobody's brushed the deserts for eons. You'd at least expect them to organise and label things. It's impossible to find your way around. I thought Morys was bad until I saw this. Perhaps they only clean up at the end of each epoch like they do on Oov. Lazy devils!

Speaking of Oov, you remember I wrote about seeing some of those ant-like chilloks? I think they were plotting to take over the planet. It backfired on them big time. Dozens of them got 'oovered up yesterday by a bear-like creature with a long snout.

Next time, I'll tell you more about eating habits here. Gross! The heterotrophs eat each other. They even eat the autotrophs! Can you believe that? What a hideous vortex of entropy! I can't wait till I finish my mission and get back to Morys.

No sign of President Carter yet. I'm going to sign off now. Say hi to polkingbeal67 for me. Tell him I'll bring him back a stick of rock.

Keep the wormhole open.

Investigator Diary 12.19.18.12.9:

Smolin9 here again, reporting from the Pale Blue Dot. I've just had a tangy vitalmados micro pill for dinner. The dopamine release is so cool. Just love the way it conjures up that feeling of cruising along the Daladax in an orbiter during a triple eclipse, while your primary tongue dips into the force field of an Oovian zeptotransmitter. Can't wait for the next one in 17 Blue Dot days! I'm still trying to get information out of the mouse with the foxp2 implant. Unfortunately for him, vitalmados always gives me wind. I just had a significant nitrogen mishap and he was gone - took off like an unstable tachyon! Just a blur of tail and whiskers. Never mind. I'll catch up with him later.

You'll be pleased to hear I've made some progress in tracking down President Carter. Well, it's sort of good news and bad news. I've been using telepathic communication with some of the life forms here. I picked up on a weird pollinator with a furry striped butt. She was broadcasting mental images of a cellular structure remarkably similar to our revered leader's palace on Morys Minor. Well, I tried out polkingbeal67's "tried and tested" mirror technique on her. You know the thing: she flicks her antenna, I flick my fingers above my head; she waggles her abdomen, I waggle mine. According to polkingbeal67, the life form is supposed to get fooled into believing we're in sync, that we're connected on a subconscious level. Well, hey, it doesn't work! She just led me to a clump of flowers and tried to sting me when she realised I wasn't another pollinator. Charming!

The behaviour of these life forms is so confusing and unstructured. They can't compete with me on an intellectual level so they resort to intimidating me physically. Don't worry, I haven't lost heart. I'll keep trying.

Keep the wormhole open.

Investigator Diary 12.19.18.13.1:

Smolin9 reporting again from the Pale Blue Dot. They say imitation is the sincerest form of flattery. Hmm. I know our code dictates that we shouldn't imitate non-human life forms except to protect ourselves under duress, but I was getting nowhere trying to find Jimmy Carter by telepathy. So I decided to use my biomimetic mutator to transform myself into a female mouse so that I could try out a honey trap on that stupid rodent with the foxp2 implant.

We started to gel straight away. I gained his confidence with some cheese and we hung out together for a while. I really went for it. He said he was into gadgets. I asked what kind of gadgets. He said he was getting into things like ladders and spinning wheels. I said that was amazing because I loved ladders. I think he was hooked at that moment. We had dinner together. After a while, the conversation stopped and our eyes met. His pupils kind of dilated. We both knew what was happening. We leaned towards each other. We kissed, tentative at first. Then he was sucking my lip and licking my whiskers. I thought – we're there: cue intimate relations, followed by intimate revelations of the President Carter kind. But it turned out he was only after cheese crumbs. I felt like giving him a blast with my micro beam plasma projector. I would have done too, but you just can't operate the gun when you're transformed into a mouse. All you've got is that prehensile tail and those ridiculously tiny feet!

Well, so much for flattery and so much for the honey trap. Preposterous rodent! I hope it rains cats and dogs! Ha ha. Tell polkingbeal67 that's a joke. There again, don't bother.

Anyway, I've just about had it with mice. I'm going to reverse the configuration on the mutator, go back to my old form and find something on this planet that's a little higher on the evolutionary tree. Uh oh! Something's wrong with the mutator settings. And now what is that mouse doing? Excuse me a moment. How do I get tech support? You know, I think that damn mouse is making amorous advances. Hey! Too late now, pal! Ugh! It keeps sniffing me. I'll have to get back to you.

Keep the wormhole open.

Investigator Diary 12.19.18.13.18:

It's me, smolin9, reporting again from the Pale Blue Dot. Guess what? I was trying to avoid that crazy libidinous rodent when I picked up a disturbance in the time vortex. Something came through the inter-dimensional doorway, hoovered up the mouse and disappeared with it. That'll teach me to leave the door open. And, damn, I've lost a perfectly good foxp2 implant!

However, I have made some progress in my investigation – President Carter is not a dolphin. It's a shame really. Dolphins are such nice, smiley creatures and it would have been fun to get to know them better. I know we'd have just clicked. Anyway, amazingly, I think Carter may be a human. At least, his language patterns match those of humans. I must admit at first I completely dismissed the idea that earthling humans could be responsible for Voyager 1. They're such an irrational, superstitious species with traits that should have disappeared from their gene pool eons ago. They have vestigial tailbones, superfluous toes and teeth, not to mention strange little clumps of hair on their bodies that serve no purpose whatsoever. Their feet have 250,000 sweat glands and, let me tell you, they are seriously smelly. You'll laugh but some parts of their faces, like their noses and ears, never stop growing and they drill holes in them!

Get this! Earthling humans spend a third of their lives sleeping! Oh yes, and they've evolved a reddening of the face that lets other earthling humans know when they're guilty of something. But it keeps malfunctioning, so sometimes they go red when they're *not* guilty. Ha ha. And boy do they breed! If the population of one of their larger land masses walked past you in single file, the line would never end because of their rate of reproduction! Their brain chemistry is similar to mice, so it may not surprise you to hear they get totally obsessed with idiotic activities like wacking balls into various receptacles. Different coloured balls, hard balls, soft balls, misshapen ones, large ones, small ones with dimples. Very odd.

I can't tell you how far they are along the path of civilisation. It's hard to make out. Some seem to have progressed beyond tool-using and cave-painting, but most of them are happy just taking in nourishment, expelling waste matter and wacking balls around. It seems gravity only became apparent to them when an apple fell on somebody's head!

Any idea how I can get the mouse back? I need to retrieve the foxp2 implant so I can embed it in an earthling human and continue the investigation.

Keep the wormhole open.

Investigator Diary 12.19.18.14.19:

Hi, smolin9 here, still trying to make sense of things on the Pale Blue Dot. I'm not at my best today. My endorphin levels are depleted and I weep for our species when I think about polkingbeal67 and what he did to me. I suppose you know he sneaked through the inter-dimensional doorway with a cloaking device and stole my mouse? Just to satisfy his delinquent curiosity. Yes I know he returned the pathetic creature, but everyone knows you've got to give rudimentary life-forms a homeodynamic disruption antidote before they can pass through the portal. Polkingbeal67 forgot. If you could only see the poor thing now. Its epithelial cells have turned fluorescent and it looks like a quivering glob of radioactive jello. With whiskers.

And now you say you want to set up a two-way communication channel between me and polkingbeal67, using the wormhole? That's just terrific. I don't see how my reports will make sense to him. The amygdala part of his brain was damaged when he used a modified plasma beam to get rid of his acne. He's physiologically incapable of feeling or understanding emotions. It's unnerving to say the least. Come to think of it, you could probably replace him with a simple piece of software.

Anyway, I've recovered the foxp2 implant. Now I've got to find a suitable human recipient. I'm still trying to get over the shock of finding out President Carter is not a dolphin or a chimpanzee. According to my research, chimpanzees were travelling in space well before earthling humans.

Actually, these earthling humans crack me up. Perhaps there's more to them than meets the eye. Perhaps the nut doesn't reveal the tree it contains. But they're still trying to figure out why quantum mechanics and general relativity aren't compatible. Some believe in string theory and some argue for loop quantum gravity. So you either get stringy humans or loopy ones. Good grief. According to a telepathic survey I conducted yesterday, most humans think neutrinos are some kind of breakfast confectionery! Let's see now: how many earthling humans would it take to change a light bulb? The answer is two - one to hold the bulb and one to rotate the universe. Ha ha. Hey, that's the sort of thing I wouldn't be able to share with polkingbeal67.

At least the implant won't need much reconfiguring. Earthling human brain chemistry is actually very similar to mice. I know I had a bad experience with the mouse, but I'm using the biomimetic mutator again and I've been fine-tuning my new earthling human look. I've decided to simulate a young Caucasian male. I've got me some big Bermuda shorts and a skateboard. Do you think I'll get along okay without eyebrows?

I've sorted out a geographical location. I've been doing some research and I like the look of the land they call Egypt. I've heard pyramids are great for skateboarding. Their culture is fascinating. All those mummies – they've really got it wrapped up! Sorry, but I've got to get all this humour out of my system before I start reporting to polkingbeal67.

Right, shorts on. Skateboard. I'm ready to navigate unknown waters as an earthling human. I'm sure I'll blend in perfectly. The nut will not reveal the tree it contains! Egypt, here I come.

Keep the wormhole open.

Investigator Diary 12.19.18.15.13:

polkingbeal67:   Greetings, smolin9. This is a holographic image of myself, polkingbeal67, and we are

	communicating using a telepresence channel in the wormhole between Morys Minor and the Pale Blue Dot. Please proceed with your report.
smolin9:	Earth.
polkingbeal67:	Earth?
smolin9:	The human inhabitants of this planet don't call it the Pale Blue Dot like we do. They call it Earth. I've found out a lot of stuff since my last report.
polkingbeal67:	Earth? Couldn't they come up with a better name than Earth? It sounds like someone being punched in the belly. Anyway, how do I look as a hologram?
smolin9:	Oh, you look resplendent. Like the first gleam of dawn on Omega Kasan.
polkingbeal67:	Thank you. No, wait, are you using that earthling humanoid sarcasm thing I've been warned about?
smolin9:	Okay, let me take a proper look at you. Smile!
polkingbeal67:	Like this?
smolin9:	Oh, stop! That's really terrifying! And, by the way, are you going to

apologise for what you did to my mouse?

polkingbeal67: Oh yes, sorry. I remember. I had a little mishap getting him through the portal, didn't I?

smolin9: Mishap? That wasn't just a mishap in a portal. That mouse had been slammed into the timewarp equivalent of a revolving door. I thought we were here to analyse these life-forms, not annihilate them.

polkingbeal67: I said I was sorry. Anyway, you'd better get on with your report. You said you've learned things since last time.

smolin9: Well, yes, according to what I learned on the microwocky during my journey to Egypt, earthling humans believe they constructed the pyramids themselves! Ha ha! A pyramid comprises about two million blocks of stone, each one weighing two and a half Earth tons. And this would have been approximately 5000 Earth years ago! Y'know, I'm starting to like these earthlings. They're so unpredictable. When I used telepathic broadcast to tell them the pyramids were built by green-snouted goopmutts fleeing from Ynonmaq Decimus, they seemed to find it funny. So I explained how the renegade goopmutts had been banished for converting Ynonmaq's oceans into liquid vitalmados. And I made it clear they were doomed to spend the rest of their days as itinerant stone tent dwellers...

polkingbeal67: Yes, yes. I know all about the goopmutts. I don't need a history lesson from you.

smolin9: Yes, but the point is .. they just laughed! One of the great tragedies of intergalactic chronology! And they couldn't take it seriously. They just kept asking me if I was the doctor.

polkingbeal67: The doctor?

smolin9: Apparently, in their culture they worship a Time Lord called Doctor Who. I couldn't believe my telepathic receptors! Earthlings engaged in time travel? But then I looked it up on the microwocky and discovered this so-called Time Lord is supposed to wander around the universe in a Type 40 Mark 3 TARDIS with a faulty chameleon circuit. There's no such thing! I checked the intergalactic database and there is no record of such a time capsule, authorised or unauthorised. This doctor has completely fooled them.

polkingbeal67:   Interesting. What else have you learned?

smolin9:   Well, it's easy to make bad mistakes here. The earthling humans in Egypt didn't think much of my Bermuda shorts.

polkingbeal67:   Curious. By the way, why exactly are you squirming around like a hyperactive flamingo on a Venus lava flow? Have you aggravated your old microwocky injury?

smolin9:   No, that's the result of something else I learned: pyramids are not for skateboarding. Gotta go now. Keep the wormhole open.

Investigator Diary 12.19.18.16.14:

polkingbeal67:   Smolin9! Smolin9, where are you? I bet he's forgotten how to configure his microwocky for the new hyper spatial wrinkle coordinates. Typical. I knew he'd be trouble. Why on Morys did they have to go and choose *him*? Just because our intelligence community thought there was a high probability President Carter was a dolphin and the cognitive processing centres of smolin9's brain are genetically similar to those of Blue Dot dolphins. So we entrust the very survival of our species to a bumbling bubble-head who thought the Egyptian pyramids were for skateboarding! Now we know Jimmy Carter is *not* a dolphin, and our revered leader *still* sticks with that sad apology for a transgalactic scout. It really worries me. We've only got one Blue Dot year to see if this planet is suitable for colonisation. Smolin9! Smolin9!

smolin9: Is that you, polkingbeal67? It's a bad line. I think we've got a missing neutrino. Well, you look amazing today. Are those butterflies or can I smell cherry blossoms woven into the long tresses of your hair?

polkingbeal67: What? Yes, I'm sure you smell nice too. Please submit your report. Hold on. I haven't got any hair. And you can't smell anything. This is a hologrammatic image!

smolin9: When I look into your eyes I see spiral galaxies pirouetting slowly...

polkingbeal67: Have you been at the vitalmados again?

smolin9: Valmados talmados shalmados. Can I share saliva with you? It's what earthling humans do. It's so lovely.

polkingbeal67: Oh god! You *have* been at the vitalmados! That's it! I'm going to terminate this connection and recommend, once again, that you're replaced immediately!

smolin9: No, no, wait! Really, I'm coming round. It's just been so lonely here. Have some pity. Our revered leader told me he'd send me to Oov as a census collector if I fouled up on this mission. I promise you I can do a great job here.

polkingbeal67: Smolin9, you'll never attain true greatness if we keep lowering the bar for you.

smolin9: You don't know what it's like down here. One false move and they'll be harvesting my organs.

polkingbeal67: No one's going to harvest your organs.

smolin9: Don't you be so sure. Let me tell you what happened to me when I left the pyramids.

polkingbeal67: Yes, do tell.

smolin9: Do I detect a little disinterest there? Well, anyway, once I discovered I didn't really fit in with

16

my skateboard and my Bermuda shorts, I redefined my image using the biomimetic mutator. I tell you, I could not have looked more like an earthling human. Not without using recombinant DNA technology anyway. So there I was, mingling happily with earthlings near the pyramid of Khafra, when all of a sudden I saw the Great Sphinx move!

polkingbeal67:   It's an ancient monument. It *can't* move.

smolin9:   I know, I know. But it *did* move. I found out afterwards it had been covered with a billion Oovian chilloks who mistook it for one of their gods. Anyway, the shock got the better of me and I fainted.

polkingbeal67:   Go on. What happened next?

smolin9:   Well, they took me to what humans must think of as a hospital. You've never seen anything like it. They conduct operations without microwave visors and actually cut people up to repair them. It's barbaric! I didn't have my microwocky with me and had to use telepathy, so I couldn't understand everything that was going on. They thought my skin looked funny. Y'know, it doesn't matter how careful you are with the mutator imagemaker, earthlings still think you're made of Teflon.

polkingbeal67:   Interesting. Did they cut you?

smolin9:   No. But I couldn't sneak away because I'd left my cloaking device at the pyramids with my microwocky. And there was this doctor who said something to me a couple of times before doing something truly horrible. I know my telepathy translations aren't the best, but I thought he was saying: 'Get ready. We're going to get you to the nebula'. For a brief moment, I thought he was one of us and he was offering to give me a tour of a cosmic gas cloud somewhere. I found out what he was really saying when I got hold of my microwocky later.

polkingbeal67:   So, what *was* he saying and what horrible thing happened to you?

smolin9:   Turns out he was saying: 'Get ready. We're going to give you an enema'. I admit I screamed like a Goopmutt. He told me he was sorry but he needed a stool. So I fetched one and hit him over the head with it. Believe me, I needed some vitalmados after that! Keep the wormhole open.

Investigator Diary 12.19.18.17.5:

polkingbeal67:	What is it? Why have you summoned me for an extraordinary transmission?
smolin9:	I'm livid!
polkingbeal67:	Thanks for the update. Goodbye.
smolin9:	No, wait! Something's happened. And it's made me angry. It would make you angry too, if you were capable of emotion.
polkingbeal67:	Didn't I tell you I've been seconded to review new supra-planetary trade operations? And didn't I tell you this is also my day-off?
smolin9:	You did.
polkingbeal67:	Didn't I make it clear you'd have to make other arrangements for your reports?
smolin9:	You did.
polkingbeal67:	So?
smolin9:	I didn't.
polkingbeal67:	Well, I'm here now. So what's happened?
smolin9:	I'll tell you, but first of all, you should know that there's a red

light on my microwocky indicating a problem with the telepresence feed.

polkingbeal67:   I know. I've got one at my end too.

smolin9:   So shouldn't you, you know, check for problems with the telepresence feed?

polkingbeal67:   It's been there for ages. It's just a warning light.

smolin9:   Isn't that all the more reason to, you know, check for problems with the telepresence feed? Whoever put it there obviously thought it necessary to warn you.

polkingbeal67:   It's just a light.

smolin9:   The feed's definitely not working now. It's really unnerving. Your eyes are where your mouth should be and vice versa. You're blinking every time you speak.

polkingbeal67:   But I don't have eyelids.

smolin9:   Exactly.

polkingbeal67:   Okay, let me try this. Is that better?

smolin9:   Yes.

polkingbeal67:   Please proceed with your report.

smolin9:	Okay, well, basically, I intercepted some primitive earthling datagrams using my microwocky and guess what? They've discovered our planet!
polkingbeal67:	Do tell.
smolin9:	They're calling it Kepler-22b.
polkingbeal67:	I quite like the name. Why are you livid?
smolin9:	Really? You like it? I think it's ridiculous! Apparently, they named it after the telescope that spotted it. So, y'know, if an earthling discovers a pimple on the chin using a shaving mirror, what would he call it? Something like ikea-2c?
polkingbeal67:	Earthlings give names to their pimples?
smolin9:	No, they don't give names to... Never mind. They're also on the verge of discovering what they think is the final elementary particle, the one that gives mass to matter. They call it the Higgs bosun. Probably because it was spotted by a senior deckhand of a merchant ship captained by someone called Higgs.
polkingbeal67:	Now you're being silly. So what is it? You're mad about the name

21

they've given our planet?

smolin9: No. The thing is – they're being incredibly rude. A number of their so-called scientists have been saying our planet can only support single-celled organisms. Bacteria, nothing else! They're saying the only life on Morys is alien pond slime.

polkingbeal67: Alien pond slime? Alien pond slime! Okay, that is rude.

smolin9: The feed's going funny again. Oh!

polkingbeal67: What is it?

smolin9: You've transformed into a muddy puddle on the ground.

polkingbeal67: [splutter!] [gurgle!]

smolin9: You're nothing more than an unsightly thick green sludge, with a few bubbles forming. Better leave it there for now. Keep the wormhole open.

Investigator Diary 12.19.19.0.7:

smolin9: I see you've sorted out the problem with the telepresence feed. It wasn't easy talking to you when you looked like a pile of regurgitated pizza.

polkingbeal67:	What is pizza?
smolin9:	It's a government-enforced source of nutrition here on Earth.
polkingbeal67:	Government-enforced?
smolin9:	Yeh. If the people don't go out to eat it, it gets sent round to their dwellings. There's no way they can avoid it.
polkingbeal67:	Interesting. Have you examined it?
smolin9:	I probably shouldn't tell you this, but I tried to ingest some when I first landed on the planet. I was hungry and didn't have time to prepare a food tablet.
polkingbeal67:	You tried to ingest it? How? Are you mad? Their digestive systems are nothing like ours!
smolin9:	Yeh, I soon found that out. Pizza doesn't work very well as a suppository.
polkingbeal67:	Humans have stomach acids to dissolve their food. We don't. I can't believe you did that.
smolin9:	Believe me, I wish I hadn't. It took me so long to pick out all the sticky cheese!
polkingbeal67:	According to our test results, the human stomach contains

hydrochloric acid strong enough to dissolve metal.

smolin9:   Frankly I'm more surprised it can dissolve that cheese!

polkingbeal67:   You crazy prokaryote! Anyway, I told our revered leader about earthlings discovering our planet. He was not pleased to hear them describe it as 'capable of sustaining nothing more than alien pond slime'. Not pleased at all. After what happened at Roswell, he said it was the last straw. So he took the invisibility cloak off the two planets vandalised by goopmutts after the Cassiopeia supernova party.

smolin9:   Oh! That explains something.

polkingbeal67:   Explains what?

smolin9:   I picked up some stuff on my microwocky – earthlings reporting the discovery of two roasted Earth-sized planets orbiting a sub dwarf B star …

polkingbeal67:   Oh, so they noticed then? Interesting. Do they know the planets were inhabited by humans?

smolin9:   I don't think so.

polkingbeal67:	I don't know why we have to be so sensitive about it anyway. It was collateral damage. A few green-snouted goopmutts had a few drinks and decided to go out shooting stars. These things happen.
smolin9:	Please try to remember we're thinking of establishing a colony on Earth. It wouldn't be very good diplomacy to ask them if they could put us up for a few eons and, by the way, we're sorry their brother and sister planets were microwaved during an inter-galactic party we were hosting.
polkingbeal67:	Point taken, but actually I think the earthlings have got colonisation plans of their own. As you know, they set foot on their moon a short time ago. According to my microwocky, the words that marked the momentous event were: "That's one small step for a man, one giant leap for mankind (Neil Armstrong)." Well it seems that it was thinly disguised code. It's an anagram for: "Thin man left planet, ran, makes a large stride, pins flag on moon. On to

Mars!"

smolin9:	But Mars is totally inhospitable to human life. It doesn't have a molten core any more. But it feels like *I* have. Ew! Gotta go. Found some more cheese. Keep the wormhole open.

Investigator Diary 12.19.19.1.8:

Melinda:	Hello?
polkingbeal67:	smolin9?
Melinda:	No, I'm Melinda.
polkingbeal67:	Melinda? I don't understand. Where's smolin9?
Melinda:	He'll be along shortly. He asked me to tell you to stick around till he gets here.
polkingbeal67:	Oh? But who are you?
Melinda:	I'm Melinda.
polkingbeal67:	Yes I know. You said. But... wait, are you an Earthling?
Melinda:	Yeh. Hi. Um, welcome to our planet, Sir. This is so erratic, isn't it? Insane. Literally. Your alien buddy and I sort of made friends a few days ago and, well, you know.

polkingbeal67:	What? No, I don't know. Okay, better wait for smolin9 then. Well, what shall we do in the meantime? What's the protocol for this? I don't have a flowchart for such an encounter. Er, do you want to exchange pleasantries?
Melinda:	Yeh. Isn't this erratic? Literally.
polkingbeal67:	Okay. I'll start. Um… Yo, s'up.
Melinda:	Ha ha! Insane! That's really good. But relax. Literally. You don't have to talk like us. Just be yourself. Y'know, I should really let smolin9 tell you this himself, but, well, we're thinking of getting married.
polkingbeal67:	What! You can't!
Melinda:	I know. I know. Literally. We hardly know each other. But…
polkingbeal67:	Never mind that. Your liaison is a flagrant breach of intergalactic law and conventions. A marriage is totally out of the question. You cannot do this!
Melinda:	But wouldn't it be good for, y'know, interplanetary relations?
polkingbeal67:	Preposterous! He's not like an earthling human. Did you know that? He's using a biomimetic mutator, er, a device that transforms his appearance. You

27

	know what? You should both see somebody, urgently.
Melinda:	See who?
polkingbeal67:	A psychiatrist? I don't know. An intergalactic, interspecies, inter..., inter...
Melinda:	Interferer?
polkingbeal67:	Intermediary. Oh help! I refuse to discuss this any further with you.
Melinda:	You want to go back to chitchat?
polkingbeal67:	Yes.
Melinda:	Okay.
polkingbeal67:	Okay. How are you? Specifically, please disclose the genetic weaknesses that run in your family.
Melinda:	Excuse me? Listen, can I get you a cup of tea or something?
polkingbeal67:	I'm sure you can. You appear to have moderate humanoid dexterity. However, I wouldn't be able to drink it. This is a telepresence simulation. I'm a hologram.
Melinda:	Oh dear, I'm so sorry. That's insane. It must be awful.
polkingbeal67:	No, no. There's nothing wrong

	with me. It's just, er, this isn't really me. I'm not what I seem.
Melinda:	Yes, you seem a bit erratic. I hope you feel better soon. So, what's the weather like there, on your, er, planet?
polkingbeal67:	Um, not bad. A few methane showers.
Melinda:	Right. Is that like...rain?
polkingbeal67:	Methane is an odourless gas produced by decomposition of organic materials in subsoils.
Melinda:	Right. Insane. Literally. So not really like our rain then. Anyway, it's been good talking to you. Smolin9's here now. I've got to go and wash my hair.
smolin9:	Oh good. You're still here. And you've met Melinda.
polkingbeal67:	Yes, what on Morys Minor is going on? You bumbling bubble-head! You left me talking to an Earthling! Who is she? What's going on? She's been talking about marriage! Oh help! What just happened? I don't feel well.

smolin9:	Calm down, p. It's all good news. It's fantastic! Melinda is the missing link.
polkingbeal67:	Between humans and apes?
smolin9:	No, between us and Voyager 1 verification. I've taken her into my confidence. She now understands all about us and she's been very co-operative. I've managed to get incredible breakthrough information. I knew I was on to something when I heard her in the bathroom singing 'Johnny B. Goode' – the song that's on the Voyager 1 golden record!
polkingbeal67:	I hate to tell you this, but I've done my research and there's no way that woman is Chuck Berry.
smolin9:	No? Oh.
polkingbeal67:	And what's all this marriage nonsense?
smolin9:	Well, we've become quite close in the short time we've known each other. She's introduced me to all kinds of earthling culture. I've been reading their literature.

polkingbeal67:	Like what?
smolin9:	I read War And Peace – only took me five hours.
polkingbeal67:	Big deal. It's only three words.
smolin9:	No, it's... Oh, never mind. Anyway, there are strategic advantages to this marriage...
polkingbeal67:	You've said that before. Remember when you fell for that jellyfish?
smolin9:	Yes, I admit that was a mistake. But you get stung and you move on. Listen, Melinda played me samples of earthling wedding music and one of them was Bach's Gavotte en Rondeau. The Voyager 1 golden disc again! It's got to be a sign. But that's not all. Believe it or not, Melinda says she knows Jimmy Carter and she's going to introduce me to him! Put that in your microwocky and process it! Anyway, Melinda and I are going to a party. I'll get back to you straight afterwards. Keep the wormhole open.

Investigator Diary 12.19.19.2.4:

Melinda:	Hello?
polkingbeal67:	Hello Melinda. Where's smolin9?
Melinda:	He's on his way. Before he gets here, there's something I should tell you. Literally.
polkingbeal67:	Oh? How did the party go, by the way?
Melinda:	So erratic. Well, it was a fancy dress party and...
polkingbeal67:	Fancy dress? What did smolin9 go as?
Melinda:	Himself. Y'know, as an alien. Literally. Insane. He wore a full length cloak, but otherwise he was... well, he was smolin9.
polkingbeal67:	Oh no. Oh help. Did he cause panic and uproar and...?
Melinda:	No. No. It's all right. There were three others who looked just the same as him.
polkingbeal67:	Oh yes, I see. Interesting. So, what was it you wanted to tell me?
Melinda:	Well, smolin9 and I are... well, we're no longer an item.

polkingbeal67:	What? What does that even mean? You're not on a list? You're not a piece of information or news?
Melinda:	Ha ha. Insane! No, we're not... well, put it this way – we're not getting married any more.
polkingbeal67:	I'm not capable of unrestrained expressions of joy, but if I was, I'd be jerking my limbs about haphazardly and singing 'Johnny B. Goode' at the top of my voice. Er, sorry. What happened? Did you come to realise a union between different organisms of different species from different planets could never work?
Melinda:	No. He just got on my nerves. Literally. It all started at that party.
polkingbeal67:	Do tell.
Melinda:	Well, I introduced him to Jimmy Carter like he asked me to. I don't know Jimmy very well. He's just someone who lives on our estate. He sold my cousin a knock-off Xbox a while back. Literally. Anyway, Jimmy introduced smolin9 to another guy who turns out to be a real low life.
polkingbeal67:	Arthropod? Fungi?

Melinda:	Arthur who? You know him? Smolin9 thought he was a fun guy. I certainly didn't. Literally. Anyway, this Arthur guy has been a really bad influence. Smolin9 has started behaving like him and talking liking him. Wait, here he comes. You'll see for yourself. I'm off. It's been totally erratic meeting you. Insane. Literally.
polkingbeal67:	Goodbye Melinda.
smolin9:	S'appenin bro? Mel tell yah 'bout us? Shame, innit. Know wot ah mean? Don' worry. We're cool. No yellin' or 'ittin' or nuffin. Yah diggin' me?
polkingbeal67:	What?
smolin9:	Ah is finkin' dat stuff on da golden record maht be a bit iffy. Know wot ah mean? Ah mean, dat Jimmy Carter. 'E knows nuffin' 'bout Voyager. Nuffin'!
polkingbeal67:	I can hardly understand a word you're saying. Is there a problem with the telepresence feed?
smolin9:	Nah! Don' fink so. Hey p, ah is finkin of resignin' ma job as spesh envoy and investigatah.
polkingbeal67:	Resigning? You crazy prokaryote! You can't do that.

smolin9:

Why can't ah den? Ah's depressed abaht dis Jimmy Carter fing an' all. I wants to jus' do some chillin' on da Erff fer a bit.

polkingbeal67:

Out of the question. You can't quit now. I've stuck up for you all through this wretched mission. Against my better judgement, I might add. Ever since you and I first found the Voyager probe while we were spacecombing with that Mark III Zeplock mineral spotter, I've tried my best to keep you on the right path, but you keep letting me down. I've persuaded our revered leader to keep you in post despite all your vitalmados abuse. Don't you see? Our reputations are at stake. Besides, I've done research and, curiously, humans don't have unique names. So you see, your Jimmy Carter may not have been the right one! You must not give up now. Our planet is depending on you.

smolin9:

Wossup wiv you bro? Chill. Join me. It'd be bonkers down 'ere on Erff knowin' all da stuff we know, innit.

polkingbeal67:

Pull yourself together. Think of the great heroes of Morys Minor. Would achilles12 have given up on an assignment like this?

smolin9:	'Oo? Oh yeh, 'e waged war massive on dem Oovian chilloks and died of gangrene when dey burrowed into 'is ankles.
polkingbeal67:	And what about Joan5 of Ork?
smolin9:	Captured by carnivorous skavaks 'n' burned as a steak.
polkingbeal67:	Okay. What about custer3? Did custer3 quit at the Battle of the Greasy Crater?
smolin9:	Listen, bro. 'E was torn to pieces by a fousand screamin' goopmutts.
polkingbeal67:	Oh. Yes. Well, at least he didn't quit.
smolin9:	Okay, okay. Ah'll fink abaht it. Keep da worm'ole open.

Investigator Diary 12.19.19.3.12:

This report was not submitted on the due date.

The following is a note from the investigator's colleague, polkingbeal67:

I can't imagine what's happened to smolin9. At the time of his last report, he'd fallen into bad company and was talking about resigning his post as special envoy and investigator. So it's possible he could have defected. Not satisfied with being just a crazy prokaryote, he may now have become a traitorous collaborator. He could be helping a combined force of earthlings and chilloks prepare for an invasion of Morys even as I write this.

I knew this would happen. All this getting clingy with other life forms – it never comes to any good you know. Frankly, I don't see why he can't be like the rest of us and conduct relationships without getting all emotionally entangled. Well, I warned our revered leader against sending him to the planet. Obviously, it should have been me. Not that I'm bitter or anything. It's just that, well, smolin9 is too sensitive. He has all that idiotic empathy thing. I'm from the mean craters of Morys Minor where even the goopmutts fear to tread. Speaking of goopmutts, here's an example of why it should have been me and not smolin9:

There we were, spacecombing in the Centaurus galaxy shortly after we'd salvaged Voyager 1, when a young cadet called yukawa3 arrived. Our revered leader had sent him out to check the Voyager artifacts we had stowed away in the hold of the ship. He also warned us there had been reports of marauding goopmutts in the vicinity. That night, I was woken by the unmistakable sound of a warlike goopmutt scream. Yukawa3 and I jumped out of our sleeping pods and saw the crested silhouette of a goopmutt in smolin9's pod. We were about to zap the pod with a couple of micro beam plasma blasts when we heard strains of 'Johnny B. Goode'. It turns out smolin9 had intended to disguise himself as a goopmutt in the event that we came under attack. So he'd configured the settings on his mutator so that he only had to flick the 'confirm' switch and he'd promptly assume the appearance of a goopmutt. Meanwhile, he'd settled down with some vitalmados pills and was listening to the Voyager 1 golden record when Beethoven's String Quartet No. 13 in B flat suddenly morphed into a trumpeting elephant. Smolin9 dropped the pills, knocked the mutator switch and got transformed into a goopmutt lookalike. His pathetic swearing was translated into the goopmutt screams that woke us up. Hardly a good example to set for a young cadet. But I'm not bitter.

I remember when we took Voyager back to Morys and our

revered leader gave us the job of investigating the Pale Blue Dot. Obviously there was a lot of research to be done before we could make any sort of contact with the planet, so we tapped into communication networks and did our homework. Eventually, we abducted a mouse for analysis. According to the information we'd acquired, we should have been able to plug the thing into a computer as a pointing device. When we clamped its tail to a microwocky connector, however, the mouse started making high-pitched squeaking sounds and the cursor got stuck. Smolin9 felt sorry for it and wouldn't let us disassemble the thing to get to the trackball. Right there, our revered leader should have known smolin9 was going to be a problem. But I'm not bitter. Really, I'm not.

Goodness knows what life-forms he's empathising with now. Before he even got involved with earthling humans, he'd fallen in love with three dolphins, a baobob tree and a jellyfish. The bumbling bubble-head! He's even started to resemble an earthling human without using a mutator. The last time we communicated via telepresence feed I swear I spotted incipient nails and some nasal hair. Which is strange because we don't have noses.

Follow-up note from the investigator's colleague, polkingbeal67:

In one of smolin9's early reports, he mentioned deciphering primitive datagrams on his microwocky and communicating with earthlings using something called Facebook. After a bit of trouble, I found smolin9's facebook page. Things are more serious than I thought. His last few status updates seem to dwell on the breakup of his relationship with Melinda. The last update he posted says he's in a black hole staring into the abyss. So, it seems he's left the Pale Blue Dot in some sort of craft and made a rather serious navigation error. I don't know if we'll ever hear from him again. But I'll keep the wormhole open.

Investigator Diary 12.19.19.4.12:

polkingbeal67:	Smolin9? Is it you? You're back! We thought you... I can't believe... How did you...?
smolin9:	Hello p. Calm down, old buddy. What are you blathering about?
polkingbeal67:	Your facebook status said you were in a black hole staring into the abyss! How did you get away? We feared the worst, I'm afraid. I've just come from a meeting with our revered leader where I reported your untimely demise.
smolin9:	I didn't know I was untimely demised. What does that even mean? Is it because I missed the last report? Listen, when I wrote about being in a black hole, I was talking metaphysically.
polkingbeal67:	You mean the age-old mystery surrounding the nature of matter, time and space at the heart of cosmology?
smolin9:	Uh, okay, in that case, I was talking metaphorically.
polkingbeal67:	You've lost me. Anyway, you're obviously okay. So, why did you miss the last report?
smolin9:	Yes, I'm sorry about that. I was at the football.

polkingbeal67:	Football? Football! You neglected to deliver a report that's vital to the survival of our species because you were at the football! It's inconsequential! Football is irrelevant!
smolin9:	An elephant? Ha ha. An elephant is an earthling creature. You crack me up, p. No, football is a game in which two opposing teams of eleven players defend goals at opposite ends of a field, with points being scored by kicking the ball into the net attached to the opponents' goal posts. Elephant! Ha ha.
polkingbeal67:	I didn't say elephant, you crazy prokaryote! I know it's a game. It could just as well be cricket, it doesn't matter, the point is...
smolin9:	I see how you're getting confused now, p. Cricket is a game but it's also an earthling creature.
polkingbeal67:	You crazy... Wait, are you mocking me? You are, aren't you? Instead of mocking me, don't you think you should just submit your report so I can have something sensible to take back to our revered leader?
smolin9:	Okay, okay. Here's my report. No, wait, mocking you is a lot more

fun!

polkingbeal67:	Please!
smolin9:	Well, like I said, I was bonding with some earthlings and we went to this football match. It was strange. There was no atmosphere.
polkingbeal67:	It was isolated from the protective layer of gases that sustains life on the planet?
smolin9:	No, I mean... well, people usually like it when their team scores goals. But this was different. We were watching a team called Manchester City. By the way, you should check out their mascot! Where does that come from? Anyway, when a City player scored a goal, he seemed to be upset about it and revealed a message on his undershirt saying 'Why always me?' The supporters were also disturbed about it. They put their arms around each other and turned their backs to the pitch as if they couldn't bear to look. What do you make of that, p?
polkingbeal67:	Interesting. Perhaps it's some kind of collective emotional turmoil. Speaking of which, are you now compos mentis and

	dedicated to your investigation of the planet?
smolin9:	I don't know. Why don't you ask this duck I brought along with me?
polkingbeal67:	What duck? I don't see a duck.
smolin9:	No? Has he gone? I must join him on the great migration.
polkingbeal67:	What?
smolin9:	I don't think I'm completely recovered yet.
polkingbeal67:	Well, I notice you've at least reverted to talking properly. I could hardly understand a word you were saying last time. I'm sure you're getting back on track. I look forward to your next scheduled report.
smolin9:	Ah. I can't make the next one.
polkingbeal67:	What? Why not?
smolin9:	I'd miss the Arsenal match! Keep the wormhole open.

Investigator Diary 12.19.19.5.3:

This report was not submitted on the due date.

The following is a note from the investigator's colleague, polkingbeal67:

Smolin9 said he'd miss this report. Well, he has. Apparently, watching earthlings dribbling spherical objects on a patch of monocotyledonous green plants is more important to him than securing the survival of an entire species of advanced sapient beings threatened with imminent extinction. He's a loose cannon and he's blown his last chance. If that crazy bubble-head thinks Mario Balotelli's undershirts hold the clue to our successful colonisation on the Pale Blue Dot, well, he... I don't know, words fail me! We can no longer entrust smolin9 with the sole responsibility for this planetary assessment and, thankfully, I've managed to persuade our revered leader that the mission requires the skills, expertise and objectivity that only I, polkingbeal67, possess. For the record, I entreated our revered leader to let me replace the bumbling prokaryote, but, apparently, for the sake of balance and alien affinity, I'm to join him and we're to work together for a minimum of two uinals.

I'm preparing myself for wormhole travel tomorrow. I refuse to adopt smolin9's low-key approach and I shall, of course, arrive wearing full Morys Minor battle dress with sherg-encrusted helmet. I intend to forge a new path for our people in a new world, a world of hope and optimism and boundless opportunity. It may be like looking for a needle at the tip of an iceberg, but I will find Jimmy Carter and we will smoke a pipe of vitalmados essence while we discuss the future of our peoples. I'll get an official apology for Roswell! I'm so excited about it, I'm experiencing an unsettling release of endorphins and I've started talking in clichés and, as you know, I usually avoid clichés like the plague.

As for smolin9, I will curb his behaviour and rectify his errors. He won't like it, but I shall put my foot down with a firm hand.

Set the controls for the Pale Blue Dot and keep the wormhole open!

Investigator Diary 12.19.19.5.18:

polkingbeal67:	This is polkingbeal67 reporting back to the mother planet from the Pale Blue Dot.
smolin9:	And me.
polkingbeal67:	And you?
smolin9:	I'm also reporting back. I was here before you, remember? I'm the one who did all the groundwork, patiently studying the life-forms and building up a network of useful contacts before you came blundering on the scene in full battle-dress and no cloaking device, terrifying two earthling humans and a dog walking in the park!
polkingbeal67:	That was no dog. It was a mutant goopmutt.
smolin9:	What do you mean? Of course it was a dog! It had five toes on its forefeet and four toes on its hind feet, with non-retractile claws. It was a domesticated carnivorous mammal of the family Canidae. It had a tail and it barked. It was a dog!
polkingbeal67:	It growled and bared its teeth, just like a goopmutt.
smolin9:	That's what dogs do when they're

44

scared.

polkingbeal67: You crazy prokaryote! It was a mutant goopmutt! Let me explain to you. If it was just a dog, why did the humans worship it?

smolin9: What?

polkingbeal67: They followed behind and collected its excrement. If that's not worship, I don't know what is!

smolin9: So, you thought it was a mutant goopmutt, eh? Is that why you ran away?

polkingbeal67: May I remind you that you ran too? In fact, you ran first.

smolin9: I'm scared of dogs!

polkingbeal67: You would never have outrun it anyway.

smolin9: I didn't need to outrun it.

polkingbeal67: Why not?

smolin9: I only needed to outrun you.

polkingbeal67: Eh? Anyway, it was ridiculous – two proud warriors from Morys Minor running in abject terror from a mutant goopmutt!

smolin9: Dog.

polkingbeal67: Whatever.

smolin9:	Well, what I want to know is – why did it just keel over and die like that? You never told me. What did it die of?
polkingbeal67:	Oh, nothing serious.
smolin9:	Nothing serious? It died, didn't it? I think that makes it quite serious for the dog.
polkingbeal67:	Goopmutt.
smolin9:	Did you shoot it?
polkingbeal67:	What? Of course not. Er, I used mind control. Have you never heard of psychological warfare?
smolin9:	You can't actually physically kill something using psychological weapons!
polkingbeal67:	Bubblehead! I didn't use mind control on the goopmutt. I used it on you.
smolin9:	Me?
polkingbeal67:	Yes. I fooled you into believing it was dead.
smolin9:	What!
polkingbeal67:	Okay, okay, I shot it! It kept coming up behind me and sniffing me!
smolin9:	I expect it was only trying to

worship you!

polkingbeal67: Okay, signing off. Keep the wormhole open.

Investigator Diary 12.19.19.6.16:

polkingbeal67: This is polkingbeal67 reporting from the Pale Blue Dot. I don't know where smolin9 is.

smolin9: I'm here.

polkingbeal67: You're late. Where've you been?

smolin9: You remember Melinda?

polkingbeal67: Oh help. The earthling woman you nearly married?

smolin9: Yes. We're getting back together and we're... you know, going to get married again. Well, not married *again*. You know what I mean. I know you don't approve, but I still think it could be a defining moment in our alliance with this planet.

polkingbeal67: Defining moment? I'd define the moment as demented, cracked, crazy, preposterous, screwball. And please remember I'm exercising a great deal of restraint here.

smolin9:	So you're slowly coming round to the idea?
polkingbeal67:	You crazy prokaryote! I said restraint, not consent!
smolin9:	There's a problem anyway. We may not be able to get married.
polkingbeal67:	Interesting. Why not? Not that I'm encouraging you or anything, but it should be easy enough. You meet her father, offer him six goats and a microwocky. Job done.
smolin9:	Well, there's the physiological incompatibility thing. I mean our biological responses to each other are so, y'know, so irregular.
polkingbeal67:	What biological responses? I trust you're not contemplating any kind of primitive carnal intimacy? What, without a test tube? I had low expectations of you, but this is just... Oh help. What will our revered leader say?
smolin9:	No, no, not carnal ... whatever. But, as you know, earthlings rely on their sensory neurons and we use telesthesia. And when Melinda touches me, my energy field emits copious quantities of ammonium sulfide. The aroma of bad eggs hangs

	around for hours. Kind of ruins the mood.
polkingbeal67:	Well, let that be a lesson to you. I've always said feelings are like chemicals.
smolin9:	The more you excite them, the more animated you get?
polkingbeal67:	No, the more you analyse them, the worse they smell.
smolin9:	Well, anyway, what have you been up to? I haven't seen you since the last report.
polkingbeal67:	While you've been enjoying your smelly liaisons, I've been putting this project back on the front foot.
smolin9:	You've been doing things back to front?
polkingbeal67:	I found Jimmy Carter and discovered he's no longer President of the earthlings.
smolin9:	So the objective of our mission is rendered null and void? We have no one to negotiate with? Your idea of being on the front foot is clearly at odds with mine. Anyway, why didn't you take me with you?
polkingbeal67:	There are times when you've just got

	to act on your own initiative and work independently without the input of your peers.
smolin9:	Well, did you speak to him?
polkingbeal67:	No point whatsoever. I'm so disappointed in him. Where's the grand palace with its guards and white elephants and golden statues? This so-called earthling leader lives in a little single-storey structure in a pitiful little one-horse town called Plains, Georgia. He lives there anonymously with his wife Rosalynn. Just an anonymous couple in an anonymous house in an anonymous street that goes pretty much nowhere at all. The two of them sit together, anonymously promoting human rights. They hold hands a lot, teach Sunday School, publish poetry, memoirs and children's books. Anonymously pathetic.
smolin9:	I don't know. He sounds like a really nice earthling.
polkingbeal67:	Nice? Come on. What sort of leader is that? What would he have done if his planet had been invaded by hostile goopmutts? Apparently, during his term of office, he didn't fire a single bullet. Never went to war. Never dropped a bomb. Never killed a single

person. A completely dismal record.

smolin9: Doesn't that sound like someone you could negotiate with? I still think I'd like him.

polkingbeal67: Bubblehead! War is its own reward. History shows you have to fight to achieve anything. Even peace. You really need to rediscover your dark side, smolin9. Well, now we've got to find the new leader and threaten him with the most despicable acts of violence. Then we'll barter with him and discuss our people colonising his planet. By the way, where's my tangy vitalmados pill? We left two of them here after the last report. One each. I've been really looking forward to it.

smolin9: Ah, yes. Well, y'know, there are times when you've just got to act on your own initiative and work independently without the input of your peers. I never lost my dark side. Keep the wormhole open.

Investigator Diary 12.19.19.7.5:

polkingbeal67: Please confirm you are the earthling leader.

President: Who are you? How did you get in here? How did you bypass my security?

polkingbeal67:   We are envoys from a planet in the constellation of Cygnus. Your security was no match for our Craterkite cloaking devices. This conversation is being transmitted in real-time to our mother planet by means of a specially configured dark energy wormhole channel. Now will you please confirm you are the earthling leader, successor to Jimmy Carter.

President: I am President of the United States of America. I am regarded as the Leader of the Free World.

polkingbeal67:   Only the Free World? Who is leader of the, er, captive, bit? Who captured them? Was it the goopmutts?

President: The Leader of the Free World is a colloquialism. The United States of America is the main democratic superpower on Earth, so its president is effectively the leader of all the world's democratic nation states. You people haven't got Michelle, have you?

polkingbeal67:   Your shell? Are you a part-time crustacean?

smolin9:   He's talking about his wife, p.

polkingbeal67:   His wife has a skeleton on the outside

of her body? Wait! It rings a bell. Let me see. Ah yes, here in the briefing notes on my microwocky it says "serious issues include health insurance, unemployment and Shell."

President: Actually I had more problems with BP.

polkingbeal67: Blood pressure? Interesting. No wonder you've got problems with health insurance.

President: You know, you guys remind me of a famous movie of ours. Do you have droids? There was this droid called, I think, yes, R2-D2. I loved that little guy. I can do a passable impression, too. Would you like to hear it? Beep beep beedle beep whirr squeee pop beep beep beedle bop whirr.

polkingbeal67: Leader of the Free World, you say?

President: Er, yes, sorry. We'd better move this on. Shall we? What are your demands?

polkingbeal67: Demands? Ah yes, well, we come from a planet called Morys Minor and our entire race is threatened with extinction at the end of the katun cycle. We're responding to an invitation from your predecessor, Jimmy Carter. He sent us a golden

	record by space probe. It wasn't properly addressed. We found it drifting around aimlessly in the Centaurus galaxy. It's a wonder we found it at all. Anyway, we want to colonise your planet and if you resist we'll blow you to bits!
smolin9:	Give him a chance, p! Oh, and ask him if I can have a souvenir from the White House. An ashtray or something?
President:	Hang on. President Carter extended the hand of friendship to you and you want to take that hand and bite it?
polkingbeal67:	Oh, don't tell me you don't want to fight! Oh help. You're just as bad as Carter. What is wrong with you earthlings? Whatever happened to blood and glory? Take over, smolin9 – do it your way. I've tried to reach out to these people in a spirit of honourable hostility and mutual loathing, but it's no use.
President:	You know, you should be aware that I don't necessarily oppose war. What I am opposed to is a dumb war. What I am opposed to is a rash war. I consider it part of my responsibility as President of the United States to defend my people against threats from foreign, er, worlds. But, you

know what? I've been going through an evolution on this issue and, you know, we could absolutely embrace visitors to this planet provided we share common principles of justice and progress, tolerance and the dignity of all human, er, humanoid beings.

polkingbeal67: Unlikely. But go on.

President: You know, it's interesting. You've made several references to things on your planet that are peculiar to us here on Earth. Katun cycles, for example. That's a reference to a calendar, right? Something to do with the Mayans – an old and famous civilisation right here on this planet. Oh yes, and the name of your planet. Well, it appears to share its name, rather bizarrely I suppose, with a small British car, now obsolete. You know, it seems to me we have some curious things in common.

polkingbeal67: Preposterous! Our calendar was introduced by our revered leader shortly after he appeared on Morys about two thousand Earth years ago. We rename our planet at the beginning of every katun and we often use information gleaned from abductees for this purpose. We ask

	them to name things they're most proud of.
President:	So you do abduct people? I always thought those people were fantasists.
polkingbeal67:	Oh help, of course we abduct people. And not just from *your* planet.
President:	Anyway, I think we have some common ground. How would it be if I was to set up an International Negotiating Committee for a Framework Convention on Interplanetary Integration? After some exploratory meetings, we could have a series of summits at the United Nations to establish the terms of reference for establishing a road map for peaceful transition.
polkingbeal67:	Oh no! Oh help! Are you sure you don't want to fight?
smolin9:	Mister President, could we get all this committee integration thing done quickly?
President:	Not till after my election. After my election I'll have more flexibility.
polkingbeal67:	Out of the question. We can't wait that long! Sir, you should prepare for war! My people will have revenge for Roswell! I don't know how you earthlings make these things official.

	Ah yes, I know – terms and conditions apply! There, I've said it.
smolin9:	I suppose an ashtray is now out of the question?
polkingbeal67:	Come along, smolin9. Terminating this report. Keep the wormhole open.

Investigator Diary 12.19.19.7.18:

smolin9:	Are you there, p?
polkingbeal67:	Well, you're looking at a virtual-holographic representation of me. Does that count?
smolin9:	Yeh, I'm pretty sure I know why, but, for the sake of clarifying things for the readers of this report, perhaps you'd like to explain why you've left Earth and you're now back on Morys?
polkingbeal67:	Well, I... I was recalled by our revered leader, uh, summoned for an urgent special consultation. So, yeh, hi.
smolin9:	Special consultation, eh? Let me see. Would that by any chance have something to do with you declaring war on Earth without, you know, any authorisation whatsoever? I'm sorry. This must be so embarrassing for

you.

polkingbeal67:	Not at all. Why are you smirking like that? I was quite within my rights. Anyway, the war became irrelevant after I shrewdly deduced what is really happening on that god-forsaken globe of rubble you're so fond of.
smolin9:	What do you mean? What *is* going on?
polkingbeal67:	Well, if you didn't have your silly bobbly head immersed in football and skateboarding, you'd have noticed that any attempts by us to colonise the Pale Blue Dot would be undermined by Oovian chilloks.
smolin9:	Chilloks? Are you kidding? What are you talking about?
polkingbeal67:	As I informed our revered leader, the chilloks have infiltrated the Pale Blue Dot in their billions and they're poised to seize control at any moment.
smolin9:	Chilloks! Seize control? Are we talking about the same things? FYI, the chilloks have been on Earth for several millennia. They're tiny, meek, docile, unassuming creatures that pose no threat whatsoever. Their

mutator technology is primitive and they can't transform themselves into other life forms. Even earthlings can control them with insecticides, like ant powder! Are you serious? Did you really use the chilloks to pull the wool over the eyes of our revered leader? You must have been really desperate to avoid a charge of unauthorised warmongering. What did he say?

polkingbeal67:   You crazy prokaryote! If you must know, our revered leader thanked me effusively and presided at a banquet in my honour. Between you and me, I think I'm in line for an Oppenheimer938 Prize. Don't worry, I'll make sure there's a footnote about you in my acceptance speech. Mm? You're welcome. Our revered leader totally agrees with me about the chilloks. Their mutator techniques are improving, you know. Already they can carry more than their body weight.

smolin9:   So you're saying there are going to be mut-ants that become gi-ants?

polkingbeal67:   What? Yes. Anyway, there are about one million of them to every human! Who knows how powerful they can become?

smolin9:   And our revered leader actually

	believes they're a threat to the planet?
polkingbeal67:	Oh help, yes. He totally expects them to claim the Pale Blue Dot any time now. He made a speech – something about the meek inheriting the Earth. Besides, there are other factors. The Milky Way galaxy is on track to collide with the Andromeda galaxy.
smolin9:	Yes. But not for about four billion years! By that time, our descendants will probably be able to steer it!
polkingbeal67:	I'm appalled you can be so dismissive. Look, it's really serious.
smolin9:	Yeh, now there's a thought – maybe I should encourage my descendants to be lawyers. Galaxies colliding? Just think of all the whiplash injuries! Wait, does that mean my mission is finished?
polkingbeal67:	I was coming to that. Uh, you might want to sit down.
smolin9:	Why? Oh no, I can sense the onset of a colon-hyphen-left-parenthesis moment.
polkingbeal67:	Huh? Your orders are to return to Morys immediately. After a thorough de-briefing, you'll be sent out to assist yukawa3 who's investigating a

planet in the Kolosimo 922 system.

smolin9: But I was going to get married on Saturday! I must speak to Melinda.

polkingbeal67: Bubblehead! It's out of the question! It's so unnatural. Absurd. Stop thinking with your heart! It's ridiculous. Do my eyes speak? Do my hands see? Do my feet smell?

smolin9: Well, since you mention it...

polkingbeal67: What? You know that whole interplanetary relationship thing gives me nightmares! Anyway, you've got a whole lifetime of asinine relationships ahead of you. How can you expect to be truly happy with a woman who insists on treating you as if you were a perfectly normal human being? The portal is all set for your return. Please prepare immediately.

smolin9: Couldn't I stay here and be like king of the ants? I'd be really nice and kind-hearted to my subjects. I wouldn't be a tyr-ant. Ha ha. No, I wouldn't walk all over them. Ha ha ha ha. Okay, okay, I'm getting ready. But I've got unfinished business here, so keep the wormhole open.

Investigator Diary 12.19.19.8.3:

Hello? I don't know if anyone can hear me out there. My name is Melinda Hill and I'm speaking to you from Camden Town. That's in London on, um, Earth. Yeh, erratic, isn't it? I'm a friend, well, fiancée actually, of smolin9's. He left this microwocky thingy behind when he left. I used to watch what he did with it when he used to send his reports. So, I know it's insane, but I'm hoping to get a sort of message through to him. He said he used a wormhole or something, but to be careful with it because it involved sub-atomic forces – like radiation and stuff. Wow! How erratic is that! There must be some bright worms out there! Ha ha. In more ways than one! It does my head in, all this time travel and so on. Perhaps none of this has actually happened yet! Literally. Totally erratic.

Anyway, you don't want to hear me wittering on, so I'll get to the point. Since I met smolin9, I've contacted other people who have met aliens like you. Sorry, do you mind if I call you aliens? I know you come from a planet called Morys Minor, so maybe I should call you Mortians or Minors or something. Ha ha. Insane. Mortians! I've spoken to abductees and all sorts. I think they're incredibly brave to come out about their encounters. I know for a fact the American President has met smolin9 and polkingbeal67, but there's no way we'll ever get to hear about it. It's like, y'know, you're so tempted to share your experience with other people, but, well, let's just say they'd give you such a hard time over it. Lots of the abductees seem to have had bad experiences, but I must say, in your defence, well, you guys are really cool. Yeh, mostly. I mean polkingbeal67 is a bit like a gorilla on amphetamines, but I suppose he's okay when you get to know him. Anyway, it's totally erratic to know there's intelligent life on other worlds. Sometimes I wonder if there's any intelligent life here on Earth! Ha ha. Totally. I love all you guys up there!

Anyway, if this message gets through to you, smolin9, I want you to know I feel terrible about being a jilted bride, but I'm not angry with you. I can't possibly understand your life but I know you'd have been there if you could have been. And I know it will have been as hard for you as it has been for me.

Obviously, I got to know your human transformation best, but right now I'm thinking of you as your true self. Literally. I'm thinking of those big, soulful, inky-black eyes and I'm imagining I see tears in them. We have a famous film here where one of the characters is a tin man who goes off to find a wizard who might give him a heart. The wizard tells him he'd be better off without one and in the end the tin man says: "Now I know I've got a heart, 'cause it's breaking."

Well, I know you didn't like us much to start with, but, eventually, you said you wanted to be more like us. It's insane, but I came to understand that you already were quite like us. You had whatever that thing is that we call humanity. You just had to tap into it. Literally. And it was beautiful. And I bet, like the tin man, you're wishing you hadn't found it, 'cause it's hurting you like hell now.

Ugh! Sorry, there seem to be ants everywhere here! So, anyway, I've got to go – I left something cooking. And no, it's not a frying saucer! Ha ha. Insane. I'm glad you touched my life. Totally. It was erratic and I loved every moment. Oh, what's that?

smolin9:	[crackle] [hiss] Hello?
Melinda:	What? Is somebody there? Hello?
smolin9:	[crackle] Is that you, Melinda? We just picked up the signal. I've been tuned to your hyper spatial coordinates for ages waiting for you to make contact!
Melinda:	Wow! Erratic or what? Hi, how are you?
smolin9:	I'm fine. Listen, we're all set up to get married over this wormhole comms link. Our revered leader is here and he's happy to officiate. And polkingbeal67 is here as a witness.
Melinda:	What? But I... I haven't...I'd have to get my dress and...
smolin9:	We haven't got time for any of that. This has to happen now. Are you happy to go ahead?
Melinda:	No. Well, yes. Okay. This is insane, but go ahead, yes!
polkingbeal67:	Can I just say I object most strongly to this union? As far as I'm concerned, smolin9, something terrible must have happened to you during the quantum entanglement process of your visit to the Pale Blue Dot. Are you sure your electrons are

okay?

smolin9:	I'm positive. Let's get on.
Leader:	Do you, Melinda Hill, take this interdimensional being, smolin9, to have and to hold from this day forward, for better and for worse, in sickness and in health, to love and to cherish, till wormhole DNA mutation or death do you part?
Melinda:	Wormhole DNA what now? Okay, whatever. I do.
Leader:	Do you, smolin9, take this earthling woman, Melinda Hill, to have and to hold from this day forward, for better and for worse, in sickness and in health, to love and to cherish, till wormhole DNA mutation or death do you part?
polkingbeal67:	Please don't.
smolin9:	I do.
polkingbeal67:	Oh help.
Leader:	By the power vested in me by intergalactic law, I now pronounce you husband and wife. You may now transmit a holographic image of yourself to kiss the bride.
Melinda:	This is just unbelievable. Literally.

smolin9:   Keep my skateboard polished till I get
            leave to visit Earth again! You'd
            better free up the channel now.

Melinda: No, *you* hang up! Ha ha. Literally.
            Keep the wormhole open!

INVESTIGATION CLOSED

2

EARTHWATCH UNCOVERED

(from the private journals of anthropologist, MMBC producer and palace adviser, nipkow4)

When studying smolin9's wormhole reports, as an anthropologist, I was much struck with certain facts in the evolution of scientific discovery on the planet called Earth, more commonly referred to as the Pale Blue Dot. These facts seemed to me to throw light on that mystery of mysteries, the inability of human earthlings to progress in a linear fashion beyond the level of hunter-gatherer-trader goopmutts. It occurred to me, towards the end of the 13th baktun, that I could perhaps make something out of this by patiently observing and reflecting on everything that could possibly have any bearing on it.

The rise and fall of civilisations. Ascents and descents. Evidence of cyclical development all over the planet: the pyramids, the Great Sphinx, Stonehenge and the Ziggurats of ancient Mesopotamia. The Aztecs, the Maya, the Incas, the ancient Greeks, the Roman Empire. The timeline of social organisation, cultures and complex technologies on the Pale Blue Dot shoots off at tangents and loops back around again. It's a bewildering roller coaster of progress, transformation, stagnation and regression. It is widely believed that the early bipedal hominids on the planet discovered the use of stone tools for tasks such as digging – and promptly buried them so that no one else could have them! Staggering advances undermined by atavistic tribal regression.

From the safe distance of our advanced civilisation on Morys Minor in the constellation of Cygnus, it is tempting to view the earthlings' plight as amusing, no, downright funny, no, absolutely hilarious, but I wanted to inject a degree of scientific objectivity to my Earthwatch project for the Morys Minor Broadcasting Corporation. With the benefit of hindsight, it was probably therefore a tad unwise to enlist the services of smolin9 and polkingbeal67. In our defence, we could not have achieved such amazing viewing figures without the idiosyncracies of the show's presenters. And, of course, they were credited for discovering the Voyager spacecraft in the first place. How could we have overlooked them? Also, you have to put the thing into context. We were under the impression that our entire race was threatened with extinction at the end of the katun cycle. Smolin9's investigation into the suitability of the Pale Blue Dot for colonisation may have been deeply flawed but it still represented a watershed moment for us. A mass migration to a planet riven by conflict, natural disasters and tribal strife would have been a devastating mistake. No one could deny that smolin9's absorption into the mainstream culture of earthling life had been instructive and illuminating. Above all, it had been entertaining in an irresistible way. We had to have him.

But that was our first problem. Smolin9 had been sent on

a mission to a planet in the Kolosimo 922 system and was enjoying himself selling "Why Always Me?" t-shirts to the inhabitants. Come to think of it, I have no idea how that worked out anyway. Not only did the Skolli people know nothing about the earthling sport of football, but also they have six arms, two heads and spinal columns the shape of giant rockcrawler treads. In the end, I appealed to smolin9's sense of romance and sentimentality and his duty to his earthling wife, Melinda. Okay, that didn't work, so I offered him a staggering three hundred shergs per appearance and he was on the next shuttle to Morys quicker than you could say Mario Balotelli.

As for polkingbeal67, well, he just leaped at the opportunity to appear as a presenter on peak-time tele-immersion. He had been working on his autobiography entitled 'Polkingbeal67: The Ultimate Fan Book', so the only thing holding him back was the same thing that was propelling him forwards into my clutches – his ego. I will put my hand up and admit I never gave enough thought to what polkingbeal67 brought to the table. In hindsight, believe me, there were times when I felt there *was* one thing I really needed from him, something only he could provide – his absence.

So there we were, the three of us, in MMBC's central meeting pod, knee deep in reports and microwocky clips of earthling behaviour, trying to agree on the focus for the first show. I would like to report that the presenters' contributions were constructive and fruitful, but the truth is: smolin9 was too busy practising his singing voice (I have no idea why) and compiling a list of football clichés he intended to drop into his patter, while polkingbeal67 spent most of the time persuading the make-up artist how essential it was that he should be allowed to wear his battle helmet.

"Reflections? I don't care about reflections," I remember him saying. "It's *got* to be shiny. This helmet... this helmet is no ordinary helmet. Why, this helmet saw the great battle of Tharsis Crater on Ynonmaq Decimus. This helmet dodged ionizer blasts during the liberation of chilloks in the Fourth Intergalactic War and led the charge against General Vog in the famous defeat of the Trox army at Ybesan..."

"You weren't actually underneath it on any of those occasions," smolin9 pointed out. "Somebody else was wearing it."

"That's not the point," said polkingbeal67, pounding the table for emphasis. Unfortunately, between his fist and the surface of the table was, well, his sherg-encrusted battle helmet. The spines punctured his skin and his face contorted with pain. "Stupid hat!" he yelled, and angrily whisked it off the table. It ended up embedded in the pod wall, quivering gently. Everyone went quiet for a moment.

"So, this Earthwatch show - are there any dance numbers?" smolin9 asked.

. . .

We moved the microwockys aside and gathered around a pile of draft scripts for the series. I thought it would be a good idea to use these as a starting point for our collaboration. As I have already mentioned, one of the concepts I was keen to get across in the series is the phenomenon whereby earthling evolution refuses to be progressive. Organisms on the Pale Blue Dot tend to adapt for survival through a process of natural selection, and yet many species do not end up perfectly suited to their environments. To some extent, this can be explained by the volatility of life on the planet. Traits that are beneficial for a particular habitat turn out to be unsuitable when the environment changes. Beset by extreme weather phenomena, earthquakes, volcanic eruptions, floods, landslides and asteroid strikes, the Pale Blue Dot has plenty to contend with, without self-inflicted behaviours such as violent conflicts, species invasions and reckless fuel and weapons generation. Throw mutation, migration and genetic drift into the mix and you've got a recipe for chaos. Tracking earthling evolution is like watching a clock – you expect it to be an undeviating measure of time, but it's just hands going round and round.

Whereas we Mortians have been fortunate enough to enjoy a linear and progressive evolution, culminating in the creation of the beautiful, adaptive, intelligent creatures that we are, earthling creatures appear to have suffered the consequences of what I call 'skewed aspiration'. In other words, they simply never make up their minds about what progress should look like. Take spiders, for example. To some of them, the best measure of progress might be the potency of a venom delivery system. To others it might be the efficiency of web-spinning glands or external digestion. Some value camouflage, others do not. Some yearn for cognitive ability, others dismiss it as pointless. They just cannot get their act together. And don't get me started on earthling humans!

Anyway, I tried to convey this to the show's presenters as I felt it was important they should be aware of my thinking behind the series. After a while, I began to realise I was not getting through. It's not that smolin9 and polkingbeal67 were dismissive of the theme. Not as such. As I remember the conversation, it went something like this:

"So, you see," I said to them. "Explaining about spiders and similar earthling species, other than humans, might be a good starting point."

"Yeh, no," said smolin9. "I hate spiders. The way they do that scuttling thing. I'm really scared of them."

"You crazy prokaryote! That's ridiculous," polkingbeal67 scoffed, while he straightened out the spines of his battle helmet. "Your fear of spiders is probably just a deep-seated, pathological anxiety about something that occurred in your childhood. You need aversion therapy."

"Yeh, that's right. Aversion. I need to avoid spiders. Yuk! Every time I think of them, it gives me butterflies in the stomach."

"Eh? Maybe it's butterflies you should be worried about."

"No, I'm okay with butterflies. Human earthlings are strange like that though, aren't they? Despite the ridiculous disparity in size, they're very nervous about little insects. *All* insects."

"Irrational," said polkingbeal67. "Is Melinda scared of insects?"

"Oh yes. Terrified. But humans are very confusing. While I think of it, there's a story I've got to tell you."

"Yes, do tell," said polkingbeal67, yawning.

"Well, it was the first time we'd slept in the same bed. Melinda was snoring away and I noticed an insect on her bare shoulder."

"Are you sure this is something you ought to be telling us?" I asked, seriously wondering where he was going with this.

"It's okay, it's okay," said smolin9. "It wasn't a spider, thank goodness. It was a butterfly. Anyway, I knew she'd be upset if she woke up and saw it there, so I sprayed half a can of insect repellent on it. It didn't do any good at all. So I ended up wacking it a few times."

Polkingbeal67 carefully placed the fully restored battle helmet on his head. "Interesting. Was she grateful to you?"

Smolin9 grinned a little sheepishly. "Not exactly. It was a tattoo."

It was at this point I abandoned the theme for the first episode. "We'll just stick to the humans then," I said.

I knew what they both *really* wanted. They wanted the first episode to tell the celebrated story of how they discovered the Voyager 1 probe. The earthling spacecraft had been towed through interstellar space by goopmutt bandits travelling at superluminal speed. In an effort to conceal their crime, the goopmutts had manipulated the data on the craft's digital tape recorder and had left it in the heliosphere where its signal could still be picked up from the Pale Blue Dot. Eventually, they had abandoned the rest of the craft in the Centaurus galaxy where smolin9 and polkingbeal67 came across it during a spacecombing trip in their Mark III Zeplock mineral spotter. It was all very fascinating, of course, but I thought it would be a distraction from the main point of the series and I was determined to resist it. I knew I would be in trouble if I failed to rein in their egos at the start of the project.

Polkingbeal67 was not too much of a problem to begin with. He was a relatively manageable mixture of bluff, bluster and bravado, but smolin9 was another matter. I swear I will understand the cosmos before I understand the astonishing dynamics and inner workings of smolin9's mind. His ego, empathy and insecurity competed for dominance like a triple eclipse on Asthenia.

We had made no progress at all and it was getting late. Reflected light from the twin moons was already shimmering on the pod wall. I was just thinking about how to wrap up the meeting, when, for no accountable reason, smolin9 finally picked up my draft scripts. Well, I suppose an egg will hatch if you give it enough time. As late as it was, perhaps we could now move on and use the scripts as a template for a constructive discussion.

"The synopsis for this episode mentions an experience involving the White Mouse!" smolin9 exclaimed.

"Bad idea," said polkingbeal67. "Even earthlings know you shouldn't work with children and animals."

"It's a typo," I said. "Should be House." Neither of them took any notice of me.

"I suppose it's a reference to the time I fitted a foxp2 communication implant to the brain of a mouse when I first visited the planet. It's important to cover that."

"No, no, I don't think so," said polkingbeal67. "We should tell the world about the one we abducted for analysis before your trip."

"But you confused it with a computer pointing device and tried to plug it into a microwocky."

"It was a typo," I said. Smolin9 and polkingbeal67 paused for a moment, gave me a quizzical look and then carried on squabbling.

"I wasn't confused. It would have worked fine if you hadn't been plying it with vitalmados."

"Mm. Should have been cheese."

"You crazy bubblehead! The comms port on my

microwocky has never worked properly since."

"It was a typo," I repeated, a little wearily. "It refers to the time you met the President of America."

They both looked at me with bewildered expressions. "You thought the President of America was a mouse?" said smolin9.

So much for the draft scripts being a good idea. I really should have thought it through properly. We had achieved precisely nothing. Nothing at all. And I told them so.

Smolin9 managed to look embarrassed, mischievous and thoughtful, all at the same time. He turned to me and said, "There's no such thing as nothing."

And there it was. I don't know how and I don't know why and I sure as hell don't know if smolin9 intended it, but we had a topic for the first episode. He was right. There is no such thing as nothing. Not in the world of particle physics, anyhow. And earthlings had recently been making laughable assumptions about the relationship between particles of matter and particles of anti-matter. It was all sorted. We would start the series by exploring the earthlings' feeble and shaky grasp of science.

Out of all the frustration and confusion, expectancy and excitement emerged blowing trumpets. Now we could get the cameras ready to roll! Certainly smolin9 was pumped up and enthusiastic. He told us he would like to spend what was left of the meeting summarising his dreams and aspirations for the series: "I start quaking from head to foot when I think about this series," he said. "We may not be great people, but there are great challenges that ordinary people may undertake. If we keep our feet on the ground while our minds take a leap in the dark..." Polkingbeal67 and I made it out of there in double-quick time.

.　　.　　.

The first day of shooting arrived. The set dressers were bustling around with props and furnishings. Over by the camera dolly, a group of engineers gathered to discuss lenses and camera angles, while others assembled the tele-immersion environment. With an air of relaxed authority, the director, onside91, monitored all the activity. I watched for a while as he stared up at the plasma lighting grid, issued occasional instructions and generally ensured that nothing was missed.

For the most part, everything had been going smoothly. The exposition, mainly comprising clips of earthling scientists attempting to explain what they called the 'Higgs bosun', had already been filmed and edited. Following a few routine discussions, all roles and responsibilities had been allocated and communicated. Onside91 was an experienced team-builder and I was confident I could rely upon him to organise and co-ordinate everything relating to the camera crew, the make-up and wardrobe people, the set designers, the art department and the tele-immersion engineers. He and I had already agreed on detailed stuff like montage sequences, special effects, inserts and cutaways. Tele-immersion sets can be insane places to work, but, although there was clearly a buzz about the place, everything felt right. And yet, I knew that even with the best planning and organisation in the world it was possible that the arrival of the presenters could reduce it all to chaos.

As it happens, it was their non-arrival that caused the problems. According to polkingbeal67, his cruiser had broken down and they had had to walk all the way to the studio pod. Given that they were only staying one muhurta away, I made the mistake of asking why they were three muhurtas late. What happened to them took a long time, but not as long as it took them to explain it! Apparently, they had had to make a detour, because polkingbeal67 thought he had spotted an approaching methane shower and was worried about getting his battle helmet wet. Then smolin9 had had to go back for his t-shirt, not once, but twice. On the first occasion, he had forgotten what he had gone back for. While he was away on the second occasion, polkingbeal67 got caught in the methane shower they had been trying to avoid. Anxious about discolouration of the shergs on his helmet, he took it off to inspect it and inadvertently dropped his universal clavis, without which he could not drive his cruiser or open his domus pod door or, most significantly, gain access to the studio. Unfortunately, he did not realise this until they were just twenty garfs from the studio pod. I realise now I should have cut this long story short, but... they went back for it, couldn't find it and polkingbeal67 could only get into the studio pod by means of holographic projection. Which didn't work too well, so, while they were telling us all this, polkingbeal67 was there, and then he wasn't and then he was...

Eventually, we sent out some of the crew and they managed to retrieve the clavis. Onside91 and I left the two presenters to compose themselves while they watched the microwocky-generated exposition. We shared a vitalmados lozenge outside the pod and returned to find smolin9 telling an earthling joke about the Higgs bosun: "A Higgs bosun goes into a church," he was saying, "and the priest says 'What are you doing here?' So the Higgs bosun says 'You can't have mass without me!'"

Polkingbeal67 was clearly unimpressed. "If I don't laugh, is it still a joke?" he growled.

Smolin9 answered with a question: "If a tree falls in the

forest and no one is around to hear it, does it make a sound?"

Polkingbeal67 was twisting his battle helmet in agitation. "If I zap you with a couple of micro beam plasma blasts, will you see stars?"

Meanwhile, the microwocky feed finished and it was time to start filming. Onside91's voice echoed around the pod: "Pan to the right and up a little." Polkingbeal67 peered at the teleprompter. "Standby on the set," said onside91. "Standby to roll. Action!"

Polkingbeal67 grinned stiffly and said: "Scientists on the Pale Blue Dot..." Then he started coughing.

"Cut!" onside91 called out.

"Sorry," said polkingbeal67. "I get a tickle in my throat when I talk about earthlings." He started again: "Scientists on the Pale Blue Dot have claimed the discovery of a new particle consistent with what we know as the treacletron. They believe this represents a significant milestone in their quest to fathom the secrets of the universe. One of their top people has described it as the missing cornerstone of particle physics."

A microwocky feed showed footage of the earthlings' particle accelerator housed in a 55,000-garf circular tunnel underneath the ground. A smirk was already playing its way over smolin9's features as he took over the narration: "The Large Hadron Collider was 14 Pale Blue Dot years in the making and cost the equivalent of 19 billion shergs. Two beams of atomic particles are fired, ha ha, in opposite directions around the tunnel and smashed together, ha ha ha ha, in an attempt to re-create the conditions from the beginning of the universe. Ha ha ha." Even polkingbeal67 struggled to keep a straight face as his co-presenter sniggered through the script. He signed off with a couple of his football clichés: "Every experiment is a cup final now, ha ha. They've just got to take one particle at a time, ha ha ha!"

The crew were in uproar. And I knew we had a hit on our hands.

. . .

Although MMBC announced record viewing figures for the first episode, we could not claim universal approval. Not even internally. I received wockyspeak messages from senior managers in the organisation criticising the programme for breaching multispecies diversity deference standards. Documentary director, winard59, said: "At a time when we are reaching out to new worlds with a view to colonisation, it strikes me as totally inappropriate to ridicule the inhabitants of the Pale Blue Dot. Although this planet has been deemed unfit for settlement, the principle of tolerance and respect for species diversity should be observed at all times."

As the end of the 13th baktun drew closer, the prospect of interplanetary migration had raised the issue of preserving Mortian cultural integrity. People generally fell into one of two camps. There were those who advocated total segregation on the host planet. Opposing them were the more accommodating types who preferred a carefully managed process of integration. Then, because mutator technology had advanced to the point where interspecies transformations had become routine and the prospect of total assimilation had become an option, a third camp emerged.

And then there was polkingbeal67. I discussed colonisation with him once and his response was blunt and unequivocal. "We should wage war on them!" he said. The topic made him as mad as a cut goopmutt. "We should choose a planet we like the look of, and wage war on its inhabitants to decide who keeps it. End of." It was not a long, protracted discussion. As for smolin9, he hopped merrily from one camp to another.

The bottom line was, we had no bottom line. If we toned things down for the next episode, the ratings would drop, and if we continued to make earthlings the butt of all the jokes, the powers-that-be would pull the plug.

It was a conundrum that knocked us off kilter during the filming of the second episode. Right from the outset, I could tell smolin9 was uncomfortable talking about earthlings' primitive interpretations of the laws of causality. The idea for the show had been conceived by the director, onside91, who had been browsing through a mountain of media material we had gleaned from the Pale Blue Dot. He had discovered a bizarre video of a highly renowned theoretical physicist known as Stephen Hawking. The translation, which we used at the start of the show, was as follows:

"I'm throwing a party, a welcome reception for future time travelers. But there's a twist. I'm not letting anyone know about it until after the party has happened. I've drawn up an invitation giving the exact coordinates in time and space. I am hoping copies of it, in one form or another, will be around for many thousands of years."

Apparently, Hawking had set out to disprove the possibility of time travel by sending out his invitations after the date of the party and then presenting evidence that no one had shown up. The video showed Hawking waiting for his guests. "My time traveler guests should be arriving any moment now," he said. "Five, four, three, two, one. But as I say this, no one has arrived. What a shame."

It should have been good. We all thought we had struck an especially rich vein of earthling goopiness. The script looked good on paper:

> *smolin9:* "Earthlings still cling to such primitive interpretations of the laws of causality."
>
> *polkingbeal67:* "I know. They don't seem to realise that the law is not absolute."
>
> *smolin9:* "Earthlings observe that things fall to the ground when they release them from their hands..."
>
> *polkingbeal67:* "...like Hawking's invitation."
>
> *smolin9:* "Good example. So what if a sudden gust of wind snatches it up and carries it up out of reach?"
>
> *polkingbeal67:* "Is that what happened to your invitation? Did you know about Hawking's party?"
>
> *smolin9:* "Yes, I got the invitation next week!"
>
> *polkingbeal67:* "Did you go?"
>
> *smolin9:* "No. I didn't see any future in it."

But, try as they might, the presenters felt constrained and failed to sprinkle proceedings with any of their customary sparkle. Many takes later, we drew a line under it and smolin9 signed off with his football-related quip: "Did he allow for time added on?"

After filming, I walked outside the studio with smolin9. As we chatted, we passed beyond the pod estate and stood gazing at the purple desert stretching to the horizon. Smolin9 told me he loved to contemplate this wide, open vista because it gave his soul room to stretch. Somehow, he said, the absence of geological features, natural and manufactured, made everything in his life seem more clear and simple and honest. Beyond the methane swamp which bubbled lazily like a fermenting vat of vitalmados, only a few rocks and bits of debris broke the tranquillising uniformity of the sterile landscape. In keeping with the spirit of clarity and honesty that smolin9 described to me, he started to divulge his feelings about the Pale Blue Dot, or Earth, as he preferred to call it. I had misjudged him previously when I had tried to lure him to do the series. Far from being unmoved by my appeal to his conscience concerning his earthling wife, Melinda, it turned out that his reason for hesitation was a fear of stirring up buried emotions. Not only was he missing Melinda, he was missing life on Earth and was desperate to return.

As the light faded and the sky turned a bruised blue-violet colour to match the desolate wastes of the desert, smolin9 turned his dark melancholy eyes to me. He said nothing. He didn't have to. His mission as special envoy to investigate the planet had been funded at considerable expense by the Mortian government at the behest of our revered leader. How was I going to tell smolin9 that there was absolutely no way the MMBC budget for the series would stretch to a wormhole visit, especially as the Pale Blue Dot was no longer a colonisation target?

.   .   .

I always felt polkingbeal67's lack of a sense of humour was unfortunate. Not just for us, but also for him. I am sure it would have helped him cope better with the rough edges of life, especially in the pressurised environment of broadcasting. Without a sense of humour, working on a series like Earthwatch is like crossing a Daladax rock gully in a jeep without tyres. I was thinking about this when I was preparing the script for the third episode. I usually got smolin9 to deliver the funny lines, especially as he came up with a lot of them himself, but on this occasion I wanted to test everyone's reactions to polkingbeal67 getting the laughs.

The topic for this episode was a narrative of Mortian trips to the Pale Blue Dot and an analysis of the effect of such visits on the earthlings.

Our biomimetic mutators offer a range of options in the realm of mimicry, imitation, disguise and camouflage, but several earthlings, including the American President, residents of Roswell in New Mexico and, of course, smolin9's wife, Melinda Hill, had encountered smolin9, polkingbeal67 and others in their natural Mortian form.

Any study of their media reveals that earthlings consider the likelihood of life on other planets to be very high, but actual contact with visitors from other planets is routinely covered up by the authorities on the planet. Sometimes the approach is outright denial, other times they prefer to airbrush such incidents with alternative explanations. I thought it would be appropriate (and entertaining) to devote some time to an examination of this phenomenon.

Polkingbeal67 said he could not understand the insular nature of earthlings.

"The truth is," smolin9 explained to him. "Their leaders are fearful of how populations would react if they knew the truth. And frankly, p,... you'd cause mass hysteria."

When we were poring over our archive of earthling media, we recognised some now-obsolete spacecrafts from Morys. "We can't use this stuff!" polkingbeal67 protested. "We're using wormhole technology now and we must forget those old rust buckets. I don't like what we're doing here. It's totally embarrassing. To present ourselves as bumbling space novices is disgraceful. Have you any idea how offensive this is to me?" He was a proud person, and anxious to show himself and his fellow Mortians in the best possible light. Anyway, I decided to fill the show with footage of the 'rust buckets' in honour of our pioneering predecessors and in testimony of earthling chicanery. Clearly, polkingbeal67 had no concept of sentimentality for the past. Nostalgia was anathema to him. So he cringed and squirmed all the way through the two days of filming. The closing lines of the script were:

> *smolin9:* "These are great icons of our spacefaring history. Did you ever make a trip in any of these?"

> *polkingbeal67:* "Oh, yeh. I've made a few trips to the Pale Blue Dot and got mistaken for a hot air balloon, a Chinese lantern and a flying cigar."

Poor polkingbeal67 glared at me every time he delivered that line. Was it really necessary for me to insist on a dozen takes? No, probably not. Ha ha. Well, obviously I thought it was amusing at the time. Later, I came to realise that polkingbeal67's behaviour was symptomatic of a deep-seated insecurity. His insistence on appearing combative, hawkish and heroic was a mechanism for protecting his fragile self-esteem. Even when I eventually fathomed this out, I was still a long way from getting to the source of the problem. But more of that later.

.   .   .

Up to and including the third episode, everything had been going perfectly. The series was becoming successful beyond my wildest dreams. In fact, if you included piracy figures, Earthwatch was generating the biggest audience for a documentary in MMBC history. You can imagine how I felt then, when smolin9 came up to me with a rather pathetic look on his face and said he was returning to the Pale Blue Dot for a while.

I suppose I should not have been as surprised as I was. I knew he had been pining and I knew he had the ear of our revered leader. For some reason, I had not made the connection between the two. I had just assumed the idea of anyone making a wormhole trip to a planet that was no longer a colonisation target would be out of the question for all sorts of political, logistical and financial reasons. But, as he had officiated at the marriage between smolin9 and Melinda Hill, I can see why our revered leader might have been sympathetic to my presenter's cause.

I do not consider myself a callous person. I like to think I had established a good working rapport with both the presenters, smolin9 in particular, but this bombshell put the rest of the series in jeopardy and I was determined to put up a fight. I will not dwell on my initial reaction to his announcement, but suffice to say the camera crew hid in the next pod with all their equipment! To be fair, smolin9 proved amenable to compromise and we all agreed to film the next three episodes back-to-back to create a window for his trip.

The first day went well enough. Our regular scans of earthling media had revealed the irresistible story of an unmanned earthling probe named 'Curiosity' despatched to Mars to poke around a crater on the surface of the planet. The presenters and the studio crew loved the story of how the earthlings proposed to deliver the incredibly fragile robotic rover from a hovering spacecraft known as a 'sky crane'. According to one of the earthling space engineers: "The entry, descent and landing is also known as 'seven minutes of terror'. We have to get from the top of the atmosphere to the surface of Mars, going from 13,000 miles per hour to zero, in perfect sequence, perfect choreography, and perfect timing. If any one thing does not go right, it is game over." None of us could believe it when the vehicle actually landed in one piece. It prompted smolin9 to entertain us with stories of other idiosyncratic earthling creations like video games and the satellite navigation devices fitted to their cruisers. "Turn around when possible!", one of the popular catchphrases on the show, was born during this session. I saw an opportunity to work some of this stuff into the script:

> *polkingbeal67:* "The sky crane thing reminds me of the time the goopmutts used something similar to construct a colossal three-tiered monument on the Pale Blue Dot in honour of their leader."

> *smolin9:* "Right. Then they made the mistake of placing eggs in it as a ritual offering. And some goopmutts became incensed, got drunk on vitalmados and demolished the structure by launching boulders at it. The ruins are still there. The earthlings call it Stonehenge."

> *polkingbeal67:* "One of the most disgraceful acts of vandalism in intergalactic history."

> *smolin9:* "Yes, but earthlings still celebrate it."

> *polkingbeal67:* "They do?"

> *smolin9:* "Oh yes. They call it Angry Birds."

'Angry Birds' was the name of a popular earthling video game. We were going to enact a parody of it for the show, but polkingbeal67 started throwing rocks around in a random fashion and we had to abandon it. None of us knew it at the time but it was the first in what became a series of on-set misdemeanours. We were about to take a break from shooting and polkingbeal67 was supposed to deliver the line: "Earthlings are going to be sick as parrots when the rover gets clamped. You're not allowed to park there!" But he suddenly flounced off the set with the cameras still rolling. When he returned, he kept growling and asking everyone if he looked fat.

I was more than a little nervous as we started work on the episode about the Olympic Games, but thankfully my fears were unfounded.

According to our research, the earthling World Badminton Federation had charged eight female players with misconduct after it emerged that they had deliberately lost their matches. As onside91 briefed the lighting operators, polkingbeal67 suddenly asked: "Why do earthlings attach so much importance to strange activities like running round in circles, throwing spears, jumping into sandpits and losing at badminton?" I thought that was wonderful and told him I would add it to the script. This obviously put him in a good mood and we rattled through without a hitch. He was positively buzzing by the time we got to the closing lines:

> *polkingbeal67:* "Do you think young earthlings are inspired by the Olympics?"
>
> *smolin9:* "Yes, 110 percent. They're already going for epic feats of endurance, like watching it on their television sets all day long."

And so we moved on to the next episode which focused on reports of an earthling called Felix Baumgartner who jumped out of a balloon from the edge of space, 42,000 garfs above the land mass known as New Mexico, breaking the sound barrier in the process. I thought it was relevant to show that earthlings certainly have a desire to 'push the envelope' and take on progressively tougher challenges, even if the constant power struggle between good and evil, fueled by their egocentric nature, ensures there is limited net gain.

It all started well enough with smolin9 sneaking in an ad-lib football reference: "They really should do something about all this diving!" The scripted dialogue progressed as follows:

> smolin9: "One thing I don't understand. Apparently, this guy said he almost aborted the dive because his helmet visor fogged up. How could he abort the dive? If earthlings have developed a way of switching gravity off, how would they do it without affecting everybody else? So you're enjoying a nice Sunday afternoon by the river, when the water all turns to globules and floats away, along with your deckchair and your picnic. What do you do – just shrug your shoulders and say 'Oh dear, never mind, old Felix must be having a bit of trouble with his visor'?"

> polkingbeal67: "I think you're jumping to a few conclusions there."

> smolin9: "Felix Baumgartner would have been jumping to a conclusion if his chute hadn't opened."

> polkingbeal67: "I'm sure even earthlings are capable of thoroughly testing these things. There's no way it would have failed."

> smolin9: "Yeh, even if it had, I'm sure they'd have given him a refund or a replacement."

> polkingbeal67: "By the way, did you notice the location of Baumgartner's jump? It was over Roswell, New Mexico, where a terrible abomination

against our race took place a little while ago."

smolin9: "Oh yeh. Now, right there – that's an example of a truly awful parachute. When our engineers said it was guaranteed to open on impact, why did no one think...?"

At this point, polkingbeal67 threw down his battle helmet.

"Cut! Cut!" shouted onside91, "What's going on?"

"Why are we making light of this?" polkingbeal67 demanded, "I am speechless! This isn't funny. What the hell is wrong with us? You know as well as I do, they did not die on impact! Those detestable earthling screwballs killed them! Innocent, space-faring Mortians like you and me. I tell you what, I'm going back to that ugly, disgusting, watery, god-awful, miserable, bug-infested hell-hole and I'm going to totally let them know what I think about them! Evil, mindless monsters who spend all their lives alternately ignoring everyone and then murdering one another! And then murdering innocent visitors from other worlds! And I'm not talking about wars. At least wars are honourable! I despise these earthlings! Most of them are just dumb automaton slaves who are just smart enough to operate their pathetic technologies but not quite smart enough to realise they're being exploited by powerful, manipulative leaders who force them to work more and more hours for less and less reward. Then they rise up and fight and the whole cycle starts over again! I'm speechless!"

We stood there open-mouthed for a moment. Polkingbeal67 kicked his helmet, impaling his foot on one of the spines, and howled in distress. "And by the way, it's my birthday!" he yelled. "Speechless!"

And that is why that particular episode finished rather

abruptly.

The following day, smolin9 was on his way to the Pale Blue Dot.

.   .   .

Two kins later, I was in the cruiser on my way to a meeting with onside91. As I approached the studio pod, a plume of dust started spinning away behind me and I enjoyed the spectacle of sunlight beams and pod shadows chasing each other over the purple terrain. I did not notice polkingbeal67's bulky form until I was just a couple of garfs away. He did not flinch. "There's no time for cheery banter," he said to me as I stepped out of the cruiser. "Answer this. Why did you let him go?"

Although he had known well enough about smolin9's intention to return to the Pale Blue Dot, polkingbeal67 had been unaccountably upset about it. Now, he was downright distraught. "I'm tormented by the thought that he won't come back," he said. "Don't you see? He's emotionally damaged and cannot function in a rational manner. His cognitive faculties are shot. He's going to come to a gruesome end!"

"That's ridiculous," I told him. "He's just visiting his earthling wife for a while. He'll be back in ten kins. This was agreed by all of us, including you, before he left."

"You don't know him like I do," he said. "You don't know the sort of people he associated with when he was there last time. Look at this." He showed me a microwocky image of random squiggles and splashes of colour on what appeared to be an earthling subway train. "Smolin9 just sent this through the wormhole."

"What does it mean?" I asked. Peering closer, I thought I

could make out some earthling lettering. "Wait, does that say 'Mommy's Socks!'?"

"No," said polkingbeal67. "It says 'Morys rocks!' Contact with earthlings has corrupted and compromised his sanity. The crazy prokaryote has jumbled his particles. The bubblehead! Let me play you the message that accompanied this picture."

Smolin9's voice crackled excitedly: "Hey bro! I can't find Melinda. But look at this wholetrain! Badass! Siiiick! See my throw-up? Yeh, some of those pieces are mine. I've totally decided to go for a spider. I'm back with the crew and tonight we're gonna get up with fresh cannons and we're gonna bomb this place! I'll get back to you bro."

I looked at polkingbeal67 in dumb uncomprehending amazement. "What?" I said. "What does all that mean?"

"What don't you understand? It's all there, isn't it? Melinda's gone missing and smolin9's convinced himself a spider is responsible for her disappearance. He's been using earthling public transport to track her down and made himself travel sick. He's lost all sense of perspective and plans to reduce the city to rubble using exploding munitions. Get back in your cruiser. We've got to go straight to our revered leader to alert him."

To be honest, I accepted polkingbeal67's conclusion that smolin9 had gone mad and was threatening to commit terrorist atrocities on the Pale Blue Dot. I readily agreed that we should consult our revered leader. But a little worm of doubt started gnawing away at me. Smolin9's use of earthling English was usually very competent, if a little colloquial. Yet the words he had used in his message struck me as odd. While the cruiser sped across the vast unpopulated flatlands, I sent a wockyspeak note to MMBC's cultural linguistics specialist, attaching a copy of smolin9's transmission.

I had never met our revered leader in person before and I had no idea what to expect. As the palace loomed into view, polkingbeal67, who had calmed down a little by now, pointed out the Voyager 1 dish antenna half-buried amongst the ponds and fountains. "Yes," he said, noticing my astonishment. "It's now home to a shoal of bugtrap pontus fish munching on each other over a bed of permanganate seaweed." I wondered aloud what the earthlings would think if they knew the fate of their precious spacecraft. "Personally, I think we should track down Voyager 2," said polkingbeal67. "It would be nice to have a matching pair either side of the drive. Besides, the earthlings should be pleased the probe got as far as it did. When smolin9 and I first discovered it, we noticed a serious problem with the Photopolarimeter System. There was a message on the console saying 'Press any key to continue'! They really aren't fit to dabble in space exploration."

The palace, cellular in structure, was poetry itself. It was as if a dozen or so pods had been assembled in a pyramid and allowed to melt slightly under intense heat. Undulating, curved walls reflected the statues, fountains and monuments of the lavish gardens. The interior was a labyrinth of beautifully sculpted volcanic magma, decorated with glass, porcelain, the finest silks and precious stones. As we followed the aged guide to our revered leader's chambers, my eyes were drawn to vast images of Mortian heroes staring out at us alongside the glimmering ceramic fixtures and exotic carvings lining the passages.

Frankly, our meeting with our revered leader was not what I expected. I had seen official portraits of him looking regal and resplendent in a crimson mantle, sporting a gold skull pin. In the flesh, he looked fragile and vulnerable. There was no gold pin, just some goopmutt horns attached to his head by means of a leather strap. A pungent-smelling flower was fastened to another strap that he wore diagonally across his body and he had obviously smeared his body with strange oils and ashes. Anyway, he listened attentively while polkingbeal67 regaled him with the reason for our visit. I remember there was an awkward long silence afterwards and then he smiled benignly and said: "Keep on asking, and you will receive what you ask for. Keep on seeking, and you will find. Keep on knocking, and the door will be opened to you. Everyone who asks, receives. Everyone who seeks, finds. And to everyone who knocks, the door will be opened." We bowed and the guide led us back through the interminable passageways.

Back in the cruiser, I turned to polkingbeal67 and said: "What just happened?"

Polkingbeal67 had a smug expression on his face. "He's authorised me to go to the Pale Blue Dot and bring back smolin9 in one piece, if I can."

"He has?" I said, completely baffled. "How did you get that from ... *that*? And, were those goopmutt horns?"

Polkingbeal67 told me our revered leader was not only happy for him to go but he had also suggested that, if the mission proved successful, smolin9 should give up his job as a presenter on Earthwatch and become his (polkingbeal67's) butler.

My head was reeling as I dropped him off at the wormhole station. There was a wockyspeak message waiting for me. It was a reply from the linguistics specialist advising me that smolin9's transmission was purely composed of earthling graffiti slang. The full ramifications of that did not dawn on me for a while.

Problems with the wormhole channel meant I had had no contact with smolin9 or polkingbeal67 and we were approaching the deadline for the next episode. Sometimes in life you have to be a phoney. You have to put on an act and fool people into believing you're something you're not. Summoned to a meeting with senior MMBC executives, who were understandably alarmed over the absence of the Earthwatch presenters, I resolved to come over as confident and relaxed and focused. I wasn't! And, unfortunately, they saw through it.

There was another backdrop to all this. The end of the thirteenth baktun was approaching and, although the thinking behind the end-of-the-world predictions had recently been thoroughly discredited and plans for resettlement on another planet were no longer a serious part of anyone's agenda, many Mortians remained adamant that the apocalypse was assured. End-of-the-world sales were going strong, Armageddon parties were being organised and many deluded fools were entombing themselves in survival pods. Not only were the MMBC top brass keen to grab as much airtime as possible to cover the developments, but also they wanted me to write and produce the broadcasts. To my mind, a compromise is an agreement whereby both parties get what neither of them wants and I was determined that they were not going to get me if they pulled the rest of the Earthwatch series. Well, the road to hell is paved with good intentions. In the end, they granted me just one more episode of Earthwatch and secured my name as executive producer of the end-of-the-world programmes. Not so much a compromise as outright capitulation.

Meanwhile, unbeknown to me, polkingbeal67 had managed to get himself an audience with the Queen of England. As I said, communications between Morys and the Pale Blue Dot were down at the time, so this conversation, recorded by polkingbeal67 on his microwocky, did not emerge until he returned:

"Greetings, O holy revered majestical leader of the Pale Blue Dot," said polkingbeal67, who had bypassed security by means of his Craterkite cloaking device.

"You may call me Ma'am. And please get up now."

"Okay, Ma'am. Sorry, my knowledge of earthling etiquette is rather shaky. We can't go nose to nose, because I don't have one. Should I curtsey or bow or put on a grass skirt and scream things with my tongue poking out?"

"I think one can dispense with that, Mister...?"

"Polkingbeal67, Ma'am".

"That's a bit of a mouthful. May I call you 67?"

"Ma'am, if you did that, we would be obliged to submerge ourselves in a vat of liquid vitalmados and fight a duel to the death. Please accept my deepest respect and this gift of crystallised goopmutt horn shavings."

"Yes, thank you. Now, Mister... Mister... whatever you said, tell me, one assumes this has something to do with the Olympics? Never mind, I assume we have some business to attend to?"

"Ma'am. I've come to warn you of a plot to bomb your lands. One of our people, smolin9, is here on your planet and is threatening to carry out terrorist operations."

"I see. That is certainly regrettable. Does he have a grievance?"

"Yes, Ma'am. He doesn't like spiders."

"How unfortunate. We have many, many spiders. There are probably thousands in this very building."

"Ma'am, your life is in danger. I respectfully suggest you find your earthling comrade, Melinda Hill. She is married to smolin9 and probably holds the key to all of this. Oh, and if I was you I would banish all the spiders. Ma'am."

Polkingbeal67 may be as stable as a one-legged drunken goopmutt on a tightrope, but he can be smarter than you might think. He secretly traced the communication link from the Queen to the palace footman to the Metropolitan Police. Then, using his microwocky, he followed a maze of enquiries of various databases and arrived, well before the police, at a room in Glastonbury rented by Melinda Hill for the purpose of running a business as a life coach. When she had lost contact with smolin9 following their wormhole-enabled wedding, she had decided to leave London and start a new life from scratch. Although they had, of course, met several times in the past, polkingbeal67 figured Melinda would be alarmed to see him, so he appeared in disguise, pretending to seek advice about being more confident and self-assertive (as if he needed to be!):

"Well," Melinda said, as polkingbeal67 waited for a suitable opportunity to unmask himself. "You've come to the right place, literally. Empower yourself and achieve your personal goals with my tried-and-trusted life-coaching tips! Okay, let's talk about your low expectations. You remember when you were young and you dreamed of being a professional footballer or an astronaut or a celebrity or something? And then reality kicked in and you realised how hard life is and how you must settle for lower goals? Well, first of all, life is hard compared to ... what? The alternative doesn't bear thinking about, does it?

Literally. So let's not go on about how hard it all is, yeh? And second of all, in what game are lower goals easier to hit? Exactly. Insane, isn't it? You see? Erratic. Remember, the best way to avoid disappointment is to take a shot and call whatever you hit the target. So try to identify your outdated expectations and don't be your own worst enemy, right? Life is already full of disappointments. My approach to it is to be full of life! Literally. Remember, a glass isn't half full or half empty. It's always full! Water *and* air! You see? Ha ha. You see what I'm saying? So it's full even when it's empty. Literally."

Polkingbeal67's patience was running out, but he still could not get a word in edgeways. Melinda continued: "I know life can be easier to get through if you don't expect much out of it in the first place, but there's a saying in my profession: 'eagles may soar in the clouds, but weasels never get sucked into jet engines'. Insane. What I'm saying is there's nothing wrong with being a weasel. Weasels are human too, y'know. And a peacock that sits on its feathers is just another turkey! Literally. Every creature has its own wonderful unique abilities. It's what separates us from the animals. So live each day as though it were your last. And remember, one of them will be! Isn't that erratic? And do you know what?..."

Polkingbeal67 could not restrain himself any longer. "Oh help! Stop!" he shouted. "Stop, for pity's sake! It's me, polkingbeal67. You remember, I'm ..."

"Yes of course I remember you. Literally. Why are you here?"

"I've come to see smolin9."

"I haven't seen him. Literally. I never thought I'd see him again. I, oh ..." She followed polkingbeal67's gaze and realised he had already spotted smolin9's biomimetic mutator on the shelf behind her. "Okay," she said. "Have you come to take him back?"

"So smolin9 *is* here?"

"Yes, he's here. Well, he's not actually *here*. He's gone out doing some of that graffiti art stuff. Insane."

Hearing a sound outside the door, she turned around. When she turned back, polkingbeal67 had vanished. And so had smolin9's mutator.

.   .   .

I do not know why polkingbeal67 recorded his meeting with Melinda, but I was delighted to find the video on his microwocky, not least because it gave me a valuable insight into his disturbed state of mind. Firstly, having gone to all the trouble of tracking down smolin9, why would he return to Morys without speaking to him? And, secondly, why would he have stolen the mutator, leaving his friend trapped in earthling human form? I had precious little time to ponder this at the time, because the end of the baktun had arrived and my MMBC commitments in that regard were keeping me frantically busy. Polkingbeal67 had lent me his microwocky to show me that earthlings had also picked up on the apocalypse prediction. He and I both found the discovery rather disconcerting as we thought the doomsday prophesy demeaned earthlings and Mortians in equal measure. Were we going to have to revise our pretensions to superiority, just slightly? Surely not. Privately, I had always concurred with polkingbeal67's portrayal of earthlings as backward and insular. After all, even at a stage in their development when they were starting to reach out to other worlds, they had not seen fit to name their own sun or their own solar system.

On my way to the studio, I stopped the cruiser and walked

around for a while. It was quiet. Dark streaks of cloud were smeared across the pink sky, but there was nothing particularly foreboding about it, nothing to suggest a cataclysmic event was about to trigger our imminent extinction. The end of the world had indeed been postponed. Sadly, however, a small part of my own particular world *had* been extinguished. The final episode of the Earthwatch series had been scratched amid speculation that smolin9 would never return from the Pale Blue Dot. I could not shake off the suspicion that polkingbeal67 was in some way responsible.

That morning, several of us were at the studio pod, collecting personal effects, packing away equipment and preparing media for archiving. Polkingbeal67 was downloading stuff onto his microwocky when I casually confronted him about smolin9's mutator.

"If he thinks being an earthling is so great, maybe he should stay that way!" he snapped.

Sometimes, halfway through a conversation with polkingbeal67, I would feel like I had got concussion. This time it hit me straight away. I was gobsmacked. "So you don't want to see him back again?" I asked. Polkingbeal67 turned away without replying. I watched him as he busied himself with his microwocky and I wondered if he was trying to get accustomed to life without smolin9. For a moment there, the thought crossed my mind that perhaps, just perhaps, he had taken the mutator to make smolin9 angry with him and make their parting easier somehow. There again, perhaps not. It was more likely to have been an act of jealous spite. To be honest, I was struggling to cope with all this emotional baggage cluttering up the place. And then it struck me.

Emotions! Unlike earthlings, our Mortian neurocircuitry is supposed to be configured in a way that precludes emotions interfering with cognitive processes. And yet, here we both were, psychologically tossed around on a sea of destructive feelings like anger, resentment, sadness, vengefulness, bitterness, anguish and depression. Had we become tainted through association with earthlings?

The rationale behind the Earthwatch series was based on the self-defeating nature of earthling behaviour, and emotional derangement was mooted as a major cause of this. It seems clear to me that logic and emotions are inextricably linked on the Pale Blue Dot. For example, all over the planet, earthlings are very angry with their governments. They think their politicians are too controlling, too intrusive and too interfering. So, what do these people actually want? They want their governments to do something about it!

Anyway, I was thinking about this and thinking how ironic it was that a series that purported to reveal how all earthling enterprise is doomed to fail should itself collapse in such self-inflicted disarray, when I noticed polkingbeal67 with his back to me, huddled over a crate of bits and pieces. He was weeping into one of smolin9's 'Why always me?' t-shirts.

At that very moment the pod door opened and smolin9 stood there, a pair of earthling headphones balanced precariously on his domed head. "Waddup!" he said. "Hey, p, what are you doing with my t-shirt? Get off! I've got a bone to pick with you. I've just spent thirty kins in an earthling prison, doing time for suspected terrorist activities. Would you like to explain that? And that's not all. You nicked my mutator, so I couldn't change form and escape. What have you got to say for yourself? Hmm?"

Polkingbeal67 just gaped at him. Smolin9 turned to me. "So when are we shooting the next episode? I've got some really cool material!" He flicked his microwocky. "Look at this, p. I made some great crop circles. Check these out!"

A silly grin tugged at the corners of polkingbeal67's mouth. I had never seen that before.

I continued to reflect on that nagging sense that Morys Minor and the Pale Blue Dot may not be worlds apart after all. We may be separated by vast stretches of space and lapses of time, but we are in thrall to the laws of gravity and we pull at each other in all kinds of ways.

3

ONE WAY TICKET

A spiral of diaphanous methane mist curled aimlessly over the ochre-coloured prairie, resisting the feeble incandescence of the red dwarf sun that peeked over the distant horizon. Morys Minor, a circumbinary planet, boasted two sunrises, two sunsets and a complex pattern of daylight hours and seasonal variation. Ironically, the inhabitants had dismissed Earth as a potential colonisation target for being too chaotic and volatile. The pale light gradually infiltrated the medical pod where Melinda Hill sat patiently waiting for the effects of the homeodynamic disruption antidote (HDA) to wear off.

Wormhole travel is a wonderful thing, but it is not without its drawbacks. At best, it feels like tying your shoe laces in a revolving door. Some life forms have even been known to suffer DNA mutation, so the Mortians administered HDA routinely to time travelers on both arrival and departure.

Melinda simmered with frustration that her first day on

Morys Minor had been spent confined to a convalescent unit staffed by four-legged androids who struggled woefully to engage in any kind of meaningful dialogue.

"So, are you like robots?" Melinda asked. "Droids or cyborgs or something? This is so erratic!"

Her previous attempts to converse with them had elicited high-pitched monotones in response, but this time the nearest android wheeled around and spoke in a surprisingly human-like voice with a soft lilt to it. They were clearly learning and adapting as they went along. "Please wait while I process this communication," said the android. "Parsing complete. Problem occurred loading translation function. Compiling, please wait. An unexpected problem occurred. Sorry, I am unable to reply to you at this moment. Please try again. Enunciate clearly and speak slowly."

"Wow! That was good," said Melinda. "You sounded almost human. Literally."

Another android approached. "Please prepare your arm for a blood transfusion." A sachet of bluish-purple blood was secured to her upper forearm and the retractable spine painlessly punctured her skin and found its target.

Smolin9 emerged through the pod door at this moment. Melinda was still trying to get used to his native appearance. On Earth, he had used a biomimetic mutator to disguise himself as a human earthling. His soft, oily, smooth skin had a lustrous quality to it, and his eyes were large, coal-black and curiously expressive. "Hi Melinda," he said. "How's it going? Are you enjoying your first day on Morys?"

"Well, I didn't expect anything like this."

"Like what?"

"Oh, y'know, the lavish reception, spectacular views, lush jungles, white sandy beaches, fantastic cuisine, a landscape teeming with extraordinary wildlife and undiscovered phemona... phonemon... strange stuff. Insane. Literally. Yeh, it's been the best experience I've had in, like, ever. Sorry, yeh, I'm being sarcastic, but, look, when am I going to get away from this freaky hospital and all these nerdy robot people? And what is this thing on my arm? Wow! Totally erratic! Am I going to have blue blood?"

"Okay, you're entitled to know about the special blood configuration required by life forms on this planet," said smolin9. "And obviously you want to know about the unique molecular signature we have that's based on enzymes with special metabolic functions like converting methane to oxygen."

"Okay," said Melinda, tentatively. "Signature function blood what?"

"Now, that's a really smart question." Smolin9 realised Melinda would not grasp even the most basic explanation of blood composition. "Let's keep this simple," he said. "Our planet is different from Earth and you need stuff in your blood to help you survive the conditions. So, well, you know how you've got red cells and white cells?"

"Of course. I'm not dense, you know. Literally. I learned all that back in school: text books, diagrams, the whole lot. Red and white cells, yeh, it was all there in black and white."

"Well, what you need is some extra cells called BBCs, blue blood cells. So that's what's going on. It won't take much longer. The medibots will check your blood pressure and your body temperature and your pulse and make sure there are no compatibility issues. Yeh, anyway, I need to talk to a few people, so I'll catch up with you later."

An android interrupted them. "Please confirm you agree to be bound by all the terms and conditions," it intoned solemnly.

Melinda pulled a face and turned to smolin9. "What?" she said. "What terms and conditions?"

"You just have to say 'yes'," smolin9 told her. "It's just a formality thing."

"Okay, but this is rather erratic," said Melinda.

"Please wait while I process this communication," said the android. "Parsing complete..."

"Just say 'yes' when it's finished," said smolin9. "See you later."

The people smolin9 had to talk to included no less than the revered leader of the planet, who had not officially sanctioned Melinda's visit and was reported to be less than happy with the turn of events. He had presided over the historic wedding between smolin9 and Melinda, the first ever between a Mortian and a humanoid from another planetary body. The ceremony had been conducted via a specially commissioned wormhole channel a short while after smolin9 had completed his reports on the suitability of Earth for Mortian colonisation. The discovery of the Voyager 1 space probe by smolin9 and his companion, polkingbeal67, had raised expectations of harmonious relations between inhabitants of the two planets, but Earth, known to Mortians as the Pale Blue Dot, exceeded volatility thresholds and was ultimately deemed unsuitable.

Melinda leaned back, closed her eyes and started daydreaming about the adventures she might expect to have during her visit. The happy thoughts of careering around in a dune buggy were soon eclipsed by disagreeable worries about the availability of chocolate and toilet paper. Everything seemed fairly earth-like in the hospital, but would there be gravity out there? Or would she have to prance around in slow motion? If that were the case, her leopard print, three-inch heel pumps were not exactly ideal footwear and short skirts might be out of the question. Where would she sleep? Should she have brought a toothbrush? Where could she get hold of some shampoo? And why hadn't she asked smolin9 these questions before she had agreed to the trip? First and foremost, where on earth (oh, she thought, that is really funny), where on Morys Minor was she going to get a cup of coffee? What if there was no coffee? What on earth (oops! there I go again, she thought) was this world going to be like? Wrestling with matters of such significance and import proved too distressing for her, so she sat up and looked around. Before long, she had resorted to type, slipping into her earthling role as a life coach and treating the bewildered androids to a fifteen-minute spiel on how to take themselves more seriously.

"Ask yourselves some questions," she said. The androids were seemingly transfixed by her earnest voice and extravagant arm and hand gestures, "I mean, what sort of life do you want? Are you doing a job you love? Ask yourselves, 'What would I do if I knew I couldn't fail?' Literally. Yeh, you never know how far you can go until you take one more step." The androids drew closer. "Then make a list of things you really want. When you have a list of, say, twenty things, put an asterisk next to the five things you really, really, really want. Then choose two of them to really focus on." Melinda glanced around at her audience and thought she detected a hint of slowly dawning comprehension. Was this an epiphany moment for them? "Literally, you owe it to yourselves to do this," she urged them. "Think it, believe it, achieve it!"

As she paused for breath, the androids retreated, wailing in high-pitched monotones. One of them pivoted around disconsolately and clattered into the pod wall.

"I know," said Melinda, her eyes responding with empathy and gentleness, her voice little more than a cadence of soft breathing. "I know. Sometimes you just got to cry it out."

.   .   .

It takes a long while for an earthling body to adjust to a blue blood cell (BBC) transfusion. Reacting with organic tissue and bone marrow, the newly introduced cells mutate and stimulate the reconstruction of host organs. This facilitates and ensures the continuous regeneration of BBCs for the lifetime of the host. Polkingbeal67 described them as "like cockroaches - let one in, and you never get rid of them." It was an analogy that made Melinda shudder as she thought about what was going on inside her body.

Later, having completed the first phase of her post-transfusion recovery, Melinda was on her way to an urgent meeting with the planet's revered leader in the company of polkingbeal67. The latter was reveling in his assumed role of planetary guide, making it his business to educate and instruct Melinda on every aspect of Mortian life.

"Wow!" said Melinda, on discovering that polkingbeal67's cruiser had no wheels. "That's insane. On our planet, they only steal the tyres!"

"We don't use wheels here," polkingbeal67 explained, as the colourless graphene cruiser accelerated away. "We use magnetic propulsion."

The G-force snapped Melinda's head back into the headrest. "Woh!" she screamed, gripping the console with both hands. "Insane! It's time you people re-invented the wheel!" Polkingbeal67 nudged a button to moderate the speed and Melinda relaxed a little. Watching the featureless landscape whirling past, she interrupted polkingbeal67's illuminating description of the cruiser's specification: "So tell me more about this blue blood and what it's going to do to me," she said, "and leave out the cockroach stuff."

"Well, imagine a rat..."

"No!" Melinda shouted, shuddering perceptibly. "I don't want to imagine rats or any kind of bug or anything that scuttles or slithers or buzzes or crawls. Or flies into me, bites me or stings me. Okay? Literally."

"Algae?"

"No! Not algae!" Melinda insisted. "Algae is slimy!"

"Right, well, it's all beneficial anyway. BBCs are the secret to our long, healthy, disease-free lives. Our experiments show that female earthlings, in particular, enjoy dramatic benefits from BBCs, and, er, effects."

"Effects? What sort of effects?"

"It's all to do with the stem cell properties of your menstrual blood," polkingbeal67 explained. "You'll find when you have your period, you will probably experience certain changes..."

"Like?"

"Like diseased cells getting zapped, teeth turning blue, hair colour changes and a general feeling of euphoria."

"Really? That dramatic?" Melinda asked as she tried to remember where she was in her menstrual cycle.

"Oh yes, one of the things the BBC does remarkably well is period drama," said polkingbeal67. "What are you laughing about? What is it?"

After a while, Melinda revealed she was nervous about the meeting they were about to have.

"Don't worry," polkingbeal67 reassured her. "Smolin9 will be there."

"Yeh, but what's this leader guy like? What's his name?"

Polkingbeal67 cocked his head slightly. "He doesn't have a name as such. He's just our revered leader. That's what we call him and that's how you address him." He noticed Melinda's baffled expression and tried to explain further, but he couldn't. "That's it," he said.

"But what if he gets deposed or overthrown or whatever? What if you elect a new leader? What will he be called then? He *must* have a name! Literally."

Polkingbeal67 took a deep breath and shrugged. "We don't elect our leader. He arrived on Morys over two thousand of your earth-years ago and he's always been our revered leader. And he always will be."

"So you people don't believe in democracy and all that stuff?"

Polkingbeal67 was stunned. "Of course we do!" he said. "We elect our government and the planet is run the way we want it to be run. Actually, there's an election due soon. It's just that we don't elect our revered leader."

"So, are we going to one of your government buildings?"

"No," said polkingbeal67, looking a little confused. "We're going to our revered leader's palace. We don't have government buildings."

Now it was Melinda's turn to appear confused. "You don't have government buildings? So, where do they... how do the government people, y'know, govern?"

"They're not physical people. Think of them as virtual people."

"Virtual people? Literally? Do you mean like androids? Your government is run by those sad androids?"

"That reminds me, I was going to speak to you about the medibots. They seemed to be in a wretched state. Have you any idea what happened to them?" He went on to explain that the functions of Mortian government were carried out by sophisticated artificial intelligence systems in accordance with the flavour of ideology determined by the electorate.

They passed a flock of spherical-shaped birds. "Totally erratic!" Melinda exclaimed. "What are those?"

Polkingbeal67 was a bit of an authority on Mortian ornithology and launched into a detailed lecture on the anatomy and physiology of the orbis bird. It did not last long. "Wait, they don't have beaks!" Melinda shouted. "They don't have beaks! Totally insane! How do they... I mean, they don't have beaks!"

Polkingbeal67 explained that the orbis tucks its wings in and lands on the top of dwelling pods so that its momentum propels it down the structure towards the ground. Its special feathers absorb the moisture as it rolls, providing it with all the nutrients it needs.

Melinda watched them in childlike awe. "That's so erratic, wonderful. Literally."

Polkingbeal67 twisted his mouth to produce what might have passed as a smile. "You're going to like it here," he said.

Melinda nodded. "I'm going to need a coffee soon, but you know what? You're right. I really am going to like it here."

"It's just as well," said polkingbeal67. "After all, you can't go back."

Melinda's face froze. "What?" she said.

"Did no one tell you? The changes to heart tissue brought about by BBCs are irreversible in earthlings. You can't go back." He became aware of Melinda's eyes staring at him in disbelief. "So it's lucky you like it here. Right?"

As the cruiser sped past the Voyager 1 dish antenna half-buried amongst the ponds and fountains of the leader's palace gardens, polkingbeal67 and Melinda noticed smolin9 careering around the lower slopes of the palace building on a modified skateboard propelled by plasma jet thrusters. As soon as the cruiser shell touched the ground and polkingbeal67 released the angel wing doors, Melinda slid out from the seat and raced over towards the marble steps where smolin9 was now waiting, jetboard in hand. As she ran, she was torn between hugging him and pounding him with both fists. In the event, she did neither. Sobbing bitterly, she stood in front of him, arms stiff by her side, unable to utter a single word.

"What's wrong?" he asked.

When Melinda finally found her voice, she spoke in a whisper punctuated with suppressed sobs. "Why didn't you tell me I could never go back to Earth?"

Smolin9 looked bewildered. "What do you mean?" he said.

"I can't go back to Earth. I've got this blue blood and it's messed around with my insides and so, apparently, I have to stay on this god-forsaken planet for the rest of my life!" Her emotions veering wildly from fear and self-pity to anger and back again, she started pulling at her hair. "Why did you do this?" she yelled, "Why didn't you tell me? You must have known I wouldn't have agreed to come here if I'd known it was a one-way ticket!"

There was an awkward silence. Smolin9 looked at polkingbeal67 with an expression of covert hostility.

Polkingbeal67 was the first to speak. "He didn't know," he said.

"I didn't know," smolin9 confirmed.

"What?" Melinda whimpered. "Why didn't you know? So who *did* know?" She turned to polkingbeal67. "Why didn't you tell him?"

Polkingbeal67 shrugged. "It's a misunderstanding, that's all," he said. "Smolin9 wasn't around when we analysed the simulation test data." He started to sound more and more defensive as the other two stared balefully at him. "Listen, I thought... I mean, I didn't know this was meant to be a temporary visit. I thought... you two being married and everything..."

"I didn't know," smolin9 said in a small voice. His mental faculties had temporarily regressed to a state of infantile helplessness. He knew well enough that he would have to shoulder the bulk of the responsibility for this catastrophe. After all, Melinda's wormhole visit had been entirely his own initiative in the first place and it was entirely his own fault that he had neglected to supervise the laboratory simulation tests.

"Anyway," said polkingbeal67, breezily. "Don't forget, you agreed to the terms and conditions. It's done now. Better get on. We're almost late for our meeting with our revered leader." He adjusted the strap on his sherg-encrusted helmet and bounded up the steps.

Melinda sat on the bottom step and took a tissue from her fake crocodile skin bag. Dumbfounded and lost for words, smolin9 sat beside her and tentatively placed his hand on her shoulder.

Melinda blew her nose. "It's not that I'm ungrateful to you for giving me this opportunity of seeing your planet," she said, folding and unfolding the tissue. "When I was a little girl, there were these little plastic 'My Little Pony' toys. Me and my friends, we all loved them. It was a real craze at the time. Literally. My favourite was Skydancer. Skydancer was a ballerina and loved to dance to the sound of the wind when it flowed through the clouds like the music of string harps, and she pranced and pirouetted in tiny circles. I simply had to have one!" She blew her nose again. "Anyway, my dad... this was before he left us... for Christmas, he got me, you won't believe this, he got me a real, live pony. Insane! There was a farm down the bottom of the road and he'd rented a stall there and everything. He said he'd show me how to feed it and groom it and muck out the stall. I was going to have riding lessons and learn how to lead it and tie it up properly and how to put a halter, saddle and bridle on it. The thing is, I was barely four foot tall. It seemed scary huge to me. It frightened me! And, the point is, all I'd wanted was a little plastic Skydancer. With rainbow hair. Literally."

The point of the story might have been a bit obscure; it

certainly flew right over smolin9's head. "Don't worry," he said. "I'll get you a Skydancer."

As Melinda followed smolin9 through the palatial labyrinth to the leader's private rooms, she gazed in awe at the architectural opulence and marveled at the grandeur that oozed from every gilded surface and every ornately decorated portal. She started to think about wealth disparity and how it seemed to be so different on Morys Minor compared to the economic inequality back on Earth, where the rich were cocooned from ordinary people's ordeals. 'Ah yes,' she thought. 'That is it. This leader of theirs clearly enjoys a life of incredible luxury and privilege, but the ordinary people don't have ordeals.' She had witnessed no evidence of poverty or hardship or discontent or social injustice.

"So what is it with all this?" she said. "All this abundant richness, all this treasure and wealth. It's insane. Back on earth, for someone to enjoy gold and precious stones and jewels like this, a whole bunch of other people, the underclasses, have got to put up with, er, well, bling and, er, designer labels, um, yeh, forget it, I guess it's not so different."

"Get ready to like us!" said smolin9. "We're the product of a complex molecular soup, but we have a social cohesion that most planets would die for. There's no corruption or sleaze. Everyone's happy with their lives."

"The soup sounds great," Melinda agreed. "Actually, can I get a cup of coffee?"

To say Melinda found the leader somewhat unimpressive would be a colossal understatement. Attached to his small wizened head were a pair of strange bone-like objects like truncated antlers and his body reeked of wet straw and fried oil. Desperately as she tried to dismiss the image, he reminded her of Gandhi with horns. When she repeated her request for coffee, he told her: "So I say to you, ask and it will be given to you." He snapped his bony fingers at one of his underlings and a brew was produced before he had finished outlining his plans for a grand televised reception to mark Melinda's arrival on the planet.

There was not much that was beyond the power of the Mortians. Most of the food resources on Earth had been sampled, analysed and reproduced in dedicated laboratories, but the greenish brown sludge the leader had managed to acquire for Melinda left her begging for the soup. She spat it out and almost gagged. "It must be the methane?" suggested smolin9.

.   .   .

Melinda took up her place between smolin9 and the Mortian leader and did a double-take when the intro to Chuck Berry's "Johnny B. Goode" echoed around the vast banqueting hall. The music from the Voyager 1 Golden Record was being played in her honour.

Thirty guests had arrived at the palace for Melinda's official reception. All were formally announced. Many, including polkingbeal67, wore full ceremonial dress, a curious ensemble of folded robes secured by graphene sashes, straps and belts sumptuously decorated with embroidered flaps and tassels. Random ornaments completed the outfit. All around the perimeter of the hall, androids were engaged in various activities that Melinda later described as 'kind of nerdy dancing'. They postured and mimed and re-enacted historical earthling events, none of which were recognised by the guest of honour.

"Are these like the top leaders and dignitaries of your planet?" Melinda whispered to smolin9, pointing to the guests.

"No, this is everyone," said smolin9. "We're all here."

"What? This is your entire population? Really? That's harrowing. Literally. But why are there so few of you?"

"It's all we need. We've optimised the link between population and resources. We love our planet and we've spent eons creating a fair and equitable state where every citizen is scrupulously engineered and has a specific role to play. Nobody gets marginalised and there are no sources of conflict. Our revered leader has always told us 'when two goopmutts fight, the grass suffers.'"

"Okay, what have goopmutts and grass got to do with it?"

Smolin9 was stumped. He had no idea. While he fretted over it, Melinda hit him with a supplementary question: "But what about polkingbeal67? He's obviously a confrontational, warmongering guy who loves fighting."

"Yes," said smolin9, "but only with beings from other planets, like the carnivorous skavaks of Ork who killed and raped millions of our people and stole an entire vat of vitalmados."

"When was that?"

"Oh, many, many thousands of your earth years ago," said smolin9, who was still distracted by the goopmutts and grass business.

"That's totally erratic. You can't go around killing people for stuff that happened centuries ago!"

Rattled once more, smolin9 endeavoured to explain: "Ah, yes, but he only heard about it *recently*, at an intergalactic history workshop."

They sat on soft piles of what looked like blossoms. In

front of them was the most underwhelming feast Melinda had ever seen. A few lozenges were arranged in perfectly geometric fashion on a low table. Melinda picked one up and inspected it quizzically. "How do you eat it?" she asked.

"Oh, yes," said smolin9. "Um, we eat them like, well, on your planet I think you call them suppositories. They're totally delectable. These are the most prestigious vitalmados pills on the planet, hand-picked for their premium quality. They fizz divinely."

Melinda placed the lozenge back on the table. "I'm not really hungry just now," she said.

After a short while, the leader struggled to his feet and signaled for silence. "May your voices have wings," he said. This was the signal for nipkow4 to deliver the first of a series of speeches celebrating Melinda's arrival. Nipkow4 had made a name for himself producing the hugely popular Morys Minor Broadcasting Corporation (MMBC) Earthwatch series aimed at encouraging interest in earthling life, and this ceremony was being recorded for subsequent broadcast to tele-immersion systems around the planet. Melinda was astonished to hear nipkow4 deliver an accurate insight into her personal characteristics along with details of her life that could only have been obtained through surreptitious monitoring, tracking and spying.

Melinda poked smolin9 with her elbow. "What the hell's going on?" she hissed. "How does he know all this?" She gaped open-mouthed as video images of her walking down Glastonbury High Street appeared on the walls. "You've been spying on me!"

Smolin9 moved closer so that he could talk to her without drawing attention. "Calm down," he said. "We didn't spy on you. Your own people did. We just used the data."

"That's insane! What spies? What data? Why would they? How could they? This is invasion of privacy with a capital 'I' and, er, 'P'."

"Sorry, but all this stuff about you is routinely recorded and stored in databases on your planet. I'm surprised you don't know about it. You must realise there's software on your communication devices that analyses your messages? It all gets used for beaming advertising at you. Your comms devices also keep track of your movements. You've got cameras in your streets and cameras scanning your vehicles. Your shopping habits are tracked by shops and credit agencies. Then there's your social media. I used Facebook while I was visiting Earth. Remember? I friended you. It's quite addictive. I used to break out in a cold sweat if I didn't see a status update for, like, ten of your Earth minutes or so. Obviously, all that stuff gets logged and stored in databases. And it's easy to see all your computer network activity. It's just basic communication data."

"Oh my gosh," said Melinda as nipkow4 attempted a public analysis of all her recent retail purchases. "I feel like an animal in a zoo. Make them stop!"

Smolin9 could feel her distress and discomfort but was powerless to do anything about it. Once the MMBC wheels were in motion, nothing short of natural disasters and acts of God could stop them. Upset about the possibility that the blue blood debacle and this new ordeal she was suffering would drive a wedge between him and his earthling wife, he cast several anxious looks in her direction. Then he drew himself up to his full height and hooted (Mortian coughs sound a bit like demented owls). "Wait," he said. "I have to stop you there."

Melinda tugged at his arm. "Don't get yourself in trouble!" she whispered.

Smolin9 suddenly felt conscious of the cameras. "Yeh," he mumbled. "All this information. Shopping and stuff... I just wanted to say..."

"Just leave it," Melinda begged him.

"I just want to say that... the lice shampoo was for me." All eyes turned on him and he visibly flinched a little. "Yeh, I, y'know, I get that itchy thing." He sat down and nipkow4 cast him a look of perplexed amusement before continuing with his speech.

Smolin9 need not have worried in any case. Melinda, for her part, felt these experiences only drew them closer together. Smolin9's naivety and helplessness lent him a vulnerability that she could clearly identify with in her current predicament and she felt a closer bond with him in consequence.

A strange, ululating chant, the Mortian equivalent of applause, marked the end of nipkow4's presentation. Then everyone turned around and headbutted the nearest wall. Footage from the Earthwatch series was projected silently around the hall as various other people made speeches. Meanwhile, some androids filled the central area with a bizarre array of musical instruments constructed out of graphene, wire and silicon. Polkingbeal67, distinguishable from the others with his eye patch and sherg-encrusted helmet, was among those to pick up an instrument and contribute to a sonic composition akin to a bear with toothache being let loose in a junkyard. Smolin9 leaned across to Melinda and said "This is nice. You know what's going on?"

Melinda gave him a wonky smile. "Not so far," she said. "Literally."

Everyone fell silent as the leader struggled once more to

his feet to formally welcome Melinda to her new planet. "Welcome to Morys Minor, Melinda. May your obstacles be stepping stones. You are with friends and we will travel together. There is a reason for this and every journey. Blind as we are, for the eye may see no more than the mind can understand, we must hope that we will recognise our destination when we reach it. We all have much to teach and much to learn." This prompted more chanting and headbutting of walls. Melinda smiled politely as everyone turned towards her. "You're expected to reply," smolin9 told her.

Melinda stood up, bowed, curtsied and smiled at the leader. "Thank you, your, er, leadership," she said. "That's totally erratic of you. I'm also looking forward to this trip, er, journey thing. It should be good. Journey with a capital 'J'! Literally. But seriously, it's really great that you've given me this opportunity to come here to this galaxy far far away, ha ha, y'know, by wormhole and everything. It's also kind of appropriate, because, as you know, I come from Earth and, y'know, wormholes, earth, yeh? And while I'm on that subject, if there's anything you can do to get me back home... well, I'm an earthworm really, ha ha!" She desperately grasped for something profound or witty to round off with. "I hope our two planets can be friends and we can wormhole to each other all the time, so that maybe one day we'll be so close it'll be like not telling which end of the worm is which! Ha ha. Insane. Thank you." She bowed, curtsied and smiled once more at the leader who presented her with a bowl of what looked like glazed purple rabbit droppings.

She sat down. "Was that okay?" she asked smolin9, taking the bowl and showing her teeth in a fixed smile. "What do I do with these?"

"That was just fine," said smolin9. "And, er, they're

supposed to be absorbed rectally."

"There's no way..."

"You have to. It will be a breach of intergalactic protocol if you don't."

"Well, he'll just have to settle for a symbolic gesture," Melinda snarled. She got up, placed the bowl on the blossoms, sat on it and smiled affably. The leader bowed, curtsied and smiled back.

.   .   .

Time went by. Well, what else would it do? But exactly how *much* time had gone by, Melinda was by no means certain. She did not know if a Mortian day was the equivalent of an Earth day and, anyway, the fact that there were two suns made it all so confusing. Mortians measure time by means of a numerical system that made no sense to her whatsoever.

Melinda was still struggling to come to terms with her exile from Earth. She had spent hours sitting alone, staring at a few dog-eared photographs of friends and relatives. Although she knew the only way she could mitigate some of the loneliness was to throw herself heart and soul into her new life on Morys, yet she refused to abandon hope of one day being able to return home. Her experience as a life coach taught her that clinging to such an unrealistic prospect was psychologically dangerous. She risked alienation from smolin9, and, worse, she risked slipping into a kind of existential death.

"What exactly is it about these blue blood cells that make it impossible for me to go home?" she asked smolin9, as they sat back to back on the prairie floor outside their dwelling pod. "Polkingbeal67 said something about changes to my heart tissue, but I don't really understand why that can't be fixed."

Smolin9 reached behind and placed his hand on hers. "I'm really sorry, Mel. I've spoken to our experts about this and it seems that although the other organs revert just fine, earthling hearts are different. They're just different, that's all. I'm so sorry."

"Couldn't I have a transplant or something?"

"Well, a transplant would work, but, well, would you really want us to abduct someone else from Earth to be a donor?"

"No," said Melinda. "I suppose not. What about a Mortian?"

Smolin9 pondered this for a moment. "Strangely enough, that would work. As you know, our hearts function perfectly okay on both planets and there's no reason why an earthling body should reject a Mortian heart. The thing is, our body parts self-heal almost instantly, so we live for centuries. Mortians only die when there's catastrophic trauma involved or the heart becomes incredibly old and useless. So no one would ever meet donor criteria. Anyone who dies on Morys is not going to have a healthy heart to pass over to you." He turned his head. "I'd give you mine..."

Melinda sighed and squeezed smolin9's hand. "Don't be silly," she said. "Literally."

Androids had been allocated the task of obtaining methane hydrates and separating the water molecules from the gas molecules. So Melinda had been drinking coffee, but she had eaten nothing since her arrival on the planet apart from some chocolate she had brought with her in her fake crocodile skin bag. "We've got to talk about food," she said. "I'm really going to have to eat something soon."

Both suns were high in the sky above them. Smolin9 faced the swollen giant, Melinda the red dwarf. The combined radiation produced a stellar wind manifesting itself as a series of sinuous, spinning vortexes dancing capriciously along the horizon. Weaving in and out of the twisting columns of gas and dust and heading towards them was polkingbeal67's cruiser. They sat and watched as it sped towards them, leaving red dust in its wake. Polkingbeal67 and the young cadet, yukawa3, got out of the cruiser and strolled across to where smolin9 and Melinda were sitting.

Smolin9 greeted them and introduced yukawa3 to Melinda. "You may have met briefly at the reception," he said.

"Yeh, I remember," said Melinda. Yukawa3's build was similar to smolin9's, but his mouth had a slightly pinched shape and his eyes were narrower. He sported what looked like a sou'wester rain hat. "What brings you here?"

Yukawa3 looked perplexed. "Er, I live on this planet," he said.

Melinda laughed. "No, I mean, um, anyway, why the hat?"

"Why the hat?" yukawa3 repeated, looking at polkingbeal67 with an expression of helpless bewilderment.

Melinda shrugged. The conversation had already become a bit of an ordeal. "Don't worry, it's a very nice hat. So erratic. My Aunt Vivienne has one just like it."

Yukawa3 cast a pleading look at polkingbeal67. "She's got an amphibian that wears a hat, sir," he said.

To be polite, Melinda sought to clarify matters. "Aunt Vivienne," she said. "Not amphibian. Amphibians are literally like frogs and toads. And they don't wear hats as a general rule." She shrieked with laughter.

Yukawa3 shot a pained glance at polkingbeal67. "Sir?"

Smolin9 brought the awkwardness to an end. "Melinda's been asking about food," he said, turning to polkingbeal67. "Have we been able to sort anything out yet?"

"You bet we have!" said polkingbeal67, sounding quite excited for him. "We obtained samples of principal earthling foodstuffs, analysed them and recreated the molecular structure of most of them in tablet form. And we've discovered a sustainable way of producing the tablets without raiding the Pale Blue Dot!" He noticed Melinda's vexed expression. "But you'll get all the macronutrients, micronutrients and phytochemicals you need."

"It is spoken," yukawa3 pronounced, nodding wisely.

Melinda looked aghast. "I don't want macro, micro stuff or fighter chemicals!" she protested. "And I don't want tablets. Literally." The thought of the vitalmados suppositories at her welcome reception sprang into her mind. "That's utterly harrowing! I'm not going to spend the rest of my days eating food at the wrong end! And that's that!"

Smolin9 understood. "Don't worry, Mel. We don't always eat like that. In fact, our primary tongues are here in our mouths." He demonstrated by poking a worm-like tube from his mouth and flicking it with his finger.

Yukawa3 was looking at polkingbeal67 and getting agitated. "Tell her, sir," he said. "Tell her about the coronation orbis!"

"Yes," said polkingbeal67, tapping his eye patch the way he did when he felt proud of himself. "We noticed a lot of your food is derived from organisms that have wings and fly, or have scales and swim, or have fur and run. So we analysed similar organisms that live here on our planet and discovered several that will be compatible with your digestive system. We found an earthling recipe for coronation chicken and discovered that the orbis bird is an excellent chicken substitute. So, yes, we made some tablets for your lunch. They're in the cruiser."

"It is spoken," said yukawa3, nodding.

Melinda was less than impressed. "But this is insane!" she complained. "So if I fancy having lasagne or sausage and mash, I just get a tablet? Why can't you use your fighter chemicals to make sausages instead of tablets? Literally."

Polkingbeal67 shook his head. "It doesn't work like that. And we can't just fetch a pig from your planet every time you want a hot dog."

"Why not?"

"Really? It would be so wasteful. One pig makes 450 sausages."

"What an amazing animal!" said smolin9. "What else can you teach it to do?"

Polkingbeal67 scowled. "You crazy prokaryote! Anyway, there's no way I could justify abducting animals from the Pale Blue Dot just to be eaten."

"Earth!" Melinda insisted. "Call it Earth!" Her mood was clearly changing.

Yukawa3 felt he should break the silence that followed. "I want to say something about this," he announced.

Unfortunately, his mental faculties were not up to it. "Let me think about it," he said.

Polkingbeal67, who had been urgently swiping and flicking at his microwocky, suddenly sprang to his feet. "It's confirmed," he announced. "They're all in quarantine right now."

"It was prophesied," said yukawa3, shaking his head for no apparent reason. He was not sure if polkingbeal67 was ready to reveal the news to Melinda, so he just waved his arms around in frantic expectation. "We must be ready for an unforeseen event that may or may not occur," he said, barely able to contain his excitement. "Sir?"

"All right, yukawa3, I'll tell her," said polkingbeal67, folding his arms to lend his words an air of importance. "Melinda, you will be delighted to learn we've arranged for some of your earthling friends to live with you here on Morys."

"It is spoken," said yukawa3. "Wait, I want to come in here." Everyone waited for him to contribute, but the pressure of having to say something intelligible proved beyond him. "You think that's exciting? Well, it is. I hope that answers your question."

Melinda rose to her feet as she struggled to digest what polkingbeal67 had said. "Did I hear you right?" she asked. "My friends? Coming to live here? Are you serious?" A pang of joy was instantly suppressed as she realised anyone from Earth would be doomed to permanent exile just as she was. "Oh my god, what have you done?"

Melinda's tone of voice put polkingbeal67 on the defensive and he made a dismissive gesture with his hand. "I went to a lot of trouble to do this. You have no idea," he said. "It costs millions of shergs to transport people by wormhole. You're just lucky our revered leader has taken a bit of a shine to you."

"It's not some can... It's not can thing... It's not something you can dismiss lightly," said yukawa3, tripping over his words. "But it doesn't matter really. It's done now and you should be grateful. No question about it, but I ask myself..."

Melinda had had enough. "Shut up!" she snapped. "Sorry, literally, but shut up! You're jabbering like a hyena. I want to know who's been brought here and what's happening with them."

"They're with the medibots. You should be celebrating," said yukawa3. "You've got earthling friends here and you'll be meeting them soon. You should be partying. This is a joyous occasion and you should be dancing and laughing, not attacking us!" He tried prompting Melinda by giggling maniacally. "Who's the hyena now?" he said. At this point, polkingbeal67 slapped him on the top of the head.

Smolin9 put his arm around Melinda's shoulder while polkingbeal67 explained that the new earthling immigrants were not actually known to her. They were a dozen young adults, six men and six women, abducted from various prisons in the vicinity of Melinda's home. In his wisdom, the Mortian leader had judged that their incarceration rendered them expendable.

Melinda was dumbfounded. "So basically," she said, "you've got hold of a bunch of criminals, possibly *dangerous* criminals, and you've brought them here for my benefit. And they're all stuck here forever. And they're all going to blame *me* for it! Well, what could go wrong? So, do tell me, what knucklehead halfwit donkey came up with that idea?"

Appalled at this blatant slander, polkingbeal67 turned on his heels and left. The cruiser accelerated away, trailing a plume of dust behind it. Yukawa3, who had been nursing his crumpled hat, gestured in the direction of the speeding cruiser. "That knucklehead halfwit deserves to be kicked to death by a donkey," he said, keen to ingratiate himself with the sobbing Melinda, "and I'm just the one to do it."

. . .

"Remember," said the Mortian leader, as Melinda left the palace to join smolin9 and yukawa3 in the cruiser, which was humming like a monk at the foot of the steps, "eagles are unsociable and don't flock like other birds. But we rejoice when the eagle soars. It is tempting to look away from the sun as it is bright and may hurt your eyes. But you should draw no comfort from the world of distorted shadows."

Smolin9 gave Melinda a quizzical look as the cruiser hovered and lurched forwards with yukawa3 at the controls. "What was that all about?" he asked.

Melinda shrugged. "Yeh, it was a bit erratic. Maybe it will make sense eventually. Right now, you need to explain to me why these people are being held in a prison camp. They may have committed crimes on Earth, but you Mortians have no right to lock them up."

The three of them were on their way to the earthling prisoners' camp on the far side of the vast methane lake known as nefeshchaya. A patrolling company of androids marked the boundary of the enclosure, but security was actually assured by means of an invisible force field that occasionally erupted in tiny sparks and crackling plasma fountains. The twelve convicts had been provided with dwelling pods, a colossal greenhouse with a closed earth-like ecosystem, some dairy animals, a food processing facility, an ice house and a random assortment of equipment, tools and materials plundered from farms and factories on Earth. There were water extraction kits and even a fully sustainable sanitation system. Some of the convicts had begun to make the best of their situation. They spent time at the camp perimeter and exchanged gossip and information with the androids. Others fumed and plotted and schemed.

By and large, the Mortians had gone the extra mile to make the earthlings feel comfortable and empowered. They were perhaps understandably upset when the convicts dubbed the enclosure a 'living tomb'.

"Why do they call it a tomb?" yukawa3 asked as the androids ushered them through a temporary portal in the force field close to one of the dwelling pods. "What *is* a tomb?"

"It's a burial chamber," Melinda explained as the convicts came towards them. "Literally. It's where our people used to bury the dead. Like in pyramids and stuff."

Yukawa3 whimpered pathetically, fell to the ground and adopted the foetal position.

Smolin9 shrugged. "He'll be fine. He's been watching a lot of old earthling movies about zombies."

Yukawa3 recovered, sprang to his feet and puffed out his chest. "Sorry," he said. "I felt a little faint. Haven't eaten today. These living dead earthlings don't actually look very dangerous. No match for battle-hardened space guerrillas like me and smolin9! Pah!"

"Well," said smolin9, "We're not armed. What do you suggest we do if it turns ugly?"

"Let me think about it," said yukawa3, sucking his lips. "I've got it - shout for help, of course!"

Melinda attempted to introduce herself to the convicts, but one of them interrupted her. "Yes," he hissed menacingly. "We know who you **** are." He spat on the ground. "You're the **** who's responsible for getting us into this. Do you realise what you've **** done?" This man, Joseph West, self-appointed leader of the twelve-strong convict community, had been serving time back on Earth for grievous bodily harm and had had previous convictions for drug dealing, racially aggravated common assault and burglary.

Yukawa3 attempted to spit, but could only produce a feeble whistling sound and a small globule of saliva that dribbled down his chin.

"It's not her fault," said smolin9. "Melinda had no idea about any of this: the blue blood cells, you people being abducted, none of it. And don't forget you were in confinement on your own planet."

"So what is this? The new **** Australia?" West countered. "At least on Earth we only had to serve our **** sentences and then we'd be free. But this... this is a living **** tomb."

"How long was your sentence?" Melinda asked.

"Eight words," yukawa3 interjected helpfully.

West spat again. "None of your **** business."

Melinda persisted in the hope of engaging the convicts in some kind of meaningful dialogue. "What were you in for?"

"Doing my **** Christmas shopping early," West lied.

"But surely that's not an offence," said smolin9.

"Yeh, well, it is if you do it before the **** shop opens!" said West with a sardonic grin that revealed red and inflamed gums. "All right, I kicked the **** out of someone. I'm no **** angel. But I don't deserve this. None of us do! It's bad enough on Earth in the **** prison. If you stick an animal in a **** cage and don't feed it properly or exercise it or nuthin', people call you **** cruel and barbaric. I mean, if a dog does a **** job on the carpet, you shout at it, right? But then you try to teach the poor **** devil another way. It might take a few times, but eventually most of 'em learn. So why the **** can't we do it with people?"

West's anger and frustration continued to simmer as he and Melinda discussed general issues concerning incarceration.

"You see," Melinda told him. "I agree with you that there are lots of alternatives to longer and longer prison sentences, but I guess it's easier for society to say: 'Take them away, lock them up and keep them away from me.'"

Yukawa3 interrupted. "I want to come in at this point," he said. "You think that's easier?" He racked his brain but only came up with: "Well, it is."

"You can't **** imagine what it's like to be confined to a small space and narrow routines for years and **** years, maybe until death," said West. "Okay, nothing terrible happens, but then nothing great happens either. There are no real dramas of any kind like in real life. It's just day after day of nothing. It's the **** nothingness that kills you."

"I totally understand that, literally," said Melinda. "And I believe people can be made better."

"Right," said West. "It's just **** wrong to strip away great chunks of a person's life, together with their relationships and mental well-being and their..." He searched for the right word.

Melinda supplied it. "Humanity?" she said.

"Yeh. In some ways, I think flogging is better. If you've got to punish people, then flog them!"

Melinda frowned. "I don't know. I think flogging is barbaric. Literally."

"It may be barbaric, but punishments, by definition, are supposed to be unpleasant, aren't they? Given the choice, I'd rather be flogged than spend time in **** prison. And justice is then seen to be done. You'd be surprised at how prison terms make people worse. They come out and feel they need to make up for everything jail took away from them. So they resort to lying and cheating and stealing to make up for lost time."

"Yeh, or they become bitter and resentful," Melinda agreed. "Not forgetting that many criminals are victims themselves. Or they're dysfunctional people who just need help to cope with their lives. Harrowing. I've helped many ex-convicts myself."

Yukawa3 could remain silent no longer. "It feels like the world is ignoring me," he said. "It is spoken."

It was some time before West and Melinda moved on to the more specific context of their situation. As soon as they did so, West suddenly resumed his hostility and turned on smolin9. "You consider yourselves an advanced **** civilisation. But you do this to us!"

The events that unfolded afterwards happened very

quickly. West pushed smolin9 to the ground, grabbed Melinda, produced a knife and held it to her throat. Yukawa3, for no particular reason, started running around in circles.

"Everyone keep still and listen!" West shouted.

Yukawa3 stopped, pointed at West and said: "Put it down! It's dangerous."

"Shut up, you **** idiot!" West snarled.

Yukawa3 was undeterred. "It's dangerous, I tell you. I once gripped the wrong end of one of those and cut my hand. You see? Who's the idiot now?"

"Don't harm her," said smolin9 in a slightly tremulous voice. "Don't you see - she's the most valuable asset you've got on this planet."

West's red gums were displayed once more as a sneering grin stretched across his face. His lips were thin and colourless. "I think she's important to you lot too, right?" he said, pressing the cold knife-blade against Melinda's neck. "Now, how do you control those robot people out there?"

Smolin9 gestured towards his microwocky and West instructed him to summon the androids. The sporadic sparks from the force field ceased abruptly and the androids approached, uttering high-pitched monotones. "Tell them to drop their weapons!" West barked.

A variety of plasma rifles and stun guns clattered to the ground and the other convicts moved to collect them. But before they could reach the weapons, a burst of plasma exploded in front of them and polkingbeal67 emerged from a pod behind West. Having anticipated trouble of this kind, he had crawled his way into the enclosure through the sewage pipes and now stood before them covered in foul-smelling sludge. His eye-patch was all askew and his sherg-encrusted helmet was embellished with blobs of slime and scraps of tissue. "Put down the knife!" he commanded.

West tossed the knife aside and Melinda broke free. Polkingbeal67 raised his rifle and took aim at West. Melinda screamed at him: "Don't you dare fire that thing! Don't you dare!" Polkingbeal67 lowered the weapon, the androids armed themselves once more and order was restored.

The dwarf sun glimmered over the enclosure as West and the convicts were ushered back towards the dwelling pods by the androids under the supervision of smolin9 and yukawa3. Melinda went up to polkingbeal67 and smiled. "I love you, you big old bear," she said. "And if you didn't smell so bad, I'd hug you to bits. Literally."

.   .   .

"Well, we certainly showed them a thing or two, didn't we?" said yukawa3, as he and smolin9 and Melinda waited for an audience with the Mortian leader in one of the palace anterooms. The walls were faced with albarium and here and there were clusters of sculptured figures, Mortian war heroes, randomly streaked with a kind of verdigris. "Hell, we stepped up big time. It was just like the old days, eh?"

Smolin9 looked askance at him. "What old days?"

"Well, you know," said yukawa3, who had a knack for reinventing history and painting himself in a better light in the process. "The three of us, intergalactic heroes. You, me and polkingbeal67 facing challenges head-on, looking them in the eye, having blind faith in each other and refusing to blink. If they kick us in the teeth, we just bite back. With both feet. In the midst of our troubles, we just keep going straight ahead. Nothing can stop us, short of death. Or, wait, yeh, maybe a tangy vitalmados pill."

"I don't know about blinking or going straight ahead," said smolin9, "but I do recall you fainting and running around in circles."

"Those weren't circles," said yukawa3, indignantly, "Those were, uh, spirals. I was trying to confuse the enemy while I got closer and closer and..." He started wheeling around the room to demonstrate his reinterpreted role in the incident at the convicts' enclosure.

"Time and place, yukawa3," said smolin9, grabbing the cadet's arm. "Time and place. And I think we all know which of us, if any of us, did anything remotely heroic."

Melinda noticed the wounded look that flashed across yukawa3's face. "I'm sure your spirals will eventually become the stuff of Mortian legend," she said, reassuringly.

Smolin9 sat next to Melinda and murmured under his breath: "I'm glad you're here. You're an eyewitness and, believe me, that's the only thing stopping me from killing him!"

Melinda patted his leg. "I want to know what we're going to tell your leader guy about what happened. Is there any way we can play down what happened? How will he react?"

Smolin9, who seldom understood anything the leader said at the best of times, had absolutely no idea what to expect. "Oh, I'm sure he'll be fine with it. We'll let yukawa3 do all the talking."

"Why?"

"Because our revered leader would never believe a word he says!"

However, before they were summoned to the leader's apartments, a special emissary, accompanied by two of the android medibots, burst into the room. "No time to lose!" he said. "Come with us immediately! We have a donor!"

Smolin9 and Melinda had time to exchange a look of shocked amazement, nothing more, before they were whisked away in a speeding medicruiser, leaving yukawa3 to explain the fracas at nefeshchaya. Smolin9 was flabbergasted. Several days previously, he had explained to his wife that a Mortian heart donor could only be possible if someone were prepared to make the ultimate sacrifice and lay down his life explicitly to give Melinda a chance of returning home.

Melinda's head was in a whirl. She, also, could not understand why anyone would do this. Her hazy recollections of the events of the day included a vague memory of the prairie rolling past like time lapse film footage. She remembered, for the first time, being aware of smolin9 actually having teeth, because he used them to chew at his bottom lip during the journey. And she remembered snatches of tense conversation.

In particular, she remembered the distraught expression on his face when she asked him: "Will I be able to return to Earth immediately after the transplant?" And she remembered him being unable to reply, his voice choked with inarticulate agony.

She remembered arriving at the medical pod and being escorted along a corridor, smolin9 in her wake. She remembered glancing into the operating theatre where the donor was lying, half-concealed by a drape. And, above all, she would never forget the adjacent table, containing, as it did, an eye patch and a sherg-encrusted helmet.

4

THE STOVE BOAT

Some eons ago – never mind how long precisely – having little or no money in his sherg-purse, and nothing particular to interest him on his home planet, polkingbeal67 thought he would sail about a little and see the celestial part of the universe. It was a way he had of driving off his gloominess and regulating his metabolism. Whenever the cold methane rain swirled around the landscape of his soul, he would take to his Mark III Zeplock mineral spotter, usually with smolin9 in tow, and the two of them would go spacecombing in the Centaurus galaxy scavenging for defunct satellites and pieces of space junk. It was on one such trip that they had discovered the Voyager 1 space probe drifting aimlessly through a shifting vapour of space dust.

Up until this point, the closest polkingbeal67 had ever come to an act of fellowship or kindness was to tackle the social problem of vitalmados abuse on Morys by confiscating it and consuming it himself. Many Mortians had felt the cold blast of his fury when they had had the temerity to question one of his odious opinions, and many had turned to him for help or sympathy only to find themselves caught in the cold, remorseless gaze of his uncovered eye (he had lost an eye during the battle of Hat Signs and wore an eye patch). So it had come as a great shock to the Mortian community when they discovered that this battle-hardened veteran of the Jatron wars had apparently offered to donate his heart to smolin9's earthling wife. It had also come as a great shock to polkingbeal67 himself, as he had had no idea what had been afoot and had been under the impression he was being offered the chance of a new eye.

"I've been tricked!" he yelled from his bed in the post-operative care unit.

Melinda, lying in an adjacent bed, had just spent several minutes showering effusive thanks and praises upon him for his heroic act of self-sacrifice. Having assumed that polkingbeal67's reaction was just an attempt to deflect her gushing adoration with gruff modesty, she simply smiled and closed her eyes in blissful contemplation. Had she kept them open, she would have witnessed polkingbeal67's wild gyrating of limbs as he descended into a frenzy of speechless rage.

To be fair to polkingbeal67, one can understand how he had got hold of the wrong end of the stick. He had arrived at the medical pod after suffering respiratory problems during the incident at the earthling prisoners' camp at nefeshchaya. The head consultant at the medical facility had been under pressure from the planet's revered leader to find a solution to the dilemma Melinda was facing, and he had frivolously asked polkingbeal67 if he might be interested in organ transplant surgery. Wires got crossed during the conversation because polkingbeal67 took this to be a reference to his eye and replied that he was definitely interested. While medibots were assembling for the heart transplant, polkingbeal67, feeling a tad uncertain about things, had tapped his eye patch and asked the consultant, "You've got a new one for me, yes?" The consultant had looked confused but replied in the affirmative. And now, there he was, still groggy from the anaesthetic, a transplanted earthling heart beating rhythmically in his chest and a shiny new patch stretched across his empty eye socket.

At this point, smolin9 and yukawa3 appeared, just in time to see polkingbeal67 flailing his arms around.

"You see!" yukawa3 exclaimed. "I told you they'd both be fine. Just look at him waving his arms! He's celebrating!" Roused into high spirits, yukawa3 seized smolin9's arm and danced around the beds singing an impromptu and very inharmonious rendition of a song he half-remembered from a party he had been thrown out of long ago: "Wave your hands up in the air! Wave 'em like you just don't care! What it is, what it is!" He rounded up a few android medibots to continue his spontaneous celebratory song and dance routine, while smolin9 and Melinda hugged each other close, savouring the moment.

"I can really go back to Earth now?"

"Any time you like," smolin9 confirmed, nodding like a parcel-shelf dog.

"This is so erratic! I can't tell you how grateful I am. Literally. I'm going to devote the rest of my life to being the absolute best version of me I can possibly be. I'm going to find my inner princess, literally! What can I do for this wonderful old bear, polkingbeal67? Is he going to be okay?"

Smolin9 continued to nod in trance-like euphoria. Polkingbeal67 sat up, cleared his throat and shouted at no one in particular: "I'm not okay! I'm not okay! Okay?" Having got everyone's attention, he thumped the bed and continued, "I'm sorry if I'm ruining the mood here, but I've been cut up like a piece of earthling meat, I can never visit the Pale Blue Dot again, I'm no longer one hundred percent Mortian and, horror of horrors, I've been given an earthling heart! This is the greatest insult since the goopmutts were credited with building the Supreme Palace of Toston Pinnacle! So, no, I'm not okay!"

An awkward silence fell like a lead blanket. It was finally broken by the muffled sound of yukawa3's voice emanating from the inside of a kind of CT scanner: "Wave 'em like you just don't care! What it is, what it is!"

.   .   .

When smolin9 and yukawa3 left, the pink and orange streaks of the first of Morys Minor's two sunsets were already reflected on the crystal wash basins and the blades of gleaming white magma that served to partition the ward into quadrangles. In one of those quadrangles, Melinda propped herself up in bed as the rays of the second sun splintered and scattered around the various dispensers, appliances and glass receptacles. Three of the android medibots, attired in crisp tunics and crisp attitudes, whirred industriously around the beds, irritating polkingbeal67 in the process. "Why do they wear tunics anyway?" he grumbled. "They're androids. They don't need uniforms. We know who they are and what they do."

Melinda graced him with an insouciant smile. "It's about hygiene," she said in her sweetest voice. "After all, it's not like they can take a shower or a bath. Literally." She thought for a second. "They'd rust!" she added, shrieking with laughter. "They'd be rustpital workers!"

"Oh please," said polkingbeal67, rolling his good eye and folding his arms.

Melinda gazed at him with a tranquil expression. She was not persuaded by his protestations about the heart swap. "You know what?" she said. "You can say what you like about being tricked and all the rest of it. I think you're totally, totally wonderful and I'm forever indebted to you. It's freaky, but I literally don't care what you've got physically beating away in there - as far as I'm concerned, you've got a big old heart of gold. Totally."

Polkingbeal67's expression clouded. "Gold? What use would a heart of gold be to me? It may be important on your planet, but gold is just a shiny metal with little value besides what is assigned to it by people who trade with it. To me, a gold heart is no more use to me than the stool sample on that shelf over there." He closed his eye and pulled the sheet over his head.

"Now you're just being grumpy," Melinda said. "You know I don't mean a heart of gold in the literal sense. Literally. Back on Earth, part of my job as a life coach involves school visits. Well, I'm going to tell you a story I like to tell the kids." Polkingbeal67 groaned loudly, but Melinda continued, undeterred. "There are these two sisters, Jawad and Fahim. Jawad is a kind and generous girl, while Fahim is selfish and greedy. One day, they're walking in the forest with their father when he suddenly disappears. Literally. They look all around but there's no sign of him. The girls are utterly heartbroken and they sit on the ground and weep. Then an angel comes down and replaces their broken hearts with golden ones. She promises to return with their real hearts as soon as she can get them repaired."

The medibots switched on the ambient photon lights and parked themselves at the nursing station. Polkingbeal67 could be heard grunting from time to time as Melinda went on: "So the two girls do what they have to do to survive in the forest. Jawad suffers and becomes weaker and weaker because every time she performs her little acts of kindness, like rescuing animals and feeding the hungry birds, it costs her a piece of her golden heart. Literally. Eventually, when she runs out of gold and lies on her deathbed, the angel reappears carrying their mended hearts. Fahim refuses to return her golden heart and runs off, never to be seen again. The angel restores Jawad's mended heart. At that very moment, the girls' father stumbles through the trees and he and Jawad are reunited."

Morose and petulant as he was, polkingbeal67 felt obliged to say something when Melinda had finished. "I have no idea what point you're trying to make, but I'll tell you what - I'll take my old heart back right now and you can have a stupid gold one."

"I know you don't mean that," Melinda said.

Polkingbeal67 rolled on to his side so that Melinda could no longer see his face. "I'm going to sleep," he said.

Over the next couple of days, they had plenty of time to exchange stories, fables and anecdotes. In a case of life not imitating art, Melinda, who was recovering well, spent her time performing little acts of kindness and took on the role of nursing polkingbeal67 while he slipped into a gradual decline. The consultant was worried about a series of complications that might be symptomatic of organ rejection.

A couple of days later, the medibots were preparing Melinda for discharge when polkingbeal67, now enveloped in a dark cloud of bitterness and resentment, launched the most acrimonious of his fables.

Melinda, excited at the prospect of leaving the medical pod and making arrangements for her return to Earth, paid only scant attention. "A Mortian elder sees a gold goopmutt in a shop window," polkingbeal67 growled. "He goes in and says he wants to buy it. The shopkeeper offers to explain the story behind it, but the elder is impatient and just wants to buy the gold goopmutt. He leaves the shop and notices straight away that he is being followed by a couple of real live goopmutts. Then a few more appear. And a few more. After a short while, hundreds of goopmutts appear and they all follow him down to the methane lake. But when the elder stops at the water's edge, the goopmutts keep going. And they drown. The elder returns to the shop and the shopkeeper says, "So, you've come back to hear the story of the gold goopmutt?" The elder says, "No, I've come back to ask if you have a gold earthling!"

"Hmm, what?" Melinda asked, applying her eyeliner and mascara. "I lost you when the guy went into the shop. What are goopmutts? Anyway, I just want to thank you for everything you've done for me. I'll never forget it. You take care now. Literally. I'll come and visit you every day until I go back to Earth. I'm totally behilden, mabolden, oh, what's the word? Bahooden, whatever, I'm melindahillden to you!"

"That isn't even a thing," polkingbeal67 complained.

"Well, it is now," said Melinda. She walked across to his bed and kissed him on the cheek.

Polkingbeal67 squirmed like a worm on a hook. He liked to think of himself as an autonomous intellectual who used analytical reason and independent critical faculties to make sense of the universe. Frankly, the tendency for human earthlings like Melinda to crave empathy and allow themselves to be drawn into the perspective of others was anathema to him. Having witnessed this appalling weakness afflict smolin9, he was all the more determined to fight it, lest it might seep insidiously, like a slow poison, into the Mortian character. At this moment, he resolved to identify the core of whatever it is that constitutes the soul of a human earthling, and destroy it.

.　　.　　.

Meanwhile, smolin9 and yukawa3 had sought and been granted an audience with the revered Mortian leader at the palace of obsidian fingers. At the second sunrise of their second day at the palace, the pair were finally led to the leader's bedchamber where they found him attired in a seaweed body wrap, surrounded by heaps of discarded fortune cookies. Greetings were exchanged and a pipe of scorched vitalmados essence was passed around.

"I have a question for you, O revered leader," smolin9 said, bowing deferentially.

The leader closed his eyes and made a sound like a cat chewing a wasp. "Every wise man started out by asking many questions," he said. "We must bathe together." With that, he flounced from the room, a couple of subservient minions and long pieces of seaweed trailing behind him, and headed for his spa room, a specially designed bath split into six separate open-top cells like a car battery. After a short while, the three of them were joined by nipkow4 and two executives of the Morys Minor Broadcasting Corporation. When all six were settled in the spa tubs, they looked like a carton of eggs.

The MMBC people set out their plans for a flagship series of news programmes, featuring interviews, analysis and investigative reports from around the universe, involving on the spot coverage spearheaded by an outstanding team of presenters. Smolin9 and yukawa3 were formally invited to join this elite team. "Your ability to juggle many tasks will take you far," said the Mortian leader, as smolin9 saw an opportunity to request a posting to the Pale Blue Dot.

Yukawa3 nipped in ahead of him. "Let me do the Pale Blue Dot!" he pleaded.

The leader shook his head. "Each day, compel yourself to do something you would rather not do," he advised.

"What's he talking about?" yukawa3 whispered to smolin9.

"I think he wants you to go to one of the other planets," smolin9 explained. That, at least, was his preferred interpretation.

"But I want to go to the Pale Blue Dot! I love those sou'wester rain hats! We ought to bring some of them back here!"

The leader, growing tired, puffed his cheeks and blew air through his thin, loose lips. "Advice, when most needed, is least heeded," he said. "Say hello to others. You will have a happier day."

"But what about the hats?" yukawa3 protested. "Everyone said it'd be a great idea to bring them back here. And it was all *my* idea!"

"An idea is not responsible for the people who believe in it," the leader intoned sternly.

Yukawa3 was assigned a mission to investigate reports of unrest in the city of Niffis on Oov. Smolin9, to his undisguised delight, was appointed MMBC correspondent on the Pale Blue Dot. Photon lights were moving in the steam from the spa, creating the impression that the water was rippling. Before too long, the leader extracted himself from his tub and began smearing his body with oils and ashes. He and smolin9 remained behind to discuss the condition of polkingbeal67.

"I'm sure he'll pull through," said smolin9, "but I'm worried about him. He seems to be taking it all very badly and seems to be grieving for his heart with anger. He could probably do with a spell away from Morys once he recovers, but of course he can't come to the Pale Blue Dot with me as his new heart won't function there."

The leader shrugged his shoulders. "You can't remove a fire, you have to douse it where it is," he said.

As the conversation went on, the leader made it clear that he had granted smolin9's request to take Melinda with him to the Pale Blue Dot on condition that he return to Morys in due course with a plentiful supply of new fortune cookies. He had made such requests before and smolin9 was only too happy to oblige. He was in high spirits as he walked through to the grand vestibule, where yukawa3 was trying on a full suit of medieval armour.

Smolin9 exclaimed, "What on Morys are you doing?"

Yukawa3 thumped the breast plate and smiled at the echo.

"Just like that earthling movie," said smolin9. "No heart. All hollow. But you don't know what I'm talking about."

"Yes I do," yukawa3 insisted. "It's a film based on a book called Crime and Prejudice. Isn't this great? I love it here. It's times like this when people like us ..." He racked his brains to think of something to add, but he had overstretched himself.

"What?" smolin9 prompted him. "People like us ... what?"

Yukawa3 had run out of steam. "I don't know," he said. "What should we do?"

"What you should do is get out of that suit before our revered leader sees you. Then we must go home and make our wormhole travel arrangements."

Before they left, smolin9 and yukawa3 were honoured with a formal ceremony at the foot of the twenty-eight white magma steps, although the parade consisted of little more than the leader and one of his minions traipsing to and fro, one trailing seaweed and the other hopping from side to side trying to avoid slipping on it. At the conclusion of the formalities, smolin9 thanked the leader for all his wise guidance and inspirational leadership.

The leader waved a frond of seaweed and said, "Help! I'm being held prisoner in a Chinese bakery!"

.   .   .

Smolin9, Melinda and yukawa3 were supposed to have had a big send-off before they left for their respective destinations, but it never took place because the Mortian leader was away attending the sixty-eighth General Assembly and Intergalactic Conference on Bridle Berg. Nevertheless, polkingbeal67, who was still battling organ rejection, entreated the three of them to join him at the medical pod for a farewell party of sorts.

The medibots turned a blind eye to the haze of scorched vitalmados and yukawa3 performed his herky-jerky turkey dance and joined the consultant for a kicking, hip-jerking two-man conga line, but otherwise it was a fairly subdued affair. Most of the planned festivities were hijacked by polkingbeal67 himself. Determined to exploit the opportunity to quiz Melinda about the nature and essence of the earthling human soul, he had been trying to get her attention all evening. His chance finally arrived when smolin9 was distracted by a tele-immersion call from the MMBC Earthwatch producer.

Polkingbeal67's plan was to be casual and nonchalant and to steer the conversation in the desired direction as subtly as possible, but no matter how well the Mortian warrior paved any route with good intentions, he invariably took the first available shortcut. "So, tell me now," he said. "What is the nature and essence of the earthling human soul? I need to know right away."

"Uh, what's that now?" said Melinda.

"You know: the secret of what it means to be an earthling human. Is it a religion thing?"

Melinda wrestled with the question and was surprised to find herself quite easily overpowered. "Well, it's not just... Religion is part of it, literally, but humanness is also about our intellectual ability and ..." She broke off as polkingbeal67 was staring at her in open-mouthed amazement.

"Sorry, but there must be more," he insisted.

"Well, y'know, the possession of a soul and that kind of thing."

"A soul. Are we back on the religion thing? Tell me about your god. Why do you have so many religions? Do you all have different gods, or what?

"Well, no, I suppose all the different religions lead to the same god. It's just that everyone has different ways of, uh, approaching the subject."

"And, according to our research, you all fight like rabid goopmutts about *which way* is the right way of approaching it. Anyway, are you sure it's the same god? When we were studying you people, we discovered there were several contenders."

Melinda sat on the side of polkingbeal67's bed. She could see this conversation was not going to get comfortable any time soon. "What contenders?"

Polkingbeal67 took a deep breath and suggested a few that came into his mind. "Oh, well, there's the one you call the supreme creator and then there's the impersonal force which some of you believe is made up of all living things and holds the universe together. A bit out there, don't you think? Let me see. There's one who has something to do with elephants and costumes. And then there's others, like the Flying Spaghetti Monster, Eric Clapton, Ryan Giggs and David Beckham."

Melinda laughed. "Oh, this is so erratic! God is an all-powerful being ..."

If polkingbeal67 had had external ears, they would have pricked up. "All-powerful? What are his weapons? Has he got laser incinerators? Plasma tech blasters?"

"Don't be ridiculous. He's all-powerful because, well, because he created us and everything in our world."

Polkingbeal67 looked distinctly unimpressed. "Is that it?" He waited a few seconds. "There's more, right?"

Melinda had never had to defend and justify God in this way before. "Look, he created the world in six days, okay. Six days!"

Polkingbeal67 considered this. "Okay, six days is not bad, I must admit. We built and populated our third moon, Jiraqa, in just over thirty days and we had a tribe of goopmutts helping with the large masonry structures. So, fair enough, six days is a good effort. All that water was a bit of a cop-out though. You don't think he's a bit of an underachiever?"

Melinda had had enough and picked up her drink. Polkingbeal67 grabbed her arm. "You can't go yet!" he said. "I need to know more. What does he look like and what planet does he live on? Is it just him or a whole species of gods?"

"We don't know what he looks like and he lives in heaven. And there's only one god. Literally. God, the Father. Although he has a son who came down to Earth."

Polkingbeal67 looked suspicious. "What about God the Mother? A son, but no mother?" As the conversation went on, the Mortian warrior misinterpreted Melinda's increasing discomfort as evasiveness. He became convinced that she was hiding something from him. Perhaps there was a mother god and she was the key to unlocking the secrets of earthling humanity. "So, he said, "If, just by chance, I wanted to visit heaven, how would I find it? What are its coordinates? What kind of place is it? Have you been there?"

"Excuse me?" Melinda was now looking around the room for an excuse to get away. "Listen, this is getting silly. Of course I haven't been there. It's heaven. You can't just set the controls and fly to it! Literally."

"If I were to take you with me, would you be able to find it?"

Melinda squealed. "What! I'm not going to heaven before I die!" She noticed his uncomprehending expression. "We go there when we die. If we've been good, that is. Otherwise, we go to the other place."

"What other place?"

"Hell."

"What's the point of going somewhere when you're dead?" said polkingbeal67, perplexed. "And who decides which one you go to? And what difference does it make, if you're, y'know, dead?"

"God decides," Melinda's patience was wearing thin. "Where is smolin9? Look, heaven is a *higher* place, with a capital 'H' and, er, 'P'. It's a holy paradise kind of thing. Literally. Hell is an inferno."

Polkingbeal67 thought about this. "So the good people get the holiday of a lifetime when their lifetime is over, and the bad people just get cremated."

Melinda beat a hasty retreat and found smolin9 crushing a vitalmados lozenge. All of a sudden, she burst into tears. Smolin9 wrapped her in his arms and implored her to forgive him. "I was going to offer you some, honestly," he said.

"It's not you," Melinda sobbed. "I just had the most erratic conversation with polkingbeal67 and I realise I betrayed my people and misrepresented them." She dabbed at her eyes with her sleeve. "He asked me to explain the nature of the human soul, but I got sidetracked by his questions about religion and I never mentioned courage, art, love and determination. Or how we're always pushing the envelope. The way we encourage and inspire each other. Or how we believe in doing to others as we would have them do to us. I never mentioned empathy and compassion. The power of a smile. The ..."

Smolin9 interrupted. "Yeh, it's probably just as well you didn't say all that. He'd have called it stumcrust."

"Stumcrust?"

"Goopmutt excrement."

Back at polkingbeal67's bedside, yukawa3 was discovering that the power of a Mortian smile made as much impact as a dollop of custard. "What's wrong, p?" he asked his former mentor.

Polkingbeal67 fixed him with a vacant stare. "Hmm? Oh, I've found out some interesting stuff about earthling humans and what makes them tick. I've been learning about their god." He proceeded to tell yukawa3 all the information he had gleaned from Melinda.

Yukawa3 looked distinctly bewildered. "Now that I have that knowledge, what do I do with it?" he asked. "I can't be doing with all those religious things. Mind you, I like the sound of the elephants and costumes."

Polkingbeal67 took hold of his arm. "Promise me you'll forget everything I just told you," he said. "And don't mention any of this to smolin9 or Melinda. The thing is, as soon as I'm fit enough to get out of here, I'm going to get the old mineral spotter serviced and I'm going for a little trip." He set his lips in a grim line. "I'm going to heaven and I'm going to find and destroy God the Mother!"

.　　.　　.

Tele-immersion producer, nipkow4, was drumming his fingers on the magma blade that served as a table in his office at MMBC Headquarters. He had failed to convince yukawa3 that there was anything glamorous or exciting about their imminent departure for the planet Oov. "Listen," he said, "When I was a young journalist like you, I had to prove myself by covering local stories for provincial news stations about things like pod boundary disputes and corruption and methane storms. You don't know how lucky you are to be sent to inhabited planets."

"Oov is inhabited by ants," yukawa3 complained sulkily.

"Chilloks are not ants."

"They look like ants."

"I know it's easy to confuse the two. Chilloks are social creatures with node-like structures and they tunnel through soil to form honeycombed mazes and they pile the excavated soil into mounds above the soil line."

"So how are they not ants?"

Nipkow4 sighed and squinted at the microwocky in front of him. "You know as well as I do they have highly sophisticated antennal lobes and exhibit intelligence way beyond even *our* understanding." He began drumming his fingers again. "And they've colonised almost every landmass in the known universe. If they were bigger, you and I would be their slaves. And you certainly wouldn't want to be caught calling them ants."

Yukawa3 leaned forwards. "I know," he said, "but polkingbeal67 always told me not to stay too much inside my comfort zone. He said it's like a bubble and I must push the skin of the bubble before it contracts and suffocates me. And I happen to know that he's about to embark on a really interesting mission! MMBC really ought to cover it."

"You can tell me about that in a moment," said nipkow4 sceptically. "But you've got to realise that good journalism is not about taking a massive risk to produce one attention-grabbing piece of work."

"What if it's so big, it could launch my career and make

you head of MMBC?"

Nipkow4 wagged a finger at yukawa3 and raised his voice a little, sounding a little aggravated. "It still wouldn't prove you're any good at your job," he said. "If you want to succeed in this industry, you need to do good work, no matter where you are, no matter what the story. Putting yourself at risk on some hostile planet as a fast track to fame is not how we do things here. You've just got to knuckle down and put in some hard graft." He looked at yukawa3 with an expression of benign paternal tolerance. "I know you're impatient to make your mark in this field and I fully understand you're anxious to get ahead of the competition. But competitiveness is not necessarily the best approach to everything. In my opinion, there's only one person you should try to be better than and that's the person you were yesterday." He paused for a moment to let his words sink in. "Now tell me about polkingbeal67."

Polkingbeal67 should have thought twice before telling yukawa3 of his plans. It was an injudicious mistake. His former cadet was about as discreet as a stampede of goopmutts.

Nipkow4 was astonished to hear such a preposterous scheme. "But heaven is an earthling fantasy planet!" he spluttered. "And even *they* don't believe in a female deity!"

"You think that's hard to believe? Well, it is. I'm just telling you what he told me."

"Well then, I have to tell *you* that you cannot, you just cannot, apply reason and logic to earthling belief systems. Their worldviews are contradictory and you simply cannot, must not, give intellectual credence to things like the virgin birth and Mohammed leaping from Mecca to Jerusalem on horseback in the course of one single night! Do you know what I find really surprising about all this?"

155

Yukawa3 nodded and then shook his head. "Is it the leaping thing?" he said. "The last time I went to the Pale Blue Dot, it was religious Christmas and I really enjoyed it. Will it be Christmas on Oov?"

Nipkow4's eyes widened. "What?" he said. "It's Oov. They're not earthlings!"

"Oh," said yukawa3 heedlessly.

"Anyway, what I find surprising is that polkingbeal67, of all people, is coming out with this stuff. If you'd told me this about smolin9, I'd have believed it and laughed it off. But polkingbeal67..." He shook his head in despair. "Something's seriously wrong."

Dismayed as he was, nipkow4 did not have the luxury of hindsight and took no action whatsoever concerning polkingbeal67. Instead, he and yukawa3 became completely engrossed in preparations for the trip to Oov. Eventually, all the equipment checks were duly completed and homeodynamic disruption antidotes were administered to all personnel. Nipkow4 consulted his microwocky for details of the rematerialization conditions at the destination site. "No problems," he said. "Warm. Twenty five dreebs. Broken clouds."

Yukawa3 seemed a little agitated. "I hope they're going to fix them," he said.

.   .   .

Melinda's return to Earth was delayed for several days by unfortunate circumstances, not least of which was her reluctance to leave Morys until polkingbeal67 showed verifiable signs of recovery. For reasons that defy any rational explanation, however, the stricken heart donor was not cooperating with anyone, including the medical staff, so it was difficult for them to assess his cardiovascular health. Then suddenly one morning, he woke up, got out of bed, arrayed himself in full Mortian battle dress and discharged himself from the medical pod.

As chance would have it, he bumped straight into Melinda as he walked through the main pod door. "Well, look at you!" Melinda exclaimed, throwing her arms around him and kissing him on the cheek. "You're up and about and everything! Literally. That's erratic and totally wonderful! How are you feeling?"

Polkingbeal67 wiped his cheek. "I'm okay," he said. "I'm fine. I've got to go. I've got an appointment."

Nonplussed, Melinda looked askance at him and smiled a crooked smile. "Did you just wipe off my kiss?"

"No, of course not," he said, impatient to be on his way. "I was just, uh, rubbing it in. When are you going back to the Pale Blue Dot?"

"Well, if you're...," she broke off as polkingbeal67 was striding away as fast as his portly frame would allow him.

The on-duty consultant, mendel8, was in a conference, so Melinda sat on the bed polkingbeal67 had just vacated and gazed out of the window. After a short while, her bottom lip trembled and tears started welling up in her eyes. She had been trained to understand and interpret human behaviour and considered herself a good reader of contextual cues, but her inability to read hostile signals from polkingbeal67 left her feeling bewildered and vulnerable. Actually, if she had been honest with herself, she would have had to admit that it was not so much an inability to read the cues but a refusal to acknowledge them. "What have I done wrong?" she sobbed. The android medibots, who had yet to become aware of polkingbeal67's disappearance, were oblivious to her distress at first. Then one of them whirled closer and spoke with a high-pitched nasal whine: "Problem detected. Please try again. Enunciate clearly and speak slowly." Another approached, offering a thin gauze-like tissue. "Where is the patient? Where is polkingbeal67?" it intoned querulously, finally noticing the elephant in the room (or the absence of one).

Melinda wiped her eyes and blew her nose. "I just don't understand," she said.

A few more medibots gathered around, offering tissues. One of them spoke. "You are a mere earthling of limited intellectual capacity."

Melinda sniffed. "Yes," she said. "Thanks for that. Literally. But I'll never apologise for being a mere earthling, as you put it. Anyway, if you're so clever, how have you managed to lose your patient? Hmm?"

The medibots scattered, emitting high-pitched squeals and odd clicking sounds. One of them came closer. "Please try again. Enunciate clearly and speak slowly."

"You may be programmed to be really smart, but I see you're not above a bit of selective hearing!" she remarked as the androids retreated to their various nursing stations.

After a short time, mendel8 came up and sat beside her. "I suppose polkingbeal67 has discharged himself," he said.

"Yes, I think so," said Melinda. "He was leaving as I came in to visit him. Is he well enough? I thought he looked quite rough and not himself at all. Grouchy and ill-disposed."

Mendel8 smiled pleasantly. "Well, it sounds like he's turned himself around completely," he said.

"Oh?"

There was a twinkle in mendel8's eye. "Definitely. He used to be ill-disposed and grouchy!"

Melinda chuckled. In her experience, Mortians were often inadvertently funny, but it was rare to encounter one who actually attempted to make someone laugh. "He's put on a lot of weight too," she said. "I know he hasn't been able to exercise or anything, but he looks like a giant lemon."

"His weight gain is a concern of ours. And I have a confession to make. When I asked him about it, he told me he was following a strict diet between meals. I must admit it didn't twig with me at first. I only paid attention to the words 'strict diet'."

Mendel8 came across as warm and friendly and had already succeeded in putting Melinda at ease. She opened up about her feelings of guilt concerning the heart swap and asked him if it was possible to reverse it.

The consultant pursed his lips and looked at her reproachfully. "Technically, yes, it's a reversible procedure." He paused for a moment to collect his thoughts. "But, first of all, we don't really do surgery on Morys. It's frowned upon. The circumstances giving rise to your heart swap were considered truly exceptional and the surgery was authorised at the highest level."

Melinda was intrigued. "But you all live for hundreds of years. What happens when you become ill and your organs fail?"

"Well, we've evolved to a point where cell degeneration is simply not the phenomenon it is for your species. We can regulate apoptosis and we can treat disease and injury trauma with highly sophisticated cell therapy techniques."

Melinda noticed polkingbeal67's old eye patch lying on the bedside table. Mendel8 read her thoughts and nodded. "It's his own choice," he explained. "He could have had the eye replaced at any time. He still could."

"He's a real mystery and no mistake," Melinda said, picking up the patch and examining it.

"And that's not all," mendel8 continued.

Melinda understood straight away. "Oh my God!" she exclaimed. You mean... Oh my God! Literally."

"Yes," mendel8 confirmed. "We can use totipotent stem cells to create new Mortian body parts. *Any* body part. Mind you, it takes a fair bit of time."

"How long?"

"The entire mitotic process to create a new fully functioning heart takes about one year."

"Is he aware of this?"

"Yes, I've spoken to him about it," mendel8 confirmed. "He knows a new Mortian heart will be ready for him in a year's time. Now please excuse me, I've got to sort out these androids."

Melinda lay back on the bed and spent a few moments in quiet contemplation. Before long, her thoughts turned to home and the life she had left behind. She felt she was now ready to make arrangements to travel back to Earth with smolin9.

Meanwhile, her Mortian husband was in an informal meeting with some of the back office staff at MMBC Headquarters. Having acquired a considerable reputation for his earlier investigative work on the Pale Blue Dot, smolin9 had his audience eating out of his hands. In fact, they were devouring every word he uttered. "Our mission," he declared, sitting on a table with his legs crossed, "is to get at the truth and do amazing things with it." He had the air of a wise professor bestowing his knowledge and life experience on a fawning group of assembled disciples. "I will be reporting on all the news and events from the Pale Blue Dot, including their current obsession with global warming and the environment. Yes, my first assignment will be a visit to one of their wind farms, where they're presumably hoping to grow some, er, wind. Make sure you don't miss it!"

. . .

The Mortian leader's health had been deteriorating for some time now. He had been treated for a number of infections over the last hundred years or so and had begun to struggle with basic activities like personal hygiene and dressing. His lips chattered constantly and he was losing his grasp of social graces, often getting up in the middle of a meeting to announce that he needed to empty his bowels. No one on Morys dared to discuss the matter openly, but in private many had started to speculate about his successor. Although there had been no change of leader for over two thousand years, everyone was aware of the tradition that the new leader had to be appointed by the current incumbent. You could sense an unspoken concern that this crucially significant task might soon be beyond a leader whose cognitive powers were becoming increasingly fragile.

If Mortians had had eyebrows, a few of them would have been raised after it emerged that the leader had made a clandestine appearance at the medipod shortly after the heart swap surgery. No plausible reason for this had been forthcoming and none of the medical staff had been privy to conversations that had taken place during the secret visit. However, when polkingbeal67 discussed his imminent trip to the Milky Way with the head mechanic at the intergalactic starship depot, he spoke cryptically of "having seen the future", a remark that would start resonating around the planet as soon as he departed in his wormhole-traversing mineral spotter.

If polkingbeal67 were to be proclaimed as the new leader, it would certainly be a popular appointment. It was common knowledge that the battle helmet belonging to this self-proclaimed war hero had seen action at the great battle of Tharsis Crater on Ynonmaq Decimus and it had been scorched by ionizer blasts during the liberation of chilloks in the Fourth Intergalactic War. It also featured prominently in illustrations commemorating the charge against General Vog's Trox army at Ybesan. Those closest to him, like smolin9, were aware that polkingbeal67 had not actually been wearing the helmet on any of those occasions and had "inherited" it from a drunken museum curator, but, let's face it, many a reputation has been enhanced by vague associations and a total lack of scrutiny.

None of this was uppermost in polkingbeal67's mind as he reclined in his mahogany and red leather pilot's chair, studying the charts for a superluminal passage to the Pale Blue Dot. As he had no celestial coordinates for heaven, his plan was to cruise the Milky Way using the Pale Blue Dot as a base and point of reference. By the time the ground crew saw the flash of light created by the departure of the mineral spotter, the journey was already over and polkingbeal67 was jabbing his leg with a syringe of HDA to neutralise the effects of neutrino oscillation. Switching over to the cold fusion and hot plasma power systems, polkingbeal67 orbited each and every planetary object, scanning for visual clues. He was in a zone of pure concentration and fanatical zeal. Occasionally, he would break out into a Mortian space shanty, a high-pitched, mewling chant of barely-decipherable gibberish which, roughly translated into earthling English, went something like this:

Our good ship is heading north and south
Both east and west we fly
Way down below they watch in awe
While we traverse the sky

Away boys, away, away we go
Away, away-o
A-hunting high and a-hunting low
Away, away-o

Sometimes we're bound for Fidderzog
Sometimes we're bound for Oov
Sometimes we don't care where we go
Come on you boys, let's move.

Away boys, away, away we go
Away, away-o
A-hunting high and a-hunting low
Away, away-o

He improvised a further verse and bellowed his way to a raucous crescendo:

We're heading for the Milky Way
Our target will be found
Fire the engines and set the course
For we'll be heaven bound

Away boys, away, away we go
Away, away-o
A-hunting high and a-hunting low
Away, away-o

But if the search for heaven had only just begun, the search for the Mortian leader's successor had already finished. At least, the vast majority of Mortians believed it had. You cannot stop the rumour mill once it gets going. Eventually, it runs out of energy or the gears wear themselves out, but until then you might as well try and catch the wind. Once the head mechanic had related his conversation with polkingbeal67 to his friends and colleagues, it was as if they could *all* see the future and polkingbeal67's name was writ large in it.

The speculation had not reached smolin9 and Melinda who were now finding their feet back on Earth. As it took a while for the HDA to really kick in, they were struggling with mundane tasks like walking up and down stairs and preparing meals. Melinda had picked up her Chihuahua from a friend who had been taking care of it during her absence and the poor dog was completely spooked by smolin9, even though the latter had assumed an earthling disguise by means of his biomimetic mutator. While Melinda searched the cupboards for something to eat, the dog jumped up and down and ran around in circles, gnashing its teeth.

"Sit!" smolin9 commanded. "Stay! Does he think I'm the postman or what?"

"Don't worry," said Melinda. "He's just not used to you. Literally. He'll calm down eventually. If it's any consolation, he's worse than that with the postman. This is nothing really. Why, he can jump as high as that table!"

Smolin9 looked perplexed. "Tables can't jump," he said.

"That's totally off the beaten cloud!" Melinda laughed. "Look, why don't you take him out for a walk? It'll give me a chance to get lunch ready and it'll give *him* a chance to get used to you." She attached the dog's harness and lead.

Smolin9 figured the dog was simply hungry, so he walked down to the corner of the road where the aroma of freshly brewed coffee and the smell of bacon wafted out onto the pavement. A little later, looking ruffled and sounding out of breath, he hurried back through Melinda's side door, unclipped the lead and watched the dog resume its frenzied jumping.

"What's up? What's happened?" Melinda asked, her eyes flicking from one to the other. "Why are you back so soon?"

Smolin9 told her he had glanced through the cafe window and spotted an empty table with a plate of full English breakfast, only half eaten. After tying up the dog outside, he had gone into the cafe and scraped the food into a large disposable coffee cup.

Melinda was concentrating on getting her fingers to grasp some cutlery. "Go on," she said. "I *am* listening. Literally."

"Well," said smolin9, "A man came out of the gents' toilet and walked up to the table to finish his meal. He was not very happy."

Before the day was out, smolin9 was broadcasting to Morys Minor from a wind farm in Avonmouth via a wormhole link.

"The power plants you can see here," he said, sporting his best snake-oil salesman fake smile, "have now fully emerged as giant fans ready to take on the task of cooling the planet." He made a flamboyant sweeping gesture with his arm. "Unfortunately, in order to print money for all the green subsidies, they've had to cut down all the trees."

.　　.　　.

"Oh my god!" nipkow4 exclaimed "It's bedlam in there!"

Yukawa3 curled his lip and rolled his eyes. "You could have fooled me," he said. "It's about as exciting as surfing in a bathtub. Nothing but ants, sorry, chilloks milling around like grit in a sand storm. Why are we here? How is this even a planet?" He kicked listlessly at the dirt. "What's our next assignment? Don't tell me - we get to cover the earthworm karate championships? We're living the dream."

"Don't show your ignorance," said nipkow4. He was crouching over a fascinating structure composed of a conical base tapering upwards into a tilting columnar spire. "There's a full-scale war going on. Get over here and check out the myrmecam. It's got macro extension tubes and you can see everything that's going on!"

To the untrained eye of a rookie reporter like yukawa3, the towering city of Niffis on the planet Oov may have looked like a fossilised tree stump about to crumble into a heap of dust, but it was actually a marvel of engineering. The sophisticated structure boasted an outer layer of tunnels and chambers leading through a latticework of intersecting and entwining passages to a series of intricate sculptured walls and receding terraces, culminating in spectacular labyrinthine subzones of stalagmites and caverns.

Niffis may have looked peaceful enough, but violence had erupted again during the night and many chilloks had sought to escape the chaos by leaping to their deaths from the upper levels of the complex ventilated structure. Yukawa3 unwittingly squashed their bodies as he approached the city and peered grudgingly through the lens.

As the sun came up on the next day, the myrmecam was linked up to the wormhole communication channel between Oov and Morys Minor. Nipkow4 was preparing for the inaugural transmission by briefing yukawa3 on the latest developments. "Listen," he said, "Around midnight, Muqu rebel fighters stormed Naaffab sleeping chambers and shouted slogans, calling their enemies aishiwas." Noticing yukawa3's blank stares and uncomprehending demeanour, he slowed down his delivery and tried his best to hold eye contact. "Are you with me? Aishiwa means 'renouncer'."

"Renouncer," yukawa3 repeated, a lost and vacant expression swimming ponderously in his eyes.

Nipkow4 continued, "In retaliation, the Naaffabs shook their antennae and chanted the word 'ramubakh' at the Muqu population. Ramubakh means 'reprobate'. Once again, this has highlighted the widening Naaffab-Muqu divide."

"I think I may regret saying this," said yukawa3, shrugging his shoulders, " but you're going to have to give me the background to all this."

"Well, the historical background to this conflict started with the death, in the ninth baktun, of the great chillok potentate, Da'Qunaa. You see, Muqus and Naaffabs both preach peace and understanding and devotion to their god, but Muqus believe in a literal interpretation of Da'Qunaa's admonition against wearing antenna rings, whereas Naaffabs have adopted a more liberal outlook."

By now, yukawa3 was simply watching nipkow4's jaw moving up and down. Nothing was getting through. "It's okay," he said. "I'll just wing it."

Nipkow4 conceded defeat. Trying to enlighten yukawa3 was as pointless as an IQ test for a goopmutt. "Roll the camera," he said.

The camera lifted, turned and panned slowly towards yukawa3, who spoke in a measured tone: "And so, another night, another outbreak of brutal sectarian violence in the power struggle between..."

Nipkow3 did his best to mouth the words 'Muqus' and 'Naaffabs', but it was no use. Yukawa3 inclined his head towards the chillok mound behind him and continued, "...the Mochas and the Frappes on the planet of Oov."

"Cut!" nipkow3 yelled. He waved yukawa3 away and provided the voiceover for the rest of the report: "The chillok news agency has reported that 79 Naaffabs and 32 Muqus have been killed in the clashes. Visual evidence of the violence is all around us here. Severed antennae lie in heaps at the foot of the city, as do the corpses of the Naaffabs who jumped to their deaths." Out of the corner of his eye he noticed that yukawa3 was peeling some of the bodies from the soles of his feet. He prayed the camera was not picking this up. "In spite of the hostility and acrimony that is everywhere in this beleaguered city, the chilloks have allowed observers and journalists free movement. In fact, our reception has been excellent. We are expecting a signal from the presidents of the Intergalactic Commission and the Oov Council condemning the violence."

Off camera, yukawa3 turned away, spread his arms in a gesture of futility and muttered, "What's the problem? A few puffs of insecticide and the war's over!"

.   .   .

Melinda handed smolin9 another tissue as the tears streamed in rivulets down his face. Christmas was approaching and the leading charities had launched their usual campaigns: heart-rending television appeals featuring malnourished children and neglected animals.

Staring open-mouthed at successive images of pitiful, shivering dogs, smolin9 was distraught. "Those poor, poor dogs!" he wailed. "Can't we do something?" He glanced at Melinda, who was painting her toenails with deep concentration. "Aren't you upset by this?" he demanded.

"Yes, of course, literally. But to be honest, you have to get a bit, y'know, hardened to it, especially at this time of year. It'll be Christmas soon."

"When?"

"Not sure. I think Christmas is on a Friday this year."

Smolin9's eyes widened. "Let's hope it's not the 13th then."

Melinda thought about explaining, but then decided against it. "So charities, yeh," she said. "They say a child dies every minute from drinking dirty water. Well, you can't cry every minute, can you? And as for these dogs, hmm, I think you have to be aware that these charities kinda construct sentimental distressing stories just to squeeze sympathy out of people. And sympathy is the key that opens wallets! It may be a bit harsh, but if these charities can afford a TV ad campaign, they've probably got quite a lot of dosh already. I mean, be serious! Have you any idea how much a campaign like this costs? So, shouldn't they be spending that money on the dogs?"

"I don't know. Shouldn't your leaders, your government, do something?"

Melinda smiled. "Well, that would certainly be a bit off the beaten cloud," she said. "We've got government ministers for all kinds of eccentric things, like homosexuality, diversity and Morris dancing, but I don't think we've got a minister for mutts! I guess dog welfare is just not considered a very high priority."

"I can't believe you're saying that. You've got a dog of your own."

"I know," Melinda said, puckering up her lips. "Who's a sweet cutie poochie, then? Come over and give me a big licky kiss!"

Smolin9 unfolded his legs and leaned towards her.

Melinda chortled. "I was talking to the dog!" she said. "By the way, speaking of sad stuff and dogs, you know the Lewis family two doors down? Their Labrador had a seizure on Sunday and had to be taken to the vet. Their son, Michael, told me about it when I was putting the bin out this morning. He seemed very upset. S'funny, he never struck me as the sensitive type. You can learn a lot about people by the way they interact with their dogs. Literally." Replacing the cap on the nail varnish, she regarded smolin9 with a look of mingled tenderness and amusement. "Do Mortians keep pets?"

Smolin9 shook his head. "No, we don't have anything suitable really." He cocked his head to one side. "Thousands of years ago, we had the goopmutts, of course."

"What exactly *are* goopmutts?"

"I suppose they're like a cross between earthling dinosaurs and, yeh, dogs. We shared the planet with them for several millennia. Together we discovered new worlds and helped create amazing civilisations throughout the observable universe. The goopmutts needed us for the technologies we developed and we needed them to do all the construction work. I suppose you could say we were the brains and they were the brawn, although eventually they became the dominant species and almost wiped us out."

Melinda looked baffled. "But if you were the smarter ones, how come they were dominant?"

"Well, they started to kill us and eat us."

"Yeh," said Melinda, nodding. "That would do it." Smolin9 was disappearing through the front door. "Where are you going?"

"Back in a minute!"

Driven in equal measure by his newly acquired compassion for dogs and his disgust at Melinda's apparent indifference, smolin9 went straight round to the Lewis's and pressed a ten pound note into Michael's hand, gushing incoherently with sympathy and compassion. The money came from an allowance Melinda had given him for personal expenses and transport costs (wormhole travel was fine for travelling vast distances, but, curiously, tiny hops caused all manner of physiological problems). On his return, he immediately set to work on a couple of campaigns of his own. One of them was snappily entitled 'Dogs Are Entitled To Welfare Too You Know' and the other, in keeping with the theme of his mission on Earth, was concerned with the melting polar ice caps.

By lunchtime the following day, smolin9's research had left him confused and baffled by all the earthling paranoia concerning global warming. He described his findings to Melinda, who had always taken man-made global warming as a given. "I don't get it," she said. "You say the met office people have significantly *lowered* their prediction of how much hotter the planet will get in the next few years?"

"Yes, and that's all rather inconvenient, not to say

embarrassing, for the plethora of scientists, politicians and policy makers who spent the last decade issuing dire warnings of melting ice caps, dying polar bears, flooding coastlines, heat waves and all the rest of it."

Melinda frowned. "Yes, but you also said global temperatures stalled fifteen years ago and have yet to rise again. So, what's going on? That's totally bizarre. Surely they couldn't have been lying about it?"

"I don't know about lying, but the experts are now backtracking like frightened lobsters."

"Erratic."

"Yeh, it seems they've been trying to create a better world for nothing," smolin9 concluded. "It's really annoying because I've ordered a whole bunch of printed t-shirts, polo shirts and sweatshirts based on the global warming science being settled beyond dispute."

Melinda glared at him. "What?" she screeched. "How much did that cost me? What's printed on them?"

"Okay, well..." Smolin9 shrugged and looked at the floor. "It's a great slogan: 'Save the Arctic. Donate ice!'"

Smolin9's reading of earthling body language left a lot to be desired, but it was sufficient to prompt a rapid retreat into the bathroom. Throwing a tight smile over his shoulder before slamming the door and locking it, he waited until Melinda's venomous tirade had abated. Then he re-emerged with an expression of innocent asininity and risked her further wrath by asking for a supplement to his allowance.

"You're joking, aren't you?" said Melinda, exasperated. "God knows how much these blessed t-shirts have cost me. And now you want *more* money? I gave you nearly a hundred pounds yesterday. Where's it all gone?"

Smolin9 flashed one of his disarmingly artless smiles. "It's gone to good causes," he assured her. "There are a lot of sick dogs in this neighbourhood and I've been helping the families cope with the distress."

Melinda was bewildered. She obviously knew about the Lewis's Labrador, but, as far as she was aware, the only other dog owners in the street were the Liveseys at No. 8, who had a perfectly healthy poodle, and Melinda herself. The root of her confusion lay in her not knowing that young Michael Lewis had shared the news of his ten pound windfall with several of his mates. This had prompted a sudden and inexplicable increase in the number of dogs in the vicinity and a commensurate decline in their health. Naturally, smolin9 had responded with unhesitating magnanimity in each and every case. It turned out that Michael himself had suddenly acquired two other dogs, both of which, tragically, had succumbed to illness almost immediately.

As Melinda was fond of saying: you can learn a lot about people by the way they interact with their dogs (both real and imaginary).

.   .   .

As smolin9 prepared to make an on-location broadcast from an ice floe somewhere in the Arctic and while polkingbeal67 probed and scrutinised the Milky Way whilst wrestling with his inner turmoil, nipkow4 persevered in his efforts to persuade yukawa3 to take the Niffis crisis seriously.

More than fifty chilloks had died in fresh violence in the city after Naaffab protesters loyal to the ousted President

Keshiak had clashed again with security forces. The latest trouble had started with a gruesome dismembering in a busy market place in the Muqu quarter of the city, when a mob, dragging the bloodied antennae of a prominent Naaffab cleric, had been allowed to parade through the trading archways while security officials stood by.

"It's times like this when ambitious, enterprising young reporters should roll up their sleeves, crack the story and go down in journalism history," nipkow4 enthused.

"Yeh," said yukawa3 lugubriously, "but what should *we* do? If I had sleeves, which I don't, I'd keep them rolled down so there'd be less chance of getting any of these pesky ants on my skin."

Nipkow4 persisted. "Come on," he said. "When the time comes and your life flashes before your eyes, you'll want to see something worth watching, won't you? When you breathe your last and people gather around to reflect upon your contribution to Mortian history, wouldn't you like to be esteemed by your peers and hear them say 'he was a ground-breaking journalist' or 'he touched the lives of the people with his famous scoops'?"

"No," said yukawa3, "I'd like to hear them say 'wait, don't bury him, he's still moving!'"

The city of Niffis, a giant chillok mound, was the only obvious evidence of 'pesky ants' on the vast expanse of parched, arid soil where the MMBC crew was stationed. To most observers, the dilapidated column, rising in bizarre isolation out of an otherwise flat landscape of red sand, could have been dismissed as nothing more than a big inoffensive pile of dirt. Expert examination, however, revealed a cauldron of street riots and seething hatreds. It was a city in torment - ravaged, ransacked and looted.

The MMBC myrmecam, a highly sophisticated device that combined visual inspection fibrescopes with a stunningly effective real-time language translator, enabled the crew to observe and interact with the chilloks in an astonishingly effective way. On arrival, the crew had been given a warm reception by Keshiak's Naaffab-led interim government. A short trek across the planet's smooth, sweeping landscapes had been followed by an illuminating guided tour of the city. But Keshiak had been toppled within two days and all pretence at diplomatic niceties had been abandoned. Representatives of the minority Muqu and Mishah communities clamoured for a coup while military chiefs and leaders of secular parties struggled to keep the peace. Every time MMBC technicians pointed a myrmecam into the labyrinthine tunnels of Niffis they were greeted with a hostile shake of the antennae and slogans such as "We will eat the antenna beads of the infidels!" and "Walk the death spiral!"

Well aware that their Mortian visitors had influence with the Intergalactic Commission, spokesmen for both the Naaffabs and the Muqus were keen to give the impression of being reasonable, tolerant people who accepted contention and dissent. The evidence of nipkow4's eyes, however, was conclusive - the chilloks were peaceful creatures only when they were not snapping off the antennae of their opponents (which was most of the time)! Their take on democracy was to insist that they were the people's choice and then kill any chilloks attempting to conduct a popular poll to prove or disprove that claim. Intrigued, nipkow4 tried to conduct a poll of his own and inserted microscopic flyers with detachable slips into the city tunnels. He was confident the words were translated correctly, but film from the myrmecams just showed chilloks tearing along the dotted lines at top speed.

The MMBC crew worked around the clock, monitoring and

documenting the violations of chillok rights that continued to be perpetrated on an appalling scale, when suddenly, one morning, an urgent bulletin was received from Mortian Headquarters. All MMBC personnel were to return home to attend a briefing by the Mortian leader.

"He's going to announce his successor!" nipkow4 concluded, visibly upset. "I'm really annoyed about this. We're doing ground-breaking work here! And we all know who the next leader will be anyway."

Yukawa3, by contrast, was like a dog with two tails and could not contain his excitement. Hopping from one foot to the other, he tried to keep his voice under control but eventually erupted in a series of barely decipherable bleats: "It is spoken. What it is! What it is! What it is!"

Like nipkow4, yukawa3 was convinced his former mentor, polkingbeal67, was a shoe-in for the leader role. Most Mortians were equally sure. But I can reveal to you now, dear reader, the true account of the event that gave rise to this expectation (you were bound to find out eventually anyway).

When the Mortian leader visited the medipod shortly after the heart swap, he had indeed spoken to a groggy and drowsy polkingbeal67. He had not, however, discussed the appointment of his successor, at least not directly. The main thrust of his message had been a lengthy discourse bemoaning the loss of gender identity on the planet, an evolutionary development that had occurred millions of years ago. According to his theory, prompted by his observations of Melinda during her short sojourn on Morys Minor, the primordial shift towards agamogenetic reproduction had left the Mortian species with an imbalance of hormones and a dearth of female attributes. He was now persuaded that all Mortians should try to rediscover their 'inner woman' in an effort to connect more empathetically with other beings. When polkingbeal67 disputed this and protested: "But we have smolin9, so we cannot possibly be accused of having too many male hormones!" the leader launched into a rambling tirade against belligerence and warmongering. Citing Melinda's caring, sharing nature, her capacity to bond with others and her ability to curb her aggression, he denounced the tendency to elevate one's own species above other beings and told polkingbeal67 of his great ambition to spread "emotional glue", as he described it, all over Morys Minor and beyond. Much to polkingbeal67's displeasure, he ended the conversation by pointedly remarking that he expected his vision to be endorsed by future leaders. "These," he said, "are the thoughts and qualities and characteristics I seek in my successor."

Exasperated, confused and frustrated, polkingbeal67 had therefore spent his recovery becoming more and more embittered and hostile towards earthlings, while the source of his anger lay on the adjacent bed, smiling blissfully at him. To his great credit, he harboured no personal hatred or animosity towards his friend's wife and refused to contemplate any notion of revenge against her. Nevertheless, his general antipathy towards earthling human nature simmered and festered inside him.

In view of what the leader had told him, polkingbeal67, unlike everybody else, had absolutely no expectations of being appointed as the next Mortian leader. When he received the summons to attend the official briefing, he completely ignored the call.

If anyone suggested to polkingbeal67 that Mortian civilisation was going down the drain, he would disagree and insist it was way, way worse than that - it was coming *up* the drain. In his view, the leader's vision of the future threatened a regression to primeval feebleness, a bubbling up of long-dormant histrionics that would render Morys Minor ungovernable and vulnerable to hostile aggression. He felt impotent and out of control, and his knee-jerk reaction to take out his anger on earthlings had not abated in the slightest. We do not know if he considered heaven a real place or a state of being or a figurative concept - the pandemonium in his mind ensured it made no difference whatsoever. Heaven represented the pinnacle of earthling aspiration and, by inference, God the Mother defined everything that irked him about earthling people and the Mortian leader's veneration for them. We can be sure that polkingbeal67 would have been intent on causing as much mayhem as possible on Earth itself, had he not been saddled with a heart that could not function there. Clearly, there was little scope for him to cause too much trouble in heaven. Ionisation blasters are woefully ineffective against figurative concepts.

Nevertheless, he soon developed an itchy trigger finger and fixed his sights on a large rogue asteroid hurtling around in the vicinity of Jupiter. Unfortunately, having zapped it with the ion blasters, he managed to steer his craft right through a shower of debris, inflicting serious damage to plasma turrets, the tractor beam emitter and a large section of the primary hull. Worried that the fusion propulsion systems had been compromised, he further compounded his problems by impulsively jabbing at the superluminal thruster without properly resetting the destination coordinates. He found himself in the vicinity of the Ring Nebula, helplessly ensnared in a thick viscous goop, like a bug stuck in jelly. Now he really was in a predicament. The space jelly, often referred to by cosmic travelers as the 'rot of the gods', adhered like molasses to the hull of the spacecraft, making both superluminal velocity and fusion propulsion impossible. Polkingbeal67 shook his head. "Yeh," he muttered to himself. "This could ruin my day." Resigned to his fate, he turned to the console and sent out an intergalactic distress call.

When the call was received on Morys Minor, all MMBC personnel, including smolin9 and Melinda, were already back home anticipating the big announcement by the planet's leader. Although polkingbeal67 had transmitted precise hyper spatial coordinates, two-way communication with him was out of the question, not least because of the growing impermeability of the space jelly. The leader was in a quandary. Should he send a rescue party and postpone his briefing? Or should he go ahead as planned and inflict a little more solitary confinement on the hapless war veteran? While he was wrestling with this conundrum, another fly appeared in the ointment. Actually it was a chillok; and it was not so much ointment as a dish of the leader's skin oil.

To explain that, we must turn the clock back to yukawa3 and nipkow4's final day on the planet Oov. The conflict in the city of Niffis had escalated in the hours immediately preceding the departure of the MMBC crew. The Naaffab leader, Keshiak, had been reinstated as President and was being held accountable for killing dozens of Muqu rebels in a formic acid attack on one of the main rebel-held sections of the city.

In accordance with the provisions and stipulations of the Intergalactic Charter, all chilloks were obliged to be routinely vaccinated with compounds that neutralised their formic acid. Keshiak was alleged to have authorised the suspension of these vaccinations for his troops in the lead-up to the current unrest. When nipkow4 challenged him about this in the course of a private interview via the myrmecam, he freely acknowledged the offence had taken place.

"Don't you have any principles?" nipkow4 asked him, incredulous.

"Of course," Keshiak protested. "But I don't let them get in the way."

"In the way of what?"

Keshiak paused for a moment to consider his reply. "In the way of doing what's right," he said. "For the record, I must tell you that I did not authorise the use of formic acid and, furthermore, all my troops have been neutralised. I have nothing to hide and I welcome inspection by any observers approved by the intergalactic community."

Nipkow4 discussed the matter with crew members afterwards. It seemed strange to all of them that the Naaffabs should have deployed these chemical weapons at a time when they did not need to use them.

"I don't get it," yukawa3 said. "He's been reinstated as President and was evidently winning the conflict."

Nipkow4 endeavoured to explain. "It's all part of a cunning plan to stop foreign intervention," he said. "You see, it works like this: Keshiak denies using these banned weapons, then he negotiates with foreign powers like us who might potentially intervene in the conflict. Using the weapons as bargaining chips, he invites inspectors to Niffis in return for promises of non-intervention."

Yukawa3 struggled heroically to get his brain around the idea. "So he wants to invite us round for chips?"

"No, no, not those sort of chips. Bargaining chips. Don't you see? He's worried about foreign interference."

"I get it," yukawa3 declared. "I totally get it. Yeh, I'm clued-in. I'm in the loop. It's so obvious when you think about it!"

"You don't get it, do you?" said nipkow4. Yukawa3 slapped

his thigh and shook his head. Nipkow4 attempted to clarify his theory. "Well, to sum it up," he began, "Keshiak is trying to persuade the intergalactic community not to take punitive action against him for using chemical weapons, which it wouldn't have done anyway if he hadn't used them. And he's trying to achieve this by allowing weapons inspectors to inspect weapons he says he didn't use and doesn't have. Right? So the weapons are bargaining chips, you see?" As the look in yukawa3's eyes turned from slightly vacant to hideously hollowed out, he added: "Bargaining chips are something that someone else wants that you are willing to lose in order to do a deal. I trust that's all perfectly clear now?"

"Perfectly clear! What it is! The penny has dropped! Wow, that's some devious cunning plan thing, isn't it?"

"You still don't get it, right?" Nipkow4 never liked to give up on anything, but sometimes defeat is the only option. "Let me put it like this: Keshiak... is inviting us round for chips."

While all this was going on, Muqu rebels were fleeing from the city, traversing the red sand under cover of their diminutiveness and concealing themselves in the MMBC starship. They remained undetected during the return trip to Morys Minor and during the bumpy trek to the palace of obsidian fingers and during the long hours they spent yelling at the Mortian leader at the tops of their voices while he swaddled himself in the remains of one of smolin9's tattered old 'Why always me?' t-shirts and a trailing whirl of seaweed fronds.

And now we are up to date and back to the moment when the Muqu rebel leader decided the only way he could attract the Mortian leader's attention was to leap theatrically into the dish of skin oil and swim backstroke like a false eyelash in a whirlpool. Eventually, the Mortian leader spotted him and called for a myrmecam to be installed. The Muqus then recited their long list of grievances against President Keshiak and the Naaffabs. Having heard them out, the Mortian leader continued his ablutions and sent for yukawa3 and Melinda.

Yukawa3 was the first to arrive. The leader received him in his lavish private chambers and told him: "I want you to deliver polkingbeal67 from his confinement and travel with him to the city of Niffis on the planet Oov. Tell him he must prove himself as a broker for peace in keeping with the philosophy of our new covenant. We must learn to dwell in harmony with all our neighbours and he who leads an ox to drink must first wet his own feet."

"It is spoken," said yukawa3 ingratiatingly. He had no idea what was required of him and only understood later when nipkow4 translated the message into a form of words that he could grasp the meaning of.

"So what exactly has polkingbeal67 got himself stuck in?"

"Space jelly," said nipkow4. "Think of it as frogspawn without the eggs, a slimy blob of goo. Polkingbeal67's craft is like a foetus in a womb and he's completely surrounded by the placenta. You'll have to use a plasma blaster to get him free." He thought about the womb analogy and made the association with polkingbeal67's quest to find God the Mother. He chuckled to himself. "You'll have to administer a caesarean section!"

Melinda described her private interview with the Mortian leader as 'literally surreal'. Recalling the bizarre conversation afterwards, she dismissed his words as the incomprehensible ramblings of a senile, demented old fool. Smolin9 and nipkow4 thought otherwise. In their view, Melinda was privileged to have been granted an audience with a revered leader whose cryptic but wise utterances would be celebrated in time as prophetic and revelatory. When she told them he had presented her with a small bag of pebbles, dried leaves and what looked like some rotting teeth, they both backed away and swayed in sheer amazement. Nipkow4 was the first to find his voice. "You are the chosen one!" he exclaimed.

"Can you remember exactly what he told you?" smolin9 asked.

"Oh, I don't know, it was all a bit erratic," Melinda replied. "He was kind of warbling. He said the sun will shine upon me and I must be sure to spread the light to others. Then there was a whole lot of other stuff, er, something about a diamond with a flaw being better than a pebble without."

Smolin9 and nipkow4 exchanged looks. They had the advantage of knowing that the reference to the sun and sharing the light was part of an ancient ceremonial chant signifying a transfer of power from one leader to the next. "You've been appointed his successor!" smolin9 confirmed.

"That's literally eccentric and ridiculous!" Melinda scoffed. "I'm not even a Mortian! Be serious!"

Nipkow4 bowed reverentially. "You have a Mortian heart," he explained. "That's all that's required."

Melinda sat down on a velvet ottoman and stared ahead, pondering this new development. Smolin9 and nipkow4 left her to her contemplation. After barely five minutes of frantic soul-searching, her mind was made up. Destiny beckoned and she would embrace it. A smile played slowly over her lips. "Yes," she said to herself. "I'll do it. I will be the next leader of Morys Minor. Literally."

. . .

Yukawa3 circled the space jelly a few times to study it and take some readings. Then he steadied the ship and fired several blasts of plasma until he could make out the battered hull of polkingbeal67's Mark III Zeplock mineral spotter. Parts of the jelly became spongy and shriveled up, making it possible for yukawa3 to manoeuvre close to the round hatch window. Polkingbeal67's face appeared. He looked well enough, a little chastened, a little chagrined, perhaps even a little humbled. The hull of the ship was scratched and pock-marked, displaying all the scars of the fateful encounter with the asteroid rock fragments.

Once polkingbeal67 had been safely transferred to the main cabin of the Acubierre shuttle, yukawa3 began the daunting task of damage assessment. As he pored over the data flashing across the screen, he stole a glance at polkingbeal67 and broke the silence with a low whistle. "Life isn't fair, is it, sir?" he said.

"Oh, it's better than the alternative," polkingbeal67 muttered darkly.

Yukawa3 resumed his work, recording and analysing the damage caused to the Zeplock by the flying debris.

"I can save you the trouble," said polkingbeal67, visibly steeling himself for the ordeal of parting with his precious craft. "She's beyond hope now. The navigation's gone, the hull has been mangled and all the propulsion systems are shot."

"But surely..." yukawa3 protested.

Polkingbeal67 was trying to be brave. "I never repeat myself," he said, grimly.

"We can salvage some parts," yukawa3 persisted. "Y'know, for keepsakes?"

"Like I said before, I never repeat myself," said polkingbeal67 as he fired up the Acubierre launch sequence.

"We've got orders to go to Oov to sort out those infernal ants. Our revered leader wants you to be a broker for peace. Nipkow4 says you're being tested." He cast a searching look at his former mentor. "Are you okay with that?"

Polkingbeal67 spoke softly and deliberately. "Yes, I understand," he said. "They're chilloks, not ants. We will go there and conduct ourselves with decency, decorum and diplomacy. It's time to put an end to the endless cycle of tribal violence in Niffis."

Yukawa3 stared for a second in utter disbelief, then he passed the coordinates to polkingbeal67, who punched them in and gripped the control column. Mere nanoseconds later, the two of them were climbing out of the hatch and gazing around at the eerie, shadowless landscape of Oov. Yukawa3 surveyed the desolate terrain. The only difference from the last time he had set foot there was a few additional wind-swept ripples. And one other thing.

"Well, where is it?" polkingbeal67 asked.

"Where's what?"

"The city of Niffis. Where is it?"

"I don't know," said yukawa3, "It was right here."

"You gave me the correct coordinates, didn't you?"

"I'm sure I gave you the exact coordinates."

Polkingbeal67 tapped his eye patch as realisation dawned

upon him. "The *exact* coordinates," he repeated, staring at the shuttle craft, nestled in the sand like a cat on a blanket.

A long silence ensued, during which the two Mortians contemplated their complicity in the intergalactic crime of the century. Neither of them knew what to say or do. Eventually, yukawa3 started scraping and clawing at some of the scorched remains that had blown to the side of the shuttle during the descent, but it was no use. He began to wish he was dead. Polkingbeal67 made as if to throttle the bungling cadet with his bare hands. But this was the new, reborn polkingbeal67, the polkingbeal67 who would henceforth resolve problems by means of compromise and negotiation and pragmatism and consensus. Putting a consoling arm around yukawa3's shoulders, he said, "You do realise one thing though?"

"What's that?"

"We can never go back home."

5

EXILE AND BEYOND

Polkingbeal67's heart was pounding. He had not expected it to do that. Having acquired an earthling human heart as a consequence of a medical blunder, he was finding it difficult to adjust to its vagaries. His own Mortian blood-pumping muscle had functioned very differently and he was now discovering that in matters of the heart nothing is quite what it seems.

To all intents and purposes, the mission to the planet Oov to broker a peace deal between warring factions of chilloks, had not been a total failure – at least they were not fighting any more! But it had been a bit of a Pyrrhic victory – he and his former apprentice, yukawa3, had spectacularly botched the operation by unwittingly landing their spacecraft smack-dab on the city of Niffis, completely flattening it. Fully aware that they had perpetrated a heinous intergalactic crime of monumental proportions, the two hapless Mortians were staring incredulously at the scene of devastation.

Yukawa3 scratched his head. "Maybe no one will notice?" he said in a small trembling voice.

Polkingbeal67 batted his head in exasperation. "We've wiped out an entire city, a living historical monument to chillok arts and technology. I mean, I've done some bad things in my time..."

"Like the time you abducted an earthling tarantula and released it in a plate of salad someone was eating in a restaurant?" yukawa3 suggested. "I hope that answers your question?"

"What question? No, not the tarantula. Well, okay, that was quite bad. But I was thinking of some of the diabolically heroic acts of war I've been involved in."

Yukawa3 shrugged. "Oh, those," he said carelessly, hoping that his former tutor would not feel the need to list them all with the usual wearisome level of detail. "Anyway, they were just ants."

Ants. Polkingbeal67 considered the word for a moment, allowing each phonetic element to metaphorically crawl around his mouth, oozing formic acid over his taste buds. Then he spat them out. "Ants!" he hollered. "Believe me, I wish they *were* just ants. I tell you what, I would *rejoice* if they were ants. I'd summon a band of tone deaf goopmutts playing violins and bagpipes and I'd dance with you till my feet became as sore as a lemchin's eyeball in an Oovian sandstorm!"

Yukawa3 shrugged again. Having worked on the MMBC documentary about the internecine conflict in Niffis, he clearly had some inkling of the enormity of the tragedy he and polkingbeal67 had perpetrated.

Polkingbeal67 continued. "This city... This *former* city boasted a whole host of intergalactically celebrated inventors and philosophers." He glanced at the young cadet to see if his message was getting through. "Niffis produced pioneers in the fields of science, aerospace, engineering and communications. Their celebrated but ruthless leader, President Keshiak, who now lies crushed somewhere under the landing gear of this spacecraft, represented his people at the Intergalactic Court of Justice, Arbitration and Conciliation."

Yukawa3 interrupted. "Excuse me, but he wasn't exactly conciliatory towards his enemies, was he? You talk about rejoicing and dancing - well, the Muqu rebels will want to rejoice! They'll hail us as heroes and liberators." A sly, knowing expression flickered across his face. He had no idea why. "We should think about that," he said.

They looked at each other like two schoolboys outside the headmaster's office. Yukawa3, who felt like he had sneaked behind the bike sheds and done nothing, broke the silence. "Hah!" he exclaimed, concluding that he had made the winning argument. "It is spoken."

Polkingbeal67, suddenly weary with the obligation of having to drum some sense into the young cadet, stepped forward and slapped him on the top of the head, crushing the yellow sou'wester rain hat he was so proud of.

While yukawa3 sat and nursed his sou'wester, polkingbeal67 returned to the craft to shift it from the massacre site. His mind was besieged by darts of hysterical self-recrimination over his role in the disaster and clouded with baleful portents of the likely consequences. In the judgement of the intergalactic community, the absence of malice aforethought would be woefully insufficient defence. In cases like this, and there have been several precedents, where the sheer colossal scale of the crime demands reprisal and redress, the perpetrators are invariably considered dishonourably negligent and therefore liable to impeachment, regardless of whether or not they intended or foresaw the result of their actions. In other words, *any* conduct resulting in mass annihilation is judged, at best, to be criminally reckless and subject to severe punitive action. The chances of getting a verdict of accidental slaughter were infinitesimal.

The Mortian 'Opportunity' craft lifted off, hovered and nudged forwards for a few seconds before the retro-thrusters kicked in. The landing became obliterated by a cloud of dust, debris and, I shudder to report, thousands of pulverised chillok carcasses. With all the detritus of the chillok city scattered to the four winds, the culpable pair sat for some time surveying the parched wasteland, their minds as arid as the desert landscape itself. Uncomfortable with the oppressive silence, yukawa3 cleared his throat to speak, uttered a strangled choke and fell silent again. A full minute passed before he felt obliged to try again. "No one needs to know," he said, inclining his head away from polkingbeal67, lest the latter should attempt another assault on the crumpled sou'wester. "There are no witnesses."

His companion, a veteran of the Jatron wars and The Great Retreat, continued to stare straight ahead with his steely eyes. "No witnesses, eh?" he murmured, almost to himself. "Take another look."

Yukawa3 followed polkingbeal67's gaze, saw nothing, stood up and scanned the entire panorama and sat down again. "Nothing," he concluded. "No one. And if you think seeing is believing - well, it is."

"Yes, it would appear that seeing and believing are both beyond your limited capacities at present," said polkingbeal67, becoming irritated. Streaming away towards the horizon, unobserved by yukawa3, were serried ranks of chilloks - survivors, witnesses and rescue workers - fleeing the decimation and ruin, carrying the bodies of the dead towards some unknown resting place in the wilderness. One of the corpses would have been Keshiak himself. For some reason, polkingbeal67's thoughts wandered back to the Jatron wars and, specifically, the funeral ceremony of a former comrade. The memory of a great crowd lining the river Qada floated into his thoughts, mourners wading through the shallow water to touch a lavishly decorated raft drifting effortlessly past emerald-green reed beds, a flock of birds in a swirling vortex overhead. It only served to make his mood even more sombre.

Eventually, even yukawa3, with his relatively dull powers of observation, managed to detect the chillok exodus. In total contrast to their earthling cousins, ants and termites, which only possess about 250,000 brain cells, chilloks boasted ten times the mental capacity of earthling humans and, since examinations of chillok brain tissue revealed a microstructure that was way beyond the comprehension of any other species in the known universe, it should have come as no surprise to anyone that these minute creatures were the first to discover all the major scientific concepts known to living beings. Not that that cut any ice with yukawa3.

For a moment or two, he contemplated eliminating the entire procession. After all, he figured, it would be simple enough to detach a hatch door from the spacecraft, attach it to a chain and squash the chilloks as they marched. He thought better of proposing the idea to his mentor, however, and a further compounding of the tragedy was averted. Meanwhile, polkingbeal67's mind was racing. What should he do? He was sure the incident would have been logged with the Intergalactic Commission by now. An emergency session of the Oov Council would be convened before the day was out. There was no way he and yukawa3 could cover their tracks, so to speak. Obviously, if they returned to Morys Minor, they would be apprehended immediately and any prospect of release pending trial would be out of the question owing to the magnitude of the crime. If they failed to return straight away, units would be dispatched to arrest them. He racked his brain to remember if the penalty for such an offence had ever been reduced owing to mitigating circumstances.

Yukawa3 suddenly slapped his thigh. "We should go on the run!" he urged. It was not just the idea itself that startled polkingbeal67. Could yukawa3's thought processes actually have been in sync with his own, or was this just one of the cadet's random exclamations? "Yeh, totally, that's what we should do," yukawa3 went on. "What's the worst thing they could do to us if they captured us and brought us to trial? The absolute worst thing."

Polkingbeal67 turned towards his excitable companion and spoke in a soft monotone. "Exile," he said. "They'd banish us. We'd have to drift from one unrecognised territory to another for the rest of our days."

Yukawa3 clapped his hands. "Exactly!" he declared, snatching his hat from his head and then replacing it again. "Is it? Are you sure?" He had been expecting a different answer. "Okay, well we might as well impose exile on ourselves! Let's go exiling around the galaxy! I can't tell you what a brilliant idea this is!" And, indeed, he could not.

But polkingbeal67 was beginning to appreciate some of the advantages of such a strategy. Sure, he thought, he would end up in exile either way, but he wouldn't have to spend months, possibly years, in captivity waiting for lawyers to crank up the big legal machinery and suck up as much money as possible from as many people as possible before the trial even took place. Yes, in many ways, going on the run made perfect sense.

"We'll be legendary outlaws!" yukawa3 enthused. "We could go to Noot, steal an argojet and cruise along the Daladax, or visit Lexis and drink the vitalmados pools dry!" Noticing the withering glance directed at him, he puckered his lips and took a different tack. "We'll make amends," he suggested, placing a hand on polkingbeal67's shoulder. "We'll go to planets where chilloks are struggling to get by and we'll help them. We'll teach them agriculture and all the useful stuff they're too smart to work out for themselves. We'll organise fund-raising events." His eyes widened and he swept his outstretched arm in front of him. "I can see it now, p," he said. "I can see it now! We'll sponsor a star-studded evening in aid of chilloks in need. I tell you - we're going to march home like heroes!" In a symbolic gesture, he went over to where the remains of the city of Niffis lay scattered, reached down, scooped up a pile of soil, mud and cellulose and raised it to his lips.

Polkingbeal67 weighed up the alternatives. On the one hand, day after day of humiliation and boredom incarcerated in a Mortian detention centre, or... He glanced in dismay at the animated cadet in front of him. Yukawa3 spluttered incoherently, his mouth dribbling moist slivers of Niffis debris, his arms aloft in a show of daring and bravado: "From these nnnnghh ruins, we will mnnnnggh rebuild and gnnnrrrl restore!"

.   .   .

Embarking on a new life is usually harrowing enough when it is the fruit of a rational process executed in a systematic and measured way by all the parties involved. When such a critical turning point is thrust upon you like an arrow out

193

of the blue, however, it makes it all the more traumatic. Finding themselves so suddenly cast as hapless playthings of fate, polkingbeal67 and yukawa3 desperately needed time to come to terms with their plight. Unfortunately, time is a precious commodity that is seldom for sale. Polkingbeal67 was trying his best to make cool decisions about plausible destinations, but his thinking was disrupted by the antics of his younger companion.

"I've got to call the laboratory technicians who fused the gametes to produce me," yukawa3 howled, his face suddenly crumpled in distress. "I just need to tell them I love them. I just wish... I just wish there was something that would bring us closer." His high spirits had completely dissipated and he sloped off towards the 'Opportunity' spacecraft, holding his sou'wester hat in one fist and punching it with the other.

"Come back and listen!" polkingbeal67 hissed. He was loathe to allow yukawa3 time alone in the 'Opportunity' while his moods were swinging from irrational exuberance to abject self-pity and despair. Who knows what he might decide to do on an impulse? "Listen to me! This is difficult to bear for both of us. But we are where we are and we've got to make the best of it." As yukawa3 had not turned back, polkingbeal67 hurried after him and the two were soon ensconced in the cockpit of the spacecraft.

Yukawa3 replaced the sou'wester on his head and nodded like a woodpecker at a tree trunk. "I know we've got to make the best of a bad job," he said. "I know, I know, I know. I totally know that. It's just, well, I've never done exiling before and I'm a bit nervous. Hey, actually, I'm freaking out here. I'm freaking out and I don't know why. I think I'm freaking out because you're *not* freaking out. What will it be like, p? Sir? Is it okay to call you p, p?"

"Don't call me peepee."

"No, I mean just one 'p'."

"Swampy? I don't think so. Listen, from now on we're going to have new identities. You're going to have to call me by a new name."

"Seriously?"

Polkingbeal67 nodded. For a short moment there, the two of them were nodding like dashboard figurines. "Listen to me. It is now our fate to wander among the stars, homeless and homesick, with a bounty on our heads, regarded throughout the universe as the scourge of mankind."

Yukawa3's face took on an expression of abject, panic-stricken misery. "I just want to clear up one thing," he said. "When you say mankind, does that include, y'know, earthlings? I couldn't bear it if earthlings thought of us as scourges."

Polkingbeal67 ignored him. Actually, he thought the idea of being a renegade outlaw sounded quite heroic, in an antiheroic sort of way. "Anyway," he said, "apart from that, we'll be okay. It'll be tough for us and, let's face it, it'll be tough for the rest of mankind too. I'm sure we'll be missed. We've just got to work out the best place to go, then launch the 'Opportunity' towards the starting point of the rest of our lives."

Daunted once more by the challenges that lay ahead, yukawa3 mulled over his mentor's words but slowly became incoherent and agitated. "We'll be fine," he repeated, mumbling irrationally to himself. "We just tough out the best launch of our lives and the 'Opportunity' will be missed..." He clapped polkingbeal67 on the shoulder. "If you think I'm beaten by this... If you think I am going to allow this little setback to derail me, ... well, I am! I'm your man! So, where are we going?"

The logical option was to proceed without delay to The Pale Blue Dot, although polkingbeal67 harboured a few misgivings. The most troubling of these was the likelihood of yukawa3 failing to integrate in a suitable manner. In actual fact, the cadet had a bit of history with that particular planet. He had already made one abortive trip there as part of a short fact-finding mission. However, remote monitors revealed he had been spending all his time squirreling away all the sou'wester hats he could lay his hands on. So when polkingbeal67 proposed that they should take their chances with the blue planet dwellers, yukawa3's eyes lit up. Eager to supplement his collection of collapsible oilskin rain hats, he was quite willing to forego the lure of more exotic locations.

They climbed out of the 'Opportunity' and ambled over to a barren ridge well beyond the elongated shadow of the spacecraft. As the sun dipped slowly and serenely towards the horizon, they reclined together on the arid soil and discussed the issues pertaining to their new identities. "We've obviously got to blend in," polkingbeal67 mused. "We've got to be discreet and inconspicuous. You understand what I mean?"

Yukawa3 started nodding again. "I think so," he said. "I'm not sure. I mean, would it be possible for you to explain it in great detail? No, no, I can do discreet. Seriously, I can do that. I can be the foot of discretion."

"I think you mean the *sole* of discretion, and anyway it's not that kind of sole - it's soul, as in spiritual stuff and the phrase 'don't tell a soul'."

"I won't."

"You won't? You won't what?"

"I won't tell a soul."

"Just shut up!" Polkingbeal67 sighed savagely and pointed to data displayed on his microwocky. "Choose a name for your earthling identity. I've worked out an algorithm to calculate the most prevalent first names and last names on the Pale Blue Dot."

"They have such weird names, don't they?" said yukawa3. "Why do their names contain more than one word and why do they use capital letters?"

"That's the sort of mess you get in if you can't devise a system for producing unique monikers. Anyway, choose from this list of common first names. I'm going for Mohammed."

"Okay, I'll go for Mohammed, too," said yukawa3, who was nodding again.

"No," polkingbeal67 protested. It was strange, he thought, that when people have the freedom to do exactly what they like, they invariably end up copying one another. "You can't... I've got Mohammed. We can't have the same name. It'll be ridiculous. You can be Sophia." He tipped the device and more data scrolled down the screen. "Here's a list of the most popular second names and underneath is a list of the most common occupations. I'm taking Wang. I'm going to be a waitress called Mohammed Wang. That sounds good."

Yukawa3 took the microwocky, flipped it a few times and handed it back. "Okay," he said. "A second name and an occupation to go with Sophia? Hmm. I'm going to be a fisherman called Sophia Gonzalez."

Polkingbeal67 cocked his head to one side and tapped his eye patch. "Wait a minute," he said. "Fisherman isn't on the list."

"I know, but I really want to be a fisherman," said yukawa3, slyly, banking on his mentor being unaware of the brouhaha surrounding his previous trip. "It's a very common occupation in coastal areas of the planet. Come on, p, let's go to the seaside! Any questions?"

Polkingbeal67 stretched and propped himself up on his rubbery elbows. At this point, he was not prepared to get into an argument about their precise destination. Although, actually, the more he thought about it, a beach lifestyle might be quite suitable. The earthling stories he loved best were those about pirates fighting on the decks. He was confident that he and yukawa3 would integrate well amongst the eccentric characters who made their living on or by the sea. Furthermore, despite some concerns he had about the composition of the sea-life food chain, the prospect of spending his exile surfing, snorkeling, fishing and swimming was a fairly appealing one.

Out of the corner of his eye, polkingbeal67 noticed that the chilloks had returned and had formed a pattern of concentric rings around the site of their former city. "Look!" he said. "It must be some kind of ceremony commemorating the dead."

Yukawa3 raised his head from the ground just enough to witness the fascinating spectacle. "A wake?" he asked.

"Of course I'm awake, you fool. I wouldn't be talking to you if I was asleep, would I?"

Yukawa3 pointed to the chillok ritual. "No, no, I mean Keshiak."

"Keshiak? Awake? I'm afraid not. I just told you - it's a funeral ceremony. No, I'm afraid Keshiak is sleeping in the comforting cellulose clouds of the great chillok paradise in the sky. Good grief! What am I talking about? What a load of swivel-eyed drivel! Must be some sort of vitalmados deprivation. Why, I'm beginning to sound like smolin9! Keshiak is dead, crushed by the nether parts of 'Opportunity'. And that's that." Realising that it would not be the height of diplomacy to proceed with a take-off while the ceremony was in progress, he stepped gingerly over the assembled chilloks and fetched a handful of vitalmados capsules from a storage cubby just below the cockpit window.

Vitalmados was an intoxicating liquor as defined in Section 3C of the Morys Minor Health Statutes. It was unlawful to manufacture for sale, sell, offer or keep for sale, possess or transport it, except upon the terms, conditions, limitations and restrictions enumerated in the statutes. Effectively, this meant that it may not be used for any purpose except, under very restricted circumstances, as fuel or ammunition. The law was almost universally ignored by the Mortians.

A by-product of Morys Minor's construction industry, vitalmados was actually derived from pulverised goopmutt waste, fermented in methane. In contrast to the debilitating effects of earthling alcohol, it distorted the user's perception of reality by manipulating and vitalising the brain. Available in quick-release tablets and capsules, as well as in liquid form, rectal ingestion of capsules was by far the most popular way to ensure rapid absorption. Ingested orally, it had a distinctive, slightly tangy taste. Essentially, it induced a euphoric state of mind, particularly in those predisposed to depression. Certain characters on Morys tried to make themselves as miserable as possible so that they had an excuse to ingest it.

The following morning, polkingbeal67 and yukawa3 were

199

still under the influence of vitalmados as they plotted their course and still far from clear-headed when they landed the 'Opportunity', erratically and bumpily, a few metres from the lapping waters of a secluded cove on the Pale Blue Dot.

They had both forgotten something quite serious. When polkingbeal67 had swapped hearts with Melinda, enabling her to visit her home planet, he had inherited a modified organ that rejected white blood cells and therefore confounded the defence system required to fight earthling infections and diseases.

.   .   .

When news of the Niffis massacre filtered through to Morys Minor, its impact was immediate and overwhelming, not least because the planet's leader was playing host to a delegation of chillok Muqu rebels seeking intergalactic condemnation of Naaffab atrocities. As we know, Niffis had been the scene of brutal sectarian violence in the power struggle between the Naaffabs and the Muqu minority for some time before the 'Opportunity' came knocking. The Muqus' joy at the demise of President Keshiak was more than offset by their grief over the annihilation of their martyred brethren. Dismissing the Mortian leader's apology as 'a hollow, half-hearted, face-saving rhetorical statement', they were convinced that the city's destruction had been 'a deliberate, blundering, heavy-handed intervention, conceived and carried out with the express intention of erasing the Niffis crisis from the intergalactic agenda'.

Melinda, now Morys Minor's leader-in-waiting, had been summoned to the planetary leader's palace for an urgent briefing. As she waited in the opulent antechamber while the leader adjusted the seaweed garland hanging around his neck and drizzled himself with various oils and aromatics, she reflected on the implications for polkingbeal67. You would naturally expect there to be a special bond between an organ donor and a recipient, doubly so in the case of an exchange, and, although polkingbeal67 believed he had been tricked into swapping his heart for an inferior earthling organ that had been clumsily modified to circulate Mortian blue blood, Melinda, for her part, could not have been more grateful for the Mortian muscle that beat so steadily in her chest, given that she could never have been able to visit her home planet without it. Whereas polkingbeal67's attitude towards her was one of resentment and anger, Melinda felt a singularly deep and enduring attachment to the gruff old Mortian warrior and she was acutely concerned about the ramifications of the Niffis incident.

The leader shuffled through the portal and bade Melinda follow him into the presidential chamber. Apart from the seaweed festooned around his neck, he wore a tattered robe of yellowish oily fabric gathered at the waist and fastened with a clip constructed from goopmutt horn. "Blimey!" Melinda thought. "It must be casual Friday."

"Where I lead, you will follow," the leader intoned. Unsure if this was a reference to her succeeding him as planetary leader, or a warning to let him boss the discussion, or simply his way of saying 'follow me', Melinda made no reply and strolled behind him until he reached a low dais upon which he sat cross-legged. He motioned for her to sit across from him, but she was disinclined to park herself on the floor, so she remained standing. Feeling distinctly uncomfortable as the leader sat silently and motionlessly in front of her, his arms outstretched, Melinda wondered if he was waiting for her to join him in performing some obscure Mortian ritual. Self-consciously and hesitantly, she raised her arms to mimic his stance and waited for guidance. Suddenly he spoke in a grave tone, "I will be your teacher and I will open the door, but you must enter by yourself."

"Okay," Melinda responded breezily. "Where are we going?"

"Only he that has travelled the road knows where the holes are deep."

"Tell me about it!" said Melinda, nervously trying to get the conversation flowing. "Back home in Glastonbury, you just would not believe the potholes! And can you get the council to come out and fix them? Like hell you can! Literally. I suppose it's the same here?"

"My first lesson is this," the leader continued huffily. "It is said that the smallest insect may cause death by its bite, and..."

Melinda interrupted him. "I know! You're not kidding! I got bitten by one the other night and you would not believe the size of the bump on my arm. I swear it was the size of half an apple. So itchy and, y'know, embarrassing. Literally."

Squirming in irritation, the leader muttered "Talking doesn't cook rice." He lowered his arms and pointed to a miniature podium behind him. To her astonishment, Melinda noticed the plinth was covered with animated termite-like creatures, which she now realised were chilloks. "Oh!" she exclaimed. "Has one of them bitten you?"

"Insects cannot enter a shut mouth!" the leader admonished gravely, making a gesture of silence with his forefinger.

Melinda, blissfully unconscious of his signal, was starting to relax. "Well," she said. "It's funny you should say that. I read somewhere that, on average, every person's mouth gets about seven insect visits a year, while they're sleeping. While they're sleeping! I know, right? Literally! Can you imagine?" Noticing that the leader's face was beginning to take on an expression of anger and vexation, she faltered and her voice became weaker. "Well, maybe it only affects earthlings. Or, anyway, if *I'm* eating them in my sleep, there's less for *you* to eat! Ha ha. Literally."

Installed in front of the podium was a myrmecam - the sophisticated optical-audio device that combined a magnifying lens with a real-time language translator, enabling humanoids like the Mortians to communicate with the chilloks in a decidedly effective way. The leader turned around and touched a button on the device, unleashing a tumultuous din of high-pitched voices speaking in what Melinda thought was rapid-fire Latin.

"Is that Latin?" she enquired.

The leader nodded. "You must speak with them," he said. "They will not speak with Mortians. They think we deliberately destroyed their city."

"Okay, but why are they speaking in Latin? That's so erratic."

"When you walk on snow you cannot hide your footprints. The chilloks love your earthling culture. You are, of course, familiar with the Myrmidons?" Melinda shook her head. "The Myrmidons were a troop of fierce warriors who fought under the leadership of the hero Achilles in your Trojan Wars. They were created from a colony of ants, who are naturally distant cousins of the chilloks." As Melinda stared in blank amazement, he added, "Also, they think Mortians don't understand Latin."

"But you *do*?"

"Yes."

"Well, I'll give it a go, but I hardly know any Latin."

"It matters little," said the leader. "They'll listen to you if you speak in English. I want you to give them a message from us. Tell them we pay tribute to the bravery and resilience of the chillok people. Assure them our prayers are with them and we will do everything in our power to apprehend and bring to justice those responsible for this atrocity." He shot a glance at Melinda and continued in an undertone. "And tell them anything else you think might help. Report back to me."

"I'll try," said Melinda, "Literally. I'll talk to them, but I can't promise they'll listen."

"The important thing is to hear what isn't being said," the leader concluded, as he trundled away. The salty smell of seaweed lingered behind, reminding Melinda of childhood trips to windy English beaches, amusement arcades, donkey rides and sandcastles. Drawing closer to the myrmecam, she rapped it with her knuckles as if it was an earthling microphone. "Hello?" she said tentatively. "Testing, testing."

A volley of Latin spat back at her, chaotic and confused at first, then congealing into a steady, insistent chant: "Minima maxima sunt! Minima maxima sunt! Minima maxima sunt!"

Melinda decided the best policy was to go with the flow, so, completely oblivious to what the phrase meant, she chanted along with them until they stopped abruptly and an awkward silence ensued. Racking her brains to come up with a suitable Latin phrase, she coughed and said, "Um, tempus fugit, and, er, vice versa." After a short, stunned silence, she added, "Habeas corpus?" One of the chilloks started chanting again. Encouraged, Melinda went ahead and delivered the leader's message in English, then waited for a response.

One of the chilloks spoke in a shrill voice: "Hoc est bellum. Audemus jura nostra defendere."

"Okaaay," said Melinda, dragging out the final syllable in preparation for her final foray into speaking Latin. "Status quo!" she blurted out. Perhaps it was prompted by a desire to lighten the mood, perhaps it was just a spontaneous, knee-jerk reaction to the phrase, but, for some reason, she found herself singing 'Whatever you want' in a weak, wavering voice as the chilloks looked on in rapt fascination. Bizarrely, first one chillok joined in, then another, then another, until finally they were all swaying and trilling in unison: "Whatever you want! Whatever you like! Whatever you say!" while Melinda conducted them with sweeping flourishes of her hands.

They moved on to 'Rockin' all over the world': "And I like it, I like it, I like it, I like it, I li-li-like it, li-li-like, here we go, rockin' all over the world!" and they were in full flow as smolin9 entered the chamber. "Wow!" he exclaimed. "Look at you! You're doing a great job here! I've been telling everyone you're going to make a brilliant Mortian leader and this... well, before you came on the scene, this lot were demanding restitution from our revered leader and it was all getting rather ugly."

The chilloks did indeed appear to be in party mood as they sang along, although it should be said they were under the impression they were reciting rabble-rousing incantations in protest at the leader's inaction and bland assurances.

Melinda tapped the button on the myrmecam and gave

smolin9 a hug. "Thanks," she said, "but I've no idea what just happened. What are you doing here?"

"I've come to say goodbye." The jet-black of smolin9's eyes clouded a little. "I've just spoken to our revered leader and he's sending me off to find polkingbeal67 and yukawa3. It won't take long, I promise."

"You're being sent to arrest them?"

"The chilloks have taken their case to the Intergalactic Court of Justice, Arbitration and Conciliation. We're obliged to present them to the Court during this moon."

"Why you?" Melinda protested. "Arrest your own friends? That's harsh. Literally."

Smolin9 shrugged his shoulders. "Well, our revered leader says I'm the one person who can figure out where they've gone."

"*Do* you know where they've gone?"

"I've got a hunch or two," said smolin9. "They can't have gone to Earth, since polkingbeal67 has your heart and can't survive there. So, that narrows the options. Don't worry, I'll find them and I'll be back within the moon."

The pair left the chamber hand-in-hand as the chilloks marched up and down on the podium, warbling furiously: "I li-li-like it, li-li-like, here we go, rockin' all over the world!"

.   .   .

A couple of hours later, when the second of Morys Minor's suns was setting behind the main pods of the Intergalactic Space Station, throwing sharply-defined shadows across the launch site, Melinda was saying goodbye to smolin9 as he prepared to embark on his voyage aboard the 'Crusader'. Her mood had darkened slightly when it had dawned on her that all the Mortians she knew well would be away from the planet and she would have to fend for herself. She glanced at her mood ring and was not surprised to find the liquid crystal molecules had taken on a deep, dark amber hue. Taking smolin9's hands in her own, she looked into his lustrous black eyes and spoke in a melancholy tone. "Why does it have to be you? Why couldn't he send nipkow4 or one of the cadets?" While smolin9 fiddled with his microwocky and considered his reply, she fired another question at him. "Can I come with you?"

Smolin9 shook his head.

Melinda lifted his face with her fingers to make eye contact. "We've hardly had any time together since we got back from Earth."

"I know, I'm sorry." Smolin9 smiled faintly. "Like I said, our revered leader regrets the imposition but he doesn't have much choice. He's having to spend all day at the moment sitting and thinking."

Melinda could not resist a barbed remark: "Are you sure he's not just sitting?"

"He's under a lot of pressure, not just from the chilloks and the ICJAC, but also from the planetary affairs committee."

"The what?"

"The ICJAC is the Intergalactic Court of Justice, Arbitration and Conciliation."

"No, I mean the planetary committee thing."

207

He detected a note of incipient irritation in her voice. "Do you want the long explanation or the short one?"

"I'll take half of the short one," Melinda replied.

"Okay, well, the planetary affairs committee is the hub of government here on Morys. Most of the policies have to pass through it. The serious ones anyway. It meets every five kins, er, days and its remit is to examine the expenditure, administration and policies of the various Mortian public bodies. The committee approves proposals from our revered leader. It also chooses its own subjects of inquiry and seeks written and oral evidence from a wide range of relevant groups and individuals..."

Melinda pulled a face and interrupted. "Are you sure this is the short version?"

Smolin9 responded by speaking more quickly. "It's chaired by our revered leader's virtual opponent, who has the power of veto over all the proposals..."

Melinda raised her hands as if to ward off his words. "Wait, wait, wait!" she said. "Did you say *virtual* opponent? Virtual?"

"Yes, well, you see," said smolin9, knowing there was no way he could make this sound good to an unenlightened earthling. "The functions of Mortian government are carried out by sophisticated artificial intelligence systems in accordance with the flavour of ideology determined by the electorate."

"So you're saying his political opponents are not real people? Really? Literally?"

"But you don't understand." Smolin9's brain wrestled vainly with the realisation that his argument might appear to an outsider to have more holes than a colander. "You see, that makes it *harder* for our revered leader. It's not easy to win a debate against artificial intelligence..."

"Oh?" Melinda opened her eyes wide. "It seems to me artificial intelligence has been no match for natural stupidity here!"

If smolin9 had had hackles, they would have bristled. "And, anyway, to be fair, his political allies are *also* virtual." As soon as he had said it, smolin9 realised he had taken a plasma gun to the colander. "You have to understand that everyone got fed up with politicians running the planet. They were seen to be corrupt, self-serving and power hungry. The people clamoured for an alternative, so we devised a new system of government – one that would give us truth, integrity and intelligence."

"So, let me get this straight. You've got to leave me here alone on this bizarre little planet because your revered leader is under intense pressure from, well, precisely no one. A virtual representative of a person. So, in fact, no one at all."

"You're forgetting the chilloks and the ICJAC," said smolin9 sheepishly.

"Oh yes, so it's pressure from no one and a few ants and some quango that hardly anyone's even heard of. Wait! I'll bet... Are there any real people on this ICJ... whatever? Are *they* virtual too?"

"Of course not," said smolin9, "Well, some of them, not all of them." Forced into a corner, he felt obliged to play his trump card. "Anyway, it's your fault!"

Melinda put her hands on her hips and inclined her head. "*My* fault?"

"Yes, well, not your *fault* exactly. Let's just say it's because of you."

"What? It's *not* my fault, but you're *blaming* me?"

"No. Yes. The fact is, our revered leader has become very unpopular for appointing you his successor..."

"Unpopular with these nobody virtual people?" Melinda glanced at her mood ring which had turned reddish purple.

"Yes. No. Unpopular with the planetary affairs committee. And I'm unpopular too, by the way, because I brought you to the planet. Anyway, the committee wanted the next leader to be a native Mortian." Smolin9 broke off while the main engines were test-fired. "The chairman can veto any proposal he thinks our revered leader is keen on. It's an ugly business. There are feuds, power struggles and shabby deals. No one can do anything about your appointment, but they can keep other proposals hostage. They may release them later, but only if they're granted favours in return..."

"Yes, I get it, he's in hock to these virtual nobodies," Melinda snapped. "How can computer nonentities have feuds and do shabby deals? It's insane. But I tell you what, this isn't going to happen when I take over as leader, I promise you! Literally. You tell me you people actually vote for them? Really? You vote for nobodies and nonentities?" It did occur to her that the situation on Earth may not actually be so very different, but she resolutely dismissed the thought. "I'll invite them all to a meeting," she went on. "And if they don't turn up in person, which they won't of course, I'll sack them!" As they talked, several technobots wheeled around industriously, preparing the 'Crusader' for flight. Humming and whirring, they went methodically through their checklists and other procedures. Some went in and out of the cargo bay doors carrying provisions and equipment, others stood around examining and adjusting the various systems they operated remotely from their specially customised microwockys.

"I'm sorry Mel, I *have* to go." Smolin9's aching heart distorted the sound of his voice and made him sound callous and truculent. Knocking him sideways, the pain impelled him to stifle his feelings and withhold affection. "I must get my suit ready for the launch. I'm sorry, but we Mortians have a strong sense of duty."

"But what about your duty to *me*?" Melinda protested. They stared at each other for a moment, both equally stunned.

Smolin9 uttered a strange snort that sounded like a stifled laugh. "I guess we're having our first fight," he said.

It was actually their second fight. When Melinda had first arrived on Morys, she had taken umbrage when smolin9 had neglected to tell her that the required modification to her heart precluded a return to Earth.

Melinda clasped his arm. "Okay," she relented. "I... I know you've got to go. It's just, well... You must know how much I gave up to come here and how much I've left behind and how much of a risk I've taken. Literally. And I'm not saying I want to go home or anything like that, but..." Her voice trailed off and smolin9's heart sank at hearing her stifle a sob. "Well, it's just, y'know, I kind of feel a bit, um, what's the word? Vulnerable. Yeh, I'm gonna feel really vulnerable when you leave me here now. When I was a little girl, I always thought I'd like to make the world a better place. I didn't realise that would entail me swapping it for *another* world! That takes some getting used to! Don't get me wrong. I don't have any regrets. Literally. It's all been just wonderful. Wonderful and weird.

And then there's us - I can't..., I can't be me without you anymore and because of that, and because all this is so insane, I don't know if I'm ready to cope with being me on my own at the moment. Not here. I haven't adapted to life here yet. We haven't even, y'know, decorated the house, sorry, pod."

"Decorate? What do you mean, Mel? What do you expect me to do? I can't... I can't take you to Ikea!"

"Why not?" Melinda protested. "I mean not Ikea obviously, but it would help so much if we could choose blinds and curtains and stuff. I mean it!"

A look of perplexed astonishment washed across smolin9's face. "But the windows adjust to the light and you can make them opaque at the flick of a switch. So why would you...?" A technobot approached, reminded him it was nearly time to initiate the launch sequence, then pirouetted and withdrew.

Melinda released smolin9's arm and almost beseechingly asked her husband, "*Why* can't I go with you?"

"You're too important," smolin9 explained. "The thing is, it's likely that our revered leader will be summoned to appear before the ICJAC on Lacuna to answer questions about Niffis. If that happens, you will have to stand in for him here on Morys."

"Well, it's nice to be important, I suppose."

Smolin9 took her in his arms and said, "It's important to be nice too." They both smiled. "I'll be back just as soon as I possibly can."

They parted with a kiss and Melinda watched the launch with a heavy heart. Could she have known that they would never see one another again?

.   .   .

"Where are we?" yukawa3 asked woozily, kicking at the sand with his feet.

Polkingbeal67 poked a finger at his microwocky and squinted at one of the miniature screens. "We're somewhere on the south west coast," he said.

"The south west coast of what? Are we on the Pale Blue Dot?"

"Of course we are, you prokaryote! We set the routefixer for the nearest coast to where Melinda used to live. According to the log, this should be Burnham On Sea, but you were steering so erratically when we switched to manual for the landing, we may have gone off course."

"It wasn't erratic," yukawa3 protested morosely. "I had to swerve to avoid some trees."

Polkingbeal67 slapped the cadet on the top of his head. "They weren't trees, bobblehead! That was the air freshener Melinda gave you! I told you not to hang it in the flight deck!"

The waves were lapping against the hull of the 'Opportunity' and a pair of gulls arced and skimmed over the blue-green water towards them. One of them perched on top of the craft, then hopped and fixed yukawa3 with a hard, inquisitive look that demanded an explanation. Or food.

"We've got to hide the craft," yukawa3 decided, rather superfluously.

"I know," said polkingbeal67. After weighing up all the

options, he felt compelled to put his trust in the Craterkite cloaking device, even though it was still subject to beta testing back on Morys. "We'll use the Craterkite," he told yukawa3.

As his mentor activated the device, yukawa3 tried to display as much comradely curiosity as he could muster. "What model is the Craterkite?" he asked. "Mark 2?"

"Mark 3. It's the latest prototype."

As the 'Opportunity' vanished in a greenish fog, yukawa3 scrutinised the nothingness left behind. "I can't see any difference. How is it better than the Mark 2?"

Yukawa3 had no idea why he found himself on the receiving end of another one of polkingbeal67's slaps on the top of the head. Battered and crumpled, the yellow sou'wester slipped over his eyes. "I wish you wouldn't do that," he complained. "I like to think of us as mates, y'know, sort of outlaw buddies, bros, comrades, partners in crime. I've always felt we could be special together, always hoped that deep down you were, y'know, secretly nice."

Polkingbeal67 was sorting through a travel bag of essential items. He took out his plasma gun and repeatedly set and reset the trigger mechanism. "I *am* nice," he said absently. "I'm a very friendly guy."

"If you were nice, you wouldn't keep flattening my sou'wester!" yukawa3 retorted. "A friendly guy would talk to you as an equal and never look down on you, maybe take you fishing, maybe buy you a *new* sou'wester..."

Polkingbeal67's eyes took on a slightly evil glint. "Tell me, have you heard of the expression 'friendly fire'?"

Friendly or not, polkingbeal67 replaced the plasma gun in the bag and retrieved the biomimetic mutators. He was anxious to get on and tackle the next task ahead of them. Having concealed the spacecraft, it was imperative that they disguised their own identities before they encountered any earthlings. "Right, pay attention," he said, configuring the mutators. "From now on, we are no longer polkingbeal67 and yukawa3 from Morys Minor. I'm a waitress called Mohammed Wang..." He paused as his physical appearance mutated. "And you," he continued, "you are a fisherman called Sophia Gonzalez."

Yukawa3 inspected the transformation of his limbs. "Okay, p," he said.

"Mohammed," polkingbeal67 corrected him, straightening his apron. "You can call me Mo for short."

Yukawa3 was delighted with his new identity. He stroked his goatee and flexed his puny biceps, grinning from ear to ear. "Look at me!" he beamed, spinning around in his ill-fitting turtle neck sweater while his white duck trousers flapped incongruously around his bony legs. "I'm just the most stereotypical earthling fisherman of all time! I'm going to sing a sea shanty right now!" Realising he did not know any sea shanties, he yelled "Yo ho ho!" lustily a few times and performed a bizarre jig that involved kicking his legs out and hopping erratically on one foot.

Polkingbeal67 observed him with thinly-disguised scorn. "You don't know any sea shanties, do you?"

"Yes, yes, I certainly do," yukawa3 insisted. "I know a couple."

"Name them."

"Well, one of them is..." To his surprise, he managed to

215

come up with a title that sounded perfectly plausible. "Yeh, one of them is called 'Haul away, haul away' and the other one..." His resourcefulness floundered like a gasping trout. "... isn't."

Polkingbeal67 knew that if they were going to blend in with earthlings they would have to think and behave like earthlings. He judged that one of the first and key considerations was to secure some form of employment. As it was early summer, he was certain there would be no shortage of waitressing opportunities in the area, so the immediate priority was to help yukawa3 apply for work as a deckhand with a fishing crew. With this in mind, they followed the coast on foot until they came upon a town with a harbour. Following an elevated pavement along the harbour wall towards a lighthouse, they were encouraged to see a wide variety of fishing boats bobbing in the water. For some reason, they descended the steps near the lighthouse only to be met by the incoming tide lapping against the wall, so they squabbled, ran back up the steps and retreated towards the town. Near the top of the harbour they approached a man who was unloading nets and lobster pots from a boat.

"Excuse me," polkingbeal67 said in his new phony waitress voice. "Are we having a nice day today? Tell me, do you have any vacancies at the moment? My friend here is an excellent deckhand with plenty of experience." He swished his ponytail and contorted his face into a ghastly smiling-for-tips grimace.

The fisherman straightened up, wiped his brow with the back of his hand and turned a withering gaze on yukawa3. "'E don't look like 'e could lift a bloody fork to 'is mouth!"

"No, really, his appearance is deceptive," said polkingbeal67. "He's struggled with a marlin for three days and nights."

The fisherman fingered his grizzled beard, coughed and spat on the shingle. "Not much marlin round 'ere," he growled. "Not much call for 'em either. Anyways, the skipper is 'avin a coffee in the shop there. Go an' ask 'im yourselves. I've got work to do." Sensing the possibility of some entertainment, he changed his mind. "'Ang on! I'll come with you. I'll introduce you."

The three of them crunched their way over the shingle towards the cafe. A solitary gull stood on the metal railing, its feathers lifting easily in the breeze as it eyed the motley crew marching past some cobble stones and an old rowing boat filled with flowers and herbs. Entering the cafe, the fisherman greeted the woman behind the counter and took a chair next to a man wearing a blue-checked shirt. "Jarek," he said. "These two characters 'ere want to know if we wanna take on any more crew."

Polkingbeal67 shook his head. "Just him," he clarified, pointing to yukawa3. "Not me."

"Yeh," said the first fisherman. "I kinda assumed that, being as you're a girl an' everything. Why doesn't your boyfriend 'ere speak for 'imself?" He fixed yukawa3 with a hard glare. "What's your name?"

Yukawa3 glanced nervously at polkingbeal67, who nodded in encouragement. "Sophia," he said. "I'm Sophia Gonzalez. Can I have a new sou'wester?"

The look the two fishermen exchanged was a queer combination of mistrust and amusement. "Hokay," said Jarek, pushing his coffee cup aside. "You're colled Sophia?" When yukawa3 nodded, he exchanged another look with the first fisherman. "Sophia, you're very fin for a fisherman. Are you strong? Which is important for, uh, fishing work. Uh, yes? No worries. Pay peanuts, get monkeys, uh? Ha ha!" He nudged his colleague, who joined in the laughter. "Next point is why you have a girl's name, uh? Sophia is, uh, a girl's name."

Straight away, polkingbeal67 suspected he had not paid sufficient attention to detail when he had constructed their earthling identities (given that Mortians have no gender and reproduce in an agamogenetic fashion, he could possibly be forgiven for underestimating the importance of gender issues in earthling life). This suspicion was confirmed when Jarek asked *him* his name and he replied tentatively, "Er, Mohammed?" The first fisherman snorted. Jarek, to his credit, kept a straight face, nodded and simply repeated, "Uh, Mohammed."

"Anyway," said the first fisherman, addressing Jarek, but pointing to yukawa3. "This character says 'e's fought a marlin for three days and nights. So, what do you think?" Neither polkingbeal67 nor yukawa3 noticed him winking conspiratorially at his skipper.

Jarek turned to the woman leaning over the counter, enthralled by the conversation. "Beryl," he said. "Hokay, can we borrow one of those, uh, crab line things?" He nodded his head towards a rack containing buckets, spades and other sand toys.

Beryl sneered at him derisively. "What do you think this is? Do I look like Father Christmas? They're two pound forty-five, includes the bag."

"Hokay, hokay," said Jarek, "No worries. As I'm in, uh, a good mood, I'll even buy my two friends here a drink."

Jarek paid Beryl the money and handed the lemonade bottle and the crab line to yukawa3. "I tell you what," he said. "You take this and catch me a marlin and, uh, you can have the job. Hokay? You can borrow my rowing boat. It's the, uh, blue and white one down there on the sand."

As polkingbeal67 and yukawa3 left the shop and made their way over the shingle, Beryl and the two fishermen stood at the window, pointing and laughing.

Polkingbeal67 was more than a little apprehensive. "Do you know how to row?" he asked.

Yukawa3 shook his head. "I wish I could," he said.

"You wish you could? Don't you want this job? Really, y'know, you've got to start saying 'I will' instead of 'I wish' all the time."

"I will I could?" said yukawa3, a tad confused. "Anyway, this boat's no good."

Polkingbeal67's frustration with the young cadet was growing. "Why?" he asked. "Why is this one no good?"

"It's upside down," yukawa3 replied. There was only a short pause before his sou'wester was subjected to another pounding.

Yukawa3 never thought to use more than one oar at a time, so it will not surprise you to hear that the quest for the giant marlin took place within a particularly small circular zone of the harbour waters. The outcome, especially given that he had neglected to bait the hook, was equally predictable - they caught precisely nothing. Nevertheless, the episode was not without its benefits. For one thing, Jarek's crew, along with several other bemused spectators, enjoyed the best part of an hour's free entertainment. Also, it gave polkingbeal67 plenty of time to reflect on the effectiveness of their new identities. The relative tranquility of the harbour was punctuated only by the dipping of the oar blade and the random cries of oystercatchers and gulls. It should have served to calm his disquiet, but polkingbeal67 grew increasingly agitated about the mistakes he had made. It galled him to think that smolin9 would have handled it much better. Eventually, the obvious solution - switching their names - dawned on him, but by then he was disenchanted with the whole project and was contemplating an entirely different strategy.

As his new game plan took shape in his head, polkingbeal67 cheered up. "I think honesty is going to be the better policy. Yes, that's the way to go!"

"Definitely. I've always believed in honesty." Yukawa3 shipped his oar and stood up, suddenly and unaccountably emboldened to deliver a heart-felt homily or two on the subject. "Honesty and integrity are..." His brain muscle flexed promisingly and then collapsed with fatigue. "...very good things." The boat rocked violently causing him to sit back down again. "I would be prepared to die for my belief in honesty," he asserted.

"Really?" Polkingbeal67 rolled his eyes. "I've told you before - you should never say you'd die for your beliefs, because what if they turn out to be wrong? Anyway, we've got to accept that we're no good at blending in with these people. Smolin9 might get away with it, but we're no good at it. We're never going to pull it off. This is the new plan - we're going to be upfront with them and get their support."

Yukawa3 gaped open-mouthed. "What? How? Why?"

"We'll go back and tell them exactly who we are and exactly what we want. Just follow my lead."

"You're right!" yukawa3 exclaimed. "This is, this is..."

"A good idea?" polkingbeal67 suggested helpfully.

"A total Rubicon moment!" Yukawa3 took a large swig of lemonade. He then learned the hard way that you should avoid reaching a total Rubicon moment while you're drinking. It makes lemonade shoot out of your nose.

Twenty minutes later they abandoned the boat, yukawa3 having failed in his attempts to manoeuvre it back to land. They waded through the water and strode purposefully back to the shop. By this time, the fishing crew had disappeared and the only customers were a couple of holidaymakers sipping coffee at a window table.

Beryl smiled a sardonic smile. "Did you get your marlin, then?"

While polkingbeal67 proceeded to tell her exactly who they were and what they were doing and why they were doing it, Beryl retrieved a broom from behind the counter and waved it in his face. "Right, that's it! Come on you two, out you get! I've had enough of your lunacy for one day! Off with you! Go back to your old Morris Minor car or your spaceship or whatever you're living in and get out from under my feet!" Brandishing the broom like a spear, she chased them from the shop and yelled at them from the doorway, "And don't come back here with any more of your crackpot stories! Go on, clear off! I've got better things to do!"

Withdrawing to the harbour wall, polkingbeal67 and yukawa3 sat in total despair and bewilderment.

Yukawa3 was the first to speak. "What happened?"

Polkingbeal67 slapped the sou'wester. "Okay, it didn't go exactly as I planned it."

·   ·   ·

You will recall, dear reader, that polkingbeal67 and yukawa3, in the frantic aftermath of the Niffis incident, had forgotten that polkingbeal67's prospects of survival on Earth had been jeopardised by a corrective procedure to his earthling heart that rendered him susceptible to earthling infections and diseases. The morning after the episode with the rowing boat, he woke to find what looked like an insect bite on his leg. Other than a little localised itchiness, it did not trouble him too much, but it did serve to remind him of the issue.

He and yukawa3 had booked into a little bed and breakfast near the harbour and polkingbeal67 had secured a part-time job as a waitress in the local diner. Despite their best efforts, and despite a switch of names, they had not found a fishing crew willing to employ yukawa3 as a deckhand.

It was four o'clock in the afternoon and polkingbeal67 had just started his shift and was cleaning tables in his section. Worried about the outlook for any kind of extended stay on Earth, particularly in view of his vulnerability to infection, he was preoccupied with his thoughts and barely noticed a customer who had shuffled into a booth near the door and had coughed to attract attention.

"What's your problem?" The words had escaped polkingbeal67 before he had had a chance to register where he was and what he was doing.

"I beg your pardon," said the customer in an aggrieved voice.

"Sorry, I just started work. I mean, what can I get you?"

As the diner was quiet, the two of them struck up a conversation and it turned out that the customer was the owner of several local fishing vessels. Polkingbeal67 realised this was an opportunity that he should not squander. Earlier in the day, he had resolved to offer earthlings some of the benefits of Mortian technology in the hope that it might ingratiate him with the intergalactic community and go some way towards atoning for the Niffis calamity. Mortian microwockys incorporated real-time video imaging and sonar technology that were way beyond even the wildest dreams of earthling naval boffins, so locating shoals of fish in the shallow waters of the Bristol Channel would be a breeze. This wasn't just about getting yukawa3 a job. Polkingbeal67 was thinking big. If he and yukawa3 could transform the British fishing industry, how long would it be before military and government officials homed in on the potential benefits? And how long then before the planet's top scientists would be knocking at his door, drooling and slavering over the prospects of other technological innovations? Obviously, he would have to be conservative about how much to reveal - it would not do to have dumb earthlings whizzing around the galaxies causing mayhem everywhere and undermining the established order. You can lead earthlings to knowledge and information, but you cannot make them think. No, it would have to be a judicious drip feed of advanced scientific concepts, such as biogeometry, thermodynamics, neurochemistry and genomics. He could, for example, push people like Stephen Hawking and Jacob Bekenstein further along the path to understanding string theory and quantum field theories without revealing the relationship between black hole entropy and time travel. Surely, if he could be instrumental in accelerating earthling civilisation in this way, it would go a huge way towards ameliorating his mangled reputation in the eyes of intergalactic society. And what if he expanded his ambitions into the cosmetic and pharmaceutical industries? Why, the possibilities were endless: if he were an unscrupulous, greedy and power hungry individual (and, to be fair, he was not), he could bask in the radiant splendour of prosperity, wealth and success for the rest of his days. Fleetingly, visions of world domination and affluence drifted seductively across his mind and only the sound of the customer, Peter Dylan, slurping his tea like a vacuum cleaner, brought him back to his senses.

Dylan stared in wide-eyed amazement at some of the features of polkingbeal67's microwocky and readily agreed to give yukawa3 a trial on one of his boats the following day. The plan was for Dylan and yukawa3 to take out a rigid inflatable boat at dawn so that they could use the microwocky to record the locations of the best shoals, and then communicate the data to the crews before they set out.

Later, when polkingbeal67 discussed the strategy with yukawa3, he strayed once more into wild expectations and had to be snapped back to reality by the stupefied expression on the young cadet's face.

"But don't you see?" polkingbeal67 enthused. "This is going to be our salvation. This will ensure that we can go home with our heads held high, a song of triumph on our lips and the hope of freedom on our minds." It was misguided and senseless, but he could not help himself. In truth, he was a little feverish. The insect bite had become swollen and full of pus.

Yukawa3 attempted to keep his mentor lucid and focused. "But what if they don't believe you or don't trust you or chase after you with a broom?"

Polingbeal67's eyes took on a crazy gleam. "They'll listen," he argued. "I'll be able to show earthlings, for the first time in their miserable existence, exactly what they are running from, and to, and why! And if they need more convincing, I'll amaze them by transforming myself into my natural Mortian form!"

Appalled at the notion, yukawa3 became flustered. "Don't do it!" he insisted firmly. "You mustn't do it. They'll lock you up. They'll carry out unspeakable experiments. Remember Roswell!"

The following morning, yukawa3 met Dylan outside the harbour cafe where a light rain had dampened the roads and the cobbles. A soft breeze rippled the water as they set off in the RIB to conduct their survey of the nearby fishing grounds, particularly the sand banks where high yields of bass and pollack could be expected. Meanwhile, the fishing crews started to assemble. Clearing the harbour fairway, checking equipment and repairing damaged trawl nets, they had plenty to occupy themselves with while they waited.

Polkingbeal67 arrived just as the RIB was bouncing the waves back towards the harbour. The aroma of dimethyl sulphide, the smell of the sea, would have greeted him, but, although the fake earthling nostrils configured and actualised by his biomimetic mutator appeared to be as authentic as the real McCoy, his sense of smell was actually weak and unreliable (like having a completely stuffed nose). What he thought he could smell, however, was the sweet smell of success as yukawa3 and Dylan disembarked from the RIB, looking confident and energised.

"Well?" polkingbeal67 prompted. "Did you record it all okay? Do you know how to get to the best shoals?"

"Don't worry about that," said yukawa3. "I've got it. I've photographed the metal identification plate on the transom."

Polkingbeal67 and Dylan looked at each other in bemused perplexity. They spoke in unison: "What?"

Proudly flourishing the close-up of the RIB's serial number on his microwocky, yukawa3 announced, "Look! Here it is! This clearly identifies which boat to use to catch all those fish!"

Dylan was aghast. "Do you mean you haven't identified the locations of the shoals?" A number of crew members and a few locals, including Beryl, the café proprietor, had gathered around to listen to the exchange.

"But I've identified which boat to use!" yukawa3 repeated. He was not so dense that he could not perceive that something was wrong and that whatever was wrong was almost certainly perceived by everyone else to be his fault. One glance at polkingbeal67's thunderstruck expression told him all he needed to know. To yukawa3, life was a wonderful enigma made intolerable by the fact that no one else shared his grasp of the rationale behind it. In abject remorse, he took off his sou'wester and offered it to polkingbeal67, who looked at it in confusion and exasperation before replacing it delicately on the cadet's head and slapping it hard.

"Get out of here, you... you... charlatans!" Dylan spluttered, almost choking with rage. "And don't come back here or we'll... we'll... we'll keelhaul you! Take your stupid sciencey toys and clear off! As if we haven't got better things to do!"

As they beat their hasty retreat, yukawa3 turned to his mentor and said, "Yeh, I think I know where it all went wrong."

Polkingbeal67 tightened every sinew to appear composed and restrained. "Oh?" he said. "And where do you think it all went wrong?"

"Well," said yukawa3. "For one thing, we'd never have got

all those men and their equipment on that boat."

Polkingbeal67 kicked yukawa3's battered yellow sou'wester all the way back to their bed and breakfast lodgings.

.   .   .

The ICJAC (or Intergalactic Court of Justice, Arbitration and Conciliation) only ever investigated allegations of crimes against humanity, war crimes and genocide (it also intervened in cases where a planet proved unable or unwilling to investigate serious wrong-doing by its own people). The Niffis incident was the first time that Morys Minor had been the object of this kind of ICJAC attention. In many ways, the Mortian leader's desire to protect the reputation of Mortian envoys was honourable, but, in the longer term, his failure to apprehend polkingbeal67 and yukawa3 damaged his own reputation and laid him open to accusations of collusion and corruption. Unfortunately, his ill-advised decision to send smolin9 in fruitless pursuit of the two fugitives was seen as further evidence of his complicity, and, impervious as he was to intergalactic hostility, he had been backed into a corner and there was no way out for him but to travel to the Court and answer the charges levelled against him.

Far from feeling intimidated and persecuted, however, the leader secretly relished being the centre of so much attention. He figured that if he was the focus of criticism, people must think he was actually doing stuff. Far better to risk being vilified than leave behind a legacy of obscurity and anonymity. Far better to strive to do something remarkable with your twilight years than wallow in mindless approval. If people judge and criticise and question you, it means you've actually stood up for something - something you believe in, something you're prepared to defend. The leader's minions and advisors tried to tell him this actually meant defending the negligent destruction of a famous chillok city, but he had made up his mind - he was going to face the music with defiance and resolve and he was not going to skulk in the shadows to avoid it.

The fact is, he had recently begun worrying that no one talked about him at all when he was not around (indeed, a few of his critics in the intergalactic arena had facetiously started referring to him as 'his irrelevance' instead of 'his reverence'). But now, galvanised by the challenge of defending the reputation of the planet, the Mortian supremo's sense of self-importance was fully restored and he had prepared for his departure by staging a raft of ceremonial activities like seaweed wrestling and blind cruiser jousting. He took his leave of Melinda by presenting her with a red and black mosaic of a double-headed orbis bird, a symbol of their joint leadership of the planet (or, more likely, a reminder that he was not relinquishing his authority during the period of his absence).

Melinda stared at the gift, not knowing how to respond. "Thanks," she said. "Literally. Um, don't I have to be officially sworn in or something?"

The leader threw a look of doubtful certainty and nodded. "Of course," he said, annoyed with himself that he had not formulated a protocol for such a contingency. "There is an ancient protocol for such occasions."

"Yeh, 'cause I know I'm just taking care of things pro tem while you're on..." She managed to grab the word 'trial' before it left her lips. "... on official business elsewhere. But I just thought..."

With a dismissive flourish of his hand, the leader interrupted. "There will be a ceremony in the Orbicular Room," he declared, "in, er, ten of your earthling minutes." He sashayed out of the reception chamber, depositing in his wake a trail of reddish-orange residue and a pungent aroma of exotic oils.

When Melinda arrived at the Orbicular Room, she was ushered by one of the leader's minions to a cushion diametrically opposite the cross-legged form of the leader himself. It was essentially a whispering gallery - the ceiling and the walls formed the top half of an ellipsoid, so that a person could hear another person whispering at the opposite focal point on the other side of the room. The leader, wearing a strange wig of dark wavy earthling hair which he was dipping in a bowl of fragrant broth, faced the wall and uttered mysterious phrases that eventually transmuted into words that Melinda could hear and, up to a point, understand: "If your desires are not extravagant, they will be rewarded. Do not follow where the path may lead; go where there is no path and leave a trail..." A few hastily summoned minions, hovering in the middle of the room in awkward silence, tried their best to look like part of a ceremony. They were the only other witnesses to the leader's bizarre monologue. "Your ability to juggle many tasks will take you far, but you should concentrate on one at a time..." After droning on for some considerable time, he finished with a question, "Are you ready to hear the task I have chosen for you?"

Melinda looked around and realised the inquiry was directed at her. "Okay," she said, forgetting to whisper. The echoes of her voice ricocheted around the room. "Sorry!" she said, forgetting once again.

The leader had to wait for the echoes to recede before he could continue. "Your task is to assign a new name to our planet."

Melinda whispered with exaggerated articulation, "Why? Why does it need a new name?" Receiving no reply, she repeated it with even more exaggerated articulation.

Eventually, the sound waves of the leader's whispered explanation reflected down from the ceiling. "We rename our planet at the end of every katun."

"But didn't the katun cycle end like quite recently?"

"Yes, but I forgot to rename the planet," the leader admitted, a hint of irritation in his voice. "I'd been very busy. We were under the impression that our entire race was threatened with extinction at the end of the cycle."

"It's okay," Melinda assured him. "We all forget things. Literally."

"Don't ask, don't say. Everything lies in silence," the leader counselled her, sounding a little peeved. "I am blessed with the happy combination of a clear conscience and a good memory. The superior person may neglect small matters but can be entrusted with great concerns." He continued mumbling as he shuffled across the room and told Melinda, "You are now free to pursue the path I have chosen for you. It will be full of hazards as all paths are, but go forward without fear and use the obstacles as stepping stones."

"Am I sworn in?" Melinda asked.

The leader smacked his lips over his toothless gums and said, "Never return to a firework once it has been lit."

Melinda was on the point of asking him what she should do if polkingbeal67 and yukawa3 were returned to Morys, but she changed her mind. On reflection, she thought she could probably do without the benefit of all that fortune cookie wisdom and just watched him amble slowly away. "If they get any sense out of him at the Court, it'll be a miracle," she thought.

Later that day, after the leader had made an ostentatious departure from the palace, Melinda visited the inner chambers where she was expected to take up residence. She was met by nipkow4, formerly a producer for the Morys Minor Broadcasting Corporation, now appointed as Melinda's senior advisor. He bowed his head and greeted her with obsequious politeness, "Our revered locum."

Melinda's eyes widened. "What? What did you call me?"

Nipkow4 bowed his head again. "Our revered locum," he repeated. "It is your title during our revered leader's absence."

Listening to nipkow4's strained and deferential voice, Melinda suddenly felt really alone, like a lost child in a crowd of strangers. Estranged from the characters that had captured her heart and soul, isolated from smolin9's effervescent earnestness and polkingbeal67's gruff blustering and even yukawa3's deranged inanity, the prospect of an indeterminate period of time on Morys suddenly felt less than appealing, a whole lot less than the ultimate otherworldly dream of utopian happy endings she had envisaged when she had left Earth. She was beginning to feel like the butt of some time travel agent's joke. Certainly, she was going to have to dig deep into her repertoire of life coach prescriptions if she was to survive the feeling of detachment and alienation, of being lost in a cosmic wilderness without a map. Literally. "Tell me, nipkow4," she said, "do you think all this is crazy? Do you think I'm just kidding myself trying to be a leader of an alien planet? I mean like, what's happening? You know what? If I so much as mentioned any of this to one of my own, er, species, they'd lock me up and throw away the key."

"But it's no accident, your reverence," nipkow4 assured her. "You were chosen."

"I guess you're right. I shouldn't doubt myself like this."

"Absolutely not, your reverence." Nipkow4 continued to bow his head every time he spoke. "You're on the road less travelled and you're discovering the pathway to success. A rolling stone gathers no moss, your reverence. Literally. So let's get out there!"

Melinda was vaguely aware that this was like listening to the Mortian leader, but it was having the desired effect. "You are *so* right," she said. "I've been focusing too much on the big tasks rather than the little ones."

"The little things build the foundation for the big ones, your reverence," said nipkow4, bowing and nodding at the same time. "You've got to make sure you have a solid foundation before you build on it."

"I'll make some mistakes along the way, but I'm going to make those mistakes with one hundred percent effort."

Nipkow4 had stopped bowing and was now executing small but dignified hops of excitement. "Yes, your reverence! Hustle out there! Run the plays! Go out there and execute! Let's have some fun out there! Worry about later later!"

They were really egging each other on now. "You'd better believe it," Melinda enthused. "I'm going to live every day as if it was my last!"

"And then some day you'll be right!" said nipkow4, no longer thinking about what he was saying. "You'll be right! Right! Right! Oh yeah!" The hops were not small any more, nor were they particularly dignified.

A commotion on the staircase outside drew their attention. Apparently, one of the servobots had picked up a transmission from yukawa3 on a wormhole communication channel. Desperately hurrying up the stairs to deliver the news, the servobot had collided with a couple of executive minions and a statue of an ancient Mortian war hero. Once the turmoil had settled, Melinda and nipkow4 learned that yukawa3 had sent a distress signal from the Pale Blue Dot appealing for smolin9 to get in contact with him.

.   .   .

In order to understand why yukawa3 issued a distress signal, knowing full well it would be picked up by monitoring stations on Morys Minor, we must acquaint ourselves with an account of the events leading up to it.

In the days after their hapless attempt to secure employment for yukawa3 as a deckhand, polkingbeal67 had tried to make ends meet as a waitress despite feeling increasingly unwell. The irregular configuration of blood cells in his immune system had been besieged by parasites introduced via the insect bite. At first, he attributed the headaches, muscle aches and general tiredness to teething troubles with his earthling mutation, but he was now experiencing feverishness, nausea and diarrhoea and he knew the game was up. On the tenth day, while yukawa3 was out shopping, he had a minor seizure. He could not ignore the situation any longer - the minute yukawa3 returned, he would break the news and prepare for their immediate return to Morys Minor.

At any given moment we all confront thousands of different paths leading to thousands of different outcomes and, unfortunately for polkingbeal67, yukawa3 had been waylaid by an encounter with a pair of sombre, earnest earthlings who had buttonholed him outside the cafe.

The taller of the two sharply dressed young men greeted him in a friendly manner and offered to buy him a coffee. "We'll tell you about God's good news," he promised as the three of them sat together at a pavement table.

"Which god?" yukawa3 asked. He had conducted a bit of research into earthling religions, analysing and comparing the various doctrines and spiritual philosophies, but, to be frank, his grasp of the subject was tenuous at best, if not downright risible. "Is it one of those gods that require the blood of your enemies to be spilled? Will you be honoured by your god when you do the killing? Are virgin births involved? Or prophets leaping from city to city on horseback? Or is it the Yembiyembi mud god? Are you going to dance and holler and rub handfuls of sticky mud on my face and shower me with flower petals? Has this god got news of an impending plague or an earthquake?"

The two young men were clearly nonplussed, but managed to smile affably enough as Beryl took their order and scowled as she recognised yukawa3. "So what would Mohammed like?" she asked sourly, stabbing her notepad with her pencil. "Or is it Sophia today? Or Doctor Who? Or, as it's Friday, perhaps it's Robinson Crusoe!" Enchanted by her own dazzling display of wit, she shrieked with laughter before composing herself and clearing her throat. "Sorry, dear, what would you like?" Yukawa3, who often struggled with long words, ordered a cappuccino and mispronounced it slightly, much to Beryl's delight. "Al Pacino?" she screeched. "Al Pacino! So that's your name today?" She went back through the door, still laughing.

"No, it's not the yebbywebby mud god," the taller man said, "Sir, we want to talk to you about how you can bring the creator of the living to your door and into your life. Do you know the world is ending?"

"Is it?" Yukawa3 stared at them in consternation. "I thought there was something odd about this planet." He leaned forward conspiratorially and dropped his voice. "Listen boys," he said. "You seem like nice guys. Me and my mentor, we can get you out of here when the time comes. We've got transport." He winked knowingly. "So what's going to happen? Will a fire come along and devour all living things? Will the sea become like blood when a huge asteroid plunges into it? Will the magnetic poles reverse? Solar flares? A pandemic? A nuclear winter? Whatever it is, don't worry, it's not the end of the world - oh, wait, yes it is! Ha ha! But really, we can all get away. How long have we got?"

The two earnest young men looked at each other, sensing that, at best, they were casting seeds on barren ground. "Sir," said the shorter man, who sported a pair of glasses with black, rectangular frames. "We have a letter for you that is the perfect word of God."

"How did he know I was here?" Yukawa3 asked suspiciously, as the coffees arrived. "Which god are we talking about again?"

"God the Father," the bespectacled man replied.

Beryl was beside herself. "The Godfather!" she exclaimed, chortling like a deranged goose. "The godfather!" She snorted and laughed and shook her head as she went over to clear the next table. A few seconds of silence, then she started up again. "The godfather. Ha ha! Al Pacino!"

Meanwhile, despite the fact that he had been prepared to divulge his identity for the price of a cup of coffee, yukawa3 was fearful that he and polkingbeal67 had been rumbled. "So this god," he said. "Is he the earthling leader? Does he sit on the Intergalactic Court? Listen, I can assure you it was an accident, pure and simple. What happened to that city was a quirk of fortune - could have happened to anyone. It was an honest mistake. I suggest we all just stop the finger-pointing and move on." He paused for a moment and stirred his coffee, vigorously, spilling most of it onto the table.

The taller man placed a reassuring hand on yukawa3's shoulder. "Are you okay?"

"My advice," said yukawa3, cradling his forehead in his palm, "is that nobody asks anybody any questions at all. None. It's called closure, okay?"

The two men smiled woodenly as yukawa3 slapped the table with both hands and yelled, "Everyone should just CALM DOWN!"

Yukawa3 was not so slow-witted that he failed to sense that he was barking up the wrong tree and had completely lost his audience. No, that's too generous - he *was* that slow-witted, but at least he managed to rein things in before the earthlings became irretrievably befuddled. "Now, for no particular reason," he added, for no particular reason, "I'm going to stir this coffee again."

The two would-be missionaries had stopped trying to make sense of yukawa3's ramblings - they just watched his jaw go up and down and talked about the Bible whenever it stopped. A miserable, slavering mongrel was slinking around in the street, looking for a snack. Beryl had put out bowls of water for the dogs to drink; not that she liked dogs - she ran a relatively successful business in the community and considered such gestures demonstrated her commitment to social responsibility (and social responsibility was good for business). A car horn sounded. In front of racks containing postcards, sunglasses and sandals, a few sparrows flitted around the chairs, searching for crumbs. Yukawa3 had drifted into a contemplative stupor that soothed his fretfulness and provided the opportunity for the earnest young men to expound on biblical scriptures at great length under the misconception that their companion was captivated by the elucidations and insights. The coffees came and went. Eventually, yukawa3 decided to invite his new friends back to the lodgings so that he could introduce them to polkingbeal67 and make arrangements for their deliverance from the end of the world.

"Do you think your friend, Sophia, will welcome the chance to hear the word of God?" asked the taller man.

Yukawa3 pursed his lips for a moment as he considered polkingbeal67's likely reaction. "Nah!" he decided. "She'll never go for that. I like all those stories about Lucifer and the Garden of Eden and all that, but when you talk to Sophia, I think you should stick to reality or she'll probably, um, throw you down the stairs!"

Not for a second did the earnest young men waver. "But what do you call reality?" the shorter man asked. "There is something greater than reality. I'm referring to absolute truth. We can help you learn about absolute truth and help you follow it. The things we teach are the *ultimate* reality. Like the menu at this cafe, we serve the right sort of food, at the proper time."

Yukawa3 could not hide his perplexity. He blinked uncomprehendingly before recovering his self-possession. "Yeh, stick with the food thing, I think. Sophia likes food and works in a diner. We should take him, sorry, her some lunch."

The man with glasses flashed an oily smile that was about as genuine as a Rolex in a car boot sale. "Work, not for the food that perishes, but for the food that remains for life everlasting." The smile persisted like a bout of indigestion.

"Don't worry," yukawa3 assured him with a dismissive wave of his hand. "She always checks the use-by dates."

The sun was now high. A woman dragged a wheelie bin from the edge of the pavement. The tranquility was broken only by a few stray voices, the padding of footsteps and a snatch of laughter on the feeble breeze. Arriving at the lodgings, the earnest young men hesitated, but yukawa3 motioned them to follow him as he opened the front door and took the stairs two at a time.

What met their eyes gave all three of them a jolt. Polkingbeal67, whose condition had deteriorated alarmingly, was sprawled face down on the bed and his appearance betrayed the failure of his earthling mutation to retain its authenticity. His skin looked shiny and anaemic. Clumps of hair were strewn on the pillow. If his body had not been trembling and his breathing ragged and uneven, they might have concluded that he was dead. It was apparent to yukawa3 that physiological processes had been set in train and polkingbeal67 was gradually and unwittingly reverting to his native Mortian form.

Alarmed, not just by his mentor's plight, but also by the prospect of having their true identities discovered, yukawa3 clapped his hands for no particular reason and yelled, "You are Chalky White and I claim my five pounds!" The two evangelists gawped at the scene and backed away towards the door. Yukawa3 turned to them. "It's the blood sugar!" he explained. "I told you we should have brought some food! Well, I'd better rustle something up for him. Maybe the end of the world can wait for now?"

At that moment, the phone rang (the landlord had equipped the room with a phone for incoming calls). Polkingbeal67 stirred, propped himself up on his elbows and croaked, "You'd better answer it."

Easily flustered by primitive earthling technology, yukawa3 picked up the handset gingerly, rather like a duchess fishing an insect out of the salad on the end of a fork, and put it to his ear. "I'm not here right now so can you just deal with it, okay?" he blathered.

The cold caller at the other end of the line was unruffled and cordial. "Good morning. How are you today? Are you looking for peace of mind in the event that you get hit by a truck? Let me assure you, we're well known for always telling the absolute truth..."

Without looking, yukawa3 turned to the earnest young men, held out the phone and said, "I think it's one of your people." They had already gone. This had already strayed way beyond their comfort zone and, anyway, they had better things to do.

It only remains to say that yukawa3 wasted no time hurrying to the masked spacecraft in order to issue the distress call that was intercepted on Morys Minor.

.   .   .

Dear readers, if you will allow, we must pause the narrative here and take a long hard look at the wonderful Mortian innovation known as the biomimetic mutator, not just because it is a fascinating subject in its own right, but also because it is central to understanding how events unravel from this point on.

This ground-breaking shape-shifting device allowed Mortians to assume the forms of other cellular beings and had been developed on Morys Minor relatively recently, certainly within living memory of smolin9's generation. Basically, it was a sophisticated technological innovation that utilised neutrino oscillation and chimera mutation to transform the appearance of the operator at the flick of a switch. It may sound simple, but it was not. Cellular metamorphosis required extensive training and specialised skills owing to the risk of potentially catastrophic mistakes.

The early days of mutator technology were littered with calamitous blunders, some of them irreversible. On one occasion, at a high-profile intergalactic scientific conference, a prominent Mortian senator demonstrated his ability to turn himself into a tiny chillok, complete with a segmented exoskeleton and fully-functioning antennae, only to be snaffled up by a hungry pinicola bird before anyone had had time to reverse the transfiguration. In consequence of such disasters, subsequent models had been restricted to humanoid mutations, although rumours abounded of a few mavericks who had managed to bypass that constraint. Other restrictions were also introduced - the deployment of same species (Mortian) disguises was outlawed and no one was permitted to duplicate the appearance of any actual person, living or dead. Again, it was widely suspected that such measures had been, or could be, breached.

Each device was uniquely adapted to its owner (or master). Once the desired disguise (or slave, as it was popularly known) had been configured using the three-dimensional blueprint software on the device, usually by means of pre-configured templates, it might be activated at any time. Given that the Mortian bodily configuration, DNA and body chemistry were far more robust than those of other humanoid species, the risks presented by the slave suffering injury or sickness were not usually significant. In any event, a degree of protection was afforded by the complete separation of master and slave DNA sequences and other genomic characteristics during the mutation process. Damage to the slave might be remedied by simply reactivating the configuration.

However, just to complicate things a little, you will recall that polkingbeal67's master configuration had been jeopardised by the implant of Melinda's earthling heart, creating problems with the separation of genetic material.

The infection caused by the insect bite had effectively crossed the barrier between master and slave, rendering both seriously compromised. All bets were now off. Not only could he not reactivate the slave, but also he lacked the strength to revert to the master configuration. That is to say, he could no longer become his native Mortian self. Worse, his physical appearance was now uncontrolled and subject to anomalous variations at any time.

I trust that clarifies things a little. The important thing to bear in mind is that polkingbeal67's affliction impacted his real self, not just his earthling disguise. I will refer to a further complication later.

Smolin9, meanwhile, had diverted the 'Crusader' to Earth as soon as he had received yukawa3's distress signal. Having landed on the moon and arranged wormhole transport to England, he had hastily assumed an earthling identity and was fretting over the prone form of his hapless friend as yukawa3 attempted to explain what had happened.

"Why did you come to Earth in the first place?" smolin9 asked, dismayed.

"Earth?"

"Here! The Pale Blue Dot!" smolin9 clarified impatiently. "Why did he decide to come here? He knew his heart wouldn't take it."

"He obviously forgot," said yukawa3, looking forlorn and bewildered. "I forgot too. We were a bit, uh, stressed. As I said, I found him like this earlier today and sent the signal straight away."

Smolin9 took a breath and cleared his throat. The effects of the homeodynamic disruption antidote had not yet worn off and he was struggling to maintain his physical and mental equilibrium. As for his emotional equilibrium - it was shot to pieces. He and polkingbeal67 went back a long way and although they seemed to be about as compatible as a balloon and a porcupine, they shared an affinity with one another that defied reason and they were fused together in an extraordinary and irrational way with bonds that neither of them understood. Smolin9 knew intuitively that he was going to be traumatised by this dreadful experience for the rest of his life. If bonds like that get torn, the rips leave open scars where the glue once was. Sighing lugubriously, he looked at his dying friend and then at the fidgeting cadet. "You know your signal will have been picked up on Morys?"

Yukawa3 nodded. "I know," he said. "What else could I do? At first, I was going to give myself up and request wormhole transport home, but polkingbeal67 told me he wouldn't be able to travel."

"He was right. The HDA antidote alone would've killed him." Homeodynamic disruption antidote, or HDA, was unfailingly taken to offset the adverse effects of time travel, but a sound constitution was a prerequisite.

Yukawa3 was becoming distraught. His hands were shaking like someone mixing a cocktail. "What are we going to do if we can't move him? What are we going to do? Okay now, don't tell me to calm down! Don't tell me to calm down!"

"I didn't," said smolin9.

"Well, everyone should just try to calm down! CALM DOWN! CALM DOWN! I hope that answers your question!"

While yukawa3 tried to make sense of the noise in his head, smolin9 worked out the only possible solution. It involved the use of an undocumented feature of the biomimetic mutator (I warned you there was a further complicating factor and this is it):

Besides having its owner's master configuration wired into its circuits, the biomimetic mutator also stored the quintessence or soul of its owner in automatically updateable codified form. To be clear, this was not confined to the neural circuitry functions of the mammalian brain. It was much more than that. It included intangible aspects of humanoid existence such as the soul, spirit, intellect, character, conscience, emotions and personality - all the non-physical attributes that define a person. The Mortians referred to this as Karma 5. Because a person's Karma 5 was stored together with but also in isolation from the master configuration, it was, theoretically at least, a transferable entity. Switching Karma 5 from one person to another was strictly proscribed by the Mortian authorities, but, at the behest of the planet's leader, a special panel had been set up to consider the ramifications. Unfortunately, the Multi-Agency Co-ordination Group for Mortian Mutator Management and Karma 5 Transferability had one of the least friendly acronyms ever generated by any bureaucrats anywhere in the universe, so everyone soon forgot about the MCCGMMK5T and it went underground. Smolin9 was a member of that panel.

If you're still following all this, you are certainly coping better than yukawa3, whose attempts to get his head round the concept caused him to shift from foot to foot like a dancing bear on hot coals. "So, what you're proposing," he said, eyes screwed tight as if in pain, "is to send polkingbeal67's Karma 5 back home in *your* body?"

"That's right."

"So, let me think about this," said yukawa3, whose

cogitative powers were now about as impressive as a drawing pin in a sword fight. "So *your* Karma 5 will transfer to Sophia?"

"No," smolin9 explained. "Sophia is just a slave configuration. My Karma 5 will transfer to polkingbeal67's body."

"And where's his body going?"

"Nowhere. It can't go anywhere because it's irreparably damaged. It's staying here."

"With Sophia?"

"With Sophia."

A summer storm was brewing somewhere off in the distance. Occasional flashes of lightning cast a ghastly aspect over the room, lending the scene a surreal and disturbing edge, particularly now that polkingbeal67's body seemed devoid of life. Through the window, smolin9 could see the dark clouds billowing up from the west. He was well aware that what he was proposing to do violated every law, edict, regulation, code, statute and convention in every book that was ever compiled for the guidance of Mortian officialdom. But sometimes risk aversion is the biggest risk of all and smolin9 knew the chance simply had to be taken. He also knew he had to counsel yukawa3 well, since the whole scheme would collapse if the nervous cadet failed to administer the HDA to polkingbeal67 directly after the Karma 5 switch and if he failed to dispatch him to Morys via wormhole without any delay whatsoever.

"You do understand exactly who is going back to Morys with you and who is staying here?" he asked yukawa3, as the latter pondered the logistics. "Let me test you: who's going back to Morys with you?"

Yukawa3 scratched his head. "Um, *you* are?"

"No," said smolin9.

"What's happening to *my* Karma 5?"

Smolin9 pursed his lips. "This isn't going to work, is it?" He wondered how many times he would have to go over it before yukawa3 could be relied upon to do the necessary. The thunder muttering and mumbling in the distance seemed to add to the sense of urgency. "Listen," he went on. "Nothing's going to happen to you. When I tell you, all you've got to do is operate polkingbeal67's mutator and follow my instructions so that he and I perform a Karma 5 transfer. Remember, polkingbeal67 is going home with you inside *my* body. I'm staying behind inside *his* body."

"Yeh, I get that. That's what I meant," yukawa3 lied. "So what do I tell polkingbeal67 when you've been switched over and we're ready to go back to Morys?"

There was a deafening clap of thunder. "That's the really important bit," smolin9 said, crossing the room and clasping yukawa3's shoulders. "He may refuse to leave, so you've got to make sure you get him away as soon as possible. D'you understand?" After waiting for a spark of comprehension in the young cadet's eyes, he continued, "Give Melinda all my love when you get back home. And tell polkingbeal67 *exactly* what's happened, okay?"

Yukawa3's eyes opened wide and he let out a gasp of shock. "Nah!" he said. "He'd never believe *that*!"

.   .   .

Melinda's tenure as acting leader had already sent a few

shock waves through Mortian society. Far from confining her executive activities to finding a new name for the planet, she had embarked on a campaign of proactive marketing to cement her dominion over the realm (although, to be fair, she would have preferred to be a sovereign who reigned but did not rule). Presenting herself as the true promoter and custodian of Mortian-ness, she had commissioned new coins and flags and, yes, T-shirts, as a declaration of, well, what it really meant to be a Mortian. Morys Minor, like most inhabited planets, was torn asunder by bitterness, hatred, conflict and strife (well, perhaps not torn asunder, but certainly more than frayed). Disparate factions pulled and tugged in various directions, straining to establish and protect their own special interests. It was clear to Melinda that she should find the common thread and bring everyone together in a meaningful, coherent, consolidated whole. To that end, she had set up a committee to define exactly 'what it meant to be a Mortian' in the confident expectation that they would plump for something like peace, love and understanding.

The inaugural meeting of the Committee on Mortian Allegiance and Non-negotiable Key Identity Nitty-gritty Definition (MANKIND) was now in session. Would it surprise you to know that Melinda thought up the name all by herself?

"So what makes Morys Minor special?" Melinda asked. "What are the things that make you proud to be a Mortian? We need to put together a Declaration of Independence or a Constitution or some other sort of planetary handbook. What ideals would you like to have enshrined into a book of rules? Come on, let's have a free exchange of views!" A wall of silence greeted her, so she made a fresh appeal, "If nothing else, you must have some sights and sounds that bind you all together and distinguish Morys from the other planets you visit and trade with?"

The assembled representatives of the most prestigious Mortian institutions, communities and organisations looked at each other in quizzical reticence.

Melinda persisted, beseechingly, "Tastes? Smells? Anything?"

Although nipkow4 was attending the meeting by means of a remote holographic feed, his sarcasm was unmistakable. "You mean like the thwack of the orbis bird on a pod roof, your reverence? The scent of methane drifting from a nearby fermentation vat? The ..."

"Okay, okay," Melinda interrupted. She did not want to be seen as peddling her own brand of planetary identity or imposing values and attitudes that were anathema to the native population. She was, however, keen to capture and promote the essential aspects of the planet's life and culture and historical institutions, so that a new shiny Morys Minor, proud of its heritage and ambitious for its future, might flourish, as she was wont to say, 'like the great fruit tree of the galaxy'. What she was after was 'the scaffolding and the bricks to make that literally possible'. When she said this, there were a few mutterings of dissent and sarcastic comments about what such a tree might look like. She surveyed the chamber with a steady, but stern aspect. "What about your beliefs and stuff?" she prompted.

"Why?" a voice finally asked.

"Why?" Melinda repeated, trying to locate who had spoken.

"Yes, why?" It was the rasping voice of Joseph West, self-appointed leader of the earthling community abducted from Earth shortly after Melinda's arrival on the planet. Trapped on Morys Minor as a result of the requisite modifications to their circulatory systems, the six men and six women (and subsequently, three babies) had been incarcerated in a prison camp close to the vast methane lake known as nefeshchaya, but Melinda had been attempting to use her influence to get them released and integrated into Mortian society. West's appointment on the committee had been the latest attempt to salvage something positive from the ill-conceived abduction. (To spare your sensibilities, dear reader, I have bowdlerised his remarks.) "These (unpleasant people) have mutilated us and imprisoned us on this (unpleasant) planet and you want me to co-operate wiv 'em and help 'em? I don't (displeasingly) well fink so!" he snapped with as much venom as he could muster. "And you are a (very unpleasant person) for co-operatin' wiv 'em! Tell me why you're (displeasingly) doin' it!"

Melinda struck a conciliatory tone as she addressed him. "Because, Joseph, we're here and this is our world now. Literally. And whatever world we happen to be part of, it makes sense to engage with it. I just want to make the world a better place. *This* world. *Our* world. Here and now."

A Mortian senator, identifiable by his oddly-shaped head, was appalled at the lack of respect shown to the interim leader. He stood up and demanded that West be removed from the chamber.

"Sit down, you (unpleasant person)!" West hissed. "You lot are in no position to act all (displeasingly) superior to us! If you're such an advanced (unpleasant) civilisation, how come you go flyin' around snatchin' people and treatin' 'em like (unpleasantness)?"

The senator bristled. "I will not be spoken to in this manner! We *are* a far superior race and you know it! Why, you're not fit to sleep with goopmutts! You earthlings are a backward race of beings, barely sophisticated enough to survive together on your own unstable planet! You cannot even..." He broke off, vaguely conscious of going further than he should have (but without at first realising why). Then he felt the heat of Melinda's withering look and sat down, shifting uncomfortably in his seat.

Nipkow4's projected image, shielded from the tension that permeated the room, coughed and spoke in a slow, methodical voice. "The thing is, your reverence, all our institutions have developed by means of conflicting accretions and compromises," he said. "But I suppose we can all agree on a few common principles," he said, "like freedom and government by consent under the rule of one law or another."

West spluttered. "Not you lot! You don't know nuffin' 'bout freedom! That's (displeasingly) obvious!" He took great delight in throwing punches, slaps and kicks at nipkow4's 3D holographic image.

Melinda turned to him, fixed him with a steely glare and asked, "Do you believe in freedom, Joseph?"

West shrugged. "Yeh," he said. "Of course."

"Everybody?" Melinda inquired. All hands went up in favour. And so, unperturbed by sporadic outbreaks of dissent and invective, Melinda painstakingly began drawing up a world view that encompassed and neutralised all the ambiguities, paradoxes and contradictions that bedeviled the prospect of harmonious relations on the planet. She did not get very far.

It was Joseph West who provoked the squabble that followed. "Fairness? Yeh, well, of course I (displeasingly) believe in fairness," he barked. "But who wouldn't? Who would believe in the alternative? This is (displeasingly) ridiculous. Like, who would start a crusade for *un*fairness? To be honest, it'd be better if you didn't do any of this. If you ask me, people don't wanna be defined by constitutions and all that (unpleasant) stuff. 'Cos when you break it all down, what really matters is, well, why don' you jus' let the planet be defined by the people in it? Y'know, people power an' all that."

The senator with the oddly-shaped head laughed scornfully. "Typical earthling ignorance and stupidity! If you want freedom and tolerance and fairness, you've got to *impose* it, you numbskull! You've got to mould it into pointed shapes and hammer it into people!"

West stood up. "Melinda, please tell me you don't believe this (unpleasant) rubbish! The rights an' values of the people come from nature, don' they? They can't be defined by committees or imposed by (unpleasant) laws! Seems to me the more laws you 'ave, the less justice you get. Because, I dunno, because, the really important rights an' values don' need to be written or rewritten. An' that way they can never be taken away from the people."

Melinda was nodding her head in stunned approval, but the senator was quite beside himself. "You're an abomination, you primitive hairy-headed goopmutt-brain! Of course you'd say that - you were a criminal on your own planet!" It was true. All the earthling abductees had, of course, been taken from English prisons. "How can you have tolerance if you don't enforce it with every fibre of your being?" He turned to the rest of the assembly and, with an exasperated gesture of his hands, appealed once again for West to be ejected. "Throw him out! Why are we trying to have a sensible dialogue with this monosyllabic moron? I refuse to be lectured by him! It's preposterous! What was the point of getting to the top of the intergalactic power pyramid? Can you imagine - these backward dimwits have a planet of their own!"

Melinda knocked on the table (the use of tables at

meetings was one of her innovations). "Excuse me," she said.

"Oh, you're different," said the senator, "You've got a Mortian heart, babe. The fact is, earthlings are..."

"Did you just call me babe?" Melinda asked, her eyes wide with shock and consternation.

Nipkow4's holographic image was breaking up a little. "I knew it wasn't a good idea to have a free exchange of views," he muttered bitterly.

"Exchange this!" yelled West, aiming a right hook at the projection.

"Hey, it's rude to hit someone in the wavefront interference patterns!" nipkow4 protested.

The senator weighed in. "What do you expect? The average IQ of an earthling is between 90 and 109! Ha ha ha ha ha!"

"Excuse me, excuse me!" Melinda shouted.

"None of them get anywhere near 1000!" the senator continued, his voice getting shriller and shriller. "They're all sub-millenials!"

"That's not even a thing," West countered, grabbing the senator by the throat. "Shows how (unpleasantly) clever you are!"

"Excuse me, excuse me, excuse me!" Melinda chanted as West and the senator grappled and continued to throw insults at each other.

Nipkow4 tried to restrain the senator, "What are you doing, senator? You should never lower yourself to the standards of an earth..." He managed to abort the remark and his image froze for a moment. A foolish grin plastered across his face, he turned to Melinda and added, "Not judging, your reverence, just trying to keep the peace."

Struggling to maintain composure, Melinda scolded him through gritted teeth, "We're not as dumb as we... We're not dumb!"

By now, a group of securibots were escorting the two assailants from the chamber, but they failed to prevent the senator aiming a punch at West, exclaiming as he did so, "Here! I'm striking a blow for Mortian tolerance!"

Not to be outdone, West responded with a right hook that caught the senator right between the eyes. "Then you should 'ave one of these in the name of (displeasing) equality and peaceful earth-style democracy, you (unpleasant) pile of (unpleasantness)!"

Forced to abandon the meeting and feeling generally discouraged and disappointed, Melinda sat alone in the empty chamber wondering how she could possibly achieve any form of social cohesion on this planet. Back on Earth, governments were tainted by sleaze and corruption and many of them pursued agendas that were ethically flawed. They swung from socialism to capitalism and back again, but all the political and economic systems just seemed to produce more and more worship of the golden calf. Surely, she thought, a more advanced civilisation such as this one should be capable of rising above all that? But no, the MANKIND project was clearly a disaster and she was presiding over a think-tank of ostriches. She put her head in her hands and wrestled with her gut feeling that her great Mortian dream had been exposed as an illusion, a myth of progress and prosperity through assimilation and brotherhood (and, er, sisterhood). Perhaps, after all, this was just not Melinda territory. Getting up and walking over to the window, she gazed at the dust storm outside. Stinging, blinding yellow-grey dirt swept this way and that across the plain, first coating the pods then brushing them clean again. Occasionally the plumes would rise up and blot out one or both of the suns, plunging the region into darkness, then they would subside, leaving the sky aglow with a faint orange-yellow light. Melinda could not help feeling there was a meaning in this, a real lesson to be learned from the phenomena of nature... don't be like dust, be like the wind, perhaps?

She was still languishing in uncharacteristic negativity when smolin9 suddenly breezed through the portal and strode towards her, his dark eyes flashing like coals. Of course, Melinda was completely unaware that the figure she now clasped to her bosom was not smolin9 at all but polkingbeal67 in the physical guise of his late comrade.

"I'm so glad you're here." Melinda spoke softly as a few tears escaped her eyes. "I'm not sure I'm cut out for this planetary leadership thing. Literally."

"Sure you are," polkingbeal67 reassured her. "You'll be fine. Rome wasn't built in a day." It would have been, he thought to himself, if only earthlings had thought to commission a gang of goopmutts to do the work.

"I know, but anyway..."

Polkingbeal67 interrupted her. "You just need some time to get your confidence up," he said, patting her shoulder, trying to think what smolin9 would say. "When opportunity comes knocking, you've just got to, uh, y'know, be near a door."

"Do what?" Melinda enquired in confusion. "But anyway..."

Yes, polkingbeal67 thought, he knew exactly what smolin9

would do - he would spout some dumb analogy. "Listen Mel, did I ever tell you about the time we sent two envoys to Skolli to investigate the market potential for selling football-themed T-shirts?"

"I think so," said Melinda, "But anyway..."

"Well," polkingbeal67 continued, oblivious. "The first one came back and said, 'There is *no* potential - nobody wears T-shirts on Skolli'. And then the second one returned and said, 'There's absolutely *massive* potential - nobody wears T-shirts on Skolli!' You get it?"

"Yeh, the second one, um, I don't know, but anyway..." She remembered hearing that the people of Skolli were not only totally ignorant about the earthling sport of football, but also they had six arms, two heads and giant spinal columns. There was no way they could possibly have worn T-shirts. "But anyway, how are you? Did everything go okay? Did you find polkingbeal67 and yukawa3? Never mind. First, I want you to just hold me for a while."

Polkingbeal67, groping in the dark corridor of uncertainty, put his arms around her, reluctantly and mechanically, like a robot.

Melinda pulled away. "What's wrong?" she asked.

"I've got something to tell you. It's not good news, I'm afraid. Polkingbeal67 is dead."

. . .

An analysis of polkingbeal67's Karma 5 would certainly reveal a cantankerous and misguided character, but not a bad one, even if he was inclined to make bad judgements when acting under duress. He had not intended to deceive Melinda. In fact, he had fully intended to tell her the whole truth about smolin9's unthinkable self-sacrifice and he would have done so were it not for the emotional turmoil that had gripped him when he had found her, despondent and depressed, in the presidential meeting chamber. Unaccustomed to experiencing emotional vulnerability, his psyche had gone into a kind of meltdown when Melinda had held him in her arms, and he had discovered he simply could not bear to inflict further pain on her. Although he had resolved to find the right time to tell her the truth as soon as possible, polkingbeal67 had found himself a victim of his own sensitivity and diplomacy, for a lie, once told, takes on a dynamic of its own and can even begin to sound like the truth.

There are those who believe that lying is an intrinsic part of human nature. Others maintain that it is always wrong to tell a lie, even if it is told for the best of reasons. Lies, at some point or other, invariably hurt the person who is lied to, but they can also hurt the liar. Polkingbeal67 now had to deal with the immediate fallout from his error, namely the plight of the cadet, yukawa3, who had been arrested immediately on their arrival on Morys Minor.

Fortunately, before they had left Earth, yukawa3 had had time to comply with smolin9's entreaties and had told his mentor what had happened, including every detail of the Karma 5 switch. Let us briefly bounce back to that moment:

Not surprisingly, polkingbeal67 became horrified and distraught by yukawa3's account of the afternoon's events. "We can't possibly leave smolin9 here," he declared. "Why did you let him do this?"

Yukawa3, suddenly stricken with guilt and remorse, keeled over and fell flat on his back. "It should have been me! Why didn't I say something? I'm not worthy to speak smolin9's name. I'm not a nice person at all. I'm just worthless and very, very ugly! I'm a horrible shape and my eyes are ugly and my nose is ugly!"

"You don't have a nose," polkingbeal67 reminded him.

This did not deter yukawa3. "If I had a nose, it would be an ugly one!"

By now, polkingbeal67 had composed himself. Time was running out anyway. Smolin9 had clearly thought everything through - once a wormhole traversal had been put in motion, there could be no delaying it. "Okay, shut up!" polkingbeal67 told the hysterical cadet. "We've got to go through with this now. We've got to leave before the HDA wears off. This is what we're going to do: we're going to go back to Morys, tell Melinda everything and tremble before the voice of Mortian justice. Listen, I believe we will not be denied. I believe that our justice system bears the fruit of compassion and understanding. I believe we will be exonerated and reinstated and free to continue our work in honour of our great friend and comrade who lies here..." He bowed his head and suppressed a sob.

Yukawa3, who had sprung to his feet, was flailing his arms around like a hellfire preacher warning of Armageddon. "Yes! Yes!" he yelled, tears streaming down his face. "I was about to say that! I was about to say that!"

The Mortian equivalent of a high-five was a head-butt. Suffice to say, there was a wild and frenzied exchange of head-butts between polkingbeal67 and yukawa3 before they took their final, grief-stricken leave of smolin9.

"Why can't we take him with us?" yukawa3 wailed. "At least he'd get a proper funeral with full state honours among his own people in his own community."

"Because he's not dead yet," polkingbeal67 reminded him

sombrely. "He wouldn't survive the HDA. Are you prepared to kill him?"

They looked at each other, aghast. The thunderstorm had abated a little, but the frequent flashes of lightning, combined with his partial metamorphosis, lent smolin9 an ethereal, luminous quality. The rain continued to lash down relentlessly. Then it became even heavier, gathering pace as the clouds careered across the sky. One last glance at their friend lying prostrate and helpless on the bed, at most a few hours from death, and they were gone, propelled through the vortex of space-time. There was a shrill protracted howl, like the banshee scream of an electric guitar outro. It could have been a rip in the fabric of space. It could have been the wind screeching through a crack in the ill-fitting window frame. It could have been a yell of anguish.

But all that had happened light years away on Earth. Back here on Morys Minor, polkingbeal67 now faced several dilemmas of his own making. Having failed to reveal the truth, he had, to all intents and purposes, abandoned yukawa3, not only to face the full force of the law on his own, but also to face the realisation that his mentor had betrayed him. Actually, yukawa3 had not yet figured out the betrayal - his mind had become fogged with confusion and disorientation. Rational thought was beyond him, much to the consternation of his defence counsel.

Having held a preliminary hearing on the planet Veritas, the ICJAC determined that the case against yukawa3 should proceed to trial. Charges against the Mortian leader had been dropped on the basis that he could not possibly have issued an order to destroy Niffis (or, come to that, any other intelligible command). Polkingbeal67 was presumed dead. No further delays would be tolerated.

An intergalactic jury was convened on Morys and the first

day of trial was in full swing in the presidential grand chamber. The Mortian leader attempted to throw a curveball, declaring the proceedings erroneous and void on a technicality. He argued that Morys Minor was no longer the planet's name and that the trial should therefore be adjourned until the paperwork could be amended to reflect this. Unfortunately, Melinda had not got around to endowing the planet with a new moniker and the leader's objection was dismissed out of hand.

Yukawa3 did not contest the facts of the charges against him. There were eye-witnesses (Muqu rebels were in court to submit their evidence) and compelling forensic testimony along with circumstantial evidence such as the discovery of a crumpled yellow sou'wester at the scene of the crime. The key element in the case hinged on the question of intent. In allegations of genocide, this had always been a controversial issue. Certainly, yukawa3 did not endear himself to the Court when he turned on the chilloks who were lined up behind a myrmecam in the witness box and told them, rather threateningly, that they should remember with gratitude how, as a child, he had probably shared many picnics with them. His prospects took another turn for the worse when nipkow4 felt compelled, under oath, to tell the prosecuting counsel that during MMBC's coverage of the Niffis crisis, yukawa3 had, on more than one occasion, referred to chilloks as ants and had proposed using insecticide to resolve the conflict.

Sitting in the court, absorbed in the proceedings, polkingbeal67 realised that damage limitation was the only viable strategy. He would have to come up with a massive counterbalancing factor that would show the hapless cadet in a new, different and favourable light - an example of yukawa3's behaviour that would be universally hailed as noble and humanitarian, an act of ethical altruism.

He took a break from observing the trial and wandered around the presidential gardens, deeply engrossed in puzzling out the problem. Then he stopped and gazed at the rusty, battered car chassis and the parabolic dish antenna half-buried amongst the ponds and fountains. Dear reader, if you had two planets, one named Morys Minor and the other Earth, which one would you think would value old classic vehicles the most? You would be wrong. On Morys Minor, abducted vehicles of all types, including Voyager 1 and a Morris Minor two-door saloon, were abandoned and left to decay under the elements.

Tapping the Voyager antenna as if expecting it to ring or start blaring out a fatuous and bombastic message from Earth, polkingbeal67 grinned a bigger grin than anyone would think him capable of. The solution to the problem had hit him like a keg of vitalmados. "This is going to be good," he said to himself. "This is going to be *very* good. It'll be the most dramatic mitigation anyone could possibly think of! And no one anywhere gets hurt or scared or anything! Ha ha! I don't think there'll be too many complaints from those earthlings about having better things to do - not this time!" He was gone from the courtroom for the rest of the day.

Yukawa3 was back in his detention pod after the day's proceedings when he received an unexpected visit from Melinda, who had pulled rank to obtain a confidential interview with the accused. Having more time on her hands following the leader's return and feeling depressed about polkingbeal67's supposed demise (her mood ring had turned decidedly grey), she had taken up painting as a hobby and had brought some examples of her work to show the prisoner in the hope that he might appreciate some diversion. Her ulterior motive was to discover a bit more about what had happened back on Earth.

"What's this one?" yukawa3 asked, studying one of the canvasses.

Melinda grimaced slightly. "It's a self-portrait."

Yukawa3 looked at it obliquely. "Of who?" he inquired.

Melinda thought there was something ironic about this. She had in fact been suffering a bit of an identity crisis, made worse by her perception that smolin9 had changed since his return from Earth (we, of course, are privy to the reason for this).

When yukawa3 responded to her tentative enquiries about polkingbeal67's tragic death by insisting his mentor was very much alive and had been sitting among them in the courtroom that very day, Melinda began to fear for the poor cadet's mental stability. She resolved to speak to the judge about it immediately. Then she left with her paintings.

The following day, it was clear that Melinda's intervention had borne fruit. The prosecution counsel was instructed that new information made the case against yukawa3 untenable pending psychiatric evaluation. Attention switched to polkingbeal67 and *his* complicity in the Niffis massacre (on Morys Minor, people were routinely tried posthumously). When yukawa3 was called to the stand as a witness to answer some routine, factual questions about his mentor's movements on the day in question, he caused a stir by pointing to the figure he knew as polkingbeal67 and saying, "Well, there he is! Why don't you ask him?" The judge took pity on him and told him to stand down and rest for a few hours.

It was late in the afternoon when long, accusing fingers of sunlight streamed through the windows and Melinda took the stand to deliver a character reference. "Your honour," she said in a voice already choked with emotion. "I know polkingbeal67 was already loved and respected here as a war hero and I don't need to point out his achievements in that respect. Literally. I just want to tell you why he was so absolutely mythical to me too. As you may know, polkingbeal67, who I think of as just a lovable big old bear, donated his own Mortian heart to me when he saw how upset I was about not being able to return to my home planet." Actually, as we know, the whole thing had been a complete mistake, because the heart transfer had taken place when polkingbeal67, largely oblivious to Melinda's plight, had been under the impression he was to receive a new eyeball to replace the one he had lost in the battle of Hat Signs. "Anyway," Melinda continued, wiping a tear from her eye, "there simply aren't enough thankyous in the universe to express how I feel about what he did for me. Literally."

Squirming under one of the fingers of sunlight, polkingbeal67 was beginning to feel utterly wretched.

Melinda went on. "If you could read my energy, you'd know how close I felt to him. And still do. He was, y'know, very supportive when smolin9 and I got married." Actually, polkingbeal67 had described their relationship as a preposterous screwball abomination and he had tried everything in his power to discourage it. "So many great memories! Obviously he had a fearless and sometimes impulsive nature and this was never more apparent than when he crawled through the sewage pipes to rescue me, smolin9 and yukawa3 during the unfortunate incident at nefeshchaya. There he was brandishing his plasma rifle thing, all covered in sludge and slime and scraps of tissue. Totally erratic! He was heroic and, er, very smelly! Oh and, boy, could he do a great impression of Winston Churchill!" Recalling polkingbeal67 growling monotonously through the celebrated 'fight them on the beaches' speech, staggering around and munching on a rolled-up sou'wester, she changed her mind. "Well, no, actually he couldn't, but no one's perfect are they? Anyway, what I'm saying is that polkingbeal67 wasn't just the tough guy he liked to appear as. I know he... well, I've described him myself as being a bit like a gorilla on amphetamines and, yes, he was strong and fierce and all that, but that was all on the exterior. Most people are nice enough if you try to really see them. As for polkingbeal67 - here was someone who loved guns and had fought in many wars and yet he was the most compassionate person who ever lived. On the inside, he literally had the softest heart I've ever known. And I should know, because I've got that heart now and it's turning to mush..." She broke off to cover her face as the tears started to flow. "I'm not going to cry!" she promised, striving to smile. "He was a very special person and part of me, my heart, believes he hasn't gone away at all!" The entire courtroom choked back a sob.

Towards the back, still singled out by one of those accusing fingers of light, polkingbeal67 had broken down and was weeping openly. "I'm sorry!" he wailed, staggering to his feet. "I'm sorry! I'm so sorry! It's me, polkingbeal67! I'm here, and I've got a confession to make to you all!"

.   .   .

Melinda sat under a sprawling invercresco tree. One of the strangest plants on Morys Minor, it looked like it had been uprooted and replanted upside down, its tangled root-like branches clawing feebly at the sky. It soaked up precious moisture from methane mists and produced fruit in the form of large green husks containing inky black fluid used in the production of synthetic building materials. Beyond the tree, undulating plains, punctuated by boulders, methane swamps and clusters of habitation pods, stretched towards the horizon under a pastel pink and blue sky. As she contemplated the web-like tracery of the tree's shadow, Melinda fingered her mood ring and waited for the suns to complete their lazy descents. Grieving for smolin9, her coping mechanism consisted of wandering off alone to sit and watch the remarkable twin sunsets. She beheld a planet of conflicts and contradictions, an enigmatic world of bizarreness and serenity. It was dull but romantic, desolate and yet rich with a unique, haunting beauty. "It's certainly not Weston-Super-Mare," she thought, "Literally." Having struggled to adapt to Morys Minor at first, she now held it very close to her heart. As she meditated silently, her eyes closed for a while, and when they opened again she knew she was looking at a planet that would henceforward be known as Smolin9.

Back on her home planet, her husband's body was lying on a steel rack in a Bristol mortuary, under scrutiny by baffled intelligence agents, who had so far failed to establish any link with the sensational international news story that had gripped the world in the last few days - the staggering reappearance of NASA's Voyager 1 space probe on the south lawn of the White House. Polkingbeal67's inspired notion of teleporting the probe to the very doorstep of the President of the United States had had exactly the desired effect - the bumbling, insular earthlings, without being subjected to any kind of scary ordeal, now knew, beyond any possibility of doubt, that they were part of a wider intergalactic community. This was hailed by the ICJAC (and many other intergalactic bodies and organisations) as a watershed moment for broader humanity. Furthermore, there could be no doubt where the credit for the masterly exploit belonged, for, attached to the outside of the probe, in place of the golden record, was one of yukawa3's golden yellow sou'westers.

No one could blame the police for missing the connection

between the return of Voyager 1 and the discovery of the mysteriously mutated body of a waitress found in a guest house in south west England. Certainly, no one could blame them for failing to realise that the strange device they had confiscated and stored in a top-secret vault was a Mortian biomimetic mutator. What *is* strange, however, is that the Mortians themselves did not realise the mutator contained a viable transferable copy of smolin9's Karma 5.

6

THE ANSWER IS ... A
PENGUIN

The air was tranquil. As yukawa3 arrived at the medical pod, a procession of meagre grey and yellow clouds were drifting slowly and solemnly across the sky like sacrificial smoke in an old watercolour painting. The sound of a space cruiser manoeuvring overhead triggered a sudden flash of deja vu that left him staring blankly into space for a moment.

Since the trial, he had experienced such episodes quite frequently. It was as if reality was fusing in some way with a dream or a memory and he would feel slightly nauseous and disoriented. Actually, if anyone were to press him to describe the queasiness, which they did not, he would have said it was more a sickness of the heart than the stomach. Apparently, no such elucidation was required - according to the senior medibot, these were simply petit mal seizures consistent with epilepsy. Although Mortians generally enjoyed long, healthy, disease-free lives, hippocampal glitches were as common as intermittent crashes and freezes on an earthling computer. And just like an earthling computer, the solution was invariably a quick-fix reboot. The neurological circuitry of the Mortian hippocampus could effectively be 'reset' by means of a quick zap from a medibot's molecoil pen.

The senior medibot, similar in appearance to a Mortian humanoid but lacking in facial expressions and a little random in eye and lip movements, swivelled around to face yukawa3 and spoke to him in a steady, nearly monotonous voice: "You've come for your reset?"

Yukawa3 sat tentatively on the edge of the examination table. "Well, yes," he said, "The problem is this deja vu thing I keep getting."

"That's right. You told me yesterday," said the medibot in a pinched, quavering tone that culminated in a suppressed chortle, suggesting that the joke had been intentional.

Yukawa3, who really should have seen that coming, wondered aloud who had been responsible for the absurd notion of configuring androids with a sense of humour. With a frown of irritation, he went on. "It's like... Something sets it off and I feel all kind of fuzzy, then I get this really strange, scary feeling and my chest feels tight and my body feels sort of feeble. Sometimes it's intense and sometimes it's not. Sometimes it's frequent. Sometimes it's not. I think the answer is..." The senior medibot cocked his head in sceptical curiosity, waiting for yukawa3 to continue. "And I think what the answer is..."

the cadet prattled on. "No, okay, I don't know what the answer is. I thought it would come to me while I was talking but it didn't. So, anyway..." At this point, the molecoil discharged its energy and yukawa3 was rendered momentarily speechless and senseless, his eyes wide open but no one at home (in truth, his expression barely changed at all, making it difficult for the medibot to recognise the moment when his patient's brain returned to normal functionality).

Periodically, the medibot's voice droned, "Is your brain functioning? Can you hear me yet?"

After a few minutes of dumb stares, yukawa3's voice suddenly let rip, "No! It's not working! What's happened? I don't think I'm going to make it! Do something!"

Recognising yukawa3's preposterous panic attack as a return to normal behaviour, the medibot replied in a pinched, quavering tone that culminated in a suppressed chortle, "Don't worry, I can assure you that as long as you're a patient here, the last thing you're going to do is die."

As he left the medical pod and crossed the cruiser park towards the avenue of trees marking the border between the civic area and the thinly scattered dwelling pods, yukawa3 felt himself sinking into melancholy. He saw sadness in everything. Whether it was the sombre hue of the sky or the drooping fruit of the inverted invercresco trees or the grimy, sparse arrangement of the residential precinct, everything seemed to reinforce the persistent echoes of smolin9's death that had plagued him ever since his return to Morys Minor (now known as 'Smolin9'). Gazing forlornly at the sky, he felt irresistibly drawn to smolin9's final resting place on Earth, so much so that while he was making up his mind to return there at the first opportunity, he failed to notice the mother of all methane rainstorms approaching from the west and got thoroughly drenched.

It was not a good time to be without one of his cherished yellow sou'westers, but he was going to have to get used to that. At the Niffis massacre trial, the President of the Intergalactic Court of Justice, Arbitration and Conciliation had acquitted yukawa3 with the proviso that the ruling should not be taken as a precedent, that the accused should continue to initiate judicious contact with alien species such as earthlings and that he should make a personal sacrifice as a symbolic gesture of atonement. Yukawa3 had been delighted with the verdict until he learned that the sacrifice would entail the loss of his collection of earthling sou'westers. As he arrived at his dwelling pod, soaking wet and shivering, he was greeted by three court officials specially appointed to supervise the sou'wester disposal. One of these, a gangling saurian from Permia, sputtered and gargled like a cat coughing up a fur ball. Yukawa3 stared blankly and then realised he had been asked something.

"Are you ready?" the saurian repeated. The words seemed to linger in the air as yukawa3 attempted to discern some shred of meaning in them.

"Are you the pest control people?" yukawa3 enquired. He had recently noticed damage to insulation in the walls and ceilings of his pod and suspected an infestation of pod rats. Having referred the matter to his domain conclave, he had been expecting a visit from the exterminators.

"Can we go in and get your hats?" asked the saurian.

By now, yukawa3 was making some sense of the garbled noise issuing from the saurian's mouth and concluded that he had asked about the rats. "Yeh," he said, making a sweeping gesture of his arm. "Go ahead. Feel free. Search everywhere and find as many as you can."

The rain had stopped and yukawa3 waited outside while his pod was turned upside down and every corner scrutinised. A short while later, the three officials reappeared, their arms laden with yellow sou'westers, including the ones yukawa3 had concealed so ingeniously in various nooks and crannies. A look of utter dismay and consternation flashed across his features and his face dropped like a sack of potatoes. Noticing this, the saurian gurgled, "It must be done. This is your symbolic sacrifice."

As the officials started to incinerate the hats and an acrid smell forced them to retreat, yukawa3 hopped around in agitation. "Wait!" he wailed. "Why don't we use *symbolic* hats?"

The incident only served to intensify yukawa3's desire to return to Earth. It represented the opportunity of a transformative experience through which he might be able to lose himself for a while and become immersed in an alternative life. As the primary sunset cast its pale purple glow onto the wall beside him, he sat with his microwocky and began the process of devising a new earthling identity using the computer's interactive voice response technology. "I've got a question for you," he announced.

The microwocky purred slightly and replied, "What is the question?"

The standard phase one microwocky was a product of advanced Mortian microplasma and nanomanufacturing technology, striking not only for its bewildering shape-shifting appearance but also for its ability to facilitate holographic telepresence. It provided real-time translations of nearly all languages and dialects, the one known exception being the strange phraseology adopted by chilloks (a myrmecam was required to communicate with this species). Boasting a myriad of sophisticated tools and applications such as insect zapping, muting all sound within a specific radius and calculating the time to your next bowel movement, the microwocky could even be configured to act as a tunnel node for the purpose of wormhole communication and travel. Users could swipe, rub, prod, poke, flick and push the surface of the device to initiate the desired functions.

According to the developers, the latest beta version could emulate the brains of other Mortian (and some non-Mortian) organisms, but pre-sales had plummeted amid mounting rumours that the new functionality did not work and was actually nothing more than a scam. According to some reports, the developers could only get the software to compile by rendering every line of code inactive. On one occasion, they tried to get a microwocky to emulate an earthling dog - everything went well until it detected incoming mail, whereupon it leaped at the developer and fastened itself to his leg.

Nevertheless, the standard phase one was an indispensable piece of Mortian time-travelling kit. Having been programmed with both rational and simulated emotional responses, it appeared to exhibit an uncanny level of true artificial intelligence - it complained when it got lonely, enjoyed conversations and loved to share jokes.

Sophisticated as they assuredly were, microwockys were not universally appreciated by their owners. On one particular visit to Earth, for example, yukawa3's mentor, polkingbeal67, had stood on a mountain gazing at a dark cloud in the distance and the conversation between him and his 'wocky went something like this:

polkingbeal67: How far away is that storm?

microwocky: Which storm?

polkingbeal67: The huge one there in the distance.

microwocky: Oh, that one.

polkingbeal67: Well? How far can we see?

microwocky: 150 million earthling kilometres.

Convinced that the device was malfunctioning, polkingbeal67 tossed it from the mountain, quite unaware that the hapless contraption had correctly calculated the distance from the mountain to the sun, where a solar storm had indeed been raging furiously.

Yukawa3's microwocky purred again and repeated, "What is the question?"

"I'm going to apply for a new assignment on the Pale Blue Dot," said yukawa3. "How should I present myself on the planet?"

The microwocky prompted him for the mission parameters. Yukawa3 scratched his head and thought long and hard about this. The way he was feeling about life at that moment, he was likely to be away for some time, so he wanted to be sure the mission was one he would be really comfortable with. "Okay, let me see," he mumbled. "I don't want anything complex. Let's keep it simple."

"The word 'simple' requires clarification," the microwocky intoned in its flat staccato voice. "Do you mean half-witted? Moronic?"

Yukawa3 shook his head. "No, no! Well, kind of. I mean simple as in uncomplicated. Black and white." He tried as hard as he could to stipulate more parameters, but his nasty experience with the City of Niffis meant he became a bit fixated with the means of travel. He wanted to be transported by wormhole because he still felt nervous about another crack at conventional space travel. "So, yeh, simple, black and white," he went on. "It should involve no flying. Got that? No flying!" Before pressing the GO button in confirmation, he suddenly remembered his favourite earthling activity and added, "Plenty of fishing! I want to catch fish!"

"Mission parameters complete," droned the microwocky. "Processing your question..."

Yukawa3 fretted impatiently. "Yes?" he blurted out. "Well? What's the answer?"

The microwocky purred. "The answer is..." It paused for a moment as if a trace of self-doubt had flickered across its mysterious circuitry. "The answer is a penguin."

.   .   .

If yukawa3 was finding it difficult to adjust to the post-Niffis, post-smolin9, post-trial dynamic, it was like nothing compared to the meltdown suffered by his mentor, polkingbeal67, following his dramatic and humiliating courtroom confession. The former Mortian war hero had not suffered such an indignity since the early days of the Jatron wars.

That was back in the heady days of intergalactic imperialism, before the evolution of the neoliberal cosmic philosophy advocated and championed by the current Mortian premier. Before he lost it in the battle of Hat Signs, polkingbeal67 had had his eye firmly set on military glory and conquest. However, while leading guerrilla troops in battles against General Vog's invading Trox army at Ybesan, he had not been averse to a little sport when the opportunity arose. And it arose one day at the beginning of the orbis bird shooting season when his regiment had been withdrawn to a reserve position where wounds were licked and lessons learned for the future following a long and bloody assault on an enemy stronghold. In those days, the beakless orbis bird had been one of the most ubiquitous species on the planet and its habit of plunging down onto a dwelling pod and rolling down the roof so that its feathers could absorb vital nutrients had driven Mortians to distraction. Given that the orbis bird population densities often reached nuisance levels, shooting them had been considered both expedient and necessary. In fact, if the leader had not insisted on protecting the birds during the nesting season, the hunting would have continued all year round.

Anyway, the shooting season had got under way and polkingbeal67 had offered six shergs to the first soldier in his troop to down an orbis bird. As they had stalked through the marshlands south of Ybesan, a covey of birds had sprung up and polkingbeal67 had blazed away with his large bore laser rifle. Disappointed at missing them, he had failed to notice at first that a couple of Trox soldiers had emerged from the marsh grass with their hands raised in surrender. When it later emerged that one of the soldiers was General Vog himself, polkingbeal67 had been feted as a hero. He had been promoted to the rank of supreme commander and a statue erected in his honour. Later, when the regiment had suffered an outbreak of disaffection and the truth had leaked out, his reputation had been so secure that many had refused to trust the new account of events. Nevertheless, he died a little inside every time he was subjected to anything approaching good-natured ridicule about the incident.

Now, at the start of the fourteenth baktun, he was aware once more of the very same tiny punctures in his self-esteem, not enough to cause lasting damage, but perfectly sufficient to cow him into silence and inertia. Having foolishly misled everyone except yukawa3 into believing he was smolin9, he had betrayed not only Melinda and all his fellow Mortians, but also the memory of his dear departed friend and comrade. Awaiting sentence for his role in the Niffis massacre, he spent the days wallowing in caged despondency. He was not literally caged of course, but he was not at liberty to leave the planet or disclose his feelings about the case.

Sometimes the fallout from a rhetorical volley can be at least as devastating as a shower of physical missiles. Pointed bullets and pointed speeches. Both have their uses. The trick is knowing when to use which. Melinda's courtroom eulogy had brought polkingbeal67 to his knees more effectively than any weapon he had ever faced and it had forced him to re-evaluate his career, his life and his beliefs. It was more than a little strange, then, that he barely looked up when she came to visit him the day before the sentencing.

After exchanging awkward greetings, Melinda asked him if he had heard the rumour about someone negotiating an unauthorised wormhole transit to Earth.

"Yes, I heard," polkingbeal67 mumbled.

Melinda was not in the mood to spin this out. "It was yukawa3, wasn't it?"

"Why yukawa3? It could have been anyone."

Melinda sighed. "Are you covering for him because you feel guilty? Because you let him down at the trial? Listen, you know as well as I do, yukawa3 could do a lot of, y'know, damage wandering around Earth on his own, unsupervised. Literally."

"Damage? What sort of damage?"

"Anything could happen. He could, y'know, get himself hurt. You know what he's like. He's not the sharpest knife in the drawer, is he? Literally."

"Oh, actually, I think he'll be in good company on the Blue Dot," said polkingbeal67, shutting his eyes tight and opening his mouth in a silent shriek of laughter. He was still not in control of his new physical appearance, but the universal consternation about yukawa3's welfare amused him in a perverse sort of way.

Melinda stared at him, baffled by his strange facial expression. "What are you saying?"

"Well, the fact is, earthlings are..."

"I don't care what the facts are," Melinda snapped. She was not prepared to listen to another one of his disdainful put-downs directed toward her own species. "The point is, how do we get him back?"

"That's not the question we should be asking." As far as polkingbeal67 was concerned, the immediate priority was to repair tarnished reputations. He may have been primarily concerned about his own authority, but he was not so self-obsessed that he did not shudder a little at the harm inflicted on the Mortian leader and to yukawa3 and to the planet itself. The adverse publicity surrounding the Niffis fiasco would eventually fade into the recesses of people's memories, but the process would be a long and ugly drawn-out one, unless there was some way someone could engineer a momentous shift in the collective consciousness of the intergalactic community. It was time for a real leader to sweep away trivial distractions and grasp the historical moment offered by the downturn in Mortian fortunes. In short, it was time for a reborn polkingbeal67 to emerge from the shadows, shimmering with gravitas and moral conviction, looking majestic in a new battle helmet, ready to lead his followers in the fight against, well, anything really. And he was now suddenly convinced that this, beyond any doubt, was the answer.

Melinda punched him. She had been watching him run through a whole range of bizarre facial contortions and grimaces and had become spooked by it. "Stop doing that!" she demanded. "Well? What is the question we should be asking?"

"I don't know," he said, wincing from the blow to the ribs. "I'm not... I mean, I've seen the future and I know the answer - I'm just not sure about the question yet."

When she got back to the palace to provide feedback from the interview, she found the Mortian leader engaged in the serious business of determining what Mortians should be called now that the planet had acquired its new name. His minions had proposed 'smoles', 'smolls' and 'smolin-niners', but the leader was unhappy with all the suggestions. Reeking like a fishmonger's stall on a hot day, he paced up and down, mumbling to himself, "Where, oh where is the sweet fruit of my bitter patience?"

Another suggestion was made, "What about 'smolinetians'?"

Melinda let out a snort of laughter which she tried to disguise as a cough. Conscious of several sets of eyes fixed on her, she made an apologetic gesture with her hands and said, "Well, I see you're making good progress with this. Literally. Maybe I should come back later?"

One of the minions stood up abruptly and shouted, "'Smolers'!"

Melinda could not help herself and laughed out loud. "It was yukawa3!" she declared quickly to deflect attention from her lapse of reverence. "It was yukawa3 who did the wormhole transit thing to Earth, er, the Bright Blue Dot, er, Pale Blue Dot. It was yukawa3."

The leader dismissed the minions with a peremptory swish of seaweed. Sitting down cross-legged next to Melinda, he closed his eyes and reached outwards. "Everything happens for a reason," he said, nodding lugubriously. "When you look down, all you see is dirt, so you must keep looking up. How is polkingbeal67?"

Breathing through her mouth to avoid the noxious odour, Melinda expressed her reservations about polkingbeal67's mental health. As she went on, she noticed the leader was starting to sway from side to side. "Do you people ever get depressed, y'know, in a clinical sense? I mean, you're obviously very advanced people, but things must go wrong with your brains sometimes, don't they?"

The leader stopped swaying for a moment. "Well," he said. "It's possible. No man is a good doctor who has never been sick himself. But I've never encountered it personally. You should speak to an expert. But wait, I think I sometimes forget things. Does that count?"

Melinda turned to him. "Really? Like what? Give me some examples."

"I can't remember any," he said, resuming his rhythmical swaying. "You think polkingbeal67 needs clinical treatment? How terrible!"

"You needn't upset yourself, your reveredness," she said. "I'm sure he'll be okay. He's the type of person who will make lemonade when life gives him lemons. Literally. But he says he has an answer without a question and he ..."

The leader interrupted her. "There are no right answers to wrong questions, or missing questions. Tell me more about this lemonade. Is it earthling medicine?"

"Well, no, but actually, yes. I mean, lemons have natural healing power. They kind of clean the liver and promote immunity and fight infection. They're good for you, no doubt about that. You should try some, your reveredness. But I think we're getting off the track a bit here. Literally."

"Has polkingbeal67 been taking lemonade?"

"I don't know what he's been taking, but whatever it is, it's either too strong or not strong enough," Melinda replied.

. . .

Well into his twilight years at this point, the Mortian leader was believed to have been abducted from an alien planet approximately two thousand earth years ago. This is disputed by most Mortians (and the leader himself), but official records show that he had 'arrived' on Morys Minor, by some means or other, on the Mortian date of 7.19.8.7.10.

After graduating from altoludus, he had been immediately appointed supreme commander of the Mortian Imperial Army, despite a lamentable lack of military training and experience. Clearly being groomed for leadership, he had succeeded joking mil only a few days before the latter's unfortunate demise at the hands of goopmutt bandits who had mistaken him for a plasma tag referee who had recently upset them. Initially out of favour with senior figures in the military for being effeminate and writing poems about ocean landscapes, the new leader had gradually wrought himself into the affections of the Mortian people with his venerable appearance and pious demeanour. He had no name as such and was referred to

278

simply as 'our revered leader'. Although Mortians had nostrils, they did not have definable noses as such. Their leader, however, boasted a very prominent proboscis which had never been explained and which was politely and unfailingly ignored by everyone who came into contact with him.

The enduring legacy of his prosperous reign was assured across the entire galaxy owing to the dramatic expansion of the Mortian space programme. During his tenure, by means of everything from the early cigar-shaped mother ships to the latest in traversable wormholes, explorers from Morys Minor had peered into the very darkest recesses of the known universe. But it could have all turned out very differently. In the early period of his leadership, he had commissioned, at great expense, an exploratory project to study various planets in the constellation of Tense Minor. A number of probes had been launched and they all blew up before they had even left Mortian atmosphere. When news of the fiasco leaked out, the leader managed to salvage his reputation by outrageously claiming the explosions had been successful missile weapon tests!

In recent years, his leadership had lapsed into inertia and his role as oracle and guiding force had diminished to the point where he could only regurgitate the contents of Chinese fortune cookies abducted from Earth. Recognisable by the seaweed garlands hanging around his neck and the sickly, heavy odour of rancid oils and aromatics, he nevertheless continued to appear at carefully selected public functions and intergalactic conferences and events. No longer required to sit on the more prestigious intergalactic courts, it would be fair to say that his function was now largely confined to ceremonial duties. Despite this, he continued to command universal respect for his apparent sagacity and unimpeachable integrity. Amid failing health and a paucity of fortune cookies, he had devoted the last part of his life to grooming Melinda as his heir apparent.

When news of the Niffis massacre first broke on Morys Minor, its impact on the leader's reputation had been devastating, not least because he had been playing host to a delegation of chillok Muqu rebels seeking intergalactic condemnation of Naaffab atrocities. Berated by the chilloks for failing to apprehend polkingbeal67 and yukawa3 at the outset, he became the object of almost universal vilification for his ill-advised decision to send smolin9 in fruitless pursuit of the two fugitives. Charges of negligence, incompetence and corruption had been levelled against him and had only been dropped when the Intergalactic Court of Justice, Arbitration and Conciliation ruled that he did not appear competent enough to have issued *any* plausibly intelligible commands to his subordinates.

So, when polkingbeal67's escape to Earth became public knowledge just a few hours before his sentencing hearing was scheduled to start, it came as no real surprise that the Mortian leader locked himself away in his privy chamber with orders that he was not to be disturbed on any account. It was the second unauthorised wormhole transit to Earth in two days, a serious security breach worthy, in itself, of the strongest intergalactic condemnation, but the most unpalatable aspect of this otherwise farcical gaffe is that it involved the same two culprits once again. Polkingbeal67, in particular, had shredded what little credibility the Mortian administration had left. It was difficult to see how the leader, now reduced to a gibbering wreck, could ever recover from such a blow.

Melinda, only too aware that the Intergalactic Court was enraged by these developments, remonstrated with him using one of his personal attendants as a conduit. She prevailed upon him to take up the mantle of leadership once more and guide his devastated people to the right path, but it made as much impression as an ant stomping on a rug. Her attempts to lure him out with seaweed and fortune cookies failed dismally. So finally, frustrated and impatient, she pushed past the attendant and hammered on the thick, heavy door of the inner sanctum. "This is a crisis and you need to man up and sort things out!" she yelled. "Now! Literally!" There was no sound from the other side of the door, so she hammered again and shouted, "Are you going to come out?"

A scrap of oil-stained paper emerged from under the door and fluttered slightly in the draught. Melinda picked it up. "No," it read.

"Why not?" she shouted. "What's wrong with you?"

A short pause and then another piece of paper appeared. "I just need a bit of 'me' time," was scribed in shaky, hurried handwriting.

"This is ridiculous," Melinda muttered to herself before hollering at the door, "Listen to me! This is not the behaviour one expects of a planetary leader! Do you hear me? You are not acting like a leader!"

In a few seconds, she snatched up the next piece of paper which read, "The man on the top of the mountain did not fall there."

"If he doesn't shape up, I swear I'm going to literally push him down his blessed mountain," Melinda thought, before shouting at the door again, "You're the leader of your people and they want to look up to you! Now come out here and listen to what your people are saying! Get your ears to the ground! Literally. Don't you want your people to look up to you?"

.   .   .

It was not easy being a penguin. Yukawa3 felt like a fish out of water (or sometimes in the water), dressed in a tuxedo and waddling about in totally naff footwear. The first problem he encountered was coping with those stiff, flipper-like wings and the difficulty of carrying a microwocky and a biomimetic mutator at the same time. He simply had to have the microwocky with him, so he buried the mutator in the snow, using his beak to mark the spot with a large cross.

There had been no extensive Mortian research into the lives and habits of earthling penguins. Antarctic exploration had been confined to one low-profile mission by smolin9: officially, he had abandoned his investigation owing to extreme weather conditions, but actually he had got fed up after trudging around for a couple of hours finding nothing but walls of blue-white ice and a few penguins doing nothing but huddle together.

As yukawa3 completed his cross, one of the king penguins, a female known as Peppermint, waddled over, cocked her head and said, "What are you doing? Me and Mothballs noticed you burying something there. What is it?"

Yukawa3 made a twitchy gesture with his wing. "Oh, it's nothing," he lied. "You know, just putting some fish in the freezer for later."

"Oh," said Peppermint. "Why don't you just eat it? Wanna share? Wanna huddle?"

Yukawa3 was astonished at how forward these creatures were. "Well I..." he mumbled as Peppermint drew closer, so much closer that they were almost touching each other.

"Maybe later. I'm new around here and I..."

Peppermint puffed up her feathers a little. "It's cold," she breathed. "Just huddle!"

"Oh my word!" yukawa3 exclaimed. "Oh, that's close..." He flinched slightly as Peppermint opened her beak. He could feel her breath on the side of his face. "Oh my word!" he said. "I guess I've got to get used to these things... Oh, that's very cosy. So much for personal space, eh? If you think that's close... well it is." Before he knew it, Mothballs, Lemon, Musky, Floral and a few others had joined in and he was in the centre of a tight cluster of penguins sharing their body heat. Questions tumbled around in yukawa3's head like socks in a washing machine. "What the hell is going on?" was one of them. Others included: "What am I expected to do? Why are they crowding me like this? Are they friendly or is some other thing going on?" As the temperature increased, more questions arrived, damp and deformed from the spin cycle, sometimes tangled together and other times drifting apart. "Why are they rubbing out my cross? What if I can't find my mutator? Are they expecting me to say something? Is this some kind of initiation ceremony? How do I get out of here?" His heart was racing and his throat was getting tight, the way he felt when he was about to have a panic attack. With a howl of desperation, he lowered his head and bulldozed his way out of the huddle. Tottering quickly away with his wings jerking rhythmically, he looked like a cheap clockwork toy about to wind down, and he was well clear of the group before he stopped and turned round to survey the situation.

Peppermint was padding towards him. He knew it was Peppermint because the wind was blowing from behind her and he caught a whiff of her body odour which was redolent of, well, peppermint. There were flecks of snow in the air and, for the first time, yukawa3 noticed the water-sculpted ice cave on the horizon. Aware, again for the first time, of the mystical, breath-taking, expansive beauty of the scene, he let down his guard a little. Impressed that this warm-hearted little creature appeared to have singled him out for special attention, he tried to smile and then realised, again for the first time, that bird beaks cannot change their form or length, so he fluffed up his feathers and shuffled towards her. Then he stopped and pulled himself together. He had known well enough that mutating into a non-humanoid life form was strictly prohibited by the Mortian authorities and he had heard the portentous warnings about the possible consequences. But yukawa3 considered himself wise enough and level-headed enough to cope with any complications a few dumb penguins might present. He recognised the danger of sentimental anthropomorphism and tried to maintain his cool and detached exterior (not that he could do anything about his exterior anyway).

Peppermint looked him in the eye. "Look, it's difficult meeting someone new," she said. "Sometimes their behaviour strikes you as bizarre, a bit weird, a bit, you know, freaky..."

"You're not freaky," yukawa3 assured her. "Just unexpectedly friendly."

"I was talking about you, you twerp!" Peppermint snapped. "You're the one that's strange! Listen, we huddle to keep ourselves warm. It's minus twenty degrees and these blinding, shrieking katabatic winds reach nearly two hundred miles an hour! It's how we stay alive, for god's sake!" She softened her tone to add, "So, you wanna huddle?"

The line between the grey-white sky and the grey-white ice was blurred and out of focus and yukawa3 felt like he was floating. His head was swimming. As they huddled together in the biting wind, he began to tell Peppermint everything about himself. It did not take too long, partly because there was considerably less to tell than he imagined, and partly because Peppermint made it obvious that she only understood a tiny fraction of what he was saying.

"So, are you saying you're not really a penguin and you don't have any parents?" Peppermint enquired with a look of incredulous scorn. "Yeah, right."

"It's true," yukawa3 assured her. "I don't have parents but I have a mentor called polkingbeal67. I chose to be a penguin, but, within reason, I can be anything I like." Failing to notice Peppermint slowly backing away from him, he continued, "Which is strange when I think back. My mentor, you see, always told me if I put my mind to it I could achieve anything I wanted. The sky was the limit, he said. Well, I was really upset since I wanted to be an intergalactic explorer! So, the way I see it, life is as confusing as a..." A flurry of snow clouded his sight as he struggled to think of a suitable analogy. "...as confusing as a difficult puzzle," was all he could manage. Peppermint was gone, and so, incidentally, was the cross marking the spot where yukawa3's mutator was buried.

.　　.　　.

His trip to Earth having been unauthorised and clandestine, polkingbeal67 had not been privy to much data relating to yukawa3's whereabouts. The wormhole travel console on his microwocky displayed both his own and yukawa3's trips to the Pale Blue Dot (Earth) but the usual supplementary information was unavailable. Unfortunately, this always applied in the case of unsanctioned travel. The trips were marked as being subject to mandatory recall, the home planet having requested the immediate return of the personnel concerned. In short, polkingbeal67 knew that yukawa3 was somewhere on the planet and that he had adopted the identity of a penguin, but he had no access to other crucial bits of information such as his precise location.

In normal circumstances, he would have been furious about yukawa3's breach of mutator protocol, but he figured the bizarre disguise would make it easier for him to track the fugitive down - how tough could it be to find a penguin in Glastonbury or Weston-Super-Mare? As far as polkingbeal67 was concerned, the unwritten rule of intergalactic travel was clear: if you make an unauthorised visit to a planet, unbeknown to your comrades, make it easy for them to find you by going to the place you last visited together. He made a mental note to himself to make it a *written* rule as soon as possible. Anyway, try as he might, he could find no trace of yukawa3 in South West England.

Having quickly obtained employment as an aquarist-in-training at Bristol Zoo, he spent a couple of days in a wet suit, cleaning up all the poop that the tank filters could not handle, while surreptitiously trying to identify which of the waddling poop-makers was yukawa3. The zoo had not realised they needed an aquarist-in-training until polkingbeal67 dazzled them with his microwocky-generated display of data relating to penguin genealogy along with records of food consumption, medical care, mating behaviour and moulting patterns. So impressed were they that they turned a blind eye when he approached each of the baffled birds with a yellow sou'wester and asked them if they wanted to try it on. The Rubicon was crossed, however, when he eventually found a penguin that tolerated his overtures and started berating the poor bird for not talking to him. One of the junior keepers and a few of the volunteer workers looked on aghast as polkingbeal67 followed the bird as it waddled blindly around the enclosure beneath the sou'wester and then subjected it to a bizarre interrogation during which the new aquarist-in-training was overheard saying, "Yukawa3! It's your mentor! It's me, polkingbeal67! Speak to me, you crazy prokaryote!"

The senior curator sighed as Simon Morry, aka polkingbeal67, limped dejectedly (the penguin had bitten him on the leg) through the gate and out of view. He had never had to terminate a probationary period quite that quickly before. "Poor chap," he murmured to no one in particular. "One of those brainboxes who could probably build his own internal combustion engine but would never pass a driving test. I feel for him. I really do."

"He was a bit wacky, wasn't he?" said one of the volunteers, a student called Neil, making a gesture with a finger against his temple.

"Well, Neil," said the senior curator, "I don't know about his mental state. The fact is, I couldn't take a chance on him, but I have to say I feel a bit sorry for him."

"I thought he was nuts! Did you hear him talking to that penguin? And what was going on with that hat?"

The senior curator got up to leave the office. "He was a very clever chap, actually," he said. "Just a bit overwrought perhaps. I don't think we could have done anything with him, but it makes you think. Yes, it certainly makes you think. We always have to remember, young Neil, especially in this job, that the way we treat creatures, human and non-human, is an index of our moral being."

When he had gone, Neil nudged the junior keeper sitting next to him and pulled a face. "Fluffy, bunny-hugging crap! I think our boss is just desperate to prove what a wonderful, caring human being he is."

The junior keeper grinned and put down his pen. "Whatever," he said. "Anyway, he sacked him, didn't he?"

Then it was just like the movies where the camera pans from one person to the other before zooming in on the momentous and prophetic words written on the junior keeper's pad... except that the words were: 'coffee, milk'.

As for polkingbeal67, aka Simon Morry, he was a little chastened by the experience, but not enough to stop him applying for positions at zoos in Torquay, Newquay and Paignton, the last of which did not even have any penguins. At the end of all this fruitless subterfuge, he felt like a spy who had come in from the cold, although of course the penguins of South West England had not had to adapt to particularly chilly conditions. Far from being discouraged, he sat on the beach at Weston-Super-Mare and took stock of the situation. The tide was far out, leaving a vast expanse of mud beyond the sand. Despite several notices warning of the danger of sinking sand, a small white dog ventured heedlessly towards the water's edge. A beach patrol vehicle passed several times, apparently looking for sinking people but not sinking dogs. Ignoring the distractions, polkingbeal67 focused on the matter at hand: where might he find yukawa3 (and did he even want to find him)? Blessed with a mind as sharp as the latest cutting edge computer gizmo (actually, in Mortian terms, it was more like an early Amstrad word processor with a perished disk drive belt, not to mention a spelling malfunction), he analysed, considered, evaluated, calculated and scrutinised all the available information and then gave up and consulted his microwocky instead.

The little white dog capered past him, now sporting a not very fetching set of brown socks. Its body language suggested it felt a little silly about its injudicious escapade.

Seconds later, the microwocky revealed its jaw-dropping capabilities by suggesting a trip to the Antarctic. Just as polkingbeal67 started to reflect on this, the marvellous little device went even further, plumbing the well of the blindingly obvious before recommending direct contact with yukawa3 via one of the microwocky's peer-to-peer communications channels. Polkingbeal67 slapped his forehead. Now he knew how the dog felt.

.   .   .

A microwocky is only as good as its capacity to function and yukawa3 was unable to make his device function properly with just a couple of stiff, flat, paddle-like wings and a beak at his disposal. He could not respond to calls because, like an earthling wearing oven mitts trying to operate a smartphone, he simply could not manage to prod, flick, swipe or rub the sophisticated gadget in a correct and timeous manner. Well, that, and he had blocked all incoming calls. Oh, and it was totally encased in ice and was about as much use as an inflatable dartboard.

Perhaps I should also mention that from the moment the Mortian authorities had rejected his application for an official assignment on the Pale Blue Dot, he had not given the tiniest seed of a thought to polkingbeal67 or anyone else from his home planet. He was, in fact, happy with life close to the frozen tip of Earth, huddling, trumpeting and foraging to his heart's content. Adjusting well to the social interaction and the general patterns and rhythm of life on the ice, he had mastered crucial techniques like the 'tripod', whereby penguins rock back and rest their entire weight on their heels and tail, reducing contact with the snow and ice. Of course, there had been one or two clumsy mishaps in the beginning, like a spectacular early attempt at the tripod when he had pirouetted about like a drunken waiter crossing a polished floor and ended up overbalancing and falling sideways on to the ice with a thump. But he had managed to turn this sort of thing to his advantage. Now, the entire penguin community of South Georgia Island was pirouetting around on the ice, theatrically flinging themselves sideways like salmon during the heroic upstream swim. They were all doing the 'yukawa3 tripod dance' and it was the biggest craze on the southwest side of South Georgia since the Great Huddle of 2010. They loved the dance and they loved him.

Peppermint, in particular, was enthusiastically assessing yukawa3's viability as a potential mate. One morning, tired of waiting for him to take the initiative, she went up to him, rubbed her bill against his and instructed him in the art of penguin seduction. "Come on, she said, huskily. "Hold your flippers out and point your bill up high."

"No," said yukawa3, believing it was a ruse to make him the butt of some joke or other. "Why?"

"Just do it!"

Tentatively, he extended one flipper, then the other and jerked his bill upward, keeping his eyes on her in case she head-butted him or tickled him under the flippers.

"Feel anything yet?"

"I feel pretty silly. Okay if I put my flippers down now?"

"No," said Peppermint, scowling. "Put them back up! Now, do you feel like, y'know, huddling or anything?"

"It's not actually so cold this morning."

Peppermint pursed her bill. "You're making this very difficult. Listen to me! Raise your bill, stick your flippers out parallel and make a loud, trumpeting call! Then waddle behind me! Go on, do it!"

Yukawa3 complied with all the enthusiasm of a limp lettuce in yesterday's salad. "I feel ridiculous," he complained. "I feel like a scarecrow in a soul band and…"

"I give up!" declared an exasperated Peppermint. "Don't you want to, y'know, reproduce?"

Yukawa3 reeled back in astonishment. "Reproduce? Reproduce! Certainly not! I'm asexual."

"A sexual what?"

"No, I said asexual. Agamogenetic. As in… that is to say, I don't have any sex."

"I'm not surprised, the way you carry on!" huffed Peppermint as she trudged off to seek solace with Mothballs, Lemon, Musky, Floral and the others. They, however, paid scant attention to her as they were having a whale of a time practising the yukawa3 tripod dance.

Penguins usually tried to avoid expressions like 'having a whale of a time', and for good reason, given the truly dire and distressing threat posed by the orcas circling menacingly offshore. Having sloped off towards the water's edge, yukawa3 spotted one of them getting up close and personal with a seal pup in the shallow surf. Horrified at witnessing this, he retreated with all the alacrity of a gazelle – a gazelle made of blubber, leaping majestically through the air on two stubby, duck-like webbed feet.

In the short time he had been exposed to the perils of life on the Sub-Antarctic Islands, yukawa3 had heard terrifying accounts of penguin-eating creatures such as leopard seals and orcas in the sea, and giant petrels, fur seals and skuas on land. As if that was not worrying enough, he had discovered that his penguin mutation was not protecting him from the complex seizure disorder with which he had been afflicted prior to his flight to Earth. If anything, the condition had worsened, to the point where the deja vu episodes were threatening to merge into a single continuous stream, which was ridiculous since he could not possibly have had any previous experience of life as a penguin in the Antarctic. He felt like his life was being subsumed somehow into a narrative that seemed curiously familiar – familiar enough to be recognised as it unravelled, but not familiar enough to foresee. As he stood there, contemplating all this, the sun rose and the glaciers started to glow pink. Gradually, his thoughts returned to Smolin9 (formerly Morys Minor) and his comrade, polkingbeal67. Perhaps, he thought, this life as a penguin, despite all the fishing, was not, after all, the panacea he thought it might be. And it might just be nice to touch base with his old mentor and catch up with news from the home planet. But where had he left his microwocky?

It was hours later when he found the device in the tender care of a particularly ferocious-looking fur seal a mile or so further up the coast. The seal had nursed it so well in its dense underfur that the microwocky had thawed out. Not only that, but random contact with the animal's guard hairs had switched it on and unbarred all incoming calls. Yukawa3 was sure he could hear polkingbeal67's voice emanating from the underside of the bulky greyish-brown creature. In fact, it sounded as if the seal actually *was* polkingbeal67 in disguise. Just for a split second the thought crossed yukawa3's mind that that might indeed be the case and he started forward with what might have been a grin on his bill, only to be greeted with a high-pitched whine. Then the seal lunged and slashed at him with its sharp fangs, missing him by inches. Slithering forward in the effort to attack yukawa3, it had inadvertently cranked up the volume on the microwocky which suddenly bellowed: "Yukawa3! It's your mentor! It's me, polkingbeal67! Speak to me, you crazy prokaryote!"

The seal, spooked by polkingbeal67's loud, reverberant voice, uttered one more unearthly howl and slipped away towards the sea, leaving the microwocky behind.

Yukawa3 waddled up with a look of utter delight on his face and then discovered, once again, that he could not manage to prod, flick, swipe or rub the device in a correct and timeous manner. Polkingbeal67's call went unanswered.

.   .   .

When problems become so formidable that you cannot even focus on where to start, most people give up and walk away. Polkingbeal67 was not one of those people. Mind you, to be scrupulously correct, he did do a fair bit of walking away to enjoy the renowned attractions of South West England, including a couple of tours exploring Arthurian legend and the sites of epic battles of the Dark Ages. But because he had not entirely given up on finding yukawa3, the problem did not recede into the distance - it followed him around like the smell of a mildewed magic carpet (it had to have been a magic one, otherwise it could not have followed him around). He may not have succeeded in establishing two-way communication, but his unanswered microwocky calls had secured one vital piece of information, namely yukawa3's precise location. But, try as he might to view this in a positive light, the prospect of retrieving the cadet from the inhospitable, frozen wastes of South Georgia was daunting to say the least, particularly as direct contact was proving impossible. Without the complicity of a third party on Smolin9 (formerly Morys Minor), wormhole travel and wormhole communication were out of the question, which left him with the prospect of a conventional expedition to the Sub-Antarctic island. But what kind of expedition? He could not contemplate embarking on such an adventure by himself, so the options were confined to a scientific, tourist or privately chartered expedition in the company of earthlings - people who were yet to come to terms with the existence of wormholes, who had yet to set foot on any other planetary body apart from their own moon and who still thought it acceptable to ride on the backs of other species for the purposes of transport. To put his trust in the extraordinarily crude forms of earthling transportation was anathema to him. Indeed, his misgivings were such that, at first, he simply could not face it at all and he disappeared on yet another trip to research the legend of King Arthur and Merlin.

As it happens, it was the Arthurian legend of the Holy Grail that ultimately encouraged and inspired him to go ahead with an expedition. He had often thought of yukawa3 as a vessel of mystical emptiness, so, in his mind, the analogy was not far off. According to his initial research, there were no airstrips on South Georgia, the only access was by boat and the passage was almost invariably a rough one. But this did not discourage polkingbeal67 any more than it had discouraged Galahad on hearing that other knights had returned badly wounded, or worse, after attempting to seek out the Grail.

To his surprise, he managed to find a global adventure travel company who had had a late cancellation on a 56-day Antarctic expedition following in the footsteps of legendary British explorer, Sir Ernest Shackleton. The object of the high profile, partly commercial, partly scientific venture was to raise awareness of environmental changes and the need to protect the Antarctic. Polkingbeal67 would leave from London at the end of the week on a 25-30 hour flight to Ushuaia, on the tip of Argentina. From there, he would board a research ship by the name of 'Malvinas Explorer' that would chart a course along the Antarctic Convergence to South Georgia. He stopped listening when the travel co-ordinator explained the rest of the itinerary and ignored the advice about bringing appropriate medications for seasickness.

Although it sometimes renders one insensible to banal (but important) information, one of the great advantages of possessing a highly evolved brain is the ability to understand, interpret and exploit the financial markets of relatively primitive worlds. I cannot tell you precisely how polkingbeal67 raised the money for his trip, but raise it he did, and within two days the full amount was safely deposited with the travel operator.

A swirling fog was threatening to erase Heathrow Airport when polkingbeal67 arrived for his flight, but it dispersed fairly quickly when a steady drizzle set in. On boarding the plane and locating his seat, he attracted the attention of a flight attendant and asked, "Can you tell me where the black box is located, please."

The flight attendant's voice was sweet and polite, but a slight twitch of her eyebrows betrayed her irritation. "There are two, sir," she said, "and they're located near the tail of the plane."

"They're always found undamaged in the event of a crash, aren't they?" polkingbeal67 enquired, fiddling nervously with his seat belt.

"Yes, sir."

"Well, do you mind if I travel in one of them?"

The flight attendant bit her lip. "That's not possible, sir. They're not that sort of box. Can I get you a drink or something?"

The engines surged from a whine to a roar and the plane shuddered slightly as it advanced to the taxi-way.

Polkingbeal67's voice echoed the length of the cabin, "I'm serious!"

If he found earthling air travel harrowing, it was as nothing compared to the excruciating bondage of an Antarctic sea voyage which was at best mind-numbingly monotonous, at worst a brutal and merciless encounter with the very margins of human experience. His lips swollen, his nose red and blistered, he clung to the rail of the ship, periodically vomiting over the side. But shortly afterwards, they left the port of Ushuaia and the voyage was underway.

Polkingbeal67 was still clinging to the rail a couple of hours later when they were engulfed in an icy fog. It was like a strange ethereal beast emerging from the ocean itself, grasping the keel and the sides of the 'Malvinas Explorer' in its freezing, invisible hands, sending exploratory fingers up and down the steep staircases.

A thin, wiry Argentine crew member, whose uncovered neck was covered in tattoos, went up to polkingbeal67 and attempted to console him. His attempts to engage the ailing passenger in a bit of Argentine-Spanish banter were greeted with an uncomprehending scowl and punctuated by polkingbeal67's intermittent retching.

"English?" suggested the Argentine.

Polkingbeal67 shook his head, then nodded and said, "Er, yes, English." The sailor introduced himself as Jorge and polkingbeal67 responded by vomiting again.

"Nice name!" Jorge joked. "It make the water look real pretty, no? Eh? Ha ha!"

Polkingbeal67 motioned at the fog. "I don't know," he said in a low undertone. "I can't even see the water."

Jorge laughed raucously. "So why you seasick, eh? Ha ha!"

The crew and passengers aboard the 'Malvinas Explorer' spent the next couple of days swaying on the ocean, gazing out at the foam-crested waves and the stunning flocks of seabirds as the ship skirted the Falkland Islands and headed towards the first port of call. At one point, a black-browed albatross, referred to by some of the crew as a mollymawk, swept past and then hung in the air for a moment, causing great excitement among all those on deck. By the time the high mountains and mighty glaciers of South Georgia came into view on the starboard bow, polkingbeal67 felt so wretched, he was reduced to crawling around on all fours. Jorge had already started referring to him as 'Old Sea Dog'.

.   .   .

Hundreds of light years away on a small circumbinary planet in the constellation of Cygnus, Melinda Hill was struggling to keep her head above water, charging from meeting to meeting, trying desperately to hold things together. The planetary leader had not been seen in public since polkingbeal67 and yukawa3 had vanished, leaving behind a forest of pointing fingers, a slew of accusations and allegations of corruption. When he failed to attend the annual celebration of multiverse portal access and then sent Melinda as a deputy to the closing ceremony of the Cygnus Gravity Free Games, rumours were rife. The consensus among intergalactic governments was that they were witnessing significant change on Smolin9. Some speculated that the leader was seriously ill, but most attributed his absence to politics. Oovian authorities had suspended aid to Smolin9 following the Niffis atrocity, prompting soaring inflation and concerns over the budget deficit. Was the old leader being shielded to protect him from the ongoing row over Niffis? Had there been a coup, bloodless or otherwise? Clearly there had been no uprising, but many commentators were suggesting that Melinda could have effectively replaced him anyway. Was she now the de facto leader of the planet?

Actually, there was no evidence that he had been shunted aside and replaced by Melinda; such a move would be unconstitutional and unacceptable to all right-thinking Mortians. But if the regime continued to struggle to secure significant investment from other planets in the galaxy, it would not be difficult to imagine a silent takeover by Melinda's advisers, supported by the military and working in collusion with the media. Fortunately, the Intergalactic Court of Justice, Arbitration and Conciliation had shown only cursory interest in the developments. Having earlier brought the leader to court to answer charges of corruption, their view was that the planet would be truly dysfunctional until such time as the leader passed away.

Having rushed from a meeting of the MANKIND commission, Melinda was taking her seat at a myrmecam-enabled conference with the senior chillok ambassador. She had been popular with the chilloks ever since she had introduced them to Status Quo classics like 'Whatever You Want' and 'Rockin All Over The World', but she considered it a chore to confer with them owing to their insistence on speaking Latin. Her adviser and translator, nipkow4, was attending the meeting by means of a remote holographic feed. "Shall we get started?" he asked cheerfully.

Melinda flicked a button on the myrmecam and the ambassador's high-pitched voice rang out, "Fiat justitia! Fiat justitia!"

"That's literally the sweetest thing anyone's ever said to me," drawled Melinda, with a resigned, sarcastic air. Her workload had become so excessive, she no longer felt inclined, or able, to observe the social niceties.

Nipkow4 shook his head disapprovingly and tut-tutted. "Our revered deputy! Really! Listen, he's saying he wants justice done." The noise pollution associated with a telepresence session is such that it is not easy to tell when someone starts (or stops) tut-tutting, but he tut-tutted again.

A series of high-pitched clucks and whistles heralded the chillok ambassador's next remark. "Faciam quodlibet quod necesse est."

Nipkow4's face dropped. "Serio?" he asked.

Faciam quodlibet quod necesse est," the ambassador repeated. "Ultio ultionis!"

"What's he saying?" Melinda enquired wearily.

"He's talking about revenge and he says he'll do whatever it takes," nipkow4 explained. "I think he's threatening us."

"Oh, spare me these melodramatic menacing midgets!" said Melinda. "Totally! Literally! Anyway, I've had enough of his antics for one day. Ant-ics! Oops! Anyone for a bit of Status Quo?"

The myrmecam erupted into excited babble.

"I think he's going to take matters into his own hands," nipkow4 cautioned.

"Really? That's so erratic! What does he think he'll do, tickle me to death? Look, I'm tired of talking to him now. Tell him we'll have a game of squash to settle it - he can try to squash me and I'll try to squash him. Who's your money on?"

Nipkow4 almost certainly tut-tutted again. "Shh!" he hissed. "He may understand what you're saying. In fact,

I'm pretty sure he does. Chilloks may seem tiny and insignificant individually, but try to remember they're incredibly powerful in aggregate. And they're a very advanced species. They harnessed dark energy and discovered wormhole travel eons before we did."

Jaundiced and disinterested, Melinda shrugged. "Tell him to stop getting his little legs in a twist," she suggested. "And tell him to stop looking at me like I'm from another planet!" There was a short pause. "Okay, I know I *am* from another planet, but... anyway, tell him... tell him something politically correct and reassuring and then let's leave the confounded insect to his rantings and ravings. Ipso facto, ad nauseam!" She looked at the ambassador and he looked at her. Their relationship, such as it was, had soured irrevocably, like a crocodile and a python blaming one another for devouring their best friend.

There was a sharp intake of breath from nipkow4, followed by a cough and another cough, followed by a frenzied attempt to placate the screaming chillok ambassador. "He's going to send a task force to the Pale Blue Dot and get justice for Niffis!" There was an edge to nipkow4's voice as if the polished veneer was peeling away.

"No, *I'm* going to Earth!" Melinda declared. "Tell him! Tell him *I'm* going to Earth and I'll sort it all out myself! Right now, I've just about had it with everybody and I'm going to my room where I'm going to lie down and I don't want to see anybody! Literally!" With that, she stormed off down the corridor. It would have been a powerful and dramatic exit were it not for the fact that her room was in the opposite direction. With as much composure as she could muster, she stopped, turned around and walked back. She switched off the myrmecam and engaged in awkward small talk with nipkow4 before pursuing her proposal to return to Earth. The pair of them discussed it calmly and rationally, like the calm, rational people they occasionally were.

"You're going to have to get there before the chilloks do," advised nipkow4. His telepresence image paced up and down nervously like a caged ghost that did not realise it could just walk through the bars.

Melinda nodded. "I know," she said. "Don't worry, I've been keeping track. I know exactly where polkingbeal67 and yukawa3 are. It happens to be just about the most erratically inhospitable place on the planet, but yeah, I know where they are."

The two discussed the logistics and strategy associated with the visit until Melinda became too tired to concentrate any longer. "I've got to get some rest first," she said.

"Are you sure about all this?"

Melinda smiled wanly. "I've got to go," she said, and fell silent for a moment. "Besides, there's another reason I want to visit Earth for a while." And she wiped a tear from the corner of her eye.

.   .   .

Yukawa3 was finding life as a king penguin tranquil, therapeutic and invigorating. Or so he told himself whenever the cruel finger of doubt bored through his soul like a red-hot skewer. Yes, he assured himself, it was proving to be every bit as appealing as he had thought it might be. Why, it had served to wash away many of the toxic cares of his life, banishing all the old uncertainties, vicissitudes and adversities. And if it were not for the insignificant and fleeting deprivations he had to endure to survive, why, the whole experience would be... oh, hell, who was he kidding? It was unhinging him completely. It was a harsh, savage and unpredictable existence that no living being should ever have to endure.

Feeling suddenly compelled to ditch this irksome and perilous identity, he launched himself into the challenge of finding his buried mutator. As the other penguins performed the tripod dance with reckless abandon, yukawa3 wandered in and out of them, scratching, scraping and poking at the snow and ice until the whole area was a mosaic of small, irregular pock marks like a giant, dirty golf ball stretched out flat. It did not help that a blizzard had set in and he could barely see what he was doing as the fine snow whipped his face, blinding and disorientating him. Nevertheless, like a dog determined to retrieve a buried bone, he drove himself almost to distraction, digging with all the demonic energy of a fish on a hook. One of the tripod dancers christened him 'Old Sea Dog'. (Now that really *was* an outlandish coincidence.)

One by one, the tripod dancers shuffled away, puzzled and alarmed by his behaviour. Yukawa3 stood alone, his fervour spent and his emotional security dashed on the rocks of harsh reality. No one showed him any sympathy. In fact, no one even approached him as he braced himself against the flurries of snow that whirled menacingly around him. Perversely, it brought him to his senses. Just at the moment when an intense feeling of confusion and desolation began to envelop him, he recalled the moment when court officials had destroyed his collection of earthling sou'westers, an incident that had prompted a self-inflicted collapse of self-esteem leading more or less directly to the predicament he now found himself in. The experience had served as a warning to him about the corrosive effects of self-pity on a person's perspective and judgement. He had been down that road before and got lost; and it was a mistake he was determined not to repeat.

As if to reward him for the mental effort he had exerted to banish his negative thoughts, the snow began to clear and at the rim of yukawa3's new world emerged the amazing sight of distant human forms advancing across the snow towards him. Most of them stopped a fair distance away and took photos, but one of them came closer. A wild hope fluttered in his heart like one of the butterflies you do not get in the Antarctic. What was the human holding in his outstretched hand? No, it was not possible, was it? It was yellow. It was apparently oiled canvas. It was... it was a sou'wester! Yukawa3 propelled himself forward to greet his old friend and mentor and immediately lost his footing in one of the shallow pits he had dug earlier. Undeterred, he scrambled to his feet and waddled on. Delighted, polkingbeal67 yelled a Mortian greeting and thrust the sou'wester down over his former pupil's head and watched as yukawa3, unable to remove the hat, wheeled around blindly and erratically, producing a fanfare of loud, trumpeting calls, falling into several more shallow pits.

Mortians can communicate telepathically regardless of the physical form they choose to inhabit. Polkingbeal67 and yukawa3 had a lot to catch up on. Mentor and pupil. Co-accused and co-accused in the trial of the decade. Old Sea Dog meeting Old Sea Dog. But they only had time to exchange a few pleasantries before two things happened. Firstly, the crew hand, Jorge, came over to warn Simon (polkingbeal67) that he should guard against becoming detached from the rest of the party, who were already almost out of sight. "We trek round to see Shackleton's grave, si, yes?" he said, tugging at polkingbeal67's arm. "He was great man. If we no have pipple like Shackleton, we play video games by candlelight, no?" Actually, polkingbeal67 was appalled to witness such ignorance. During the flight from England, he had researched the career of the heroic explorer and had been deeply impressed by the story of his remarkable leadership, particularly the account of his expedition in the Endurance. The ship had become trapped in pack ice and Shackleton had managed to deliver every one of his crew to safety following a desperate trek for survival in the harshest conditions imaginable.

"No, I'll catch you up," said polkingbeal67. "Shackleton's not going anywhere and I need to do some research on these penguins."

"Verra cruel research, no?" observed Jorge, as yukawa3, half-hidden under the yellow sou'wester, continued to stagger from one hole to another.

"Er, yeah, hypothermia is a leading cause of penguin deaths, so we're, er, experimenting with protective clothing."

Jorge pointed at yukawa3. "So now we have pinguino with wrapper on, si? Ha ha!"

The second thing to happen, only moments after Jorge had disappeared, was the sudden emergence of Melinda Hill, shivering, cringing, doubled up with the cold. She had remembered to take a homeodynamic disruption antidote (HDA) pill to offset the worst aspects of wormhole travel but had neglected to bring warm clothing and survival gear. Displaying great presence of mind, polkingbeal67 hauled her to her feet and half-dragged, half-carried her towards the ship. "Hu-hu-hu-who are you?" asked Melinda, her teeth chattering uncontrollably.

"Simon," replied polkingbeal67. "But you know me better as polkingbeal67. Try and run! It's not far."

Still ensconced under the sou'wester, yukawa3 tottered around in ever-decreasing circles, trumpeting forlornly from time to time, wondering what on earth was going on.

He had to wait at least an hour before polkingbeal67 re-emerged with Melinda in tow. Now encased in thick layers of warm clothing and a hot drink thawing her out from the inside, the deputy leader of the planet now known as Smolin9 slowly recovered her faculties and released yukawa3 from his canvas confinement.

"He says 'thank you'," said polkingbeal67.

Melinda gave him a puzzled look. "He didn't say a word." She bent down to look into yukawa3's eyes. "Can you talk?" she asked him.

Yukawa3 cocked his head at Melinda, then cocked his head at polkingbeal67 and replied in an absurdly loud voice: "No."

However paradoxical it may seem, it was strictly accurate: yukawa3 could not speak like a human, apart from uttering a sound that resembled the word 'no'.

"He can communicate with me telepathically," polkingbeal67 explained. "He can't talk to *you*, except by making penguin noises, one of which sounds like 'no'."

"Right. Is he okay? Ask him how he's feeling."

"You can talk to *him*. He'll understand you just fine. He just can't talk back, except to say 'no'."

"Oh," said Melinda, and then turned to yukawa3. "Well, how are you? How are you feeling?"

"I'm fine, thank you," said polkingbeal67, decoding the telepathic signal.

"No, I was talking to *him*, literally," said Melinda, nodding her head towards yukawa3.

"Yes, I know. I'm translating for you."

"That's so erratic!" Melinda squealed. "How will I tell if *you're* saying it or *he's* saying it?"

"I don't know," said polkingbeal67.

"So, did *you* just say that?" Melinda asked polkingbeal67.

"No," said yukawa3.

Polkingbeal67 sighed, defeated. "This isn't going to work, is it?"

They eventually agreed on a system whereby polkingbeal67 raised his hand whenever he was speaking as yukawa3.

With polkingbeal67's hand going up and down like a fiddler's elbow, yukawa3 clarified his predicament concerning the buried mutator. Melinda, in turn, enlightened the other two about the situation back on their home planet. "So now you know why I'm here," she said. "And you must understand that I've got to take you back with me. You certainly haven't done yourself any favours by running away. What were you thinking?"

Polkingbeal67 pursed his lips and shook his head. "I don't know," he said, "I just thought yukawa3 and I could do a great job reaching out to earthlings and getting them to embrace the intergalactic community. I just thought we could put things right, you know, kind of make up for..."

"Destroying the city of Niffis? Committing perjury? Deceiving everyone into thinking you were smolin9? Deceiving *me* into thinking you were my husband?"

"I know, I know, I'm sorry. But it's not all bad," polkingbeal67 protested, "I returned the Voyager space probe to the earthling president and..."

"And that's one of the reasons why the charges against yukawa3 were dropped. I know, literally. And it was very good of you to make sure he got the credit for it. But," she said, fixing him with a stern expression, "there's no way you should have run away before your sentencing hearing. It just looks so terrible! Literally."

During yukawa3's trial, polkingbeal67 had arranged for the teleporting of the Voyager probe to the very doorstep of the President of the United States. The intergalactic authorities had hailed the action as a watershed moment for broader humanity. Melinda considered it a watershed moment in the transformation of polkingbeal67 from a self-styled gung-ho war hero into a more caring, thoughtful and sensitive human being.

Polkingbeal67 raised his hand. "I'm not going back," he said.

"Oh yes, you are," Melinda insisted.

"That wasn't me," polkingbeal67 explained. "I had my hand up. Yukawa3 says he won't go back. And, actually, he doesn't have to. He was cleared by the court."

Melinda turned to yukawa3. "Why would you want to stay here anyway? It's literally a nightmare. The air freezes in your lungs when you breathe. It's irrational to want to live here."

"How dare you call me irrational!" said polkingbeal67, with his hand raised. "I might be crazy but I'm certainly not irrational. And there are definitely worse places to live."

Melinda was in the mood for an argument. "Name one good thing about this god-forsaken hell-hole."

"That's easy," said polkingbeal67, hand still raised. Yukawa3 thought for a moment, then another moment and then realised it was not quite as easy as he had thought. Finally, polkingbeal67 translated his best effort: "For one thing, you won't get run over by a bus!"

Polkingbeal67 and Melinda exchanged glances and shrugged. "Name one thing you can do here, apart from huddling and fishing," Melinda persisted. "Why, you can't even play hide and seek!"

Polkingbeal67 raised his hand once more. "But that's a good thing," he said. "No one and nothing can get lost here."

"You lost your mutator," polkingbeal67 reminded him. Then he raised his hand and shouted: "Nerk!"

"Nerk? What's that supposed to mean?" asked Melinda.

"Nothing," said polkingbeal67 with his hand down. "He's just going native."

At this point, Melinda announced her intention to pay her respects to her late husband at his last resting place. Polkingbeal67 expressed his support for the idea and insisted on accompanying her. As it happens, Melinda had no intention of letting him out of her sight in any case. "Okay," she said, "but if we're all going together, we won't be able to use wormhole travel." She knew that any requests for wormhole travel involving polkingbeal67 and yukawa3 would be vetoed unless the destination was Smolin9.

"Don't worry. I'll get us all on the ship somehow," polkingbeal67 assured her, speaking in a low voice so yukawa3 would not overhear. At that moment, the tour party appeared in the distance on their return from

Shackleton's grave at Grytviken. "I'll speak to them straight away. Here they come now. We'll have to continue with the expedition, but we'll get to England eventually."

Melinda cast a quizzical glance over her shoulder at yukawa3. "You might have trouble persuading them to take a penguin with them. Literally."

"I'm not worried about that," said polkingbeal67. "The problem I've got is explaining what *you're* doing here."

.   .   .

"Seriously," Melinda whispered to polkingbeal67, "I'm not leaving him here. Why does he insist on staying?"

"His mutator's buried here somewhere. He won't leave without it. He'd be trapped inside the body of a penguin for ever."

Melinda thought about this long and hard before giving up and asking: "What shall we do about it?"

Polkingbeal67 raised his shoulders in a gesture of fake nonchalance. A flurry of ideas and thoughts came charging into his mind; most of them skidded to a halt and backed out again, but one of them persisted. "It's nearly November, isn't it? According to my research, this part of the coast should become ice-free in a couple of weeks."

Yukawa3 overheard this. Polkingbeal67 raised his hand and relayed the cadet's thoughts: "So my mutator would be lying on the beach in plain view!"

Melinda and polkingbeal67 looked at each other. "That's it, then!" said Melinda decisively, "I'll come back to get your mutator. Literally. You're right, p, I swear it's feeling warmer already. And look! There are insects around!" She flicked away what she thought was an ant from yukawa3's back.

Yukawa3 started trumpeting with wild abandon. As the expedition party approached, he broke into a joyous tripod dance. The forty or so weary trekkers, all clad in waterproofs, ski gloves, sunglasses, boots and hats, would have arrived sooner but for the distraction of a black-browed albatross appearing above them with its long, narrow wings held out stiffly as it wheeled and glided elegantly along the shore. Streaks of sunlight on the horizon prised open a band of low black cloud, cloaking the restless, rippled sea with a tattered gown of gold silk.

The captain of the Malvinas Explorer was a man of few words but, as the cliché goes, when he spoke it was worth hearing. At least it may have been worth hearing if you understood Argentine Spanish. Anyway, judging by the effect his words had on his crew, he appeared to speak with the authority that can only come from real experience, like maybe someone who was blinded by conker shrapnel as a schoolboy and who then spent his life lecturing at schools about the dangers of playing conkers. As a matter of fact, though, he was not too hot on health and safety issues. Pedro Fernandez, for that was his name, was notorious in nautical circles. Stories of his outrageous exploits were legion. A few years before he secured his current position as captain of the Malvinas Explorer, he had skippered a high-speed ferry when it failed to navigate a narrow inlet channel and collided with a tug. His crew had been impressed with his cheerful and philosophical reaction to the incident and had gratefully gulped down the whisky he had offered them. No one noticed that the skipper's glass had remained untouched during all the camaraderie, but the reason for this dawned on them when the Argentine Coast Guard arrived.

Fernandez had the letter 'P' tattooed on the back of his left hand and the letter 'S' on his right. Some thought the letters stood for his two daughters, Paula and Stefania. A popular but uncharitable joke doing the rounds after the ferry debacle was the alternative suggestion that the letters stood for 'port' and 'starboard': an aide memoire for a bungling navigator. For all his faults, he was considered by many to be a very personable and affable man. Acquaintances said he was the sort of person who could tell you to go to hell in such a suave and agreeable way that you found yourself preparing for the trip with relish.

Pipe and tobacco in hand, he stood before Melinda, polkingbeal67 and yukawa3 with an expression of placid kindness mingled with well-disguised remonstrance. He mumbled something in Castellano, which Jorge proceeded to translate: "He say 'como andas'. Who this lady? Why she here?"

"How do you do?" said Melinda. "I'm Melinda Hill from Glastonbury in England. I'm here because..."

Distrustful of Melinda's ability to think on her feet, polkingbeal67 interrupted. "She's... she's a stowaway! She's a penguin expert specialising in the field of, er, bird communication. She lost her funding from the, er, National Science Gang and couldn't buy a ticket, so, as she was desperate to join the expedition in the name of science, she hid in the undercarriage..."

Jorge was wide-eyed with astonishment. "National Science Gang?" he parroted. "She hide in what?!"

"I think he means the, um, cargo hold," said Melinda hesitatingly. "Yeah, literally, the place where you hold your, er, cargo?"

The captain's arms were folded in barely-concealed hostility. As if enveloped by the tension in the air, the black-browed albatross soared past really low and dipped a wing into the water before flying off again.

"Hokay," said Jorge, trying to diffuse the situation. "We sort this out back on ship."

They all turned and started walking back towards the Malvinas Explorer, yukawa3 included. When Fernandez realised the penguin was accompanying them, he stopped in his tracks, gesticulated towards yukawa3 and directed a stream of voluble invective at polkingbeal67. No translation was necessary.

Melinda was not inclined to beat about the bush. "He's coming with us!" she declared. "The penguin is coming with us and that's that. Literally."

Jorge shook his head in silent but firm objection. "No possible. He is cold-weather pinguino," he remonstrated, picking up a handful of snow to illustrate his point. "He like snow. He like ice. Si?"

Melinda was adamant. "He's coming with us, even if we have to keep him in the fridge!"

Polkingbeal67, fearing they were in danger of losing the argument, stepped forward and tapped yukawa3 affectionately on the bill. "This, ladies and gentlemen," he intoned theatrically, "is no ordinary penguin. This is an especially receptive animal whose unique cognitive and emotional processes are particularly attuned to Melinda's extraordinary communication skills. Please allow us to demonstrate. Melinda will talk to the penguin and I will translate his responses for you. I will raise my hand to signify when I am speaking the penguin's words." As the passengers and crew gathered around, intrigued, Melinda squatted down on her haunches and looked yukawa3 in the eye. She spoke with exaggerated clarity: "Tell these people - will you behave yourself on the ship?" Yukawa3 cocked his head. Polkingbeal67 raised his hand and said, "Yes."

The group of onlookers immediately looked sceptical and one or two of them laughed. "Well, hokay, how we know pinguino iss saying 'yes'?" Jorge scoffed. "How we know really?"

Melinda quickly tried to retrieve the situation. "Does one and one make three?"

"No," said yukawa3. And that certainly piqued the interest of the passengers and crew. They drew closer still, listening with rapt attention.

"Is Paris the capital city of Russia?" asked Melinda.

"No," replied yukawa3. Some of the passengers applauded. One of them, a tall American, asked: "What's going on here? Are you a ventriloquist or something?"

"No, I'm not a ventriloquist, literally," Melinda assured him. She wondered how long she could carry on asking yukawa3 questions that would elicit the word 'no' in response.

The American could evidently read her mind. "Make him say something else," he prompted suspiciously.

Melinda was on top form. Without batting an eyelid, she instructed yukawa3 to nod his head and, to the delight of the assembled company, the penguin duly obliged.

"Flap your wings!" ordered Melinda, now really starting to enjoy herself. The group clapped their hands and laughed heartily as yukawa3 moved his flippers up and down, finishing with a real flourish by spinning around, first one way and then the other.

"Dance!" commanded Melinda, whereupon yukawa3 launched into his tripod dance, entertaining everyone with the zaniest rendition he could muster. The passengers and all the crew had been won over. They were enraptured, their faces aglow with wonder. By now, even Pedro Fernandez was applauding. A smile snaked across his face. It was a smile that suggested more than mere amusement. It was the smile of a man for whom life held no innocent joy, just opportunities to exploit and control. Putting his pipe and tobacco back in his pocket, he motioned towards the ship and everyone followed him.

.   .   .

It goes without saying that yukawa3 was the centre of attention during the remainder of the expedition cruise. From time to time, the ship stopped and everyone converged on the bridge deck to witness him take to the water to swim, fish, perform tricks and generally show off. Retrieving him from the icy, rolling sea was a challenging exercise involving the use of a specially adapted fine mesh net, but it gave Fernandez a break from his main chore - navigating the ship through the hazardous Antarctic waters where small icebergs known as growlers lurked only a few feet above the ocean's surface.

On one of the rare occasions when he had time alone with polkingbeal67 and Melinda, yukawa3 chose to confide in his mentor about the strange deja vu episodes he had been experiencing.

"Yes, I've heard about this before," said polkingbeal67, uncharacteristically sympathetic as he spoke in a low, quiet voice. "If I remember rightly, it's something to do with a defective adjustment to time dilation caused by an inadequate dose of HDA subsequent to wormhole travel. At least, that was the diagnosis put forward by the lead researcher." He raised his hand to signal that he was now speaking the words yukawa3 was conveying telepathically: "I don't understand a word of that. The medibots gave me a reset back on Smolin9, but it hasn't done any good. Have you heard of any other diagnoses? I really think I might prefer a different one."

"Could be something you ate," Melinda chipped in.

"Yeah," said polkingbeal67 with his hand still raised, "I prefer that diagnosis. The trouble is, I get the symptoms all the time."

"You might be allergic to fish!" exclaimed Melinda, clapping her hands together. "Literally!"

"Really?" said polkingbeal67, still speaking as yukawa3. "Do you think that might be it?" Scowling, he lowered his arm and muttered: "That's ridiculous! Melinda, please stop filling his head with nonsense!"

But Melinda was adamant. "No, seriously," she insisted, "I've got a cousin who's got a fish allergy. We always had to go to a chip shop where they cooked the fish and chips in separate dedicated fryers, y'know, to avoid cross contamination." Noticing polkingbeal67 scowling again, she continued: "Okay, funny story time! You'll laugh, literally. We went on holiday together once, and after a long day on the beach, we went to the local chippy and Alice, my cousin, asked them if they had a dedicated fryer for the fish and chips. And the girl behind the counter said yes, they did, but he didn't start till half past six! Ha ha!"

Polkingbeal67 drew a deep breath and released it slowly. He did not have time to respond before Melinda started talking again. "Oh yeah," she said, "and can we drop this whole 'hand up, hand down' thing now? It's driving me mad! Literally. And anyway, thinking about it, why don't you just say 'he says' when you're speaking for yukawa3?"

Desperate to learn more about his condition, yukawa3 besieged polkingbeal67 with more and more questions. Melinda, who could tell by the glazed look in polkingbeal67's eyes that the pair were communicating psychically, became irritated by their failure to bring her into the conversation and demanded to know what was going on.

"He says he wants to know what other diagnoses have been considered and I say they're not important and he says he still wants to hear them and I say he'll be sorry he asked and he says go ahead and I say are you sure and he says yes and I say well if you're sure and he says..."

Melinda sighed. "Okay, do the 'hand up, hand down' thing."

"Well," said polkingbeal67, with his hand lowered. "I heard some speculation that these kind of symptoms suggest interference from a parallel universe, a characteristic effect of quantum entanglement." Raising his hand and glaring at Melinda, he said: "No, no, I like the fish allergy best."

The penny dropped and Melinda finally saw where this was going. She started back-pedalling furiously. "I'm sorry I mentioned it. Look, you're a penguin. You *have* to eat fish. Literally."

Yukawa3 shrugged his flippers in tacit apology. He was now emphatically resolved to stop eating fish and krill, and once he had made up his mind he seldom wavered.

Polkingbeal67's face darkened. "This is your fault," he accused Melinda with a look of stern disapproval, like a judge who has just stepped in something unpleasant. "You talked him into it. Now you can just talk him out of it!" With that, he stalked off towards his cabin.

"Where are you going?" asked Melinda. "I can't talk to him without you here, you know that."

"It's *your* problem now. I've got stuff to do. Good luck."

"Okay," said Melinda, "you just go! Literally. Run away! I guess you're predisposed to it anyway."

Polkingbeal67 stopped and turned round. "What's that supposed to mean?"

"Well, it's what you do," replied Melinda. She did not want to fall out with him but was becoming increasingly frustrated and annoyed by the whole situation - not just yukawa3's behaviour and polkingbeal67's unhelpfulness, but the general lack of progress in her mission. No, this was about more than just the mission. Emotionally, she was no longer handling things particularly well. Settling on a new planet and then losing smolin9 had caused her to tumble through euphoria into a deeply buried anxiety. A piece of her soul had been torn out of her and it had not had time to regenerate. In a curious and perverse way, spending time with polkingbeal67 only served to inflame the conflicting emotions she had been struggling to reconcile. There was a momentary pause while the two of them exchanged hostile glares. "What did you do when your space craft flattened the city of Niffis?" Melinda asked. "Did you stay and, y'know, make reparation?"

Chastened, humbled and conscience-stricken, polkingbeal67 did not know how to respond and waited for Melinda to finish her point. "When you realised the full implication of what you'd done, did you turn yourself in straight away to face the music? No, you went on the run. And when, eventually, you faced trial, what happened? Right before the sentencing hearing, you ran away again! Like I said, it's what you do!"

The muscles in polkingbeal67's face tightened as he struggled to avoid looking as devastated as he felt. He said nothing. Melinda also said nothing, bit her lip and dropped her gaze to the floor. Yukawa3 made a short honking sound and span around in a tight circle. A whole minute passed before Melinda's face crumpled. Stepping forward, she took polkingbeal67 in her arms and sobbed as though her heart was broken. First-time experiences can be daunting, but slowly and tentatively, polkingbeal67 reciprocated the hug with one arm, and then, finally, the other.

Later, when they talked all this through, polkingbeal67 attempted to summarise Melinda's analysis. "So," he said, "you were saying I have an ingrained behaviour pattern characterised by a tendency to flee challenging situations. You were saying I have a deep-seated fear of disapproval and an inability to face up to my responsibilities. And you were saying that my excessive self-concern invariably overrides doing the right thing... "

"I was?" asked Melinda, totally mystified but secretly gratified that her words had been worthy of such an impressive-sounding interpretation.

"Well, at least you weren't calling me a coward."

"I wasn't?" asked Melinda, quite nonplussed.

A look of alarm flashed across polkingbeal67's face. "Of course not," he said. "If you had, we'd now be submerged in a vat of liquid vitalmados, fighting a duel to the death! Besides, cowardice comes from over-thinking things."

"Right," said Melinda, with a bit of a twinkle in her eye, "and, that would never apply to you, of course. The only thinking you did was with your legs! Literally."

Again, first-time experiences can be daunting, but the first hint of a glimmer of a smile tugged slowly and tentatively at the corners of polkingbeal67's mouth. It hovered for a second or two and vanished so quickly that Melinda later wondered if she had imagined it.

You would probably be interested in knowing what thoughts were running through yukawa3's mind while all this mental and emotional jousting was going on. After all, it was his harrowing refusal to eat fish that had caused the upheaval. He tried to interject a telepathic message. "Anyway, I'm still not going to eat fish," he said, but no one was tuned in at the other end.

.   .   .

After negotiating the stormy seas of Drake Passage, the Malvinas Explorer approached Barrientos Island, one of a series of volcanic islands just to the north of the Antarctic Peninsula. Although the winds were still high and light was fading, Fernandez decided to risk a landing. One of the tour leaders delivered a garbled speech of cautionary instruction. Warning the assembled company of possible encounters with 'homicidal wildlife', she advised everyone to give animals the right-of-way at all times and to maintain a precautionary distance of at least five metres. As she spoke, the rocky spires of several of the Aitcho Islands, tinted with twilight pastels as the sunset progressed, could be discerned behind her. There followed the obligatory inspection of everyone's outer clothing and accessories to minimise the threat of introducing foreign plant material to the fragile ecosystem, then everyone piled into inflatable dinghies powered by outboard motors and, a few minutes later, sea legs became land legs once more.

While the passengers engaged with the playful Gentoos, skuas flew overhead with an air of urgency. In marked contrast, a pair of giant petrels soared slowly and lazily along the shore, aimlessly changing direction every now and again. A fur seal flopped over the rocks in ungainly fashion and barked at yukawa3, who passed close by, apparently intent on making the acquaintance of a group of chinstrap penguins clustered on a rocky outcrop, preening, gathering stones and displaying. Further along the beach, a dozen or so elephant seals, the only residents to show no interest in the visitors, were totally engrossed in fighting boisterously among themselves. Polkingbeal67 surveyed the scene with a feeling of calm excitement that he had never experienced before. The contrast between the unfathomable beauty of the landscape and the brutal, finite territoriality of the creatures that populated it filled him with wonder. It represented a fascinating disconnect between the narrow horizons of primate social life and the intimations of immortality suggested by the vast natural beauty stretched out beyond it. It was a dichotomy, yes, but it was a fusion at the same time, in much the same way as the spirit or soul is disconnected but fused with the body. He viewed it all with non-judgmental appreciation. It did not depress or disappoint him; it simply engaged his senses in transcendental contemplation. Staggered by this, he stopped reflecting on yukawa3's mental health for a moment... and started worrying about his own.

The deteriorating light cut short the trip and no one had time to wander far beyond the beach area. As they re-assembled to board the dinghies, they were treated to the bizarre sight of yukawa3 being pursued by an angry chinstrap penguin, much smaller than himself. To the astonishment of the onlookers, yukawa3 was tripping and tumbling during the chase and would easily have been caught, had it not been for the timely intervention of 'homicidal wildlife' in the form of a belligerent fur seal. The incident provoked debate about yukawa3's physical condition. It had not gone unnoticed that he had foregone his usual fishing sorties. Polkingbeal67 and Melinda were no longer alone in feeling very anxious about yukawa3's refusal to eat fish and krill.

Fernandez, on the other hand, along with one or two of the tour leaders and other crew members, knew that food deprivation in the short term did not constitute a life-threatening emergency for king penguins. The male birds, in particular, are capable of fasting for several weeks, especially during the incubation process. For all his faults, Fernandez understood and appreciated wildlife. As Jorge often enjoyed telling the passengers, a spider had lived in the skipper's ear for a whole week on one expedition! Anyway, as far as Fernandez was concerned, he was satisfied that there were no animal welfare implications relating to the penguin, at least not for the remaining duration of the expedition. It did occur to him, though, that an opportunity was dangling before him like low-hanging fruit and he was not the sort of man to pass up a chance to make some money.

"What happened out there?" asked Melinda, eyes scrunched up against the driving spray as the rolling waves slapped against the hull of the dinghy.

Polkingbeal67 raised his hand and translated while yukawa3 nodded gravely: "You saw nothing, okay? Let's just move on from this and forget about it."

"No, come on, what happened?" Melinda persisted. "You looked like you were in a bit of trouble back there. Quite literally."

"The stupid bird accused me of stealing his stones! I mean, what the hell? There are stones everywhere! The whole beach is covered with them. Anyway, please tell me how anyone can actually *own* some stones? You can't *own* a stone."

"You took his stones?"

"No, not at all. Well, not exactly. I thought I'd be friendly and I introduced myself and, I don't know, I thought it might be a good idea to demonstrate the tripod dance. I mean, what's wrong with that?"

Melinda shook her head. "Yeah. No, probably not a great idea when they're all getting ready for the nesting season."

"Well, maybe I slightly dislodged some of the stones he was putting together and maybe they kind of slightly rolled down a slope. What? They're just stones! I mean, I... What is the point of... anything?"

At that point, just as a large wave buffeted the dinghy, a greenish haze formed around yukawa3. As Melinda described it later, he became "fuzzy" and indistinct as if he had become a distorted holographic image of himself. The phenomenon only lasted a few seconds but it left yukawa3 unable to stand unaided until they reached the ship.

Having left the ailing penguin to recuperate in his cabin, polkingbeal67 discussed the incident with Melinda up on deck. "He says he felt another one of those deja vu feelings, like before but really intense. It doesn't make sense but he says he didn't feel like time was repeating - he says it felt like it was disappearing, pulling away from him. I don't get it - even if he had an insufficient dose of HDA, he shouldn't still be suffering the after-effects. Not after all this time."

Intelligent as he was, polkingbeal67 had overlooked another possible cause of yukawa3's affliction, though, to be fair, it was about as implausible and outlandish as anyone might dream. Given that Melinda had not even mentioned the chillok ambassador's threat, we will surely forgive polkingbeal67 for not realising that yukawa3's

Karma 5 may have become infested by vengeful chillok spirits (a Mortian's Karma 5 comprises all the intangible attributes that define a person, such as intellect, character, conscience, emotions and personality). Disembodied chillok entities may have implanted themselves in the hapless cadet with the aim of applying hypnosis or perhaps inflicting psychological disorder - it was certainly the kind of sinister tactic they had deployed in the past. If polkingbeal67 had had any inkling of such an eventuality, he would have recognised that it represented a mortal danger not only to yukawa3, but also to himself.

Before too long, the captain and a few crew members approached, inspecting the ice forming on the deck. Fernandez, evidently keen to make conversation, grabbed Jorge's arm and instructed him to act as interpreter. "Hola," said Jorge. "Ze captain, he say where is pinguino? He wanna try pinguino tricks."

When polkingbeal67 explained that yukawa3 was feeling unwell and was resting in the cabin, Fernandez barked: "How you do pinguino tricks? Es secreto?"

When polkingbeal67 responded by chuckling and answering evasively, Fernandez turned to Melinda and fixed her with an accusing stare. "You are stowaway, si? I give you cabin."

He was invoking the principle of reciprocity and Melinda indicated with a nod that she understood her obligations in that respect. To remove all doubt about it, Fernandez made a gesture suggesting he would throw her overboard if she proved uncooperative.

Jorge translated his threat: "He say: you want port or starboard?" Fernandez nodded for emphasis, furtively checking the tattoos on his hands.

"Yeah, okay, I get it," said Melinda. "What is it you want again?"

"He want do pinguino tricks," said Jorge.

Melinda tried to give herself time to think. "Okay, but it's difficult. Remember, I've got a PhD in, er, Interpenguin, er, ..."

Polkingbeal67 rushed to her assistance. "Noise Studies," he prompted.

"Yeah, of course, Interpenguin Noise Studies. It's a challenging field. Literally."

Fernandez and Jorge both looked at her with sceptical eyes.

"No, iss trick," said Fernandez, winking conspiratorially, "Iss trick, si?"

"No, no," replied Melinda, "it's not a trick. It's complicated. Communicating with animals like penguins requires you to develop a sophisticated set of, um, ..."

"Ears?" suggested polkingbeal67.

"Perspectives," said Melinda, nodding, trying desperately to sound well-versed in the vocabulary of animal linguistics. "Yeah, literally, I'm not the world's greatest expert of course, but you have to understand their perspective." She smiled self-deprecatingly. "Etcetera," she added, for good measure.

"Etcetera?" Jorge echoed.

"Absolutely, yeah," said Melinda. "You have to actually, literally think like a penguin."

Jorge echoed her words derisively: "Think like pinguino?"

"Yes, of course, precisely."

"Swim? Eat fish?" Jorge asked incredulously.

Melinda persevered. "Exactly, but you have to go further than that. You've got to waddle like a penguin, huddle like a penguin; you've got to actually *be* a penguin. Try waddling like a penguin! Go on, everyone try it! Like this!"

Not wishing to offend anyone's aesthetic sensibilities, I will draw a veil over the rest of this encounter. Suffice to say that many of the passengers had been taking the air on deck that evening and YouTube saw a sudden surge of video uploads from the vicinity of Barrientos Island.

.   .   .

Later, when they were alone, Melinda and polkingbeal67 discussed the captain's interest in learning the science of penguin communication. "It's really curious, isn't it? What do you think he's up to?" asked Melinda, leaning against the railing. They both gazed at the indistinguishable grey-black junction between the night sky and the dark, menacing ocean that rolled and churned under the ship causing it to heave with each successive wave.

Polkingbeal67 scratched his head. "Maybe he's thinking of providing some on-board entertainment?"

"But why would he want to get involved himself? Why not just get me to do it?"

"Would you agree to do it?"

"Would I have any choice? Didn't you hear him threaten to throw me overboard? I was like, you can't do that in this day and age. Literally. But, y'know, I wouldn't put it past him."

Polkingbeal67 nodded. "Okay, yeah, good point. So, maybe he *is* up to something."

Despite the best efforts of animal rights organisations and despite being banned outright in large Argentine cities including Buenos Aires, circuses were still popular family entertainment (and therefore big business) in certain South American countries, even in some districts of Argentina. Fernandez had a brother who owned a travelling circus that was touring in Paraguay. From the moment he had witnessed yukawa3's performance on the South Georgia beach, the prospect of making a few pesos out of the engaging and talented bird had been crossing and re-crossing his mind until the tangled web totally ensnared his waking thoughts. Oh yes, Melinda and polkingbeal67 were absolutely right - he was up to something, and that something was a plan to kidnap yukawa3 at the conclusion of the expedition.

The fact is, however, most of us are inclined to trust people we do not know until such time as they actually deceive us, and by the time the ship docked at the wharf in Ushuaia, any incipient misgivings Melinda and polkingbeal67 may have had about the captain's motives had evaporated. Yukawa3's malaise had regressed and he had been unable to leave the cabin for the remainder of the trip. Undermined by physical weakness and fatigue, his lethargic state had been interrupted only by occasional fits of delirium. Fernandez had impressed Melinda with his attentive manner and expressions of concern. Even polkingbeal67 agreed that the captain's conduct towards all three of them during the latter part of the cruise had been exemplary and above reproach. So when he offered to take yukawa3 to a top veterinary facility recommended by a close acquaintance, no one suspected anything untoward. In fact, it offered not just an opportunity to get some expert treatment for yukawa3, but also it gave Melinda and polkingbeal67 time to ponder the daunting challenges they faced in transporting a penguin to England.

Fernandez, with yukawa3 cradled in his arms, wrapped in a blanket, escorted Melinda and polkingbeal67 from the wharf to the Hotel Austral, just a couple of blocks away from the noise and bustle of the main shopping street. Swollen grey clouds greeted them and the thin, wind-driven sleet stung their faces. A few heads turned, but most people were oblivious to the contents of the blanket. They shuffled past, their bodies hunched against the cold, their eyes fixed on the pavement in front of them. It was not the sort of day to fully appreciate the dramatic backdrop of the Andes mountains. With a few bows, a couple of handshakes and a flurry of incoherent parting words, Fernandez left them at the entrance to the hotel and hurried off with yukawa3 in search of a taxi, having promised to call back at the hotel later in the afternoon.

Watching them disappear into the street, a few pangs of foreboding suddenly flicked at polkingbeal67 like the sleet against his skin. "We trust this Fernandez, right?" he asked as calmly as he could.

Melinda caught the anxiety in his voice and felt a need to express reassurance. "Yeah," she said, "absolutely, yeah. Literally."

Try as he might, polkingbeal67 could not dispel the disquiet in his heart or quell the toxic doubts that besieged him. Rushing through the hotel foyer, he demanded that the receptionist look up the name of the veterinary facility Fernandez had specified. The perplexed receptionist looked up from her screen, shrugged, looked again and shook her head. "No, sir," she said. "It's not in Ushuaia, anyway."

Once you shake the apples from a tree, you cannot restore them. And so it is with trust. It was particularly galling for polkingbeal67, for this was the first time he had ever put his faith in a stranger, someone outside his close circle of Mortian friends. A deadly pallor spread over his face. "We've abandoned yukawa3!" he exclaimed. "We've left him in the clutches of a perfidious stranger and there are no guarantees that we'll ever see him again!" With that, he dropped his bag and ran off in pursuit, Melinda close behind. The pair of them sprinted down the street, weaving in and out of pedestrians, vendors and stray dogs on the pavement, polkingbeal67 outpacing Melinda at every turn. Slipping on some ice, polkingbeal67 lost his balance and landed spread-eagled on the ground. When Melinda caught up with him, he was mumbling Mortian swear words and uncurling from a foetal position. "We mustn't waste another second!" he said, checking his reflection in a shop window and grooming his hair with his fingers.

"Where are we going?" asked Melinda wheezily as they set off again on their helter-skelter whirlwind chase through the centre of the southernmost city on Earth. Up and down steep streets, past tacky gift shops, casinos and restaurants, then a jumble of rusty old vehicles and wooden houses protected by sloping sheet metal roofs designed to prevent accumulations of snow. Panting and puffing, Melinda yelled her question once more: "Where are we going?"

Polkingbeal67 turned his head as he slowed to a jog. "I don't know," he shouted. "Where would you go if you wanted a taxi?"

"The railway station?" Melinda suggested. "Yeah, literally, the railway station."

Melinda asked passers-by for directions. The first woman,

wary of being mugged by such wild-looking creatures, hurried on without making eye contact. Eventually, a couple of tourists, probably skiers, stopped and engaged with them. "El Tren del Fin del Mundo?" one of them asked. He was referring to the Southern Fuegian Railway, dubbed the Train of the End of the World, a narrow gauge steam railway originally built as a freight line to transport timber to the prison of Ushuaia, now operating as a heritage railway into the Tierra del Fuego National Park.

"I don't know," she said. "We literally just want the regular railway station." As the tourists exchanged baffled glances, she turned anxiously to polkingbeal67, who shrugged in helpless confusion. "Well then," she continued. "I suppose we'd better go where you said. Will there be taxis there?"

"Taxis? Si, yes," said one of the tourists. "There are taxis at the End of The World."

There was not really time to ponder the incongruity of the statement, but, nevertheless, the nuances reverberated cruelly through polkingbeal67's mind like laughter in a church.

"You want taxi?" inquired another one of the tourists, pointing to a cab parked just a hundred metres away down the road.

Throwing themselves into the cab, polkingbeal67 and Melinda collapsed on the back seat like dishevelled and disoriented fugitives. After some seconds, the driver looked around and arched an eyebrow. A silence descended on them like a pack of rabid, hungry dogs trapped in a vacuum. Slowly and painfully, the realisation was dawning on them - they did not know where to go or what to do.

Polkingbeal67 slumped back into the seat and closed his

eyes. "The End of The World," he said. The driver put his hands back on the wheel and drove off.

. . .

Back on Smolin9 (formerly Morys Minor), nipkow4 was ensconced in a meeting at the leader's palace. In the office suite below the leader's private chambers, he was holding forth on the agenda for the pre-meeting briefing on the strategy relating to the consultation with representatives of the Intergalactic Court of Justice, Arbitration and Conciliation.

Before she left for her trip to Earth, Melinda had asked him to deputise for her and had dispelled his misgivings by telling him it was his opportunity to really walk the talk. In the short time available to her, she had taken him under her wing and made him her protégé. They were both fully aware that his ability to keep intergalactic pressure at bay during this testing period would be sorely tested. Under her expert direction, he had quickly learned how to live and breathe confidence. However, he soon found that the more he inhaled confidence, the more he exhaled doubt. It was the old story of ambition and aspiration tethered by the constraining reins of reality, an encounter with a disagreeable reflection in the mirror, a dispute between a person and what that person might have hoped to be.

Right now, immersed in a meeting that threatened to test all his skills in diplomacy and statesmanship, he became fearful of broaching the subject of polkingbeal67's flight from justice and acquiescently allowed the delegates to get bogged down by the thorny issue of whether or not to approve the minutes of the previous meeting.

"I think it would be helpful to have an overview of the minutes before we're asked to approve them," suggested the saurian from Permia, spitting and sputtering like bacon in a hot pan. "My planet insists on an overview! I have been asked to present a petition to that effect." With exaggerated formality, he stood up, walked slowly and deliberately towards nipkow4, bowed and produced a rolled-up parchment, neatly tied with a red ribbon. Impressed by the solemnity and dignity, a few of the delegates applauded. When nipkow4 dutifully reminded them that clapping was not considered appropriate for officialdom or ceremony, he was rewarded with an enthusiastic round of applause.

Opening the scroll, nipkow4 perused the contents and uttered a snort of disdain. "There are only six signatures on here!" he exclaimed. The Dwingeloo commissioner, sitting on his left, nudged him and whispered, "There are only six people on Permia."

"I agree with the saurian," said one of the Lacuna delegates, "we should have an overview. And perhaps a roadmap discussion?"

The saurian nodded in approval. "Yes, absolutely," he enthused, "followed, I suggest, by a brainstorming session. What about you, nipkow4? Have you got an opinion on this? Or has Melinda not told you what it is yet?" There was a sharp intake of breath followed by one or two sniggers, then propriety reasserted itself.

Nipkow4 let it go without comment and an intervention by the Dwingeloo commissioner delivered him from his distress. "Can we please get on!" she urged. "I want to know what's going on with Melinda's mission to the Pale Blue Dot."

The saurian made a sound like a half-clogged drain. "Why are you Mortians so obsessed with that infernal planet anyway?" he protested. "Totally overrated if you ask me. Have you seen the reviews on TripCrit? Three and a half stars! Wait a minute..." His fingers drifted lazily like spider's legs over a microwocky-like device. "This is what someone from Epimetheus has posted: 'the people are volatile and unwelcoming but the trees are nice. Three stars.' Why, even Oov gets an average of four stars!"

Nipkow4 did not feel inclined to defend Earth's reputation and remained keen to defer discussion of Melinda's progress. She had been in close contact via wormhole channel during the early part of her trip but communication had been patchy in the last few days. No one could understand why it was taking her so long, having apprehended the fugitives, to return with them to Smolin9. "I must rule on the point of order first," nipkow4 insisted.

"No one raised a point of order," the saurian pointed out, twitching his spindly arms in agitation.

Nipkow4 went on regardless. "We have seriously deviated off-topic," he said. "I think we need to reach a consensus on the matter of approving the minutes. I want to be sure everyone is satisfied that we've identified all the issues..." Suddenly, the nervy, jerky flow of his otherwise wise and erudite words was interrupted by the sound of something thudding against the window. "Was that an orbis bird?" he asked, turning on his heels. It was not. It was a microwocky falling from the window above.

Frustrated by Melinda's prolonged absence, the planetary leader had demanded the use of a microwocky in order to make direct contact with her. Unfortunately, he had never mastered the skill of operating the device and, in a fit of pique, had tossed several of them through the window of his private chamber, insisting they were malfunctioning. His mood had been foul ever since his discovery that the Voyager 1 dish antenna had disappeared from his palatial gardens. Polkingbeal67's notion of returning the probe to the south lawn of the White House may have met with almost universal intergalactic approval, but the Mortian leader had been apoplectic with rage when he had learned about its removal.

Gazing out of the window, nipkow4 noticed a crisply defined funnel-shaped cloud looming menacingly towards the palace. "We're in for a storm," he observed, as the door to the office flew open and the Mortian leader crossed the room towards the table, trailing seaweed and matted braids of earthling human hair. It was his first appearance in public since polkingbeal67's disappearing act. Two of his personal attendants could be heard calling after him in anxious whispers. Appearing at the door, they stood transfixed as the leader stepped on a chair to climb up onto the table, slipped on a rogue frond of seaweed and proceeded to crawl around in random circles, uttering strange oaths and cryptic proverbs. Stopping in front of the terror-stricken saurian, he growled, "When the lion comes down from the mountain to the plains, it may be challenged by the dogs!" Fixing the next delegate with a baleful stare, he shouted, "But you have climbed the mountain and entered the cave of the lion!" With that, he scrambled to his feet, whirled a piece of seaweed and roared at the top of his voice, "Grr!" If a real lion had roared like that, it would have been banished from the pride and become the laughing stock of all the hyenas in the land. Nevertheless, the assembled dignitaries and officials fled in disarray, completely unnerved by the bizarre turn of events. The Mortian leader yelled after them, "Behold, behold the crane standing amidst a flock of chickens!"

As the leader was being escorted back to his private chambers, nipkow4 read a message on his microwocky. It was from Melinda: "Hi nippy! Wish you were here! The cruise was great. Very cold. Saw glaciers and all sorts of penguins and a leopard seal and stuff. Got lots of pictures to show you when I get back. Some of them are a bit random. Ha ha. How's it going standing in as planetary leader? I'm sure you're doing a fantastic job as deputy. Is that erratic, or what? Anyway, we've got a problem with yukawa3. He's not eating and strange things keep happening to him. I know he's a penguin and everything but it doesn't explain all the weird stuff. Anyway, I must dash. I'll get back to you later. Take care. Give my love to everybody. Literally."

At this point, nipkow4 became aware of a pair of tiny compound eyes trying to attract his attention. They belonged to the senior chillok ambassador, who had been forgotten during the exodus from the meeting and was still perched on the special dais erected for him at the far end of the table. He was unable to make himself heard because the myrmecam had apparently broken down. It is, of course, possible that it had been deliberately or inadvertently switched off at some point during the meeting. One propitious consequence of this was that the delegates had been spared the ambassador's unrelenting, hysterical, mocking laughter during the Mortian leader's deranged intervention.

As he fiddled with the myrmecam controls, nipkow4's brain started processing two apparently unrelated thoughts - Melinda's recent alarming news about yukawa3 and the memory of the threat the ambassador had issued during the conference that took place immediately before Melinda had left. In short, he put two and two together and arrived at a staggeringly big number. Pointing an accusing finger at the chillok, he ranted and railed, accusing the dumbfounded ambassador of instigating a reprehensible assault on yukawa3 in what amounted to "an utterly repugnant breach of intergalactic conventions".

As far as the chillok ambassador was concerned, it was a provocation too far. "Casus belli!" he shrieked, as nipkow4 left the office. "Casus belli! Casus belli! Casus belli!"

.   .   .

Polkingbeal67 and Melinda got out of the cab at The End of The World Station, partly because they never thought of going to the airport instead and partly because Old Sea Dog felt car sick and almost threw up in the back of the cab. They made their way to the cafeteria and parked themselves near a window with a couple of coffees, listening to the buzz of convivial chatter, the sporadic laughter of small children, a hissing coffee machine and the constant rattle and clatter of cutlery.

"What do we do now?" Melinda asked, after a short while. "We'll never find Fernandez and yukawa3 if we just sit around here."

"I need a minute to think," said polkingbeal67, both hands clasped around his coffee. Staring at the steaming liquid, he contemplated the many perils to which yukawa3 was exposed. His mind wandered. Totally absorbed by the thin, unfurling wisps of steam and the eddies of cream swirling around lazily like a flattened-out barber's pole, he pondered the fragility and tenuousness of life. Being a Mortian accustomed to longevity, he was not given to reflections on mortality and found it very disconcerting. This and his concern for the welfare of his protégé were not the only strange emotions to infiltrate the fortified ego of this estimable battle hero. Long-held tenets were crumbling inside him. Condemned to make way for a radical new makeover, his entire raison d'etre was now being swept aside by the compelling blasts of new insights.

According to earthling sociology, people define themselves in terms of in-groups and out-groups. In-groups are social groups to which people feel they belong and to which they feel loyalty; out-groups, by contrast, are groups to which people do not belong and to which they feel no loyalty. Compatibility and affiliation with groups may be based on such factors as religion, politics, race, nationality or occupation and it stands to reason that group influence has the potential to affect an individual's behaviour in both positive and negative ways. If that all sounds a bit simplistic, rest assured it gets a lot more complicated. Like a Venn diagram gone mad, intergroup cohesion gets blurred by group interdependence, group overlapping and the effect of superordinate identities ('umbrella' groups). Some would say this has a civilising effect, offsetting the dangers inherent in bonding hormones that undermine a person's conscience and render that individual disposed to demonise and dehumanise those perceived as being members of an out-group.

Polkingbeal67 had certainly been guilty of a bit of demonising and dehumanising in the past, but things had changed. His affinity with his Mortian in-group had not been compromised as such, but he now saw it in the context of a more complex hyper structure. He was developing a sense of kinship and connection with other forms of life and it shook the very foundations of his being. In short, he felt awed by a new sense of connection to other beings. Powerful coffee indeed. If this was the end of the world, it was full of hope and wonder - a Lazarus moment, the metamorphosis of a spiky caterpillar into a winged butterfly.

It is important to keep your feet on the ground when your mind takes a leap in the dark and, in timely fashion, Melinda brought polkingbeal67 back down to earth. "I need to pee," she declared, "And after that we should take a bus back to the city centre. Then, as soon as we find yukawa3..." Her voice trembled slightly. "And we *will* find him!"

"What?" Polkingbeal67 prompted her.

"What?"

"You said 'when we find him'..."

"Yeah, when we find him, we'll go straight back to Morys Minor, I mean Smolin9."

"You realise that'll mean sending me to my doom?" polkingbeal67 pointed out, eyes downcast. "They'll make me do compulsory planetary service on Oov. I'm not cut out for building ant heaps, I mean, er, chillok cities!"

Melinda placed her hand on his. "You've changed," she said, "and I'm going to see to it that the court recognises that."

"They won't listen to you. They certainly won't listen to *me*. Everyone back home now thinks I'm a liar."

"I find that very hard to believe," Melinda assured him. They exchanged looks and burst out laughing. Melinda wondered if it was the first time she had ever heard him laugh. Wiping tears from her eyes, she went on, "I think we understand each other better now. You see, I know why you came here and I know it wasn't because you wanted to escape justice. Literally." She looked deep into his eyes as if she were delving into his very soul. "When I came to visit you the day before you were due to be sentenced, you told me you'd seen the future and that you knew the answer. You said you just needed to find out what the question was. Do you remember?"

Polkingbeal67 nodded. "The answers are out there," he said. "They're everywhere. Everyone's got some. But the tricky bit is coming up with the right question. I'm only

337

just beginning to understand that. It feels like... I don't know, it's like having a great opportunity but knowing you'll only see it retrospectively. I feel like I've been born for a purpose but I don't know what it is."

"But you thought you might find the question here, didn't you? Like yukawa3, you felt kind of drawn here." She squeezed his hand. "I literally, sincerely hope you find it. Just be careful you don't pursue it too hard. It might, y'know, keep running away."

"That's true," polkingbeal67 confirmed, "and I think yukawa3 is closer to the question than I am. The trouble is, he comes up with spectacularly bad answers."

Shortly afterwards, they boarded a pale blue double-decker bus and sat behind a party of people in ski gear carrying snowboard bags, chatting away excitedly. The bus weaved through the congested, snow-slicked streets and the windows started to mist up. As they approached a junction, Melinda noticed a large crowd that had gathered outside a diner. Wiping the condensation from the window with the palm of her hand, she stared hard. "Quick, look! It's him!' she exclaimed. "It's him! It's him! Literally!" They scrambled off the bus and ran back towards the diner. Arriving at the back of the crowd, they craned their necks and peered over shoulders to see a sickly-looking penguin performing half-hearted tricks at Fernandez's behest for the entertainment of the slack-jawed bystanders, some of whom tossed a few pesos into a yellow sou'wester lying on the pavement. Unable to force their way through the throng, polkingbeal67 and Melinda waved their arms and called out Fernandez's name.

What happened next was a blur of frenzied noise and activity. Spotting polkingbeal67 and Melinda at the back of the crowd, Fernandez made a grab for yukawa3, who chirped shrilly in distress and clumsily dodged the captain's flailing arms. Undeterred, Fernandez seized the sou'wester, scattering coins everywhere, crammed it over yukawa3's head and swept him up into his arms. Later, polkingbeal67 would say he saw a cloud of flying ants ascending from the scene, but, given that it was late October, this was extremely unlikely. What he probably saw was the shower of coins flying from the sou'wester. Struggling feebly, like a worm on a hook, yukawa3 attempted to bite his captor, but Fernandez refused to relinquish his grip and clung on tight as he ran away down the street with polkingbeal67 and Melinda on his heels. Suddenly, yukawa3 became enveloped in a bright, phosphorescent green light and Fernandez dropped him. The immediate area around the penguin became engulfed in a greenish fog. It cleared almost instantaneously to reveal a sight that would be etched in the minds of those present for some time to come.

Yukawa3 was apparently embedded in the pavement and only the top half of his body was visible. He opened his beak to utter something, but no sound came forth. Eyes wide, hand to mouth, Melinda was frozen to the spot. Fernandez looked at her. "Iss trick, no?" he asked, half in horror, half in inquiry. He stooped to pull the hapless bird from its confinement, at which point there was another shimmer of green light and Fernandez was left grasping at thin air. Yukawa3 was gone.

.   .   .

"Come on, cheer up!" said Melinda, noticing what may have been tears in polkingbeal67's eyes. "We've rode these sort of storms before. All is not lost."

"So where the hell is it then?"

"Where's what?"

"All of it," said polkingbeal67. "We've lost smolin9 and now yukawa3 too. When do the good things start? That's what I want to know." His new-found sensitivity and empathy had taken its toll on him, leaving him broken, jaded, a little more cynical and a whole lot wiser. They were sitting in the Avon coroner's office waiting to speak to someone about the death of Sophia Gonzalez (smolin9's earthling identity at the time of his demise). They had travelled separately, polkingbeal67 using his airline return ticket, Melinda making a wormhole transit.

"Listen," said Melinda, "there'll be good stuff, I promise you. Joy and contentment are going to switch places with all this pain and adversity. Literally. You'll see. We'll make it happen."

Polkingbeal67 was unconvinced. "I won't hold my breath," he said. "When good stuff happens, it's like a fault on your earthling televisions." He noticed Melinda looking at him quizzically. "That message – 'normal service will be resumed shortly'."

Melinda got up and took a couple of paces towards the window. "What's keeping them? We've been waiting ages. And this office is so small and stuffy. You couldn't swing a cat in here."

"Why *would* you?" asked polkingbeal67 with artless simplicity.

An official appeared with an armful of papers and an expression of harried urgency and impatience. "So," the tall, bespectacled man said, "You say you're Sophia Gonzalez's sister?"

Melinda nodded. "Yes, we weren't very close. I, uh, emigrated and we lost touch."

The official gave her a long look of dubious indecision. "What were you told about the circumstances of your sister's death?"

Polkingbeal67 drew the conclusion that the man did not even know what had happened. "Have we come to the right place?" he asked. "Do you conduct post mortems on dead people here?"

The official sat on the desk and removed his glasses. "Oh yes," he said, with a twinkle in his eye. "We conduct *all* our post mortems on dead people." He bared his teeth in a slightly demonic grin. "Mind you, I personally have not conducted *any* post mortems. I'm not a pathologist. I'm just a liaison officer. You're probably aware that there was an inquest?" When Melinda nodded, he continued, "The pathologist's evidence was inconclusive and the jury returned an open verdict."

Sweetly and politely, Melinda interrupted. "To be honest," she said, "all we want to do now is find his final resting place so we can pay our respects. Sorry, I mean *her*! *Her* final resting place."

The liaison officer lowered his voice until Melinda could barely hear him. "I'm sorry," he said. "There was no family around at the time. We didn't know about you. The CIA got involved. They said your sister's body was potentially a crime scene. Apparently, they made some sort of link with something that happened in the States. You remember that big hoo-hah about the Voyager space probe?" He shrugged and spread his hands. "Don't ask," he said. "I've no idea. Anyway, they flew your sister's body to Washington."

Devastated that she was not going to be able to pay her respects in the proper way, Melinda began to cry. As polkingbeal67 placed a comforting arm around her shoulders, the liaison officer shuffled his papers in awkward silence for several moments before continuing, "If it helps," he said, "at the diner where she worked, her colleagues raised some money and erected a memorial bench. It's in the square just around the corner from the diner."

Later, polkingbeal67 and Melinda arrived at the square and located the bench under an impressive ash tree. They stood for some time fondly recalling their respective memories. "How do you make sense of it?" Melinda asked rhetorically, tracing the letters on the plaque with her fingers.

A gust of wind rattled some dead leaves from the tree. A puddle near the bench reflected the remaining leaves hanging like a colony of yellow bats. Melinda went on: "I suppose people live on in their children, if they have any, or in the memories of other people. In fact, if you think of famous artists and poets and musicians and statesmen and stateswomen, their lives seem more important *after* they die. It's like, if you want to be considered truly great at something, the first thing to do is be dead. Literally."

A solitary, shivering leaf fell right in front of them, like a feather from a tormented bird. "We are but petals on the winds of time," said polkingbeal67.

"They're leaves," Melinda pointed out. "Leaves. Not petals."

"Petals or leaves, it makes no difference. Like stars and tears, they delight or sadden us for a time. Ephemeral joy, fleeting moments of sadness. They assemble and scatter."

"And then fall without a sound," Melinda added.

They sat on the bench, lost in thought. Shadows

lengthened, people came and went, colours drained away.

Polkingbeal67 broke the silence. "Have you arranged for us to return home?"

Melinda's fingers pecked at her microwocky. "Yes, it's got to be authorised, so we've got a bit of time to kill."

"And that's the thing," said polkingbeal67. "You can't kill time. We spend our lives trying to control it, trying to make sense of it, seeking answers to the questions it poses."

"But you Mortians have got that thing, haven't you? That karma thing?"

"Karma 5."

"Yes, doesn't it offer you some kind of immortality? In fact..." Her heart leapt with the sudden realisation that both smolin9 and yukawa3 had left behind mutators containing copies of their Karma 5. Yukawa3's device was now the occasional plaything of penguins on a desolate beach on South Georgia Island and smolin9's was locked away in a top secret facility in Nevada. "If we could just find..."

Reading her thoughts, polkingbeal67 took her hand. "No," he said. "It's strictly forbidden."

"But why?" she asked, linking her fingers imploringly in his. "It's transferable, isn't it? In fact, your Karma 5 was transferred to smolin9's body, and vice versa. So, surely... Surely that's the answer, isn't it?"

"That depends on the question," he replied cryptically. "Anyway, our switch was carried out while we were both alive. No, it's not the answer. We can't bring them back. But I'm sure we'll find other ways to hold on to them in our lives."

They remained sitting on the memorial bench in each other's arms as occasional flutters of wind swirled around the square and more leaves twirled from the tree in silent surrender. Polkingbeal67 turned to Melinda as if to speak, but she put a finger to his lips. "Shh," she said. "I'm holding on."

7

WHEN PARALLEL WORLDS COLLIDE

One moment he was embedded up to his wingpits in the grey concrete of a pavement in Ushuaia at the southernmost tip of planet Earth; next moment there was a shimmer of green light and yukawa3 was hurtling along winding labyrinthine passageways in a totally alien environment, propelled forwards by a relentless, heaving, tumbling stream of kindred penguins. At one point, a small group of them stumbled on top of one another before scrambling upright to resume an apparently aimless stampede. As they struggled to recover their balance and dignity, yukawa3 attempted, if only for a brief moment, to catch their attention. "Where exactly are we going?" he asked with a note of bewildered irritation in his voice. Without checking their headlong pace, the penguins in the immediate vicinity threw back their heads and trumpeted loudly.

Having had the good fortune to secure his microwocky (along with his yellow sou'wester) before he had been so rudely wrenched from planet Earth, he was surprised and distressed to find the device could not decipher the sounds emitted by his new penguin neighbours. He relied upon it to provide real-time translations of virtually *all* the languages and dialects in the known universe, the one exception being the strange tongue adopted by chilloks. Horrified at the prospect that his 'wocky might not function in this strange new environment, he stopped to adjust some settings, only to find himself unceremoniously bundled into a wall. "Listen!" he yelled as he continued to be bumped, shoved and jostled by the surging crowd. "Why don't we just stop for a minute and, y'know, huddle or something?" He spread his wings beseechingly. "Wouldn't a huddle be good?" he asked, prompting more throwing back of heads and loud trumpeting. Difficult as it was, he managed to carry out a complete functionality check on the microwocky. On discovering that there were no faults or anomalies, he was simultaneously reassured and alarmed. "But I don't understand these penguins!" he wailed. "What are they saying?" Grabbing a passing penguin by the flipper, he yelled at the hapless bird: "Tell me what's going on! Speak proper penguinese, please!" All this intervention achieved was a multiple penguin pile-up that took some time to get straightened out. "This isn't going to work is it?" he observed, somewhat redundantly.

It was said (generally by Mortians) that nothing could confound the rational powers of a Mortian brain for long. Generally speaking, yukawa3 provided plenty of evidence to refute the assertion, but on this occasion the beleaguered cadet shrewdly concluded that there were two possible explanations - either this was *not* part of the known universe or the penguins were speaking the language of Formicidae chilloks. He cringed at the prospect of either scenario, so one can only imagine the anguish he would have felt if his rational powers had grasped the fact that *both* scenarios applied.

Desperate to discover where he was and what was going on, he stepped boldly into the oncoming stream, raised his flippers and shouted: "Stop! Let's just see if we can go the other way instead!" The ensuing chaos and tribulation furnished those present with further evidence, if any were needed, of the profound shortcomings in Mortian rationality (at least as far as it applied to yukawa3).

The fact is, the Muqu chillok community had sentenced yukawa3 to what amounted to life imprisonment for his role in the destruction of the city of Niffis and they had despatched him to a parallel universe way beyond the comprehension of mere human beings.

Perhaps that last remark is a trifle unfair - at this stage in intergalactic history even earthling physicists were entertaining the notion of detecting quantum information and were vaguely developing nanotechnologies to manipulate matter on an atomic and molecular scale. Indeed, they were already using tools such as particle colliders to analyse the structure of the subatomic world and the laws of nature governing it. As for Mortians, they certainly understood the concept of multiple universes, but lacked the intellect required to locate and navigate to one. Their knowledge of subquantum strings was still only theoretical. No, it may have been difficult for humans to accept, but chilloks remained the only species capable of crossing through trans-dimensional portals. Assuming, dear reader, that you are a human being yourself, you will of course find it baffling that these diminutive creatures could be endowed with such superior intelligence. After all, in common with other members of the Formicidae family, an individual chillok brain has about 250,000 brain cells compared to the 100 billion neurons in an earthling human one. As a matter of fact, an earthling adult human brain loses more cells in an earthling month than a chillok brain possesses in total. The answer to the conundrum is the chillok capacity for telepathic networking on a colossal multi-universe scale.

Not that any of these deliberations mattered to yukawa3 right now. Having been flattened and battered during his attempt to go against the tide, he had since been swept up and held aloft as the great surge continued unabated. But gradually, the twists and turns of the passageways became less and less aggravating and he found himself drifting into a shallow, dreaming sleep.

He dreamed he was back on his home planet, Smolin9 (formerly Morys Minor). Everyone was assembled in the gardens of the leader's palace in preparation for some sort of ceremony. The atmosphere was solemn and reverent. People talked in hushed tones. He spotted polkingbeal67 and Melinda deep in conversation.

"It's so erratic to have a funeral service without a body," said Melinda in a sombre, almost inaudible tone. "It's like having a wedding without a bride. Literally."

"Whose funeral?" yukawa3 enquired. "Whose body? What's happened?" Neither Melinda nor polkingbeal67 could see or hear him, so he tugged at Melinda's sleeve. She felt nothing. In fact, his hand passed straight through as if Melinda's arm did not exist.

An open casket containing a yellow sou'wester served as the central focus of the ceremony that now occupied everyone's attention.

"Why are they burying a sou'wester?" yukawa3 mumbled to himself, having realised that his presence could not be detected. "How do they know it's dead? How do sou'westers die anyway?"

Melinda turned to polkingbeal67. "Why did he always love those daft hats?" she asked. "I never did understand what was going on there. Did he have a reason for collecting them?"

Polkingbeal67 shrugged his shoulders and sighed. "He didn't need a reason. He just needed a head."

Finally, the penny dropped. "They're talking about me," yukawa3 muttered to himself before declaring aloud, "You think I'm dead! I'm *not* dead! I'm here! Look! I'm alive!" He attempted to clutch polkingbeal67's arm but his hand passed through without meeting any resistance. "I'm just not feeling very, y'know, physical, at the moment," he said. Mortians do not possess eyelids but even if they did, no one would have batted one.

"Shouldn't we say a few words about him?" polkingbeal67 suggested, squeezing Melinda's arm reassuringly. "Do you want to go first?"

"What should I say?" Melinda asked, more than a little agitated.

"Well, there was the incident at nefeshchaya, remember? The earthling prisoner insurgency?"

"I remember the incident well enough," said Melinda, perplexed, "but what exactly did yukawa3 contribute? All I remember is him running around in random circles."

Yukawa3 could not have been more indignant. "What!" he exclaimed, for no one's ears but his own. "Those circles confused the enemy and left them exposed to polkingbeal67's counter-attack! Don't you understand? I'm a space guerilla! It was a classic military tactic!" Staring at

Melinda with a look of defiance and triumph in his eyes, he added, "I hope that answers your question!"

"Okay," said polkingbeal67, "what about his broadcasting work for the MMBC?"

Melinda frowned. "I don't think so," she said. "I don't have to remind you how that all ended. Literally."

"Right, yes." Polkingbeal67 scratched his chin as he tried to dismiss the painful memory of the spacecraft flattening the chillok city of Niffis. "I see what you mean. Well, maybe we should just stick with the Voyager space probe thing," he said reflectively.

"I know *he* got the credit for it, but the truth is, it was all *your* doing," Melinda pointed out.

"I know. But as far as all these people are concerned, yukawa3 arranged for it to be returned to the earthling president. And it was *his* sou'wester that was attached to the probe in place of the golden record."

"Isn't there anything else we can say? Are there no other highlights of his life and career?"

Yukawa3 felt he should break the silence that followed. "I want to say something about this," he said. Unfortunately, when it came to it, he could not come up with anything at all. Not that it would have mattered - no one would have heard him anyway. He consoled himself with the thought that he was not actually dead yet, so there was still time to create some highlights.

As the casket was lowered into the ground, Melinda sniffed and dabbed at her eyes with a handkerchief. The planetary leader, draped in long ribbons of seaweed that trailed behind him, shuffled forward like Marley's ghost to say a few words himself. "There is many a good man to be found under a shabby hat," he said in a fragile, tremulous voice. A dignified silence fell.

"That's right," said yukawa3 gratefully. "It is spoken."

Crepuscular rays streamed through gaps in the clouds. As he delivered the rest of his eulogy, the leader's words were slurred with tiredness, emotion and a little too much vitalmados. "Here lies... taken too soon... sorrowful occasion... but the saddest thing, my friends... the saddest thing is the death of the hat, er, heart of a dear friend."

As the sou'wester disappeared from view, tears welled up in yukawa3's eyes and he turned to embrace Melinda and rest his head on her shoulder, only to glide straight through her and fall headlong into the grave on top of the casket. At this point, as he clutched the sou'wester and the first shower of dirt swept through him, yukawa3 could not have been more uncertain whether he was dead or alive.

"Stop! I'm alive! I'm alive!" he yelled in a tortured scream that should have echoed up from the grave and reverberated like Gabriel's trumpet call throughout the palace grounds (except, of course, it could not be heard at all).

It was a voice that echoed from somewhere deep in his subconscious when he finally emerged from his dream and found himself still being carried aloft by penguins scurrying manically from passageway to passageway. Realising there had been no change in his situation, yukawa3 threw back his head and trumpeted loudly.

.　　.　　.

Polkingbeal67 and Melinda were strolling through the grounds of the leader's palace immediately after the

351

memorial service. The secondary sun was totally obscured and pale beams from the primary sun barely penetrated the thick cloud cover. Off in the distance, over the clicking and thudding of people's footsteps and the distant hum of spacecruiser traffic, the plaintive jabbering of orbis birds lent a melancholy tone to the late afternoon. Although the rituals had finished, a few mourners were still lying prostrate on the ground, arms extended above their heads, palms outstretched.

"I thought that was very worthwhile," said polkingbeal67. "A really fitting tribute, don't you think?"

Melinda glanced back at the grave where the commemoration casket had been buried. "Uh-huh, I suppose so," she said. "Are all funerals like that here?"

"Well, first of all, like I keep telling you, it wasn't a funeral service - it was a commemoration service. And second of all, people hardly ever die here. We live for hundreds, sometimes thousands of your Earth years, so we just don't have these sort of services very often. This one was actually based on your earthling ceremonies. Third of all, it's not finished yet - tonight there's going to be a laser show complete with sonic blaster concerto."

"Laser blaster what now? Is that like a fireworks show?"

"Fireworks?"

"Yeah, y'know, Guy Fawkes and all that. Er, yeah, so he was this guy, ha, who tried to blow up the country's rulers."

"Well, why didn't he?"

"What – blow them up? I can't remember. Maybe his lighter didn't work or something," Melinda said abstractedly, contemplating polkingbeal67's face, which was actually the face of her late husband. "Can I talk to you about something that's bothering me? I know it's not your responsibility, but I don't understand - we've just had a service for someone who's disappeared and is presumed to be dead. Literally. But we haven't had *any* sort of service for my husband, who we know for sure is definitely dead. Why haven't we had any sort of funeral or commemoration thing for smolin9?"

"But we had a grand ceremony when the planet was renamed in his honour."

"That was supposed to be a funeral service?"

"Memorial," polkingbeal67 corrected her. "It was a special event to solemnly honour his life."

"I didn't realise." Melinda looked at the ground uncomfortably. "That's eerie. I wish someone had told me. I thought it was a purely celebratory thing. I would have done stuff very differently."

"Yeah, okay, that explains a few things," polkingbeal67 mused, pursing his lips. "Like your choice of music, for example."

Melinda looked mortified. "Oh no!" she wailed. "I see what you mean." 'Oh Happy Day' and 'Stayin Alive' now seemed such a curious choice of songs.

While the other guests and grievers headed towards the spacecruiser park, polkingbeal67 and Melinda were met on the steps of the leader's beautiful and impressive residence by the palace adviser and translator, nipkow4, who spread his hands, palms upward, and let them drop again in a courtly gesture of sympathy. Addressing Melinda respectfully, if a little long-windedly, as "our revered deputy leader and heir apparent", he advised her that the senior chillok ambassador was requesting an audience with her, presumably to seek further redress for the Niffis atrocity.

As they passed through the reception hall, bedecked with seaweed, volcanic magma, porcelain ornaments and figurines fashioned out of goopmutt horn, alongside various portraits of Mortian celebrities, the revered leader emerged from a corridor and beckoned to them. Following a complicated ritual of bows, bobs, curtseys and hand waggles, the leader looked askance at polkingbeal67 and said: "It's bad luck to return for something you've forgotten."

Polkingbeal67 made a slight gesture of incomprehension with his hands, so nipkow4 offered an interpretation: "Our revered leader believes you should not have returned."

"Beware, lest you give your enemies the means of your own destruction," said the leader, nodding meaningfully and shooting a glance towards the small ante-room where the senior chillok ambassador awaited them. "As a dog returns to its vomit, so fools repeat their folly."

Placing a hand on polkingbeal67's shoulder, nipkow4 explained, "You'd better make yourself scarce. The chilloks probably don't know you're here." He hesitated for a second. "Er, and don't come back."

Polkingbeal67, who was only too aware that he was the prime target for chillok retribution, nodded in agreement, but he felt a surge of anger erupt inside his heart. Believing that the spirit of a war hero coursed through his blood, it tore him up to be reduced to this kind of humiliating retreat. "Running away from an ant!" he muttered bitterly through what would have been clenched teeth if he had had any. Suddenly overcome with feelings of disgrace and dishonour, he curled into a foetal position and made a low growl in the back of his throat.

The leader turned to the translator with an innocent, almost childlike look of inquiry.

"He's trying to suppress a sense of anguish and betrayal," nipkow4 clarified for the leader's benefit, before moving closer to polkingbeal67 and hissing, "Don't do this!"

If polkingbeal67 had had any eyebrows, he would have arched one of them. As he did not, he settled for a vinegary scowl. Melinda, unsure how to react to this exchange, waited quietly and patiently with a sympathetic look on her face.

The leader set a determined jaw and folded his arms resolutely. "Do not believe that you will reach your destination without leaving the shore," he warned.

Nipkow4's expression turned to one of puzzlement and concern. He turned from one to the other before venturing a cautious, "Er, get going? And you'd better travel well away from here?"

"Okay, I'm going," snapped polkingbeal67. "Maybe that Guy Fawkes had the right idea after all," he added darkly.

As he left the building, trailing gloom and despondency, the others went into the ante-room where the senior chillok ambassador was waiting for them in the middle of a small circular magma table, standing on his back legs like a tiny rubberised poodle with an excess of limbs, craning over towards a myrmecam, pre-installed and pre-configured for translation purposes. "Urbes constituit aetas, momentum temporis dissolvit!" he snarled, flicking his antennae at the Mortian leader.

Nipkow4 translated: "A city built during a lifetime is destroyed in a moment."

The ambassador, barely allowing time for nipkow4 to finish, spat again into the myrmecam: "Si vis pacem, para bellum!"

"If you seek peace, prepare for war!"

While the Mortian leader gathered up his garlands of seaweed and fidgeted in anxious agitation, Melinda approached the table and spoke defiantly. "Really?" she said, "Are we going to start this conversation with negative attitudes and threats? Literally?"

Slightly nonplussed, the chillok did not reply, just stared at Melinda and waved his antennae with hesitant animosity.

"Sit down!" she barked at him. "Or whatever it is you do."

A little fazed, the ambassador duly dropped down on all six legs.

Melinda pressed home the advantage. "Right," she said. "Are you sitting down? Literally?"

The ambassador swished his antennae in irritation, walked up to the myrmecam and butted it.

Melinda dismissed the theatrics with a withering look. "Whatever," she said. "Listen, you're just trying to provoke us so as to have a pretext for war. Well, we're not having it! Not by a long chalk. Literally. To declare war on us, you've got to be able to justify it, you've got to be able to show, er..."

Nipkow4 came to her assistance. "Just cause," he said. "And a just war can only be waged if it carries sufficient moral weight. The Intergalactic Court is perfectly clear on this point."

Determined not to flinch again, the ambassador remonstrated with nipkow4, arguing that the Niffis massacre was sufficient provocation for all intergalactic treaties between the two peoples to be revoked. His people were determined to put right an egregious wrong. No terms short of unconditional and immediate surrender of polkingbeal67 by noon the following day would be acceptable to the Muqu chilloks. These, he insisted, were generous terms that were offered without prejudice.

Nipkow4 turned to Melinda and spoke in a low undertone, "Do you think we should do it?"

"What, knock him onto the floor and stamp on him?" Melinda responded as calmly as she could.

Genuinely shocked, nipkow4 coughed, stepped up to the myrmecam and bowed obsequiously to the ambassador. "Excuse us a moment," he said deferentially. Switching off the myrmecam and taking the leader aside by his arm, he murmured, "What he's offering is a compromise that we should probably accept."

Nodding in agreement, the leader whispered, "The sheep has no choice when caught in the jaws of the wolf." They both knew that the failure of diplomacy could have dire consequences. The loss of polkingbeal67 could be considered a small sacrifice if it allowed them to deal with the chilloks in anything approaching a rational discourse. They exchanged glances and then quickly turned to Melinda. It was glaringly obvious that any such deal would be totally unacceptable to her. Nevertheless, they looked at her entreatingly.

"What?" demanded Melinda, shaking a finger in reproachful disapproval. "You're going to give up polkingbeal67 just like that?"

The leader raised his shriveled and trembling hands beseechingly. "We must not attempt to extract a tooth from the tiger's mouth," he counselled. As Melinda just fixed him with a blank, uncomprehending stare, he tried something else: "When it's raining you should not refuse an umbrella."

"Excuse me, but if I was some sort of animal dentist, I wouldn't want an umbrella. I'd want a roof!" Melinda protested, her exasperation mounting steadily. "Why would a dentist work outside anyway? Literally. Listen, just stop it with all your stupid wise sayings and tell this ridiculous insect where to get off! There's no way we're going to let him take polkingbeal67 prisoner! Right?"

Retrieving some nail clippers from her purse, she advanced menacingly towards the table, flicked the switch on the myrmecam and bared her teeth at the ambassador. "Look, chief," she said, "I'll fix your teeth for you!" The ambassador recoiled in fright. Melinda continued, "I may be a rubbish deputy leader, whatever, but you... you're an insect, a bad insect, a very small and helpless insect!" Nipkow4 snatched the clippers, switched off the myrmecam and ushered her outside.

The Mortian leader stood rooted to the spot while the chillok ambassador hurled Latin curses and invective at him. Challenged like never before to represent his people and shelter them from the threat of war, the leader drew himself up to his full height, raised his right hand and spontaneously delivered the most impressive speech of his entire career, a speech clever enough to outwit the most cunning of villainous masterminds, moving enough to make rocks weep, powerful enough to inspire an entire auditorium to rise to its feet in joyous acclamation. He had always known he had a speech like that in him (after all, he had spent years studying the most celebrated speeches in human history). As he nodded to the ambassador to signify that he had finished, he realised that the myrmecam was switched off and his oratory had fallen on deaf ears.

You can never repeat the magic of the original. And so it was with the leader's second address to the enraged chillok ambassador. Upset and flustered, he started badly by raising the wrong hand and allowing a capacious garland of seaweed to slip from his shoulders and collapse in a pool at his feet. "We bow before the wisdom of the chilloks," he began, stooping to pick up the seaweed. "Let us never negotiate out of fear, but let us never fear to negotiate. This is not the beginning of the end for our special relationship. Nor is it the end of the beginning. Rather, it is a joyous daybreak to end the long night of our misunderstanding. We judge you not by the number of your legs but by the content of your character. Never have so many legs been marched by so many around so few. Once bitten, we shall fight the urges to scratch those parts of our body to soothe the pain. We shall fight them with growing confidence and growing strength in the air; we shall fight them in the hills; we shall never surrender." Bewildered and exhausted, he put his hands on his haunches and added, "I have a dream."

Not only was this officially the end of the conference, it was also officially the start of hostilities between the Mortians and the Muqu chilloks.

.   .   .

The senior chillok ambassador had stage-managed the whole thing. Not just the declaration of war, which bothered him no more or less than a rogue pheromone on a food trail, but much, much more, including the mental deterioration of the Mortian leader and his appointment of

Melinda Hill as his successor.

To understand how he could have achieved this, you need to be aware that Mortians were peculiarly susceptible to braintuning, an insidious practice whereby chillok entities implanted themselves in the brains of unwitting hosts for the purpose of inducing temporary hypnosis or, indeed, applying longer-term psychological modifications. Rumours of these brain-invading entities, often described as disembodied rogue spirits, occasionally flew around the intergalactic community, but the Mortians were only vaguely aware of the sinister technique, labouring under the misapprehension that its use was largely theoretical and that the Muqu chilloks, as full signatories of the statutes governing the Intergalactic Court of Justice, Arbitration and Conciliation, would never have dared to commit such a violation for real. As it happens, such deluded thinking may have been as damaging as the braintuning itself. The fact is, not only had the chilloks infiltrated the mind of yukawa3 to prepare him for exile in a parallel universe, they had also accelerated the cerebral decline of the Mortian leader as part of their agenda for a large-scale colonial Muqu settlement on Smolin9, their plan being to replace him with a popular but inexperienced leader who would be incapable of resisting their imperial ambitions (Melinda Hill from Earth fitted the bill quite nicely). I might also mention that they had braintuned the Mortian aphids to surrender themselves in droves. There was nothing loftily ambitious about this - they just found the sweet, sticky substance excreted by the plant-sucking insects utterly, utterly irresistible!

No one knew it, but the entire population of Mortians had been at the mercy of the chilloks even before any formal declarations of war. The hapless planet was like a festering, partially cooked chicken infected with salmonella, and the future looked unutterably grim for all concerned (except, of course, the salmonella germs). They say the greater part of our happiness depends upon our dispositions and not upon our circumstances, but if the Mortian people had had any inkling of the plight they were in, they would have been about as happy as ducks in a desert.

If the intellectual superiority of the chilloks was at the heart of the debacle, the acquiescent conduct of the Mortian government was certainly a contributory factor. A policy of preferential treatment for disadvantaged peoples had spiraled out of control. The authorities espoused a doctrine known as 'identification', a programme for social inclusion and respect for diverse lifestyles and cultures across the entire panoply of interplanetary relations. It seemed noble enough in its intent, but critics were becoming wary of a system that required them to respect civilisations they considered abhorrent. It had come to the point where ordinary Mortian natives were beginning to feel decidedly second-rate, convinced that they were being denied the rights enjoyed by non-natives. Hamstrung by its own political correctness and self-defeating groupthink, the government had blinded itself to the abominable intentions of the chilloks, who, not in spite of, but precisely *because* of their diminutive stature, were prospering in the hospitable climate afforded by these liberal sensibilities. Even before the Niffis incident, the chilloks had harboured thinly-veiled contempt towards Mortians (and others), but the planetary administration had seen fit to compromise the rights and status of the indigenous population by refusing to entertain the notion that such a disadvantaged species as the chilloks might subvert or infiltrate Mortian society. To make this a whole lot less clear, the Mortian government actually consisted of an array of artificial intelligence systems programmed in accordance with the ideology determined by the electorate. So, of course, despite all their protestations and dissent, the Mortians only had themselves to blame.

It could have been worse by a factor of the x and y components multiplied by the GPS coordinates. The chilloks would have achieved intergalactic dominance long ago, were it not for the bitter schism between the Muqus and the Naaffabs. Deeply held resentments had simmered for eons, but renewed tensions had flared up on the chilloks' home planet of Oov during the last baktun when trouble broke out during a festival to celebrate the birthday of the great chillok potentate, Da'Qunaa. The celebrations culminated in a giant parade through the subterranean passages of Niffis, when the Naaffabs suddenly reneged on a promise to avoid ostentatious rattling of antenna rings, provoking a violent response by the aggrieved Muqus. The death toll was such that chillok society had remained polarised along sectarian lines ever since.

Polkingbeal67 knew as much about these issues as a goopmutt knows about ballet dancing, so there was a good chance he was not contemplating them as he made his way to his demipod. However, his encounter (or rather, his notable non-encounter) with the senior chillok ambassador had left him feeling decidedly jaundiced towards the consummate arthropods who held his fate in their miniscule mandibles. His mind went back to a few random incidents that had occurred during his last visit to Earth, like the time Melinda had flicked away what she thought was an ant from yukawa3's back when they were on South Georgia Island, and the time he had thought he had seen a cloud of flying ants ascending from the pavement in Ushuaia right before yukawa3 had vanished forever. For a brief moment, he wondered if these apparently innocuous incidents might signify chillok involvement in the cadet's disappearance, but his mental equilibrium was so out of wack that the simple matter of putting two and two together eluded him and he dismissed his suspicions as misplaced distrust.

Yes, dear reader, you are right - this wishy-washy forbearance was quite out of character, probably symptomatic of an undiagnosed and mysterious medical condition, or so polkingbeal67 himself concluded later when he reflected on the day's events over a vitalmados lozenge. If you suspect that the chilloks were attempting to braintune polkingbeal67 in the same way as they had braintuned yukawa3 and the Mortian leader, then you would be right. But it was more complicated than that. Yes, they could easily have dispatched him to a parallel universe prison (well, I say easily, but it had taken a few abortive attempts before they had finally succeeded in ensnaring and incarcerating yukawa3), but the chilloks had other objectives to consider. Avenging the Niffis massacre was obviously high on their agenda, but it was secondary to their overriding pursuit of intergalactic dominion. If anyone should doubt that destiny has a sense of humour, they should reflect on these tiny creatures endowed with the fiercest and most relentless ambition.

Given the networked nature of their intelligence, the chilloks did not have a need for leadership as such. While it is true that they had a senior ambassador, this was a largely symbolic role concocted for the purpose of cooperating with the Intergalactic Court. They all aspired to the same deeply held but unwritten ideals and they all knew intuitively that if they wanted to win the dirty game of intergalactic politics, they would have to pay at least lip service to the rules. That is why they were represented on the ICJAC. That is why they made every effort to conceal their designs on Smolin9 and other planets. And that is why they had attempted to use diplomacy rather than force to bring polkingbeal67 to justice. Yukawa3 had been considered an easy target, but polkingbeal67, a high profile Mortian war hero, was a far stickier proposition. Not that they were ever likely to back down. Like all members of the family Formicidae, chilloks were tenacious and they would never quit. If they had it in their minds to get somewhere and you stood in their path, they would find another way. They would climb over, under, around, and keep looking for a solution. Eventually, they would get where they intended to go. In this case, although their patience was nearly exhausted, they were loath to fly in the face of intergalactic law. The Niffis issue was a controversial one. Contrary to nipkow4's analysis, the ICJAC was actually quite ambivalent about 'just causes' of war. Broadly speaking, it may have been considered legitimate to seek redress for an act of aggression, but many affiliates of the Court insisted that a war of punishment could never be a 'just' war.

Polkingbeal67 decided he needed a plan. Life had been conspiring against him recently and it was time to show initiative and wrest control of his destiny from those who wished to subjugate it. It was not going to be easy and would require the stimulating effect of a foaming vial of vitalmados. Several vials later, he still needed a plan. At one point, he was sure he could visualise a plan hovering fitfully on the far side of his demipod. Gossamer-like and translucent, it trembled like a floating veil and he dashed across the room to seize it, but it evaded him like a slippery fish and he collided heavily with the wall like a cartoon dog getting wacked with a frying pan. Sitting there, nursing his wounds, sipping another vial of invigorating vitalmados, he took stock of his situation and tried to recover his resolve. Nothing, he told himself, would be better than a good plan. So nothing was exactly what he did.

.   .   .

Obviously it did not exactly help, but the vitalmados was not the only thing that prevented polkingbeal67 from constructing a plan to change the direction of his life. The chillok incursion into his brain facilitated a braintuning technique known as neutralisation. In other words, every time he developed a thought that was potentially injurious to chillok sensibilities, it was effectively snuffed out at the neuron level. It was like Lucy pulling the football away from Charlie Brown every time he aimed a kick at it. He conceived one option after another for confronting the chilloks, but they were all snatched from his conscious thoughts before he had a chance to rationalise them. After a while, he knew what the inevitable outcome was going to be but he could not help himself and refused to give up.

The neutraliser was often used in conjunction with a related technique known as transposition, whereby each thought was replaced with a contradictory one. This was cutting-edge neuroscience, even for the chilloks, and the beta-phase disasters were still deeply etched in their collective consciousness. Indeed, two of the pioneering practitioners were still locked in a perpetual argument about who discovered it first:

"No, *I* did!"

"Yes, you did!"

"No, *I* did!"

"Yes, you did!"

As it was not possible to determine whose thoughts were being transposed, no one could find a way to terminate their circular argument and the two antagonists could not be separated.

Early the next morning, Melinda made her way over to

polkingbeal67's demipod. A bank of slate-grey clouds concealed both suns and threatened rain. Arriving at the demipod, it took her several minutes to rouse him. He appeared groggy and disoriented when he finally operated the door.

"We've upset the chillok ambassador," Melinda announced.

Polkingbeal67 rubbed his eyes and managed to haul himself upright at the second attempt. "Really?" he asked with all the enthusiasm of a patient undergoing a colonoscopy.

"We refused to hand you over as a prisoner and he's basically saying we're now at war."

Polkingbeal67's eyes glazed over slightly, partly owing to the effects of the previous night's vitalmados binge and partly because he felt drained of his newly-acquired ability to empathise and emote, but mostly because his responses were being manipulated on the fly by chillok interference. "I should hand myself in," he said, "freely, voluntarily, without duress. Yes, that would be the right thing to do."

"What!" Melinda exclaimed, "No, no, no, no, no! You're totally *not* handing yourself in, do you understand? I'm not having it! No, no, literally, no! Y'know what? If they want war, they can have it. Who do they think they are? Demanding this, demanding that. Where do they get off thinking they can trample all over us like this? We should let them *have* their war and I tell you what - we'll trample all over *them*! What have we got to lose? They can't hurt us anyway, can they? What can they possibly do to us?"

She had to wait a few seconds for polkingbeal67's reply to issue from his lips, reconceived and repackaged as a consequence of chillok tampering. "They would annihilate us, extinguish our future generations and feed on our remains during the victory celebrations," he drawled.

"Are you all right?"

Polkingbeal67 had begun to realise he was definitely not all right. "No, yes," he said, now struggling against the process being triggered in his brain. "Yes, I'm all right. The chilloks are a wonderful people and should be obeyed."

"People? Wonderful? Seriously?" Melinda stared in disbelief.

Polkingbeal67 shook his head. "No, ignore me! I mean, certainly, yes, seriously. Wonderful people."

"So-o-o-o," Melinda fixed him with a quizzical, almost suspicious look. "You think I should just turn you over to the chilloks?"

"For mercy's sake, no! Don't! I mean, yes, that would be the best thing for all concerned. They are very caring and considerate people and they will treat me well."

"They will?"

"They're cruel, cold-hearted fiends! I mean, friends. They're cool, gold-hearted friends and will take good care of me, just as they've been taking good care of yukawa3."

"Yukawa3?" Melinda echoed in confusion. Her eyes widened with incredulity and then narrowed in mistrust. "Yukawa3? Are you saying the chilloks are holding yukawa3 prisoner?"

"Yes, they are tending to him with great care, ensuring all his needs are met. The chilloks are wonderful people and they treat their prisoners in a humane and civilised way at all times."

"How do you know this? How do you know he's their prisoner?"

"I beg you, don't listen to this!" By now, the time lapse glitch in the chilloks' transposer process was clearly evident. "I mean, I beg you to listen to this. Yukawa3 is in good hands and I know this because I, uh, learned about it from, uh, reliable sources."

Of course, it would have made the chilloks' task considerably easier if they had infiltrated Melinda's brain too, but they had never envisaged a scenario where it would be necessary (earthling brains were not thought to be sophisticated enough), so they did not and could not. They were stuck with having to use their dubious powers of suggestion and persuasion to influence her.

"Codswallop and balderdash!" Melinda snapped. "Reliable sources! Reliable sources? What are you talking about? I don't know what's going on here, but something's not right and I'm going to get to the bottom of it!" She may or may not have meant this literally, but she picked up an AmbiTemp cushion and wacked polkingbeal67 on the posterior with it.

"What's that for?"

"That's for being a total alienated idiot! Why are you suddenly coming out with all this 'chilloks are humane... chilloks are wonderful forever... it doesn't get better than chilloks' garbage? Really? So, okay, what you actually want is to give up the fight, punish yourself for something you didn't intend to do, subject yourself to god knows what retribution these infernal chillok creatures might conjure up and..." Incensed and exasperated, she flopped onto the bed and stared blankly at the floor.

"Someone's not thinking straight here," said

polkingbeal67.

Melinda looked up at him with scrunched eyebrows. "Is it me?" she asked sarcastically.

"The chilloks will keep me in an environment that's consistent with my values and concerns."

"Oh, they will, will they? Like what exactly?"

"Like, well, I don't know... pirates! They'll keep me captive on a pirate ship plundering the high seas. I'd like that. Do you know who yukawa3's cell mates are?"

"Don't tell me," said Melinda. "Penguins, right?"

I do not know who was more surprised - polkingbeal67 or the chilloks monitoring his thought processes. "How did you know?" he asked.

Melinda ignored the question. "Can I just remind you of one thing? This planet, *your* planet, the planet you've loved and fought for since the day you were born, is at war with the chilloks. Your people are waiting for you to stand up and do what's necessary. Literally. You're expected to save the planet!"

"The chilloks do not threaten the planet," said polkingbeal67, eyes wide with appalled disbelief at the sound of his own words - words that gushed out in fits and starts like water from a faulty tap. "They will take good care of the planet. Trust them!"

"What? Is it my ears? What in the name of anything that's holy? Are you seriously... What?" Melinda resorted to expressing herself in non-verbal language and started beating the cushion with her fists. Then she buried her face in it.

369

She heard polkingbeal67's voice as a kind of distant, muffled echo. "We, er, sorry, the chilloks have a glorious manifesto for running the planet. Give us, sorry, *them* a chance and we, sorry, *they* will sort out all your, er, sorry, *our* problems."

Melinda suddenly sat bolt upright and dropped the cushion. "You've been got at!" she declared. "What's going on? Look at me! Have you been brainwashed?"

Conscious that the transposition tactic was going pear-shaped, the chillok entities decided to play the percentages and avoid incriminating utterances. "I don't recall," said polkingbeal67 in a clipped monotone.

Grabbing him by the shoulders, Melinda pulled him around to face her. "Listen to me," she said. "We're not going to let any ant creatures outsmart us! Do you understand? What are they doing to you?"

"I don't recall," said polkingbeal67.

"Are they here? Are they in the room? Tell me!" She dropped to her knees and scoured the floor for traces of insect activity.

"I don't recall," said polkingbeal67.

"Did anyone call here before I arrived? Did you notice any infestations or, I don't know, swarming or whatever else these creatures do?"

"I don't recall," said polkingbeal67.

Melinda clasped his arms in her hands and looked earnestly into his face. "Stay here!" she said and flew out of the door with a look of steely determination.

. . .

Most Formicidae are divided into three castes: reproductive queens, reproductive kings and sterile, wingless workers. A chillok colony, on the other hand, boasted a fourth caste, cerebrum ambulans, elusive microbe-sized creatures that invaded human skulls and interfered with brain function.

Chillok workers varied considerably in size, the senior ambassador being a striking example of one of the largest, but their body parts conformed to the standard Formicidae design - head, thorax and abdomen. They boasted an impressive pair of elbowed antennae, but the real distinguishing feature was a blue, rotating petiole segment between the thorax and the abdomen. Similar in general appearance to the workers, the kings possessed pale, delicate, diaphanous wings and disproportionately large eyes relative to the size of their heads. Their sole purpose was to mate with the new queens, who were by far the largest of the castes. Three or four times the size of workers, the queens were endowed with antennae that were twice the length of their bodies. Although they started life with beautiful, lustrous, veined wings, they lost them after mating. The kings and queens took the credit for all the chilloks' achievements and were the prime movers behind ideological orientation, but they never lifted an antenna to help with the toil and strife. To be perfectly frank, they were mainly concerned with the reproduction side of things.

Although they had advanced well beyond the intellectual capabilities of Mortians, earthlings and other humanoid species, chilloks had ploughed their own furrow in terms of technological and scientific progress. In the fields of cell signaling, neuroscience and wormhole travel, they had left others languishing in their wake, but they had never designed any physical forms of transport and, perhaps because they did not envisage a need for it, they had never developed mutator technology to disguise themselves. It may seem odd to you, therefore, that they appeared to yukawa3 as sub-Antarctic earthling penguins in the context of the alternative reality that served as his prison. Rest assured that the reason for this will become apparent before very long.

When we last left yukawa3, he was being carried aloft like a victorious football coach by penguin forms hurtling around a labyrinthine megalopolis. We find him now lording it over an audience of admiring penguins in an isolated, dome-shaped chamber, accessible only by a steep, narrow passage that was generally ignored because it seemed to plunge forever, deeper and deeper into execrable darkness. Having introduced his new devotees to the heady delights of the yukawa3 tripod dance, he had seduced them further by plying them with syrup in return for a regular supply of fish and prawns. He did not know where the fish and prawns came from, and they had no idea whence he obtained the syrup. You don't always need to know the insipid little details: as long as the big things happen, who cares? To yukawa3, life felt good once again. Despite the constraints of the language barrier, he felt like a demigod. His only qualm was the lack of water, but if there *had* been any around, so great was his sense of self-importance and worthiness, he would probably have attempted to walk on it.

It had not been smooth sailing all the time, not by any stretch of the imagination. The first few strikes of yukawa3's charm offensive had been random efforts to use anything he could find as bait. This literally backfired when he offered them some pieces of wood he had discovered at the back of the chamber. The penguins chewed it and chewed it and everything looked good until their tails suddenly went up and they sprayed long projectile streams of sawdust all over him. The slightly sweet but subtle fragrance had lingered for some time afterwards and had conjured up memories from the past that he had forgotten. In fact, the memories were more recent than he had thought - the aroma teasing his senses had derived from invercresco trees native to his home planet.

It is, of course, a cliché, but prison changes people. Even if the regime is not cruel or inhuman and the conditions are not particularly harsh or degrading, inmates and guards alike undergo psychological changes brought on by nothing more traumatic than the routine business of adapting to incarceration. Factors such as being deprived of privacy and liberty, the imposition of a diminished status and sparse material resources combine to diminish self-esteem and produce dysfunctional relationships. Nevertheless, perhaps because his self-esteem had already been about as stable as a kite in a tornado and perhaps because most of his relationships had been dysfunctional even before his confinement, yukawa3 had been coping well. In fact, his thoughts had already turned to escape.

A penguin's body, with its streamlined shape, webbed feet, paddle-like flippers and well-developed wing and breast muscles, may be superbly adapted for an aquatic environment, but frankly it's not much use for anything else. When his guards were otherwise engaged, yukawa3 spent a lot of time pecking with his bill at the floor towards the back of the chamber, only to fall through to the chamber below where some of the other birds were huddled together in sleeping posture. They were not best pleased, especially as they were largely only figments of yukawa3's imagination.

In reality, of course, the 'penguins' were chilloks going about their business in the normal way - tunneling, foraging, secreting toxins and devising plans to conquer the universe. Having interfered with the neurons in yukawa3's brain to synchronise his thoughts with their own and thereby ensnare him in an alternative reality (or parallel universe), it seems they had not anticipated the extent to which a Mortian brain would resist and oppose their efforts. In other words, they were not responsible for him perceiving them as penguins - he was supposed to perceive himself as a chillok!

Having acquired the opportunity to experiment with yukawa3, the chilloks had been using him as a guinea pig to test one of their new pet theories. They had recently started to embrace the notion that thoughts are energies capable of existing independently of a creature's physical body and capable of being connected with another creature's consciousness. Prevailing upon yukawa3 to adopt aspects of a chillok identity had all been part of this radical new approach to braintuning. What the Mortian cadet had construed as hero worship on the part of the penguins, apparently hanging on his every gesture, was actually the chillok neuroscientist workers reveling in the spectacle of their own work!

Needless to say, however, members of the cerebrum ambulans caste felt threatened and were afraid for their future. All was not rosy in the chillok camp and things had been threatening to come to a head - actually, yukawa3's head - for quite some time.

Eventually, when yukawa3 picked up yet another hypnotic suggestion that he should forage for more syrup, the cerebrum ambulans microbes neutralised it and forced yukawa3 to reinterpret it as a yearning for escape. When he tumbled headlong into the workers' sleeping chamber, it could have served as an omen, a premonition of the future collapse of chillok civilisation.

There were further examples of this contention between

the neuroscientists and the cerebrum ambulans. Receiving a synchronisation thought advocating a tidy up of his hidden chamber, the braintuning cerebrum ambulans refashioned it for yukawa3 as a cunning new escape plan employing ingenious forms of camouflage or disguise to escape detection. Wearing his sou'wester as his disguise, he endeavoured to find a passageway leading from the chamber, but he was blinded by the ill-fitting hat and collided with wall after wall until he was staggering sideways and one of his flippers was quivering like the bottom lip of an actress in a third-rate soap opera. The pitiful farce continued until he rammed a wall with so much force that his bill remained embedded in it for several minutes.

.   .   .

Unlike most of us, Melinda did not experience many moments when she felt helpless, confused and lonely, but that was how she felt right now. She did not know who to trust or who to believe or who to turn to for help. Clearly, polkingbeal67 had been got at by someone or something and, although she was confident the planetary leader was still himself and not subject to the will of anybody else, she entertained the notion of consulting him only very briefly before dismissing it. Frankly, she thought, what difference would it make if he was under someone else's spell? He never said anything sensible anyway! As for nipkow4, he was so inhibited by political correctness and concerns about upsetting intergalactic cohesion, she would need a team of wild goopmutts to drag him off his moral pedestal.

She felt as if she had been hurtling along a road, and there before her was the next bend enveloped in a thick shroud of fog. For the first time, she paused to take stock of the half-dream, half-nightmare world in which she was now so deeply immersed. Thoughts of home on Earth began to flood through her mind. They ebbed and swirled like the Stygian waters of the river Lethe, leaving her numb and stunned and disconnected. Ultimately, these reminiscences served to turn and point her towards earthling humanity for encouragement and illumination, and, without any further delay, she set out for the earthling prisoners' camp at nefeshchaya.

A rooster-like tail of red dust arced up into the air behind her as she sped off in polkingbeal67's graphene cruiser across the featureless plain. As she approached the methane lake, desultory flashes and sparks on the far shore illuminated the force field marking the camp perimeter. A few garfs from the lake, she actuated the brakes. Waiting for the dust plume to pass over the cruiser, she opened the angel wing doors and stepped outside. Behind her, grey clouds edged with gold and purple presided over the aching beauty of the Mortian landscape. The lake itself glittered with violet in the sunlight. A capricious gust of wind blew a lock of hair across her eyes but still her gaze sought the beautiful vista before her. Slowly, imperceptibly, it restored her spirits. The surging waves of panic and homesickness receded, leaving a tidemark of jumbled scraps of memory - the flotsam and jetsam of her past strewn along the shore to whet the appetite of beachcombers and flies and gulls. Yes, by and large, she was happy for a while, sifting through her own detritus, picking through the driftwood and broken green bottles and little porcelain jars, but in her heart of hearts she knew one thing - she was not ready to return to Earth, not just yet anyway. She picked up one of the bottles, which was not easy, given its metaphorical nature, and withdrew the metaphorical message concealed within it. All metaphorical messages in metaphorical bottles say the same thing. It said: 'Help!" Although, as a life coach, she had always taught her clients to avoid looking for answers at the bottom of a bottle, she took this as a sign that she should stay and rescue her new friends. One of the suns broke free, painting moving shadows of the sparsely distributed invercresco trees, before vanishing again. She climbed back into the cruiser and looked around once more. "I love it here," she thought. "I'm going to figure this out. I can make a difference. Literally."

Not prepared to tolerate any nonsense from the androids patrolling the enclosure, she flounced right past them and smiled on hearing their aggrieved voices wittering away behind her as she strode towards the dwelling pod:

"Stop! Halt! Who goes there? Identify yourself! Who is she? Where's she going? What do we do? Should we stop her? Do we shoot?"

"Don't get your circuits all crossed!" she called over her shoulder. "It's me: Melinda. Stand to attention and quick march or left turn or something! I need to speak to the prisoners. Left! Right! Left wheel! Right wheel! As you were!" She left them careening around wildly, colliding with each other while emitting a cacophony of angry hums and high-pitched yelps.

Joseph West, the self-appointed spokesman and leader of the earthling abductees on Smolin9, wore his sincerest expression as he sat and listened to Melinda. Every time one of the other prisoners laughed or sneered or whispered, he silenced the offender with a sharp, frowning glare. He had mellowed during his time in exile and was astute enough to know when to listen and learn. Having heard her out, he calmly placed his cup on the table in front of him, displayed his crooked, discoloured teeth in a mirthless smile and launched into a long tirade of snarling, spitting invective.

"No swearing!" Melinda interrupted him. "Literally, no

swearing! Look, I know it must seem intolerable to you, but I just thought... you see, I'm here to ask for your help and advice." West opened his mouth to speak and she cut him off. "Look, I know I'm indirectly responsible for you being abducted from Earth and for you being held as prisoners and everything. And I know you can't go back to Earth and I guess I'm partly, okay, indirectly to blame for that too. And, yeah, so I know you've got every reason to hate me and, uh yeah, I accept that hate. I do, really. I accept it. Literally. I just... Isn't it just possible we could have some kind of, I don't know, a kind of meeting of minds or something. I know I'm in a more privileged position than you and you obviously don't exactly owe me any favours, but is there... Is there any chance we could all sit down together and just talk about this stuff? Any chance at all?"

West sat back and contemplated the pod ceiling for a few seconds. "Okay," he said. "So you're afraid an ant is gonna crawl into your head and learn all your thoughts? Is that it?"

"No," said Melinda, "I hadn't actually thought of that. Although I suppose..." She dismissed the idea with a slight shiver.

The tension melted. West offered her a cup of tea and they all sat around and chatted in a relatively relaxed, participatory and congenial atmosphere. "This is nice, y'know?" said Melinda, after a while. "This could be the first chapter in a new history of cooperation between us. It's a chance for us people from Earth to come together and do what we English people do, what we're famous for and..."

"You mean stay at home, drink beer and watch football?" West interjected.

"No, I mean, I was thinking of Winston Churchill, fighting them on the beaches and never being defeated and all that."

"I bet he liked football."

Melinda suppressed a sigh and let the conversation wash over her for a while. The prisoners, on the other hand, were animated. Interrupting one another and shouting at cross purposes, they were energised by a rare sense of focus and urgency. Ideas and suggestions tumbled out of them like frogs from a child's jar. Most of them hopped into oblivion, but a consensus gradually took hold, evolving into a scheme to turn the camp into a factory for producing and stockpiling militarily significant quantities of insecticide. One of the prisoners, a chemist convicted of drug violations back on Earth, insisted that, as methane was proven to be highly effective in destroying insects, they should find a way to get access to the lake outside the camp, because he was confident he could develop a technique for extracting methane hydrate from the water.

"What do you think?" West asked Melinda, who appeared to be distracted by something over by the kitchen units. "Hello? Are you listening to this?"

"Yeah, literally," Melinda mumbled absently, her attention still held by something in the kitchen area. "Can anyone hear a tapping sound?"

West continued. "So if we could supply you with the poison, you and the Mortians could take out these chillok creatures one colony at a time, right?"

"Uh, okay," Melinda replied, nodding earnestly. "Wait, is that all right? I mean is that like, y'know, using chemical weapons or something?"

West rolled his eyes. "What's wrong? Don't tell me," he drawled sardonically. "Churchill wouldn't approve. Is that it?"

"Oh, he definitely wouldn't have used chemical weapons!"

"What if his books and paintings and stuff got infested with ants? What if they got at his cigars? He would've used ant powder, wouldn't he?"

"I don't think you can smoke cigars if you've sprinkled them with ant powder. Anyway, did I tell you? I had a dog just like the one Churchill had. A poodle."

"A poodle?" repeated West, shaking his head and gesturing incredulously. "I thought it was a bulldog. Anyway, what's that got to do with anything? Did his dog smoke cigars?"

"No, it's just that you can't use ant powder if you've got pets around the place."

"Pets!" West sputtered. "We haven't got any pets! This is ridiculous! Listen, these chilloks - they're like ants, right? We're talking about insecticide. Come on, it's not like they're humans."

"Okay then, makes sense, so... Can anyone hear that? That tapping noise?"

West shrugged. "Uh, let's cut to the chase. If we do this, what's in it for us?"

"I thought you'd ask that. It's something I've been thinking about for some time now. Literally. You see, I think we've reached a point where we can all trust each other enough to get along like civilised people. And I'm going to use my influence to get this camp closed down and get you integrated properly with the Mortians."

West stared at her in appalled disbelief. "What! No way! Leave us alone!"

"But don't you want to get out of this prison?" Looking around, she saw all the prisoners gawping at her in horror. "Listen, this isn't good. I expect you've become institutionalised and incapable of independent living. What are you worried about out there? Is it all the family breakdown and economic recession?"

"Don't you see?" West drew a deep breath. "I'll put it as plain as I can. We're happy here and we don't want to mix with the Mortians!"

Directly behind West in the kitchen area was an open cabinet containing various tins, jars and bottles abducted from Earth. There was flour, crackers, cereals, cake mixes, pasta, seasonings, syrups and other foods with a long shelf life. While she spoke, Melinda became conscious of a particular bottle of syrup that appeared to be moving. "That's a bit erratic," she said, mesmerised by this bottle that teetered and rocked back and forth. "Uh, yeah, I'm going to get you all released," she promised West. "I don't think the Mortians have any right to imprison you and I..." Suddenly, the bottle fell on its side, revealing a small hole in the wall behind it. "Did you see that?" she asked West without taking her eyes off the bottle.

As West turned around to follow Melinda's gaze, a section of the wall about the size of a large trash can lid toppled into the room sending shelves and their contents flying across the floor. In amongst the splattered mess were several hundred chilloks looking disoriented, waving their antennae and assuming defensive postures. But what really caught the eye was a dazed-looking king penguin, half-hidden under a yellow sou'wester.

Melinda's eyes bulged and her jaw dropped in a mixture of

disbelief and joy. She was the first to break the stunned silence. "Mister West, I thought you said you didn't have any pets!"

.   .   .

Melinda dropped to her knees, removed yukawa3's hat and pulled him into a slippery hug, only releasing him when she could no longer tolerate the rancid odour of dead fish. If West was stunned by these dramatic events, his face did not show it. Sitting with his arms crossed, staring implacably at yukawa3, he mumbled something indecipherable under his breath and then turned to Melinda. "A penguin," he said, nodding sagely and composing his face into an expression that misleadingly suggested some innate understanding of events. "So did you know about this?" he continued. "This penguin hiding behind the wall with these chillok ant creatures? Has it been fraternising with the enemy or something?"

"No, I didn't know about it. Literally," she explained, shaking her head. "And he wasn't fraternising with the enemy. Actually, he was their prisoner and he's escaped."

West raised a sceptical eyebrow. "He's not going to be happy then."

"Why not?"

"Because he's escaped from a prison *into* a prison. Anyway, does a penguin even know what a prison *is*?"

"Yeah, uh, he's not really a penguin."

"Really? Look at him! He's got a black back and a white belly, a beak and two flippers. He's waddling about on webbed feet. That, for my money, is about as close to being a penguin as you can get."

"Yeah, well, I know he *looks* like a penguin. Except for the hat, obviously. But, y'know, appearances can literally be deceptive. Think camouflage."

West grunted in amazement. "Camouflage! Are you telling me he, er, this - whatever it is - is trying not to be noticed? And he thinks the best way to do that is to jump out of walls disguised as a penguin?"

Realising how absurd this situation must appear to the prisoners and realising there was no rational way of explaining it, Melinda abandoned the attempt. "Sorry, you're confused, aren't you?"

"Thank God," West muttered. "I wasn't sure it was coming across."

"You see," said Melinda, deciding foolishly that she *should* attempt to explain it after all. "He's actually a person. One of my best friends, in fact."

West pursed his lips. "A person," he echoed.

Yukawa3 chose this moment to relieve himself on the kitchen floor. "Nice company you keep," West observed.

"Yeah, it's probably all the excitement. Listen, I can't explain right now. I've got to arrange some stuff, like urgently."

"Wait!" said West, taking her arm. "What about these chillok ant things? There are hundreds of them! What shall we do about them?"

Her thoughts temporarily wandering elsewhere, Melinda answered vaguely, "Oh, I don't know. Uh, tread on them!" With that, she scooped up yukawa3, who squawked in appreciation, and hurried outside.

Having composed themselves after their earlier ordeal, the androids had resumed their patrolling duties outside the pod. When they saw Melinda crossing the yard towards the gate, they clustered together in a defensive formation and adopted a bogus air of disinterest.

One of them caught sight of yukawa3. "What's that?" it asked. "There's no data for it in the field guide catalogue of organisms. Stop them! She could be smuggling out one of the prisoners."

Another android was unconvinced. "I don't think it's an earthling humanoid, unless it's a very small, formally dressed one."

As Melinda arrived at the gate and opened it with a swish of her universal clavis, the androids continued their agitated debate.

"It could be a mutation," said one.

"Earthlings can't mutate," said another.

"It could be a weapon."

"It's got wings. It's a UFO! Should we shoot it?"

As she climbed into the cruiser, Melinda coughed and announced breezily, "Excuse me. He's a penguin."

"Look up 'penguin'!" urged one of the androids.

Another responded a short while later after accessing its internal databanks: "Aquatic, flightless bird from the southern hemisphere of the Pale Blue Dot." Melinda's cruiser was well out of sight by now, racing towards the horizon.

"Flightless?"

"Yes."

"So, not a UFO then?"

"No."

"That's okay then. They may pass." Satisfied that all formalities had been complied with, they proceeded to take up their usual positions along the edges of the enclosure.

As far as Melinda was concerned, her immediate priority was to obtain yukawa3's mutator, last seen on a godforsaken beach on South Georgia Island. Although other Mortians could communicate with him using their telepathic powers, Melinda really wanted a normal, direct conversation with him. Having arrived at the leader's palace, she instructed nipkow4 to take whatever steps were necessary to retrieve the device so that yukawa3 could assume his natural Mortian identity, but she met resistance not just from the Mortian administrator but also from yukawa3 himself. The wildly misguided cadet was adamant that being a penguin represented his true calling in life.

Melinda became more and more exasperated as the discussion went on. "So," she said. "You're a member of an advanced civilisation that can zip around the galaxies using wormholes, but you'd rather be a bag of oily feathers that slides about on its belly and huddles with its mates in the freezing cold? I don't get it, literally."

"He loves the ocean lifestyle," nipkow4 explained. "All the diving, swimming and fishing and so on."

"Yeah, yeah," said Melinda wearily, "I know. The ocean lifestyle, whatever. It's Zen-like and idyllic, bla, bla, bla. About as idyllic as a picnic with a T-Rex, if you ask me! Listen, do me a favour and just get the damn mutator back again! I can't argue about this any more right now!"

When nipkow4 left the palace antechamber to supervise the wormhole retrieval of the mutator, Melinda and yukawa3 stood eyeing each other in perplexed silence. A full Earth minute must have passed before yukawa3 saw fit to celebrate his penguiness by launching into an impassioned performance of the 'yukawa3 tripod dance', complete with twirling pirouettes, half-twists, side dives and breathtaking back dives, culminating in an elegant belly-slide across the polished magma floor. As he tottered somewhat gracelessly to his feet, Melinda reached down, fixed him with the darkest of looks and slapped him on the head.

Later that day, not only had the mutator been retrieved from South Georgia Island, but yukawa3 had succumbed to Melinda's persuasive charms and appeared before her in his native Mortian form. During what can only be described as the briefest debriefing ever, yukawa3 divulged everything he had learned from his time with the chilloks: "I thought they were penguins."

Melinda, one of the least violent people known to Earthling anthropology, felt desperately inclined to smack him for the second time in one day. "Is that it?" she asked at last. "You thought they were penguins. And you've got nothing else?"

"I think you'll find that's very relevant," yukawa3 insisted.

"Go on," prompted Melinda.

"Go on what?"

"Tell me how that's relevant."

"It's obvious if you think about it," said yukawa3, trying

(and failing) to narrow his eyes perceptively. "You have to get into the mindset of a chillok. They're very cunning, you see. And their plan is to freeze the planet until they kill us all off. They'll use no weapons and no one will suspect a thing. They'll survive, of course, because, at a given signal, they'll mutate into penguins and huddle together in solidarity until the warmer weather arrives in the spring and the blossom appears once more on the invercresco trees and the birds sing their songs for all to hear..."

"Seriously?" Melinda interrupted. "You want to carry on with that?"

"I hope that answers your question. It is spoken," proclaimed yukawa3.

Unable to contain herself any longer, Melinda notched up her second smack of the day, dislodging yukawa3's sou'wester and eliciting a howl of anguish.

"That's no way to treat someone who was thought to be dead," yukawa3 protested sulkily. "Everybody thought I was dead. You thought I was dead, didn't you?"

"Tell me, how did you figure out you weren't?" Melinda retorted scathingly.

Yukawa3's thoughts ran aground on a disturbing half-memory of attending his own funeral and he half-described it to Melinda, who was astonished to find his half-recollected observations chimed perfectly with the full reality of the memorial service that had actually taken place. "I suppose it was a dream," he said.

"A dream?" Melinda mumbled to herself, "That's really bizarre." Unwisely, she revealed that what he had described had really happened.

"Really? You see, I dreamed I was awake. And I was supposed to be dead but I was alive. Then I woke up and found myself asleep. I've spent so much time recently just wrestling with reality."

"I think you may have finally overcome it," Melinda observed dryly.

While the march to asininity progressed towards its logical conclusion - a suggestion by yukawa3 that he should adopt his penguin disguise once more, infiltrate one of the chillok colonies and spy on them like he failed to do at the previous opportunity - Melinda hatched a plan to summon all the Muqu chilloks on the planet to a peace summit at the palace to pave the way for power-sharing negotiations. The real objective would involve poisoning them with a toxic methane vapour while they were all assembled in the Grand Hall. Convinced that this was a reasonably sound strategy (actually she thought of it as an epiphany moment), she rushed off to find nipkow4.

She found him in conference with the planetary leader in a small room adjacent to the newly designated War Council chamber.

"No, they wouldn't come to a peace summit," nipkow4 asserted. He was alarmed by the very thought of brokering a power-sharing deal.

"Why not?" Melinda looked genuinely surprised.

"There are things about the chilloks you don't understand," nipkow4 advised, wearing an expression of passive indifference. "For one thing, they worship a supreme deity and they believe this God requires the blood of their enemies to be spilled."

"Well, I'm not religious, literally, but I'm kind of spiritual.

And I like to think I respect other people's faiths. But still, why does their religion make any difference? I don't see why they wouldn't want to talk peace."

Nipkow4 scrutinised her. "Don't you see? They believe that those who kill their enemies will be honoured by their God." Suspecting that he was not getting through to her, he simplified the message. "That's *us*. *We're* now their enemies. They think their God will reward them if they kill us."

"Yeah, okay, I get that." Melinda's voice was tinged with irritation and mounting anger. "Are you saying they wouldn't want peace on any terms? That's outrageous! Ridiculous and obnoxious and immoral! Who do they think they are, really? It's like totally unacceptable to refuse to negotiate! No civilised society would act like this!"

"I hardly think we're in a position to take the moral high ground," nipkow4 pointed out. "May I remind you, honoured deputy leader, that you were intending to double-cross them and annihilate them with poison gas."

"Yes, but I was going to propose a ceasefire first."

At this point, the planetary leader intervened. Sitting back, puffing at a cigar made of dried seaweed, he coughed and intoned pompously, "The supreme art of war is to subdue the enemy without fighting."

Melinda nodded. "You see?" she said, in a self-righteous tone. "Subdue them. That's exactly what I was going to do!"

"Anyway," said nipkow4, massaging his head with his fingertips. "Even if you destroyed all the Muqus on the planet, it wouldn't achieve anything. They'd simply send for reinforcements from Oov."

"But how could they send for reinforcements if they're dead?"

"The chilloks on Oov would detect the outage in their network and send investigators."

The planetary leader, who had been listening intently while chomping vigorously at his cigar, drummed his fingers on a table and said, "When you're arguing with a fool, make sure the fool isn't doing the same thing."

Melinda and nipkow4 both assumed he was having a pop at the other and both said, "Exactly!" Then they both thought about it a little more and the room fell into an embarrassed silence. Eventually, Melinda, who no longer bothered to seek approval from the leader, told them she intended to go ahead with her plan. Nipkow4, brimming over with frustration and anger, left to arrange a briefing with the senior chillok ambassador.

The myrmecam was not only a sophisticated voice-translation device designed to facilitate real-time communication between humans and chilloks, but it also incorporated a hotline to the ambassador. So it did not take nipkow4 very long to arrange the meeting. Melinda barely had time to visit the bathroom before everything was ready and the ambassador, having appeared as if out of thin air, was twitching his antennae impatiently.

Much to nipkow4's surprise and consternation, the ambassador responded positively to the idea of a peace summit and agreed to an immediate ceasefire, subject to a few pre-conditions relating to the agenda. Melinda, who should have known better, sought clarification that the ceasefire would include the cessation of any "sneaky brain-fiddling tricks" associated with polkingbeal67's flaky mental state. Predictably, the ambassador denied any knowledge of "this unfortunate calamity". The summit was scheduled for the following day.

.   .   .

Nipkow4 branded the twenty four hour timescale as "completely ludicrous". Certainly, neither he nor Melinda had time to sleep, eat or do anything that did not involve setting up the Grand Hall or drafting a plausible power-sharing proposal.

Melinda, in particular, was in her element amid all the frantic preparations. Directing the palace minions, instructing the androids, arguing with nipkow4 about logistics and politics and answering the questions which were showered upon her by all and sundry, she was as animated and excited as a jumping bean on a pinball table. She was determined to create a lavish event of ostentatious magnificence, offering something for every palate and every disposition. "Well, there should at least be vol-au-vents and dips, aphids for the chilloks and, uh, paper flowers," she told the palace staff. "Oh, and, uh, a string quartet?"

"At what point do you intend to gas them?" asked nipkow4, weary with constantly having to point out flaws in the plan.

Racing across the hall to supervise the ribbon arrangements above the top table, Melinda shouted over her shoulder, "At the end of the meeting, I think. Or right at the start, when they've all arrived. Like a pre-emptive strike. Wait, no, yes, literally, right at the start."

"So what's the point of drawing up proposals if we're never going to get as far as presenting them?"

"Okay, you're right," Melinda conceded. "We'll do the peace negotiation stuff and then kill them straight afterwards. Tell me, do you think we should dress formally or..."

"Are we going to offer them shared residence of the palace?"

Melinda was totally engrossed in the business of avoiding breaches of sartorial protocol. "Black dress suits and evening gowns, do you think? What about name badges?"

"I'm going to assume that responsibility for programming the androids will still lie with us."

"Themed sweatshirts?"

Nipkow4 shook his head in exasperation. "We usually insist on both parties signing an agreement document. Do we make an exception in the case of the chilloks? Or do we get the ambassador to paddle around in some ink? Wait, do you mean the hoodies with the goopmutts waving peace signs? I love those!" Never distracted for long, he quizzed Melinda further about the power-sharing negotiations and recommended setting up a joint arbitration tribunal.

Now absorbed in finding a location for the myrmecam so that it would not detract from the sweeping arrangement of the paper floral garland, Melinda scoffed at the idea. "Let's just keep it simple," she said. "I'm sure we all believe in democracy. We'll put it to a straightforward vote."

"May I remind you, deputy leader, there are approximately one million chilloks for every humanoid on the planet."

"Okay, cancel democracy and do the other thing then."

Time got swallowed up like a minnow in the path of a great blue whale. As the scheduled hour for the summit drew near, canisters of poison gas arrived from nefeshchaya accompanied by the chemist's scrawled message explaining that the noxious fumes, released through the ventilation system, would mix with the air in the hall and, as soon as the methane concentration approached fifty per cent, the chilloks would asphyxiate and die.

Nipkow4 and Melinda exchanged glances. "Right," said Melinda, suddenly getting cold feet. "I wonder if... I don't suppose... Well, we've exhausted every possible means of resolving things peacefully, haven't we? Tell me, what would the Intergalactic Court say about all this?"

"According to the Court, all members shall refrain in their intergalactic relations from the threat or use of force against the territorial integrity or political or cultural independence of any people or species as defined within paragraph F of subsection 114C. In short, what you're contemplating will shock the moral conscience of humankind across the universe."

"They wouldn't approve then." Melinda chewed her lip. She was now racked with doubt and self-distrust. "But what if it's the only way to stop the triumph of evil?" she asked. "Oh, I don't know. Maybe I'm just not cut out for a life as a genocidal murderer."

Nipkow4, aware that Melinda had instructed the earthling prisoners to trample on the chilloks floundering on the prison camp kitchen floor, pursed his lips and tutted. "That ship has sailed, my friend."

"Oh God," said Melinda. "You must think I'm some kind of ruthless chillok-crunching exterminator person. Literally."

"I'm not sure that's a thing," said nipkow4, "but if it is, you shouldn't take it personally. Your species is notorious for it."

"What! That's a bit harsh, isn't it?"

"No, not at all. While we've been trying to unravel the secrets of the universe in a reciprocal, collaborative and harmonious way, you earthling humans have been staying at home exploiting, slaughtering and consuming most of the other species on your planet."

Melinda thought about it and decided to concede. "Okay, curse you, I suppose you're right."

The appointed time arrived and the entire population of Mortians, all thirty of them, including polkingbeal67, were greeted by androids bearing trays containing decanters of liquid vitalmados. After a few minutes' conversation, they took their seats and waited for the chilloks to show up. Tense and edgy already, Melinda began to fret about being duped by the ambassador - it looked as if nipkow4 had been right and the chilloks were going to boycott the summit after all. Worse than that, she suspected that they might be looking to exploit the situation - all the Mortians being assembled in one place - for some heinous design of their own. One of the Mortians called out, "Look! Over there!" All heads turned to see three or four chilloks scurrying along one of the magma borders. By the time they turned back, the entire hall was filled with the diminutive creatures, hordes of wingless workers obscuring every scrap of furniture that was not occupied by Mortians. They blanketed the floor and scuttled along the ribbons; winged kings and queens were arranged like thousands of tiny torch beams along the windowsills, preening and displaying, while the ambassador flexed his antennae behind the myrmecam on the small stage at the far end.

Melinda, standing in a pool of light to the left of the myrmecam, got the proceedings underway with a short presentation, welcoming the attendees and setting out the agenda for the meeting. As she was about to introduce nipkow4, polkingbeal67 stepped up on to the stage and a spotlight moved across and settled around him. "Sorry," he said. "Is it okay for me to say a few words?" Melinda and nipkow4 exchanged flustered looks but nodded in assent. After clearing his throat, bowing to the ambassador and blinking a few times in the light, polkingbeal67 spoke very slowly, as if his thoughts were wrestling with the cerebrum ambulans implanted in his brain. "I'm painfully aware that I'm in no small part responsible for the hostilities between our peoples and I am therefore grateful to have this opportunity to speak to you all. And I intend to try my utmost to bring us closer together in peace and harmony."

He was squeezing the words out like each one was the final glob of toothpaste in an empty tube. Melinda was convinced that foreign interference was responsible for this and was in two minds whether or not to intervene. She glanced again at nipkow4 who shrugged his shoulders in confusion.

Polkingbeal67 went on: "What happened to the great city of Niffis was a tragic event and it grieves me to speak of it. You may or may not believe that it was part of some systematic pattern of cause and effect, contingent on the actions and intentions of cognisant beings and therefore punishable under intergalactic law. You may or may not consider it a consequence of the vagaries of fate or the whim of a god. You may or may not dismiss it as a pure accident - one of the terrible effects of living in a universe where people attempt to impose their free will on the savage forces of nature, and fail. Whatever you believe, I implore you to accept that if I was a perpetrator, I was an unwitting one; one who has wrestled ever since with the enormity of what happened; one who is chastened and filled with sorrow at the loss of so much life." His delivery still very studied, slow and deliberate, he paused for a moment and then continued. "We believe we are the masters of our fate. And, indeed, to a degree, we are equipped with the tools to mould our lives. We can decide what to do with our time and what to spend our energy on. We can choose what we eat and drink and when to sleep and who to speak to. We can control what we say and what we think..."

On hearing this, Melinda immediately wondered if he was being intentionally ironic. Was he trying to issue some kind of cryptic warning? Was it a paradoxical reference to being mind-controlled? One thing was sure, she had never heard him string together such articulate words and phrases. This was not the polkingbeal67 she had come to know so well. When she finally managed to focus back on what he was saying, he was speaking a little more fluently. "... we try to understand these things but we are mere fish trying to get on with our lives in total ignorance of tides and currents and floods and droughts. For we are all at the mercy of something greater than ourselves, something beyond our comprehension, something that does not respect our efforts to be the architects of our fate. And yet," he said, leaving the words hanging for a moment, "and yet we must act as if we *are* in total control, for it is the only way to nurture and respect the wonderful gift of life. Like the gardener who will not allow his garden to become overrun with weeds, we must bring order out of chaos by applying the constraints of a universally accepted rule of law, a social contract established among ourselves as societies of cognisant beings. I bow before the judgement of the Intergalactic Court and I make no plea for special consideration. What concerns me is not my personal case but the conflict between us that my actions have triggered. And that is where I think the law must be improved. The law speaks of 'just cause' as a pretext for waging war. Friends, there is no such thing as 'just cause' for war."

Melinda shuffled imperceptibly towards nipkow4 and the pair talked in hushed, frenzied whispers, while the disposition of the chilloks slowly changed from bored indifference to thoughtful interest. Polkingbeal67 went on: "We have never looked beyond the eye-for-an-eye paradigm that has shaped our law for eons. But if we care to look, there *is* another paradigm. Instead of committing ourselves to the judicial equivalent of a black hole - cognisant society collapsing in on itself as we punish each other to the point of mutual destruction - we should stand together and look towards the light of the ever-expanding universe and aspire to enrich ourselves with the treasure it offers. Let us all revel in that light! Friends, we must reject punishment and welcome reconciliation! No more shall we counter violence with yet more violence! Together we shall strive to underpin the intergalactic community with laws and principles we *all* believe in, for, without a set of common values to glue it together, civilisation is always liable to disintegrate. And now, as I look into your eyes, and into the eyes of all my friends across the galaxies, I say to you, 'I will not hate you. I would rather die than hate you.' Earthlings, Mortians and chilloks, we must join together and spread the word! And the word is life! We must honour and celebrate the sanctity of life in all its diverse forms!"

"What the devil is he talking about?" Melinda whispered hoarsely. "Has he gone totally mad? Have they taken his mind completely? What shall we do?" The chilloks, meanwhile, were enraptured. The kings and queens were rubbing their wings against their bodies to produce a hum of approval (which Melinda misconstrued as an expression of angry protest). Waving her arms to attract polkingbeal67's attention, she hissed, "Shut up! Literally. Get off the stage!"

But there was no stopping polkingbeal67 now. He was

punching the air in time with his words: "And where we find empty minds we will fill them. And where we find closed minds we will open them. And where we find minds that are full of poison we will cure them with antidotes. Be assured we will find those who oppose and confront our values, those who will stand in our way and refuse to let us pass, those who will beat us and knock us to the ground. But we will take those beatings and fight back, not with weapons of destruction or the deployment of armies, but with the most powerful weapons at the disposal of cognisant beings - knowledge, understanding and education. Armed to the teeth with the tools of learning, we will prevail upon our enemies to change. And though it will seem onerous to devote so much time and effort on those who would destroy us, still we will consider it worth the investment. We will emerge as friends. We will emerge wiser, better and stronger. The world is our mirror! You are my reflection and I am yours! We are one and the same and we will never strike at the mirror again!" Just before Melinda careered across the stage and tackled him to the floor, he managed one more exultant entreaty: "Behold the mirror and smile!"

The chilloks hummed ecstatically. Some of the kings and queens flew around the hall in joyful abandon, while the ambassador yelled into the myrmecam: "Behold the mirror and smile! Behold the mirror and smile!"

"It is spoken," said yukawa3, nodding his head in fervent approval. As the Mortian equivalent of applause took the form of headbutting the nearest wall, all thirty of them turned around and gently beat their heads against the unforgiving magma while Melinda and polkingbeal67 dragged themselves to their feet. It now occurred to Melinda that it made no difference whether polkingbeal67 or the chilloks were behind this ridiculous charade - it had served the purpose, albeit bizarrely, of uniting the two factions and averting the need for her to inflict an act of genocide on her unsuspecting guests. Polkingbeal67 brushed himself down with shaking hands and crossed the stage to the right, only to find the steps were on the opposite side. As he turned back again towards Melinda, the chillok ambassador headbutted the myrmecam. "He may not be your leader," he said to Melinda, straightening his crumpled antennae, "but you should not let him pass without honouring him."

Melinda bowed her head, overcome with a conflicting array of emotions.

.   .   .

Several hundred chilloks were crawling over one another, crowding around the myrmecam, singing at the tops of their voices:

"And I like it, I like it, I like it, I like it

I li-li-li-like it, li-li-li-like it

Here we go

Rockin' all over the world"

Occasionally the song would give way to repeated chants of 'Behold the mirror and smile!' The discordant voices, high, piping and wavering like a damaged cassette tape, drifted out into the cloisters where Melinda, nipkow4, polkingbeal67 and yukawa3 had assembled to take stock of the situation.

"Let bygones be bygones," said yukawa3 for no particular reason except that he thought he should say something. "Oh heavenly days! If you think everything is coming up roses, well it is. And I hope that answers your question. You are my reflection and I am yours! Behold the mirror and smile!"

The frown on Melinda's face knitted her eyebrows together like a pair of caterpillars kissing. "You have no idea what that means, do you?"

"Yes, I do," said yukawa3 defensively. "It means: if I look in the mirror and I'm not smiling, then if the reflection is smiling, well, it would be yours but I would think it was mine because it's, y'know, a reflection."

The other three looked at him and then turned to each other. "Are we really out of the woods now?" asked Melinda. "I mean, is the war over?"

Nipkow4 sucked in some air, rolled his eyes and shook his head. "No, no, no, nooooo!" he said. "Well, yes, it is, as such, in the literal sense, but sometimes solving one problem creates two more. You see, I think the chilloks have interpreted polkingbeal67's words as a paean to some kind of sun-dappled utopia - a hippy-like, power-sharing fantasy that can only mean one thing to them."

"That, deep down, they really want to be peace-on-earth-property-is-theft-tree-hugging dropouts?" asked Melinda.

"No. It can only mean this: they are persuaded that *we* are happy to surrender sovereignty of our planet. If chilloks had nostrils they would have been overwhelmed with the smell of weakness."

Polkingbeal67 sought to clarify his remarks. "Ultimately, civilisations have to be judged not only by how they help the most vulnerable and disadvantaged people in their societies, but also by how they deal with the most obnoxious and loathsome in their midst. All I was saying is that pan-galactic respect, freedom, equality, dignity and fairness, underpinned by access to education, are the core

400

values we should all aspire to."

Nipkow4's jaw dropped in disbelief. "Dangerous nonsense!" he exclaimed.

"Wait a minute," said Melinda, still struggling to rationalise a range of conflicting emotions. "Earlier on, you were dissing my people for being ignorant and having no empathy with other species, while you Mortians have been collaborating and harmonising and whatever. So, what's going on here? Have you changed your tune?"

"Being *interested* in other species is one thing," nipkow4 expostulated. "*Living* with them is an entirely different thing! This is tantamount to treason! Do you think we should just roll over and let the chilloks take over our planet?"

"The time for alienating people is over," polkingbeal67 contended, smiling beatifically. "We have to get over our notion of being the centre of the cosmos. *Their* planet. *Our* planet. It doesn't matter any more. What matters is celebrating our connection to the great web of life. My philosophy is to avoid harming any creature regardless of size, species or any other characteristic. I know that won't be easy."

"Damn right it won't!" Nipkow4 was becoming apoplectic. "It's sheer lunacy! If you're attacked by stinging insects, won't you swat them? Since time immemorial, the natural balance of ecosystems has always been controlled by territorial conflict and the demands of the food chain."

Polkingbeal67 was unmoved. "There are times when we have no choice but to kill, but we should always try to respect and celebrate every life."

"I've got something important to say about all this,"

yukawa3 announced. After satisfying himself that everyone was paying attention to him, he coughed, forgot what he was going to say, coughed again and said: "If I was stung by an insect, I would think about it and celebrate the life of the insect and then, when it gets too painful, I'd swat it like a bothersome, no-good, er, insect."

The other three looked at him and then resumed their debate.

Meanwhile, the euphoria among the chilloks in the Grand Hall had abated and their thoughts turned to the implications of sharing a planet with another species. Although moving from their home planet on a permanent basis would resolve the problem of the Muqu-Naaffab conflict, it would expose them to the hazards of co-existence with other species. Having the ability to take over the brains of Mortians was a significant factor in their favour, but there were also earthlings on the planet – people who possibly could *not* be braintuned. And, in any event, chilloks still managed to get eaten, poisoned or squashed by just about all the other life-forms they encountered. It was a sobering thought.

Eventually, matters came to a head when the issue of braintuning came to the fore. Members of the cerebrum ambulans caste fell out spectacularly with chillok neuroscientist workers and the dissension began to seriously destabilise the entire chillok network communication system. The powerful dynamic of their shared intelligence was breaking, disintegrating. As their vital sixth sense diminished like a sputtering candle, they vanished from the hall in some disarray, individually and in small groups; and those that remained became more and more disconsolate. Looking distracted and fatigued, the senior ambassador attempted another chorus of 'Rockin' all over the world', but it was all in vain. By the time he got to 'Here we go', the hall was deserted except for him and the Mortian leader, who had been left behind, forgotten, still puffing meditatively at his seaweed cigar.

.   .   .

The halls and corridors of the leader's palace echoed with a long, desolate howl, full of woe and despair, such as one might make on missing a favourite programme by recording the wrong channel. A microwocky flew out of one of the palace windows like a wingless bird, contributing to the debris decorating the ground below. It was like a scattering of synthetic conkers fallen from an invisible tree. Unable to operate the devices and convinced that they were faulty, the planetary leader was frequently observed tossing them through the window of his private chamber.

Melinda and yukawa3 stared at him with a mixture of curiosity and pity. The brain that had once been as sharp as a coral reef was now little better than a clump of the rotting seaweed he loved to wrap himself in. He insisted that he still had a firm hand on the rudder in such matters as foreign diplomacy and the domestic economy, even though he was considered to be the catalyst for three of the last four Mortian wars and he had, by his own admission, nay, by his own proud boast, forecast five of the last three fiscal crashes. According to his memoirs, smolin9 had died on three separate occasions and Melinda had originally been abducted to check the plumbing.

Winding a frond of seaweed around his arm, he glanced at Melinda with a look of serious disappointment and disapproval. "So you want to leave?" he asked.

Melinda had announced this intention after a great deal of soul searching and deliberation. "Yes, I've decided to go back home, back to Earth." It was not a decision she had made lightly, but, following the unexpected emergence of polkingbeal67 as an enlightened and statesmanlike figure on the intergalactic stage, she was convinced it was the right one. She had stretched the skin of her comfort zone to breaking point and had enjoyed the experience, but the social cohesion of the entire intergalactic community was now at stake and she felt she had to give way to altruism, reason and the lure of Glastonbury High Street.

"Earth?"

"The Pale Blue Dot," Melinda corrected herself.

Peering at her with dim, sullen eyes, the leader inquired, "But I thought you had your heart set on being the next leader?"

"Yes, I know. I did, but I've had a change of heart."

"Ah, I remember. You've got polkingbeal67's heart."

"Yes, no, that's not what I meant."

"So what do you mean?"

"Mm, I mean, the thing is, I've, uh, changed my mind and I'm, well, I'm going back to my home planet."

"Well, you understand you can't be deputy leader, or my successor, if you're not going to be resident here?"

Melinda was fully aware of the provisions of the Mortian Code relating to the designation of a planetary leader. "I know," she said. "What I'm saying is - you'll need to appoint someone else."

"But who?"

Given the traumatic fallout from the Niffis crisis, Melinda was unsure how to broach the subject of polkingbeal67's credentials. "Well, while we're on the subject of hearts..."

An enlightened expression flashed momentarily across the leader's face and he lifted a quivering finger. "Polkingbeal67 has your heart!"

"Yes," said Melinda encouragingly, "and I think he's matured into the perfect natural successor to yourself. It's all happened very quickly and I suppose you'd have to consider him a work in progress, but he's transforming himself into a true visionary with a passion for undertaking missions relating to, uh, human advancement. Totally."

"It is spoken," murmured yukawa3 solemnly.

The leader suddenly looked up beseechingly at Melinda. "We rejoice when the eagle soars, but I fear our skies will grow dark without you. Will you reconsider? What you do now will shape all our destinies."

Melinda nodded. "I think my destiny is no longer here. Literally."

"Take care lest you are simply fleeing to avoid it," the leader advised sternly. Then his voice softened. "If you pursue happiness too vigorously, it may slip from your grasp."

"No, I'm not avoiding or pursuing anything," said Melinda earnestly. "I can't believe all the stuff that's happened to me here. It's all been so erratic! And I've loved it all. But the time has come for me to create my own destiny and allow others to fulfil theirs."

"It's true," said the leader, surprisingly lucid and now resigned to losing his prodigy. "If we fail to control our futures, others will do it for us."

Yukawa3, eager to contribute a philosophical insight of his

own, added, "Yes, like if we want to, uh, not appear fat, then we must avoid mirrors and weighing scales. That way, we can control the, uh, shape, of our, uh, destiny. I'm going to stop and think about that." He forgot to start again for quite some time.

Melinda and the leader embraced. This was a rather disagreeable experience for Melinda, who smelled of pungent oils and seaweed for hours afterwards. Nipkow4 arrived and they all discussed arrangements for a ceremony to mark both her departure and polkingbeal67's confirmation as leader-elect.

Two days passed. The certainty and profound peace of mind that had enveloped Melinda when she had announced her decision to leave the planet had disappeared in a fog of doubt and uncertainty, made worse by spending considerable time with polkingbeal67, with whom she had developed a strong spiritual attachment. Cruiser rides across the magnificent, wild Mortian terrain, while a reflection of the double sunset stretched over the placid waters of the lake at nefeshchaya, were also sure to make her feel a pang or two of indecision and regret. It should come as no surprise, then, that she spent the opening part of the ceremony close to tears.

Assorted exotic beasts, abducted from various planets across the galaxy, were slaughtered for the feast. Splendid culinary creations adorned with truffles, prawns, bonbons and whirls of champagne cream were arranged for the visual delectation of the guests, none of whom, except possibly Melinda, would actually eat them. The walls of the Grand Hall were decorated with the utmost extravagance. Based on research of the most luxurious residences in the galaxy, gilded magma carvings, silks and ornamental structures of stylised flowers bordered the colossal mirrors and imposing portraits of Mortian heroes. A drape of peach-coloured silk concealed a new portrait, rumoured to be that of Melinda herself. At the far end of the hall, a band plucked, blew and hammered away at a motley array of graphene, wire and silicone instruments, creating a sound akin to finger nails on a blackboard in a ship's engine room. Strange ululations gave rise to sporadic displays of headbutting as polkingbeal67, resplendent in his ceremonial robe, eye patch and sherg-encrusted helmet, made his entrance. The helmet did not fit as well as it used to before he had acquired smolin9's body, and he had to steady it with one hand lest it should fall to the floor. "Is everything okay?" he asked Melinda, noticing the tears welling up in her eyes.

Dabbing at her face with the back of her hand, Melinda nodded. "Yes, of course," she said. "I'm just, y'know, in different places emotionally right now. Literally." Just as one should never test the depth of water by jumping in with both feet, so it is with emotions. Having taken the plunge of publicly declaring her intentions, the bitter pang of heartache at the prospect of parting from these people now seeped into her soul like the leading edge of a tidal wave. Nipkow4 seized polkingbeal67 by the arm and dragged him away for an urgent conference, leaving Melinda and yukawa3 to make nervous, stilted conversation, made all the more awkward by the realisation that it could be their last.

"So, what do you think about all these lavish decorations?" asked Melinda, determined to avoid lapsing into emotional incontinence.

Yukawa3, who had ingested a little more vitalmados than was good for him, felt ill at ease but was keen to avoid giving the impression of mental torpidity. Whether or not he succeeded in this is debatable. "Well, the carvings are quite bendy," he remarked, nodding judiciously, "with some pointy bits." Observing a small rotating, circular platform, flush with the floor, containing a spectacular cake on a marble stand, he said, "Look, it's going round. Round and round. And, uh, round."

The new portrait, a stunning likeness of Melinda and polkingbeal67 together, was unveiled. Then, a dizzying succession of presentations, passionate speeches and emotional tributes, interlaced with musical performances and bouts of headbutting, morphed into a wild and tumultuous commotion that lasted for several hours, at the end of which Melinda, sobbing openly, said her final farewells. As the guests started to leave, she folded polkingbeal67 in a prolonged, fond embrace, kissed him on the cheek and whispered, "I'm leaving the planet in good hands. I'll never forget you." A pained sigh broke loose and the tears fell freely. Neither of them noticed yukawa3, on his back, spinning slowly on the circular platform, intermittently yelling out "Verily, we're all in this alone!" Executing the yukawa3 tripod dance in the physical form of a penguin had been difficult enough; attempting it as a humanoid crossing onto a revolving stage had proved completely impossible.

Legend has it that, on that night, the stars arranged themselves into a slowly spinning likeness of Melinda and polkingbeal67, exactly as they appeared in the portrait. They say you can still see the image forming in the night sky today, from Earth as well as from Smolin9. Like many such whimsical fabrications, I am sure the power of repetition has elevated it to a level of credibility out of all proportion to the truth, but I still find myself gazing up at the sky on a clear night and checking, just in case.

.   .   .

And so ends that particular chapter of my mother's life. She returned to Glastonbury and continued with her career as a life coach for a couple of years before meeting and marrying my father.

From the perspective of the end of the twenty-first century, it is interesting to reflect on many aspects of her story, not least her decision to shroud the whole thing in secrecy. For me, even publishing it now, decades later, represents a difficult judgement call, but at least now it does not matter if people believe it or not. If she had come out and revealed these events at any point in her lifetime, she would have opened herself to scorn and ridicule so great that her life would not have been worth living. As far as I am aware, I am the only one privy to her experiences with the Mortians. None of it was disclosed to my father, who would certainly have feared for her sanity had she seen fit to tell him. Of course, she was not the only one who had had a story to tell and, for whatever reason, elected not to. The no less illustrious names of Queen Elizabeth II and American President Barack Obama feature on the list of people who had had first-hand acquaintance with smolin9 or polkingbeal67 or both. Certainly, the CIA and the British secret services will have had in their possession highly confidential documents relating to the demise of Sophia Gonzalez. But perhaps the most remarkable conspiracy involves the extraordinary appearance of the Voyager 1 space probe on the south lawn of the White House and the impressive cover-up orchestrated by the FBI, the CIA and various branches of the Department of Defense at that time, much to the chagrin of the intergalactic community.

Obviously, polkingbeal67, yukawa3 and any number of other Mortians may have returned to Earth following the incidents involving my mother, but, if they did so, I have no knowledge of their visits. Almost a century further on, we still have no real understanding of wormhole travel or parallel universes or some of the advanced technology my mother was exposed to. Of course, we have the equivalent of microwockys, magnetic propulsion cruisers and jetboards at our disposal, but mutators and myrmecams continue to be the stuff of science fiction. As for the chilloks, there were the devastating insect swarms of 2047 in Nebraska, when the sky turned black with billions of mysterious ant-like bugs - could that have been some kind of attempt at an alien invasion by the phenomenal creatures from Oov? Who knows?

And that brings me to the most disturbing aspect of the whole thing, namely what evidence is there that any of it actually happened? Among the most prized of my mother's possessions are a battered yellow sou'wester and a few photographs that bear witness to her account of things, including one extraordinary shot of her holding a penguin on a ship presumed to be the Malvinas Explorer. I have seen for myself the memorial bench dedicated to the memory of Sophia Gonzalez. And, of course, there has been no resolution to the mystery of the 'escaped' prisoners. But, no surgeon ever had the opportunity to examine my mother's heart and discover its incredible derivation, and, at the end of the day, all the evidence that remains is purely circumstantial or inconclusive.

I know this was something that vexed my mother. At one point, she developed a penchant for taking preposterously long walks and I occasionally accompanied her, particularly at the weekends when I could get away from work, and it was during one of these exhausting hikes that she told me her story. Confiding her innermost thoughts to me, she said it felt as though her Mortian heart, beating fit to burst from her chest, sought synthesis with the person whose life it had previously sustained. An aching, longing, restless yearning for reunion took hold of her and drove her on as she walked and walked, heedless of distance, heedless of time, heedless of physical laws and constraints. It drove her beyond rational thought, beyond feeling, beyond pain, beyond the relentless grip of circumstance, beyond herself, until she teetered on what she imagined might be the threshold of polkingbeal67's universe. And still she walked. And why? Because something haunted her. Something tortured and disturbed her for years, right up until she died. It was the thought that she might have imagined the whole thing. Literally.

Other books by David Winship

Stirring The Grass, 2013, ISBN 978-1492952725

Off The Frame, 2001, ISBN 978-1482793833

Talking Trousers and other stories, 2013, ISBN 978-1484898420

Printed in Poland
by Amazon Fulfillment
Poland Sp. z o.o., Wrocław

52752160R00235